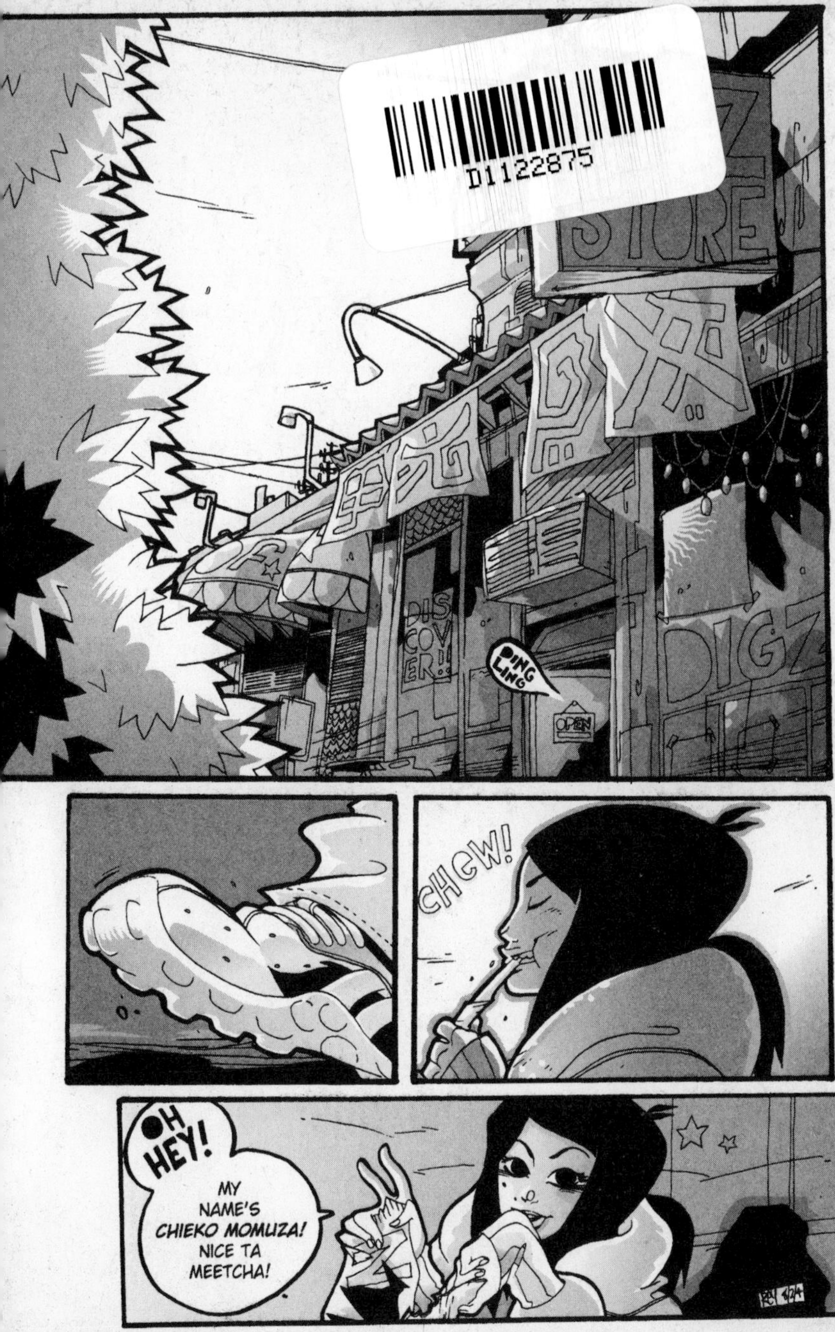
STORE
DIS
COVER!!
DING LING
OPEN
DIGZ
CHEW!
OH HEY!
MY NAME'S CHIEKO MOMUZA! NICE TA MEETCHA!

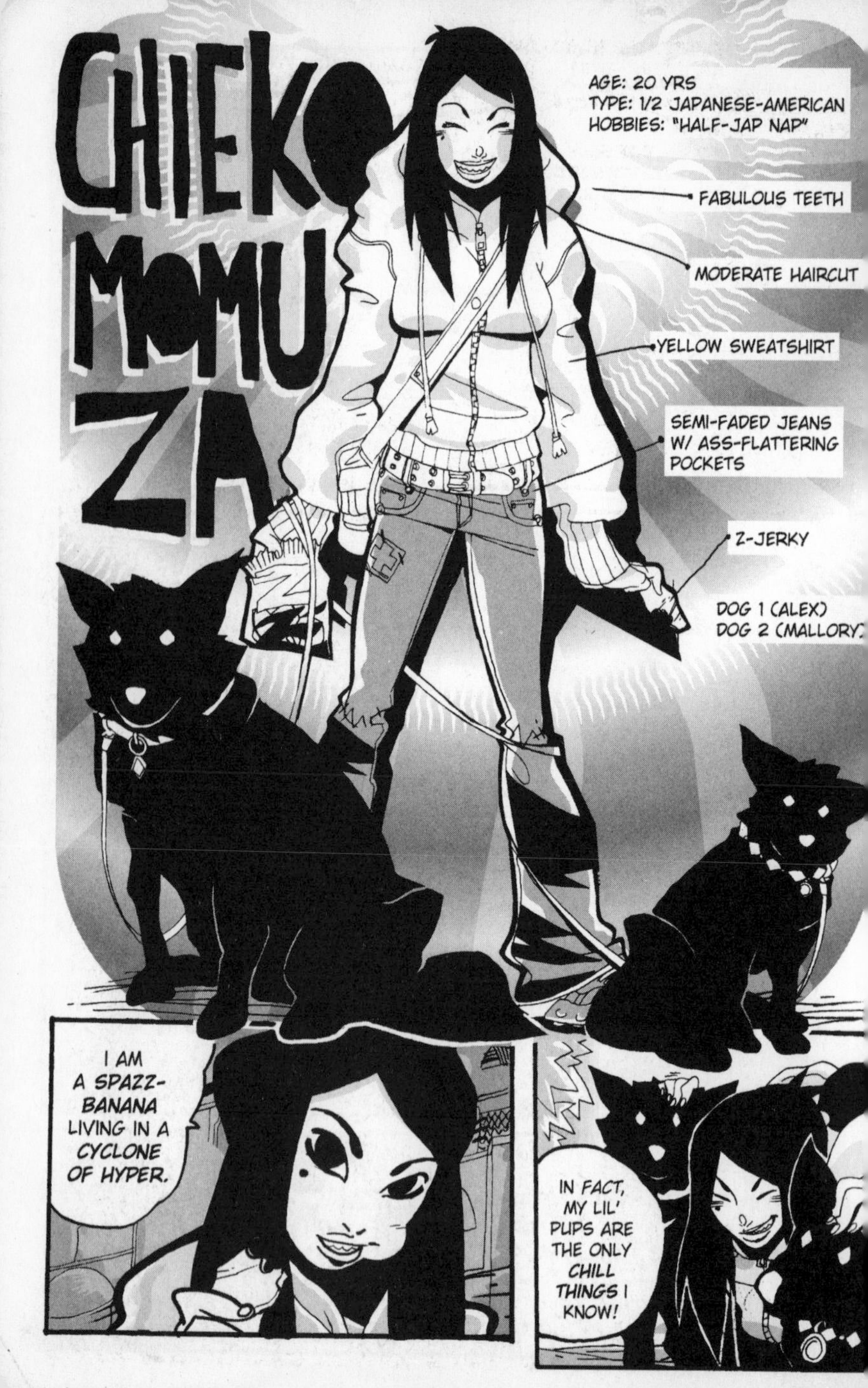
CHIEKO MOMUZA
AGE: 20 YRS
TYPE: 1/2 JAPANESE-AMERICAN
HOBBIES: "HALF-JAP NAP"
FABULOUS TEETH
MODERATE HAIRCUT
YELLOW SWEATSHIRT
SEMI-FADED JEANS W/ ASS-FLATTERING POCKETS
Z-JERKY
DOG 1 (ALEX)
DOG 2 (MALLORY)
I AM A SPAZZ-BANANA LIVING IN A CYCLONE OF HYPER.
IN FACT, MY LIL' PUPS ARE THE ONLY CHILL THINGS I KNOW!

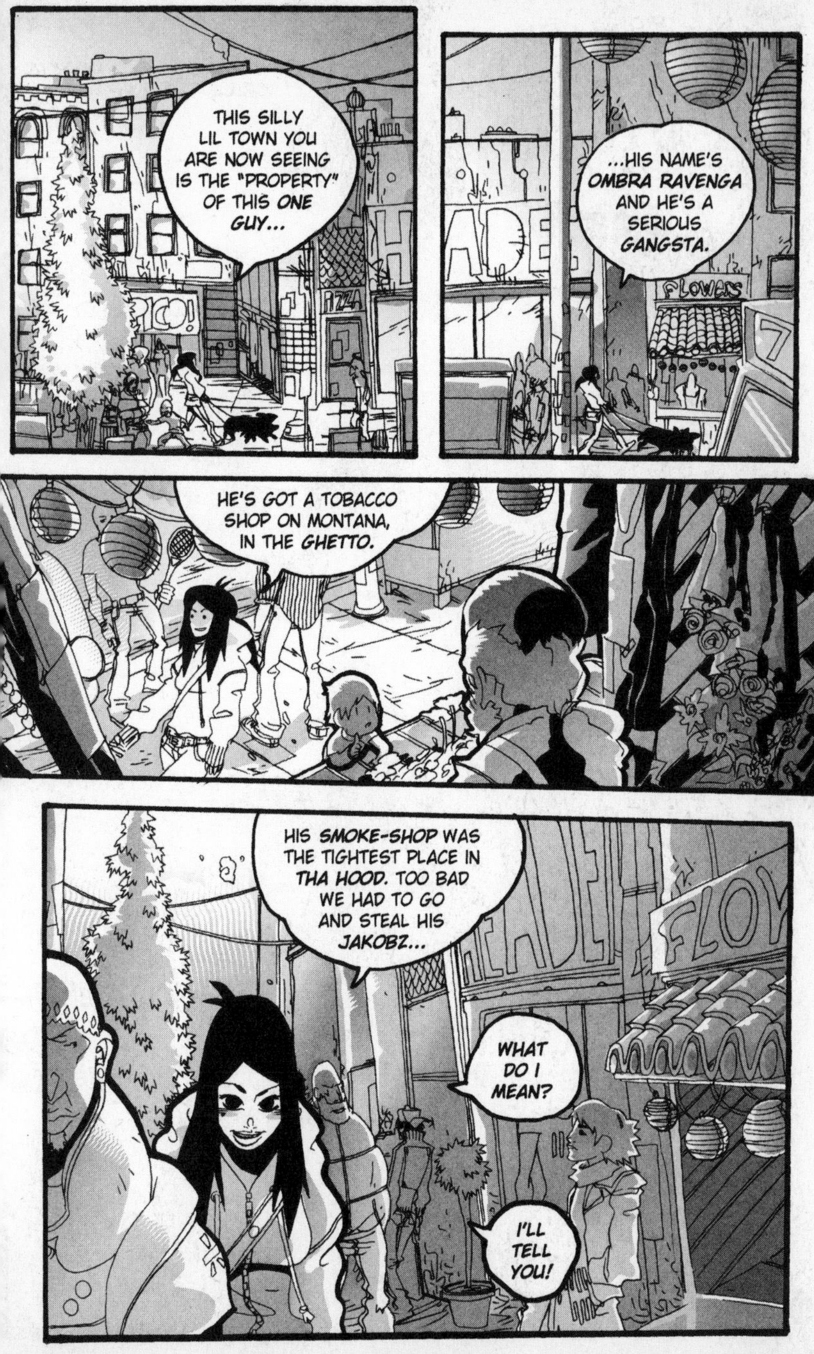
THIS SILLY LIL TOWN YOU ARE NOW SEEING IS THE "PROPERTY" OF THIS ONE GUY...
...HIS NAME'S OMBRA RAVENGA AND HE'S A SERIOUS GANGSTA.
HE'S GOT A TOBACCO SHOP ON MONTANA, IN THE GHETTO.
HIS SMOKE-SHOP WAS THE TIGHTEST PLACE IN THA HOOD. TOO BAD WE HAD TO GO AND STEAL HIS JAKOBZ...
WHAT DO I MEAN?
I'LL TELL YOU!

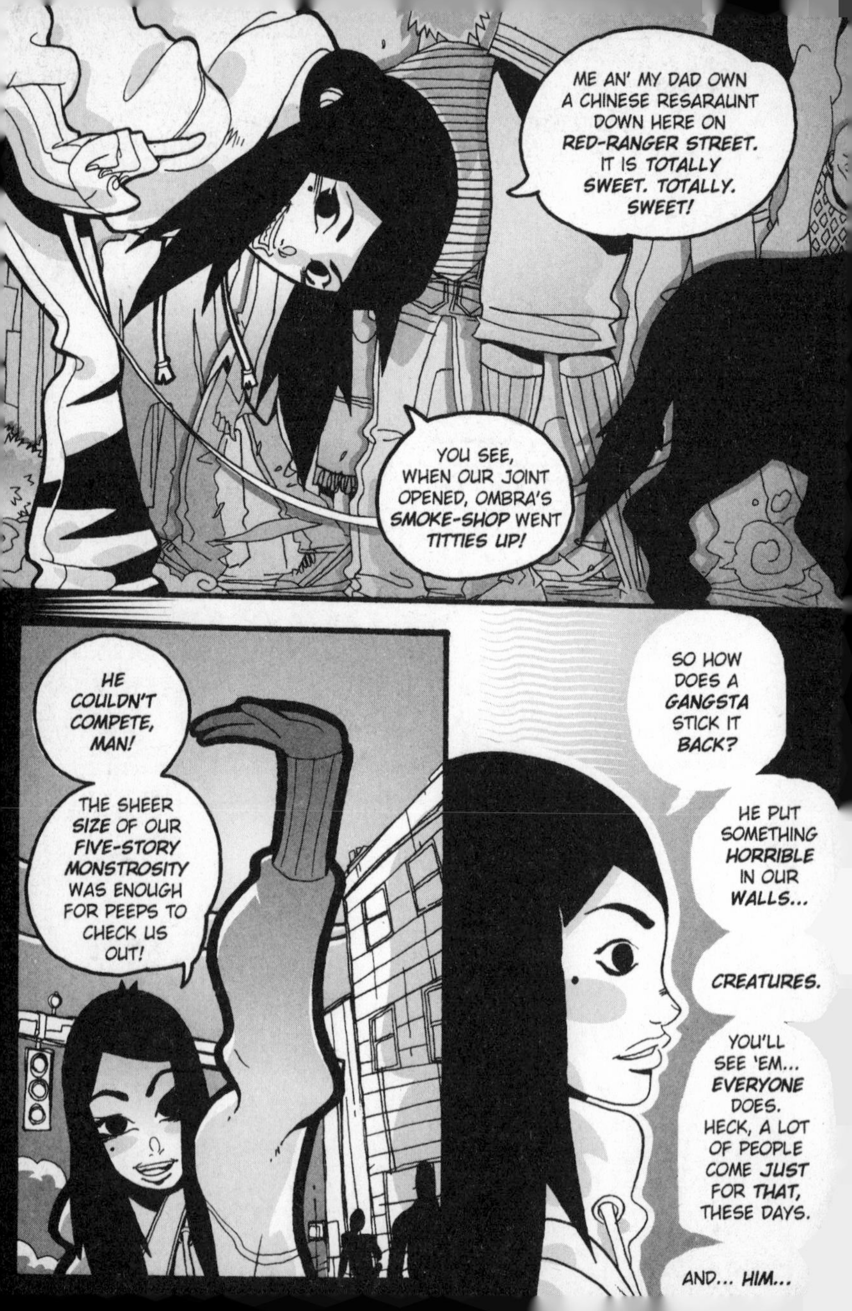
ME AN' MY DAD OWN A CHINESE RESARAUNT DOWN HERE ON RED-RANGER STREET. IT IS TOTALLY SWEET. TOTALLY. SWEET!
YOU SEE, WHEN OUR JOINT OPENED, OMBRA'S SMOKE-SHOP WENT TITTIES UP!
HE COULDN'T COMPETE, MAN!
THE SHEER SIZE OF OUR FIVE-STORY MONSTROSITY WAS ENOUGH FOR PEEPS TO CHECK US OUT!
SO HOW DOES A GANGSTA STICK IT BACK?
HE PUT SOMETHING HORRIBLE IN OUR WALLS...
CREATURES.
YOU'LL SEE 'EM... EVERYONE DOES. HECK, A LOT OF PEOPLE COME JUST FOR THAT, THESE DAYS.
AND... HIM...

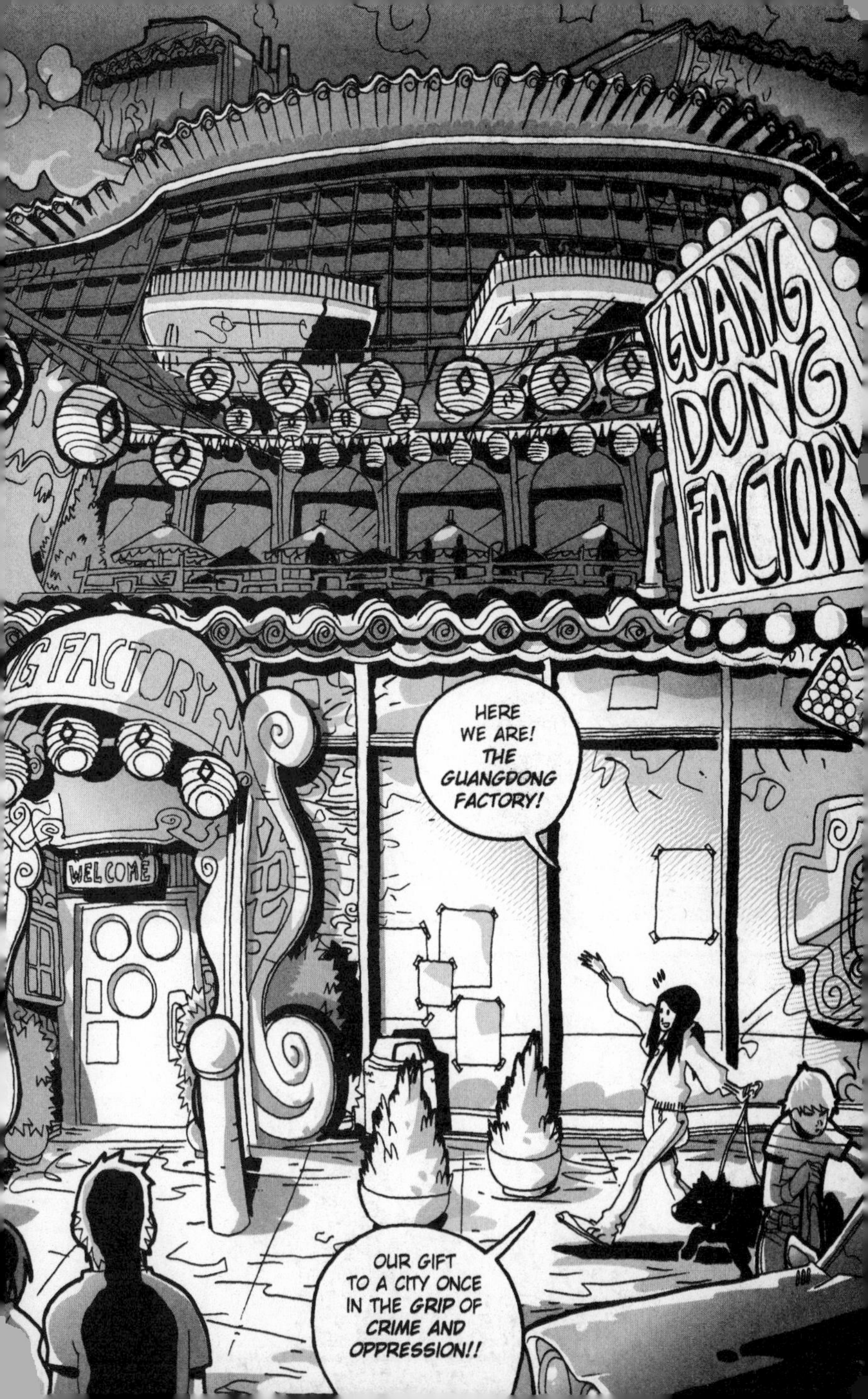
GUANG DONG FACTORY
G FACTORY
WELCOME
HERE WE ARE! THE GUANGDONG FACTORY!
OUR GIFT TO A CITY ONCE IN THE GRIP OF CRIME AND OPPRESSION!!

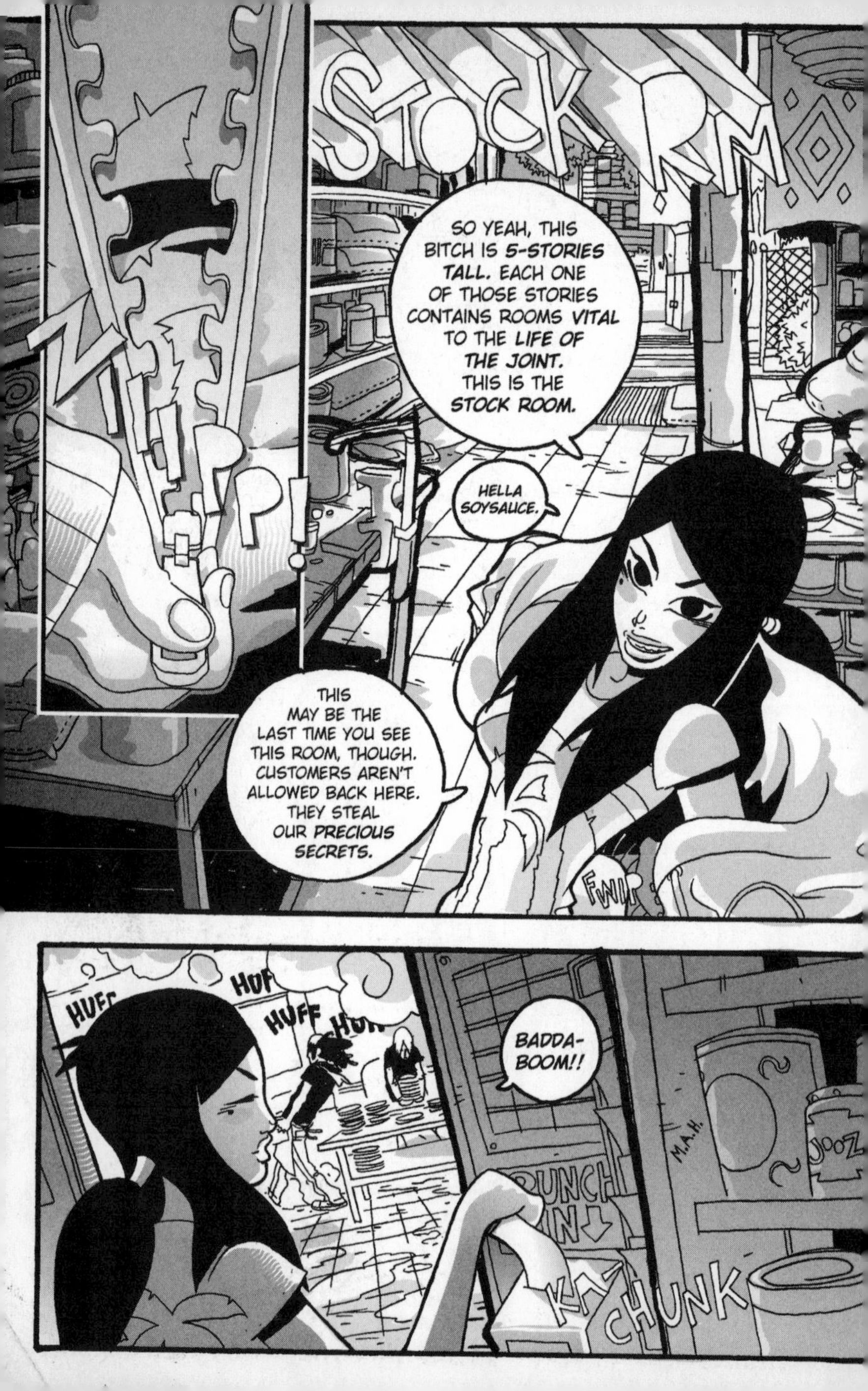
ZIIIP!
STOCK RM
SO YEAH, THIS BITCH IS 5-STORIES TALL. EACH ONE OF THOSE STORIES CONTAINS ROOMS VITAL TO THE LIFE OF THE JOINT. THIS IS THE STOCK ROOM.
HELLA SOYSAUCE.
THIS MAY BE THE LAST TIME YOU SEE THIS ROOM, THOUGH. CUSTOMERS AREN'T ALLOWED BACK HERE. THEY STEAL OUR PRECIOUS SECRETS.
FWIP
HUFF
HUF
HUFF
BADDA-BOOM!!
M.A.H.
JOOZ
KA-CHUNK

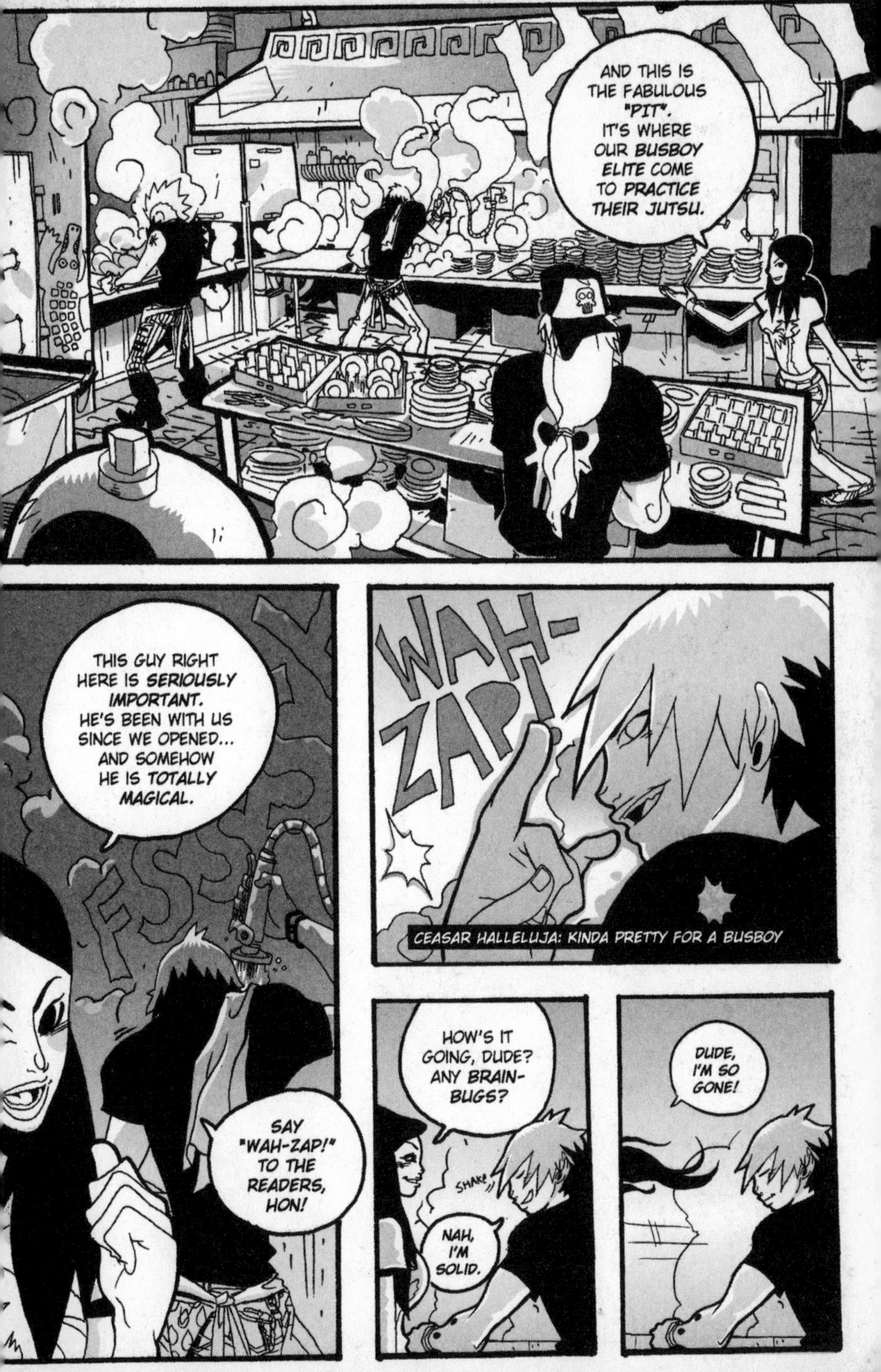
AND THIS IS THE FABULOUS "PIT". IT'S WHERE OUR BUSBOY ELITE COME TO PRACTICE THEIR JUTSU.
THIS GUY RIGHT HERE IS SERIOUSLY IMPORTANT. HE'S BEEN WITH US SINCE WE OPENED... AND SOMEHOW HE IS TOTALLY MAGICAL.
FSSS
SAY "WAH-ZAP!" TO THE READERS, HON!
WAH-ZAP!
CEASAR HALLELUJA: KINDA PRETTY FOR A BUSBOY
HOW'S IT GOING, DUDE? ANY BRAIN-BUGS?
SHAKE
NAH, I'M SOLID.
DUDE, I'M SO GONE!

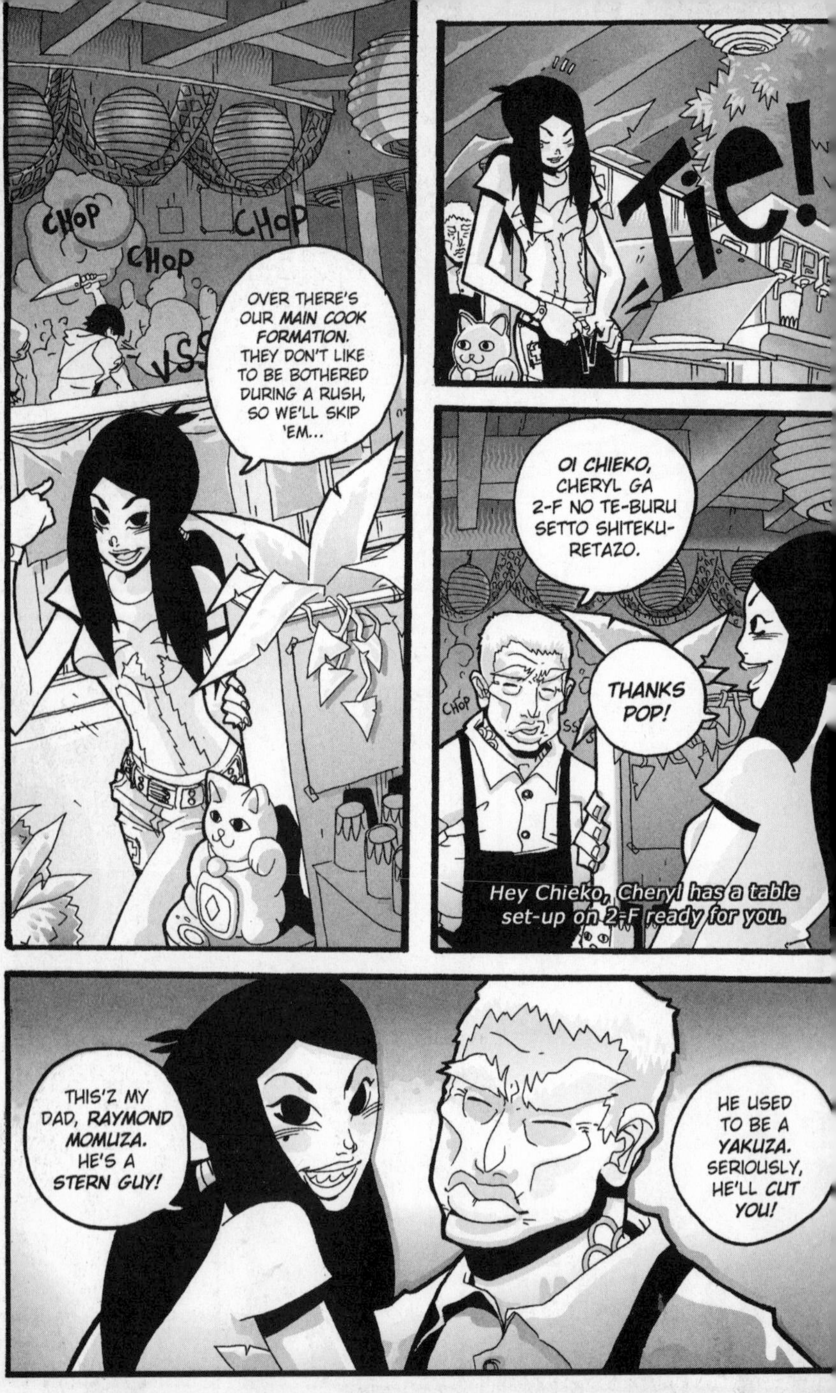
CHOP
CHOP
CHOP
VSS
OVER THERE'S OUR MAIN COOK FORMATION. THEY DON'T LIKE TO BE BOTHERED DURING A RUSH, SO WE'LL SKIP 'EM...
TIE!
OI CHIEKO, CHERYL GA 2-F NO TE-BURU SETTO SHITEKU-RETAZO.
THANKS POP!
CHOP
Hey Chieko, Cheryl has a table set-up on 2-F ready for you.
THIS'Z MY DAD, RAYMOND MOMUZA. HE'S A STERN GUY!
HE USED TO BE A YAKUZA. SERIOUSLY, HE'LL CUT YOU!

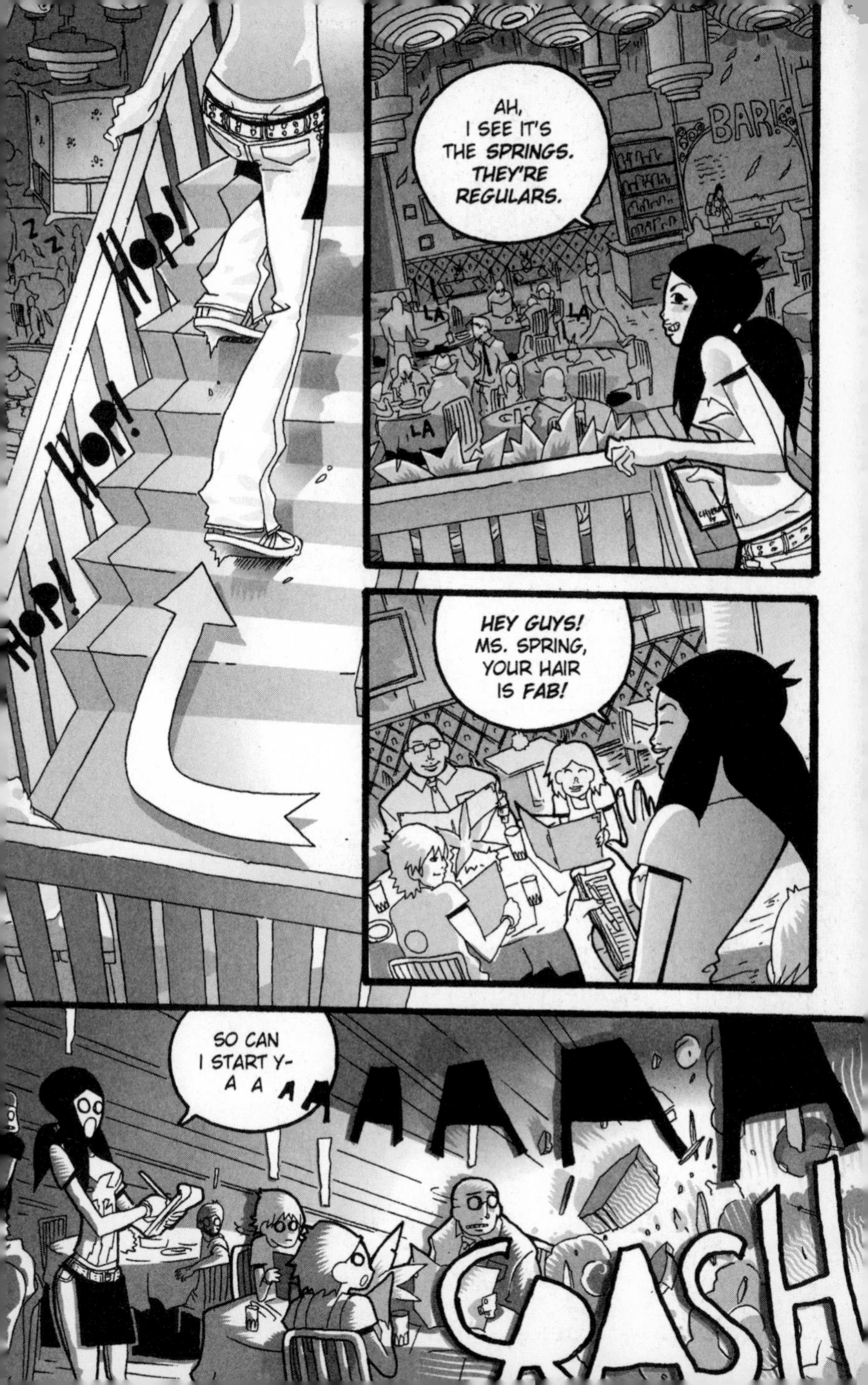
HOP!
HOP!
HOP!
Z
Z
AH, I SEE IT'S THE SPRINGS. THEY'RE REGULARS.
BAR!
LA
LA
LA
HEY GUYS! MS. SPRING, YOUR HAIR IS FAB!
SO CAN I START Y- A A A A
AAAAH
!
!
!
CRASH

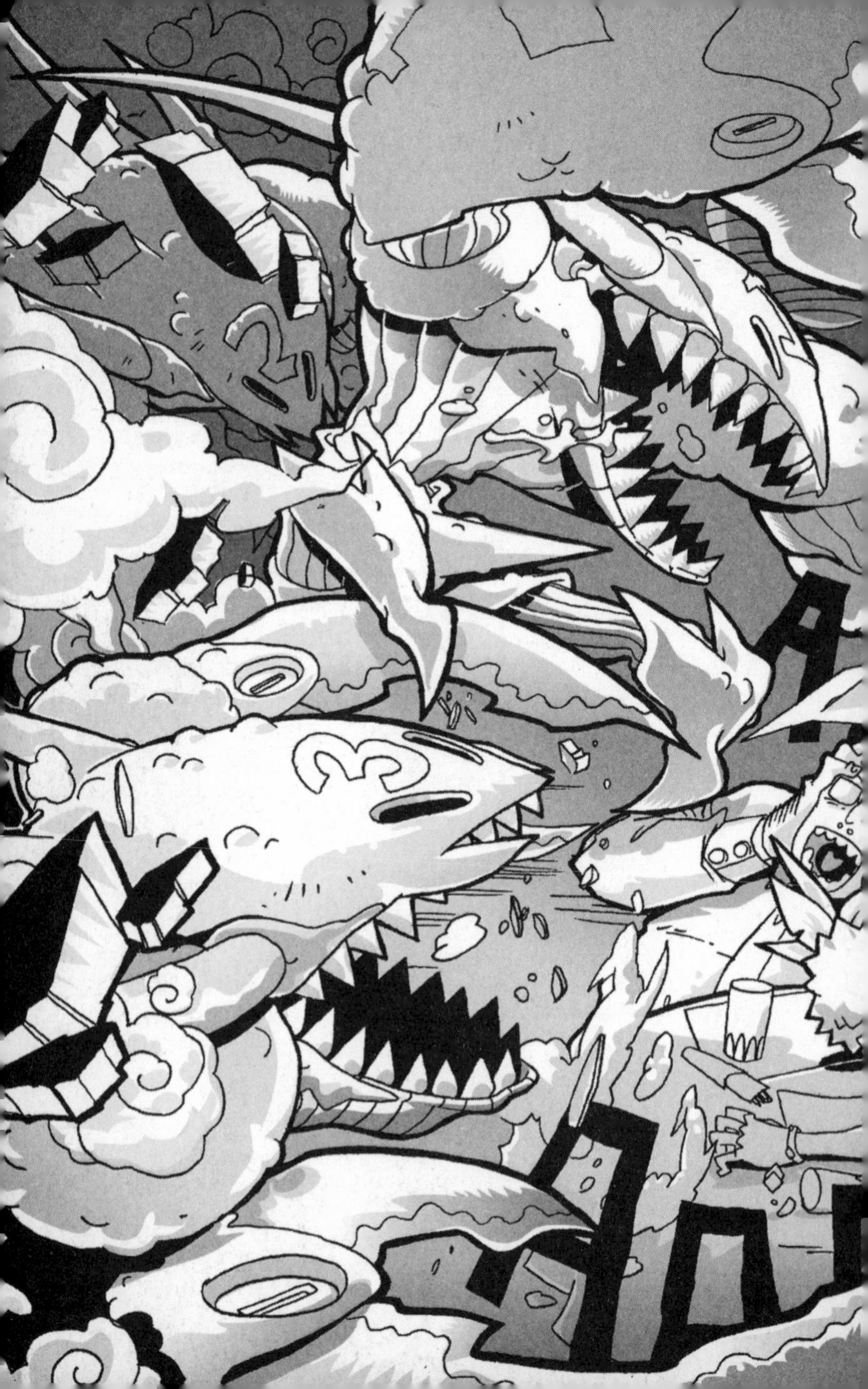

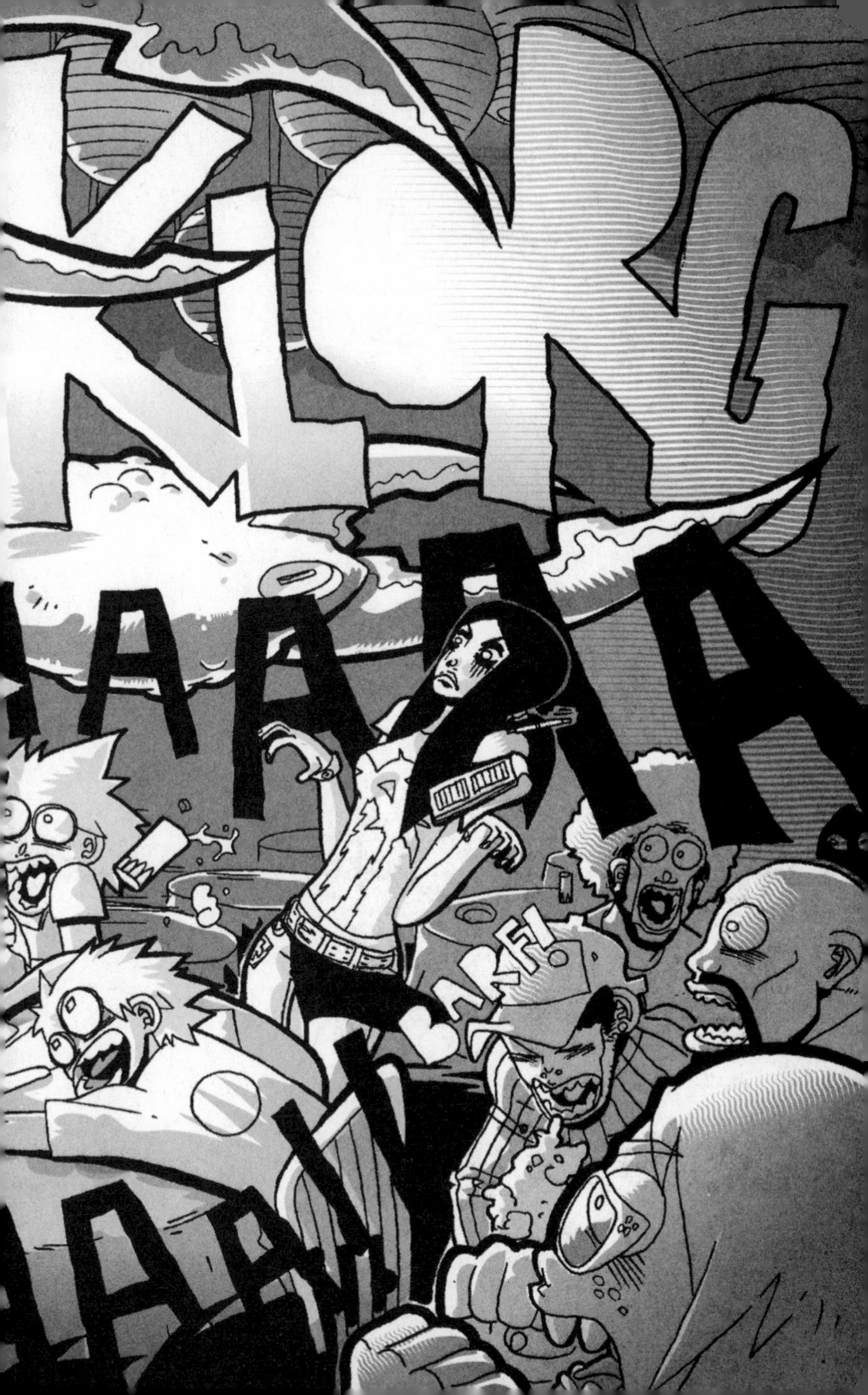
ARF!

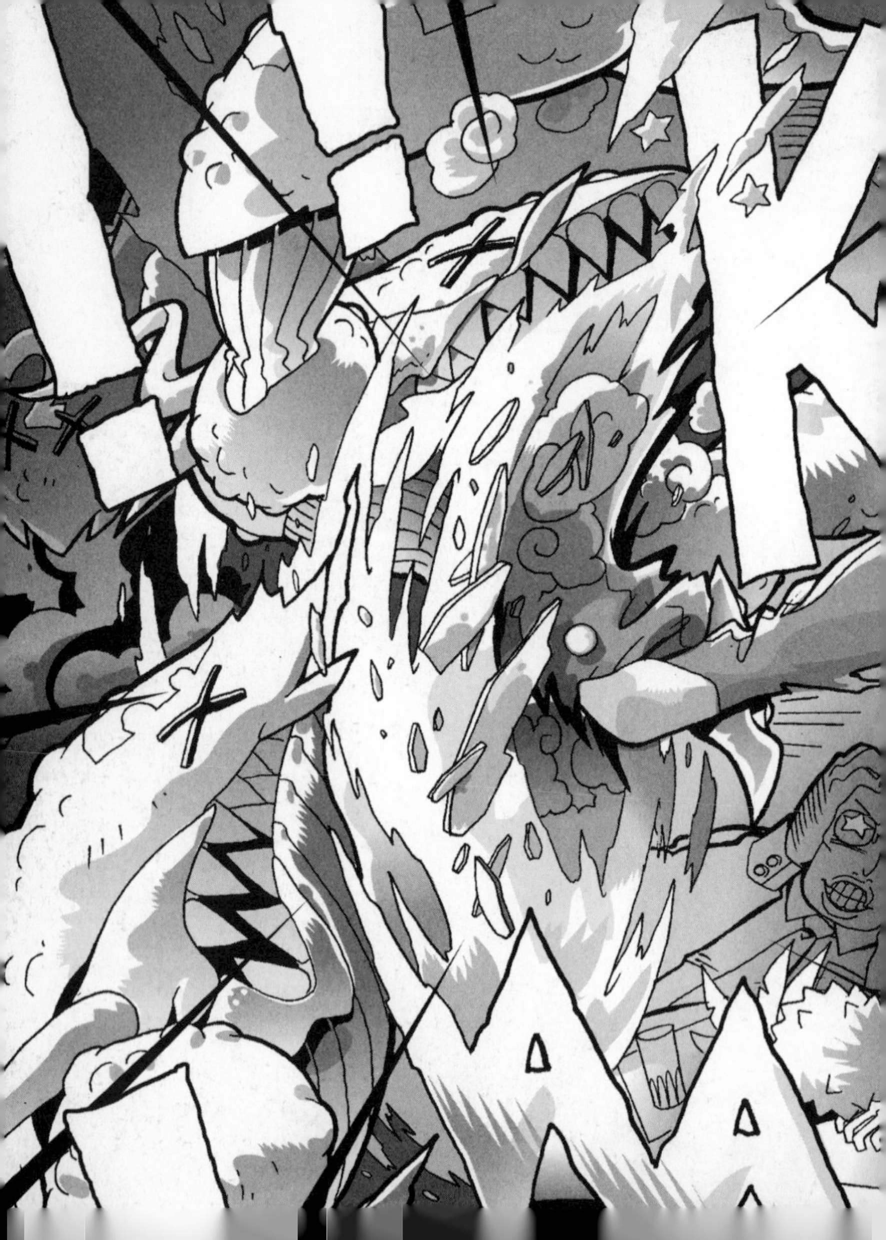

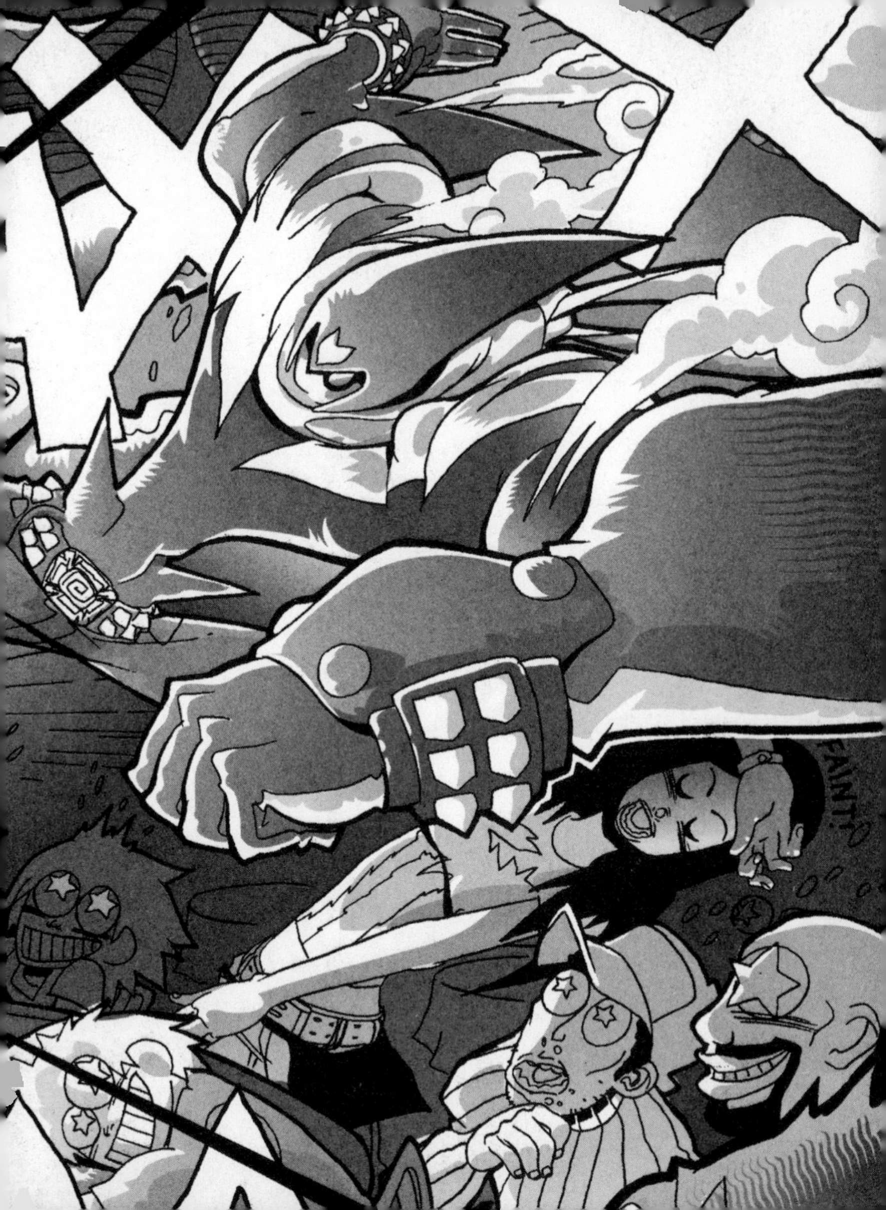
FAINT!

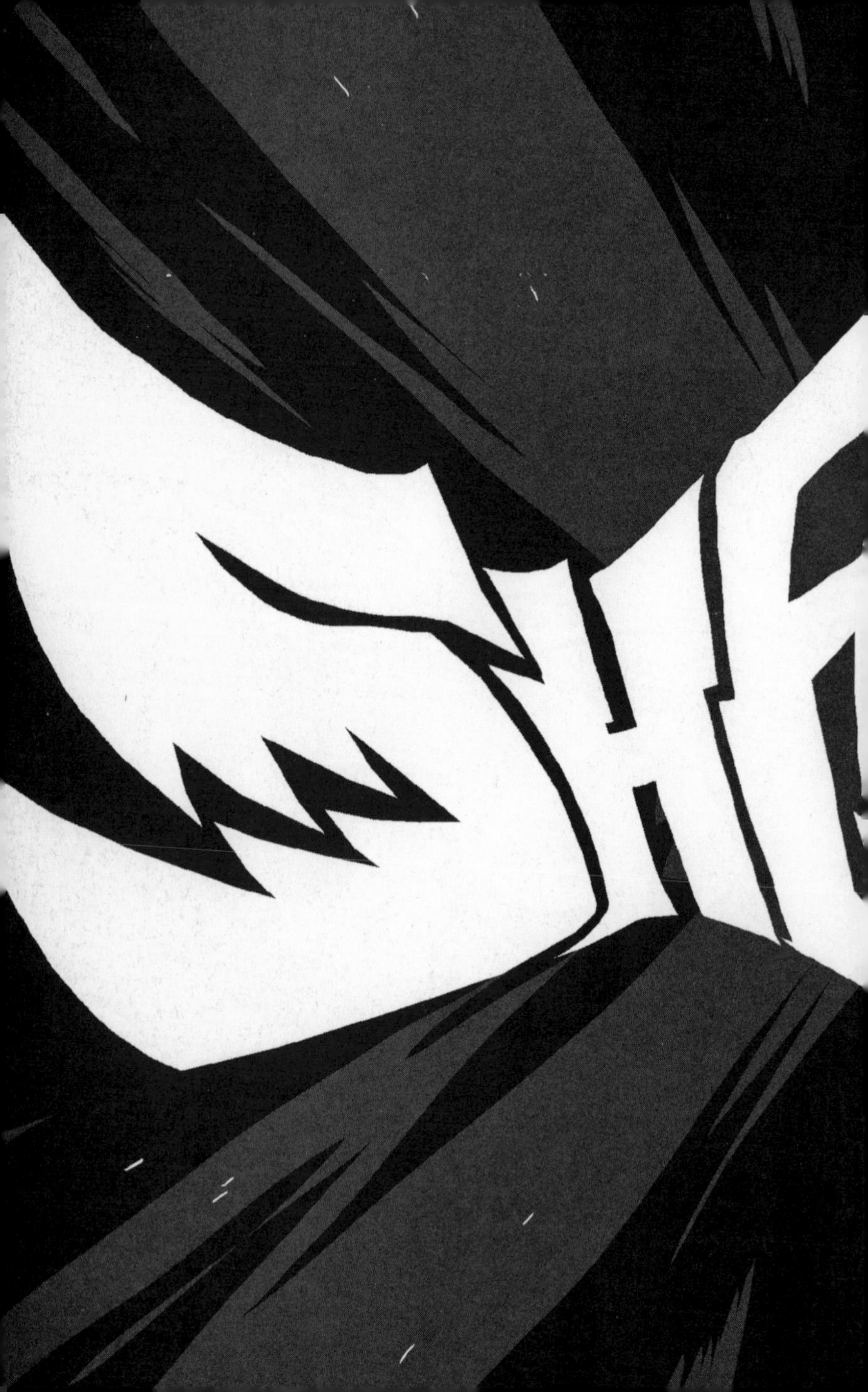

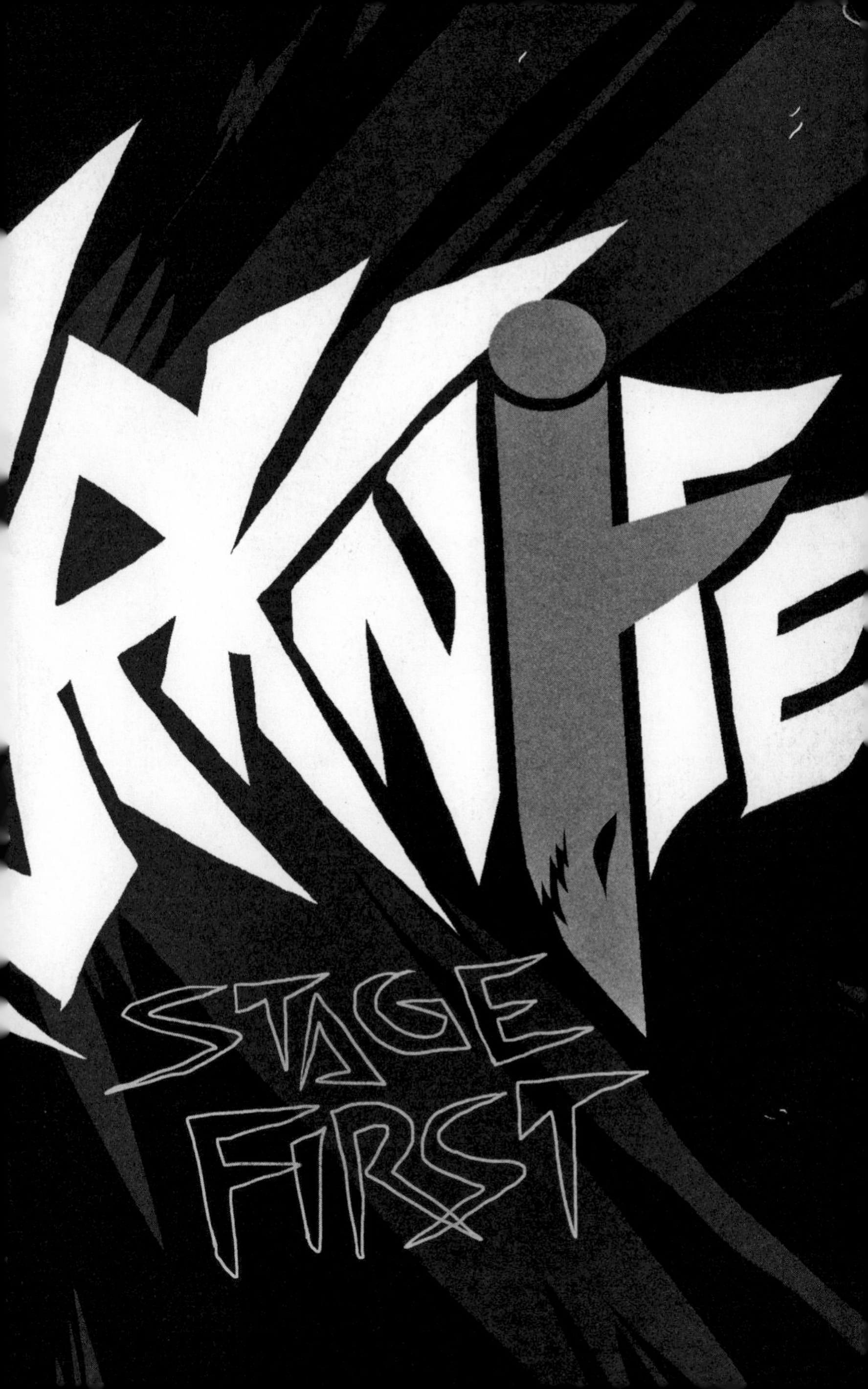
STAGE
FIRST

SHARKNIFE

BREAKER 1

SHARKNIFE'S SPIRAL EXPLOSION!

FIGHT
LOVE
SWIM

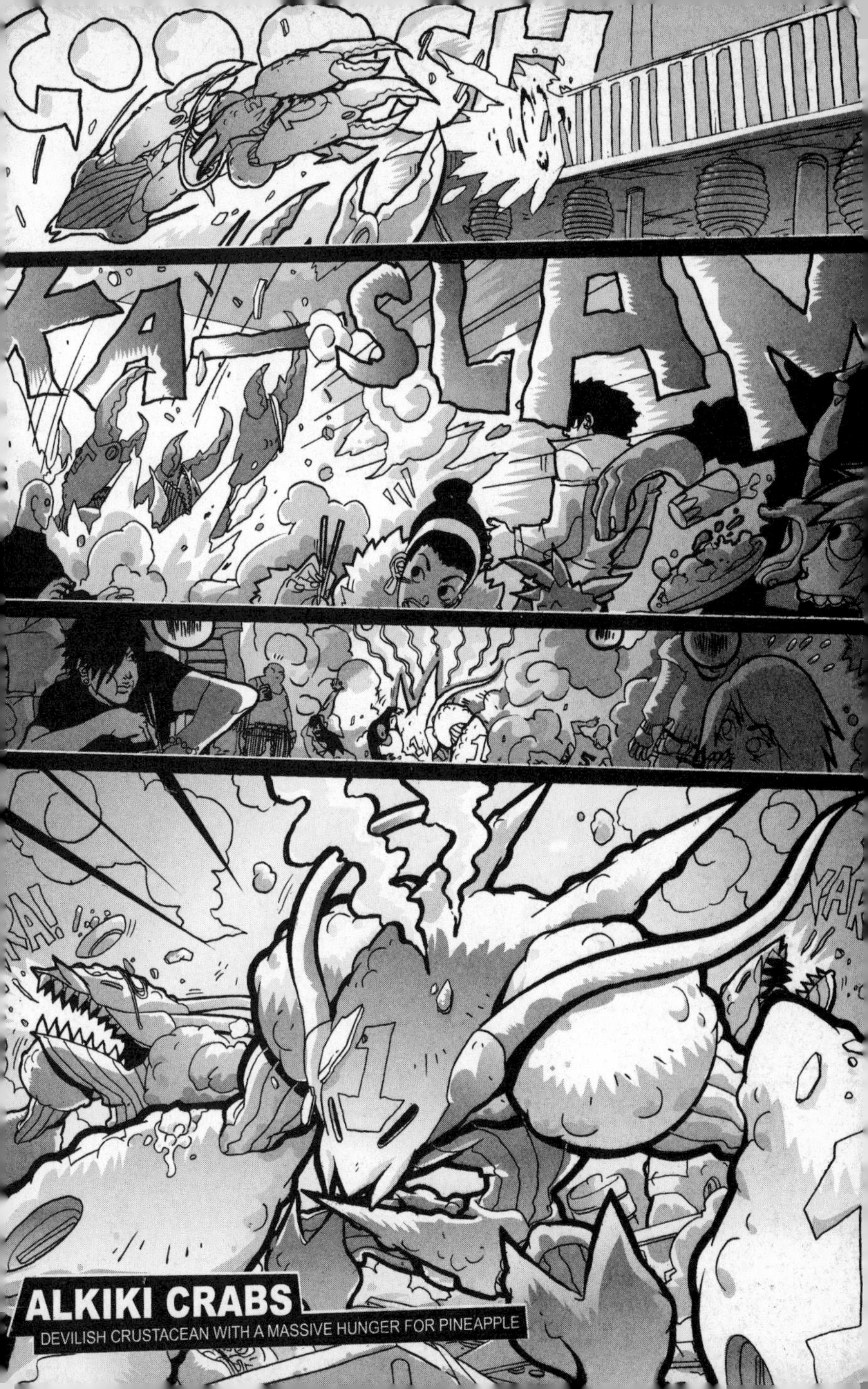
GOOOCH
KA-SLAM
ALKIKI CRABS
DEVILISH CRUSTACEAN WITH A MASSIVE HUNGER FOR PINEAPPLE

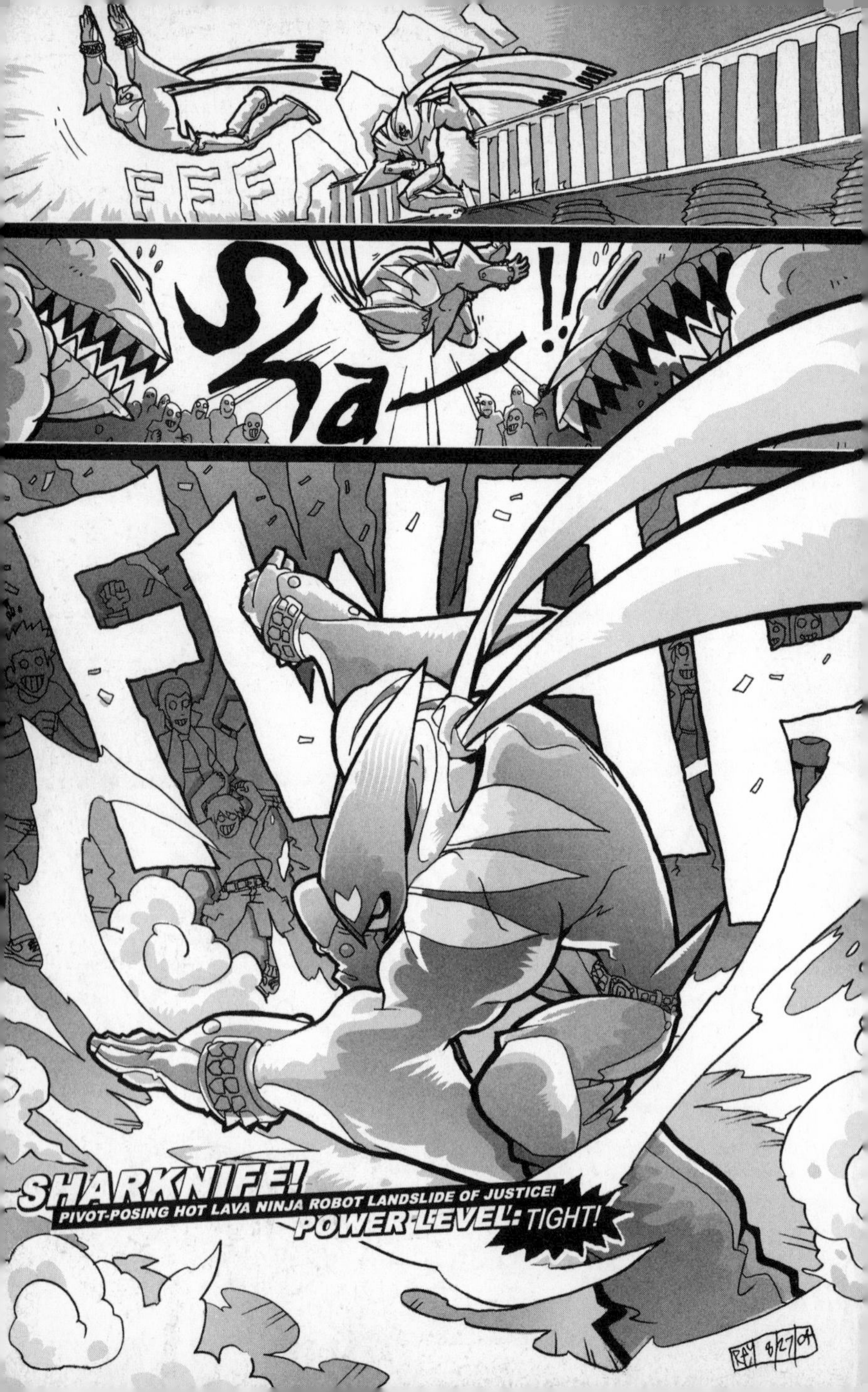
FFFF
Sha!!
SHARKNIFE!
PIVOT-POSING HOT LAVA NINJA ROBOT LANDSLIDE OF JUSTICE!
POWER LEVEL: TIGHT!
RAY 8/27/09

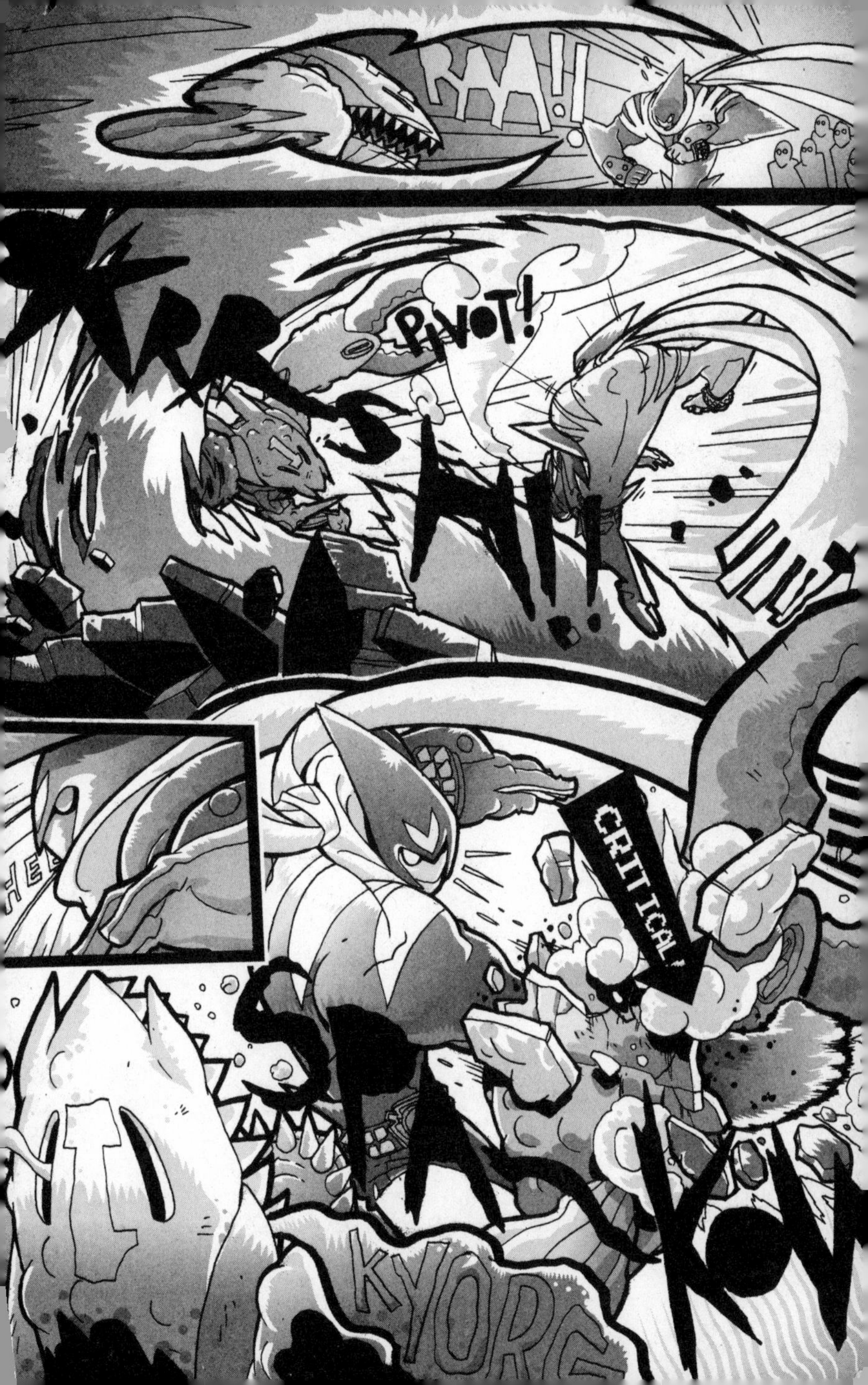
RYAA!!
PIVOT!
CRITICAL

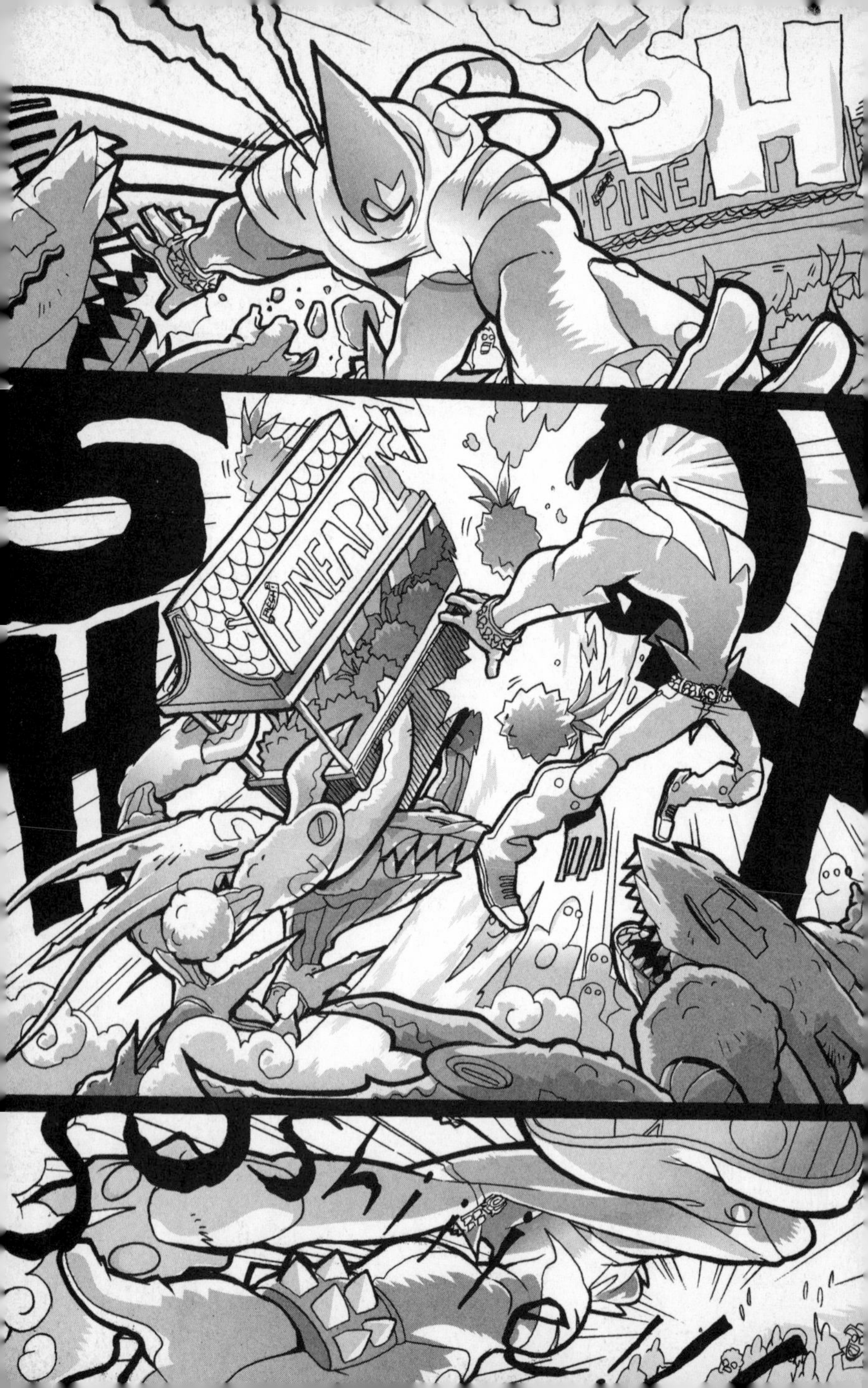
SH
PINEAPPL

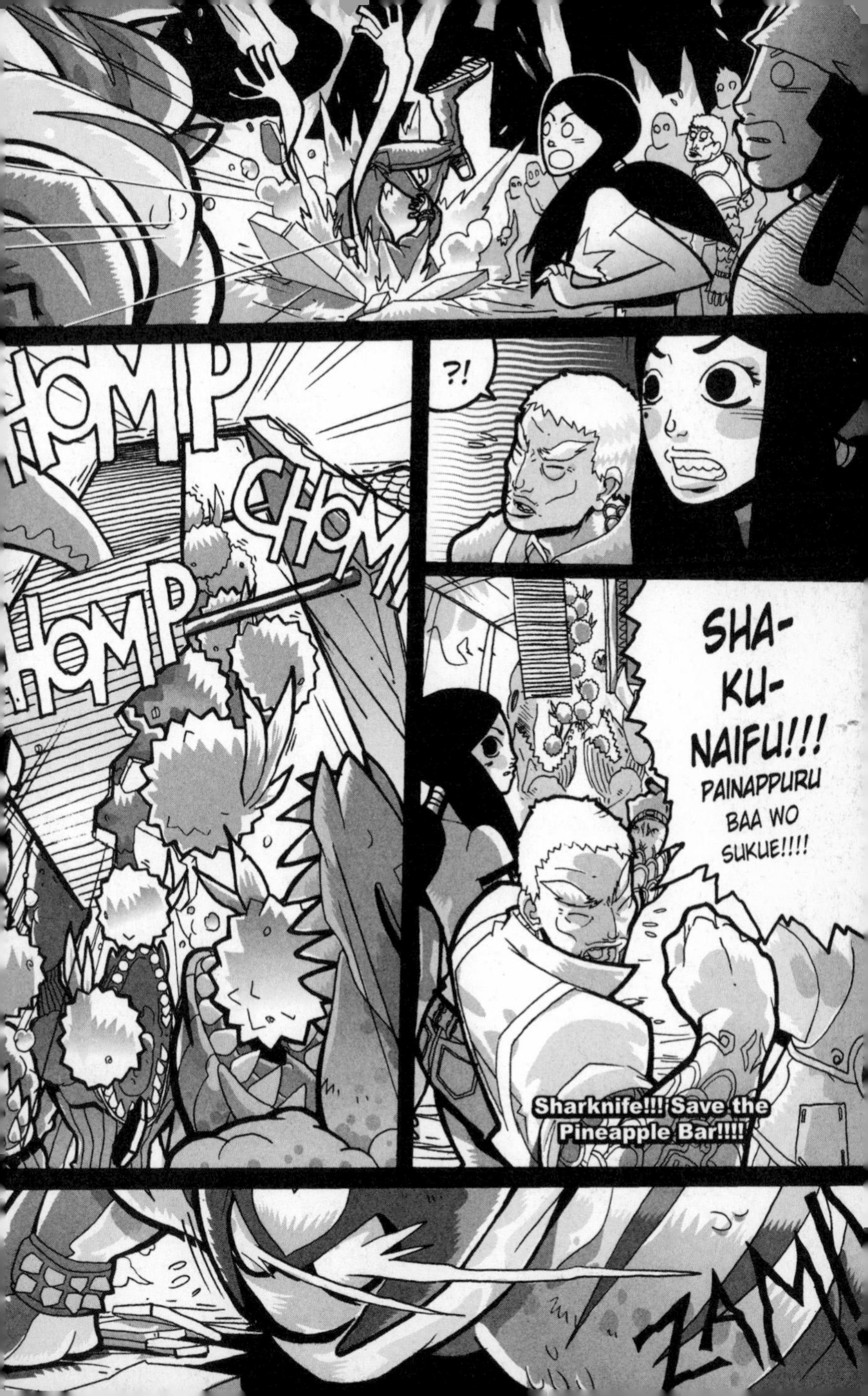
CHOMP
CHOMP
CHOMP
?!
SHA-
KU-
NAIFU!!!
PAINAPPURU
BAA WO
SUKUE!!!!
Sharknife!!! Save the
Pineapple Bar!!!!
ZAM!

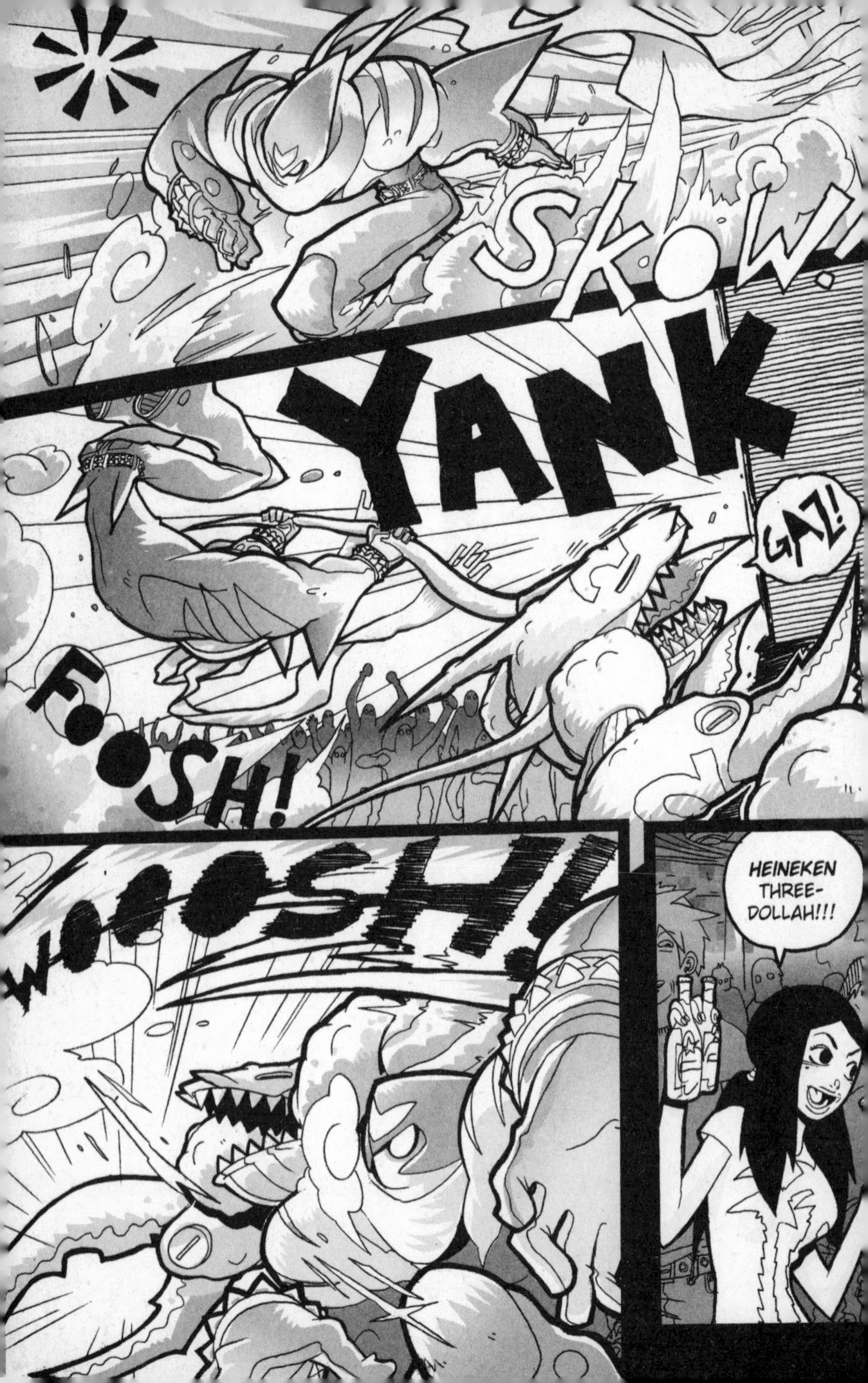
SKOW!
YANK
GAZ!
FOOSH!
WOOOSH!
HEINEKEN THREE-DOLLAH!!!

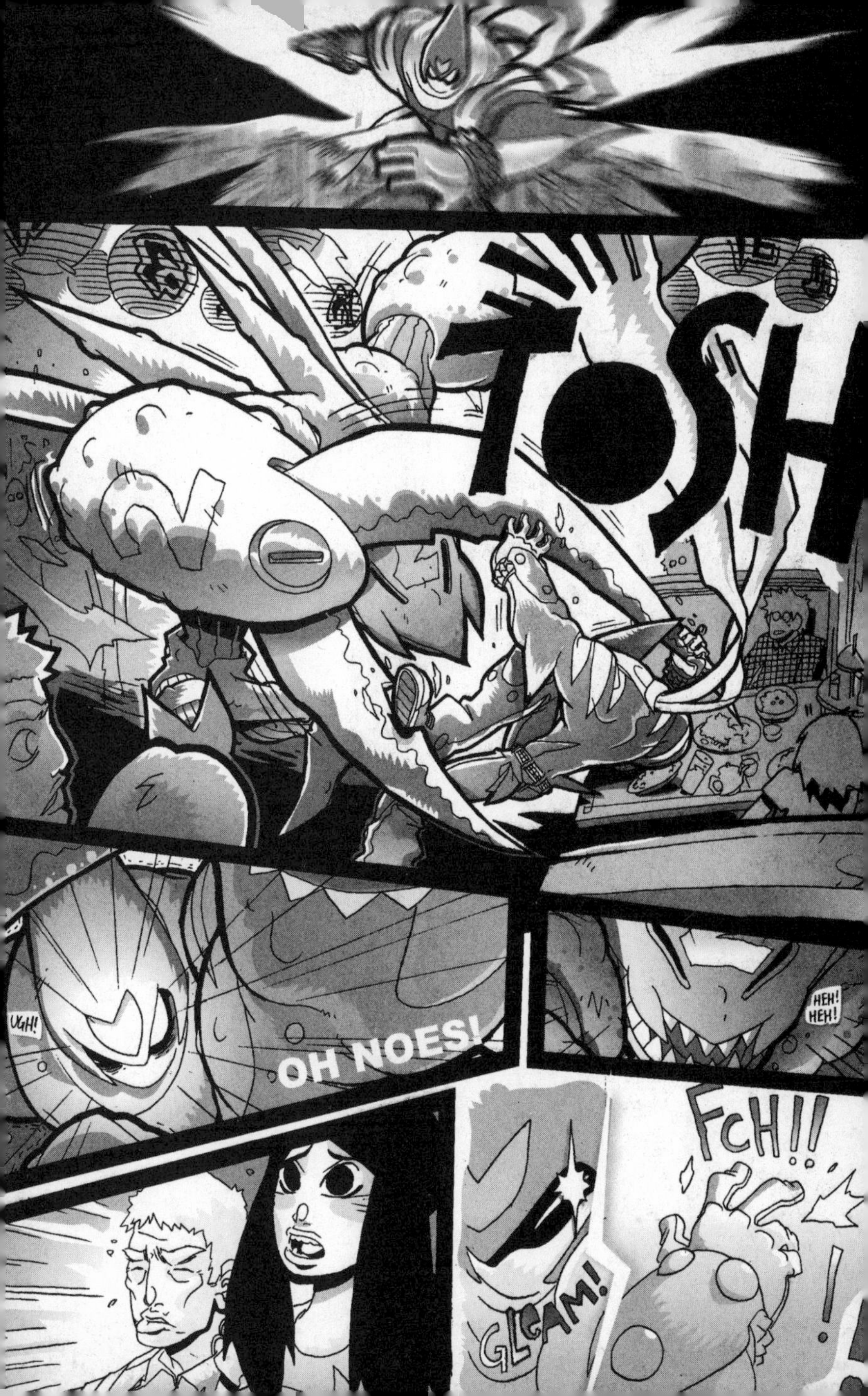
TOSH
UGH!
OH NOES!
HEH! HEH!
FCH!!
GLEAM!
!

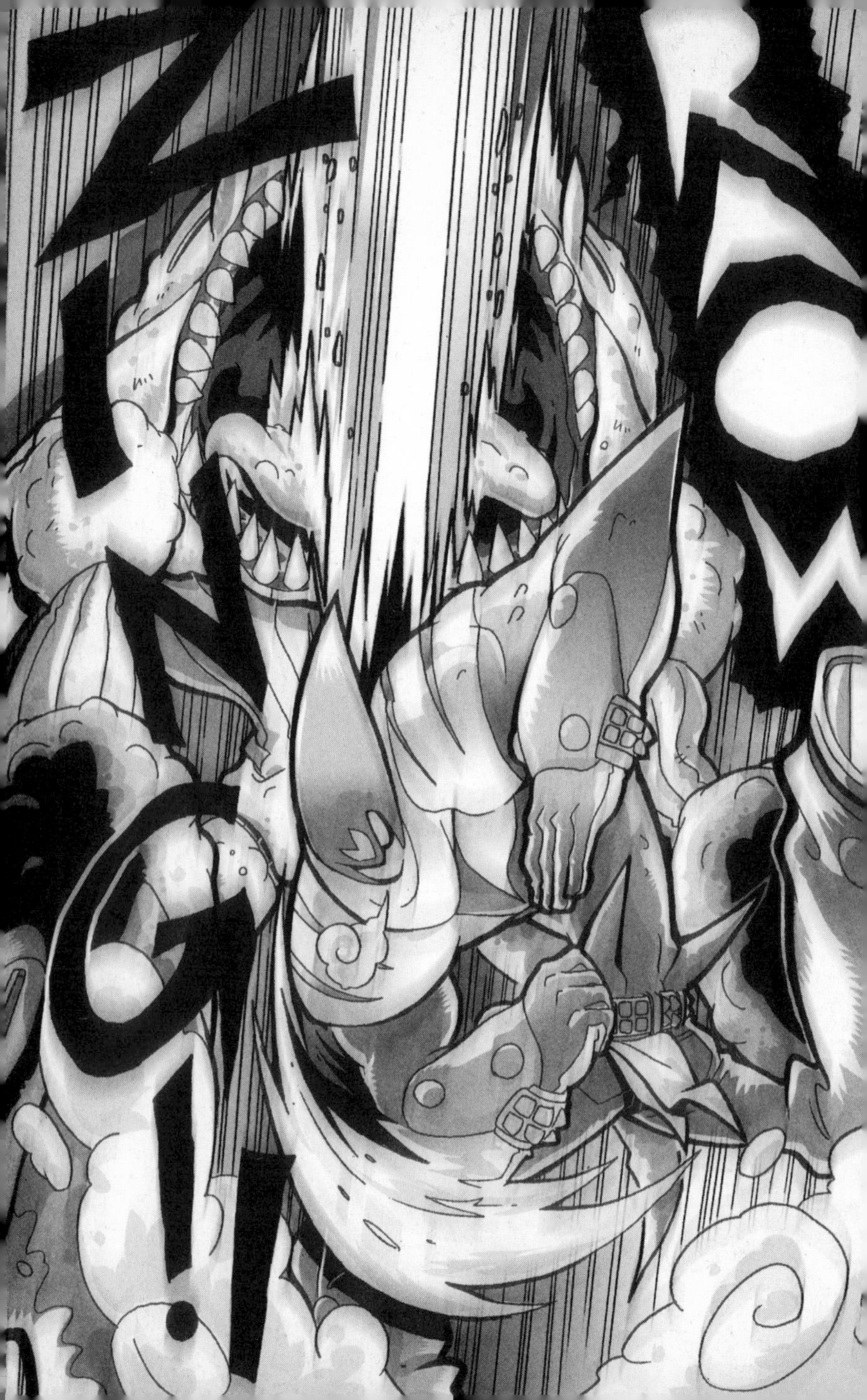

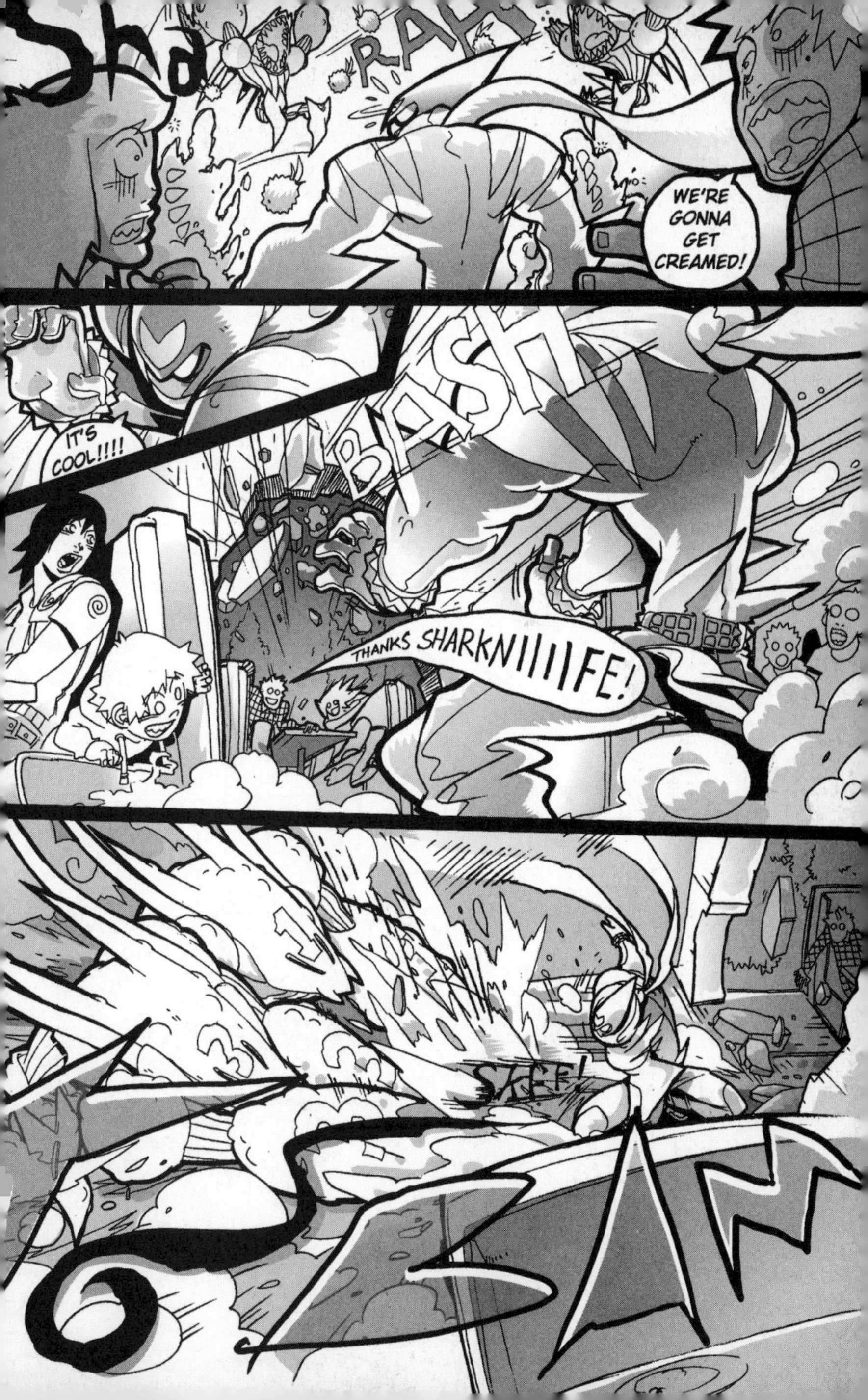
Sha
RAH
WE'RE GONNA GET CREAMED!
IT'S COOL!!!!
BASH
THANKS SHARKNIIIIIFE!

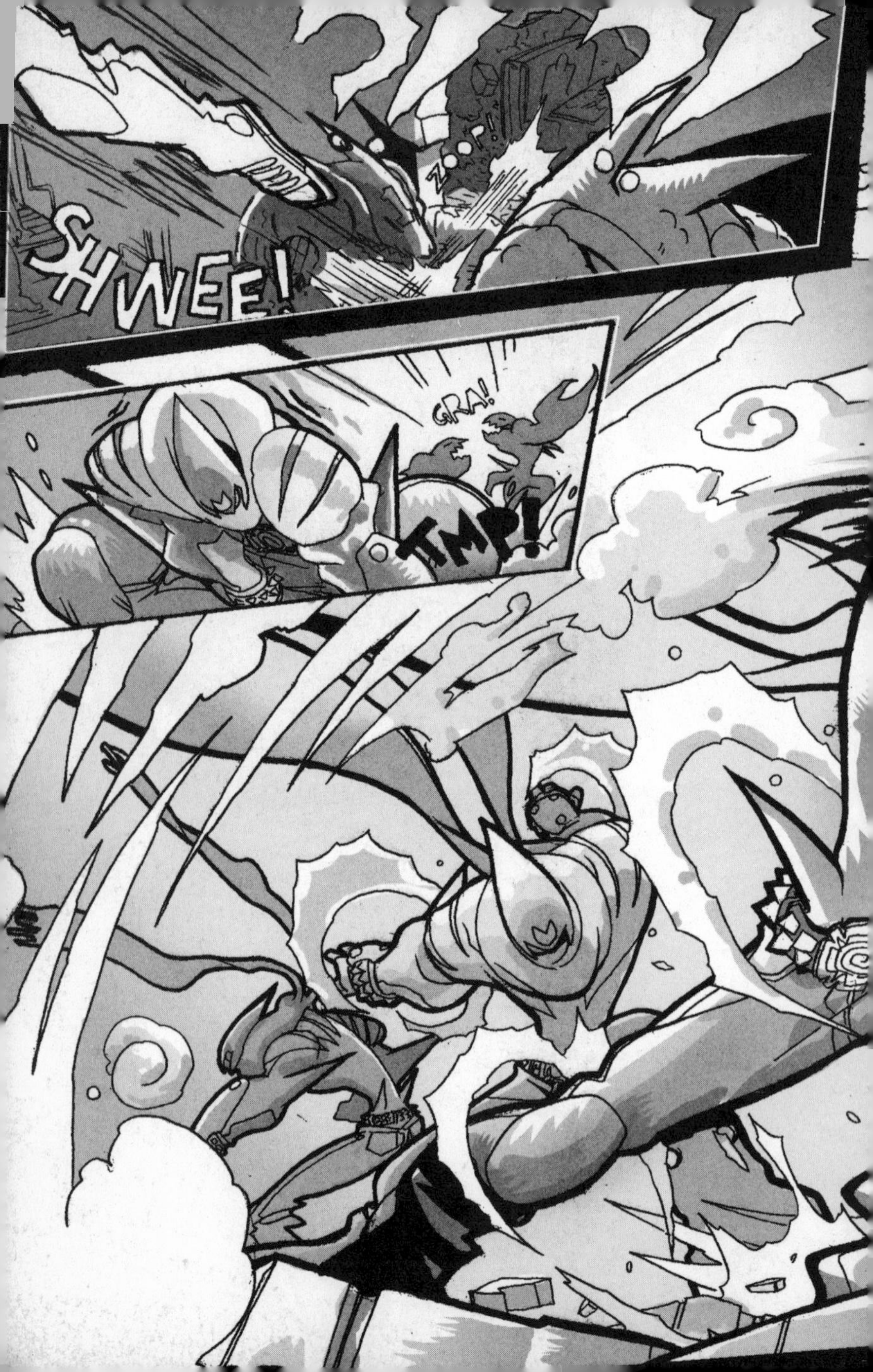

SHWEE!
ZOOP!
GRA!
TMP!

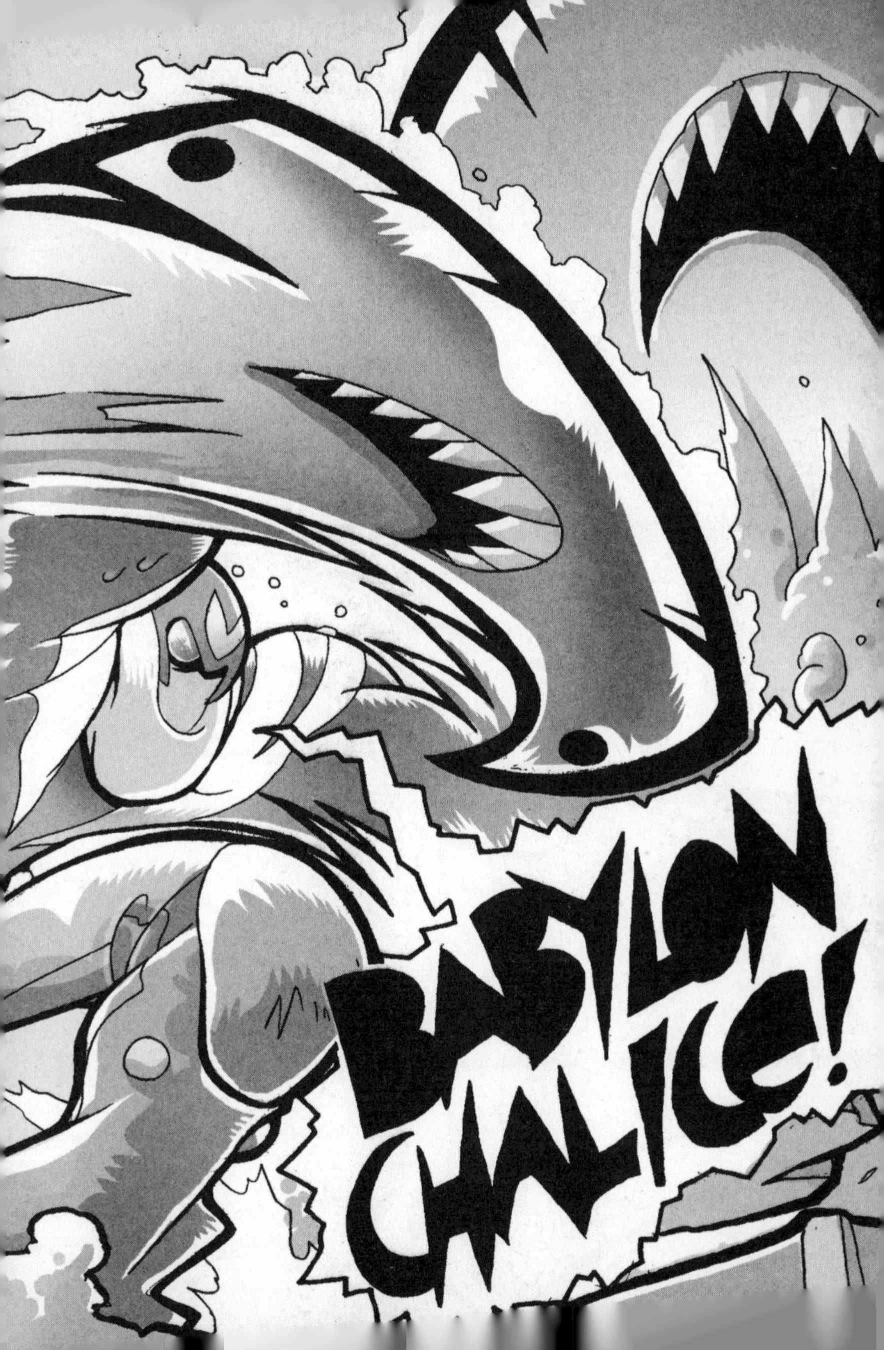
BABYLON CHALICE!

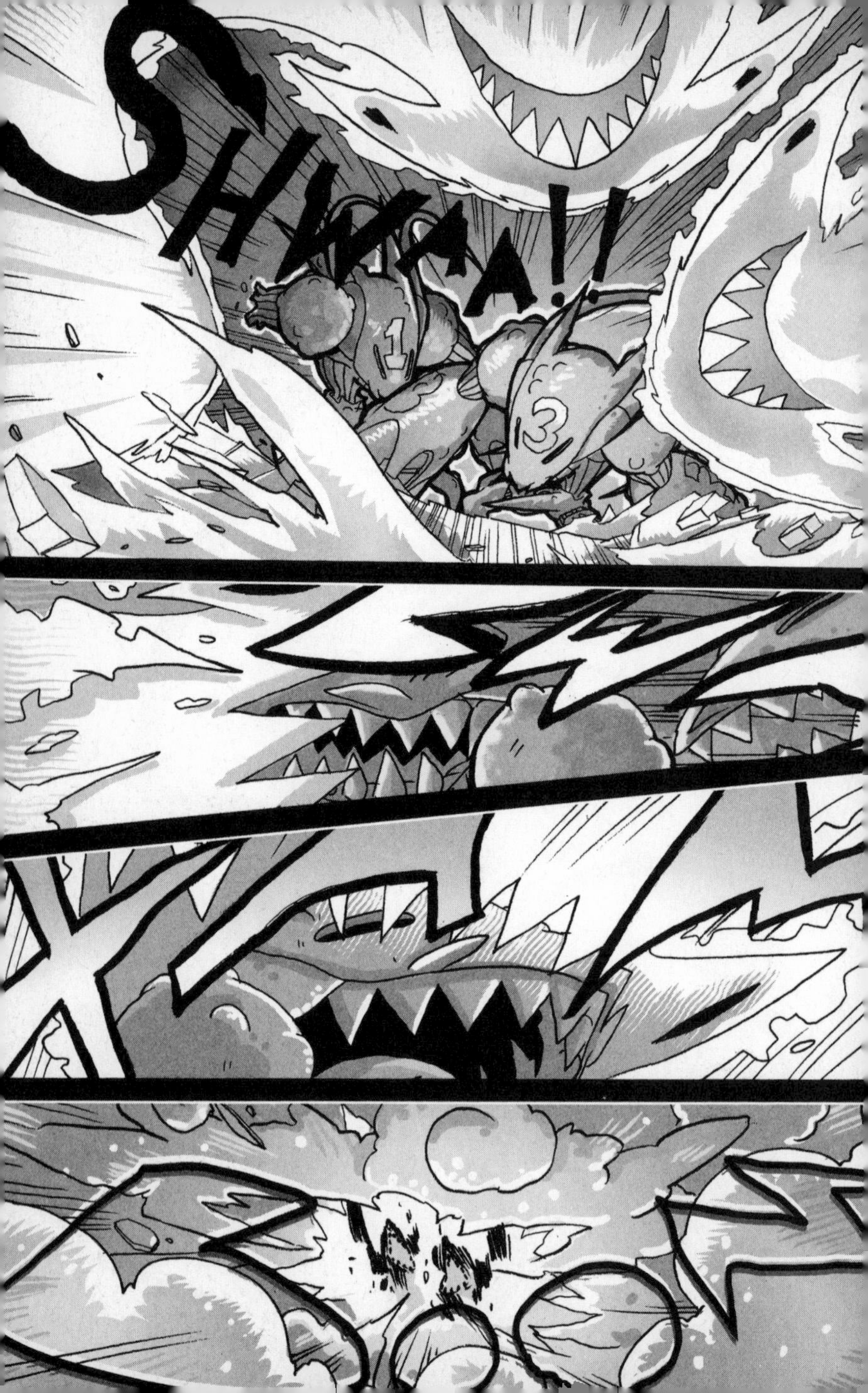
SHWAA!!

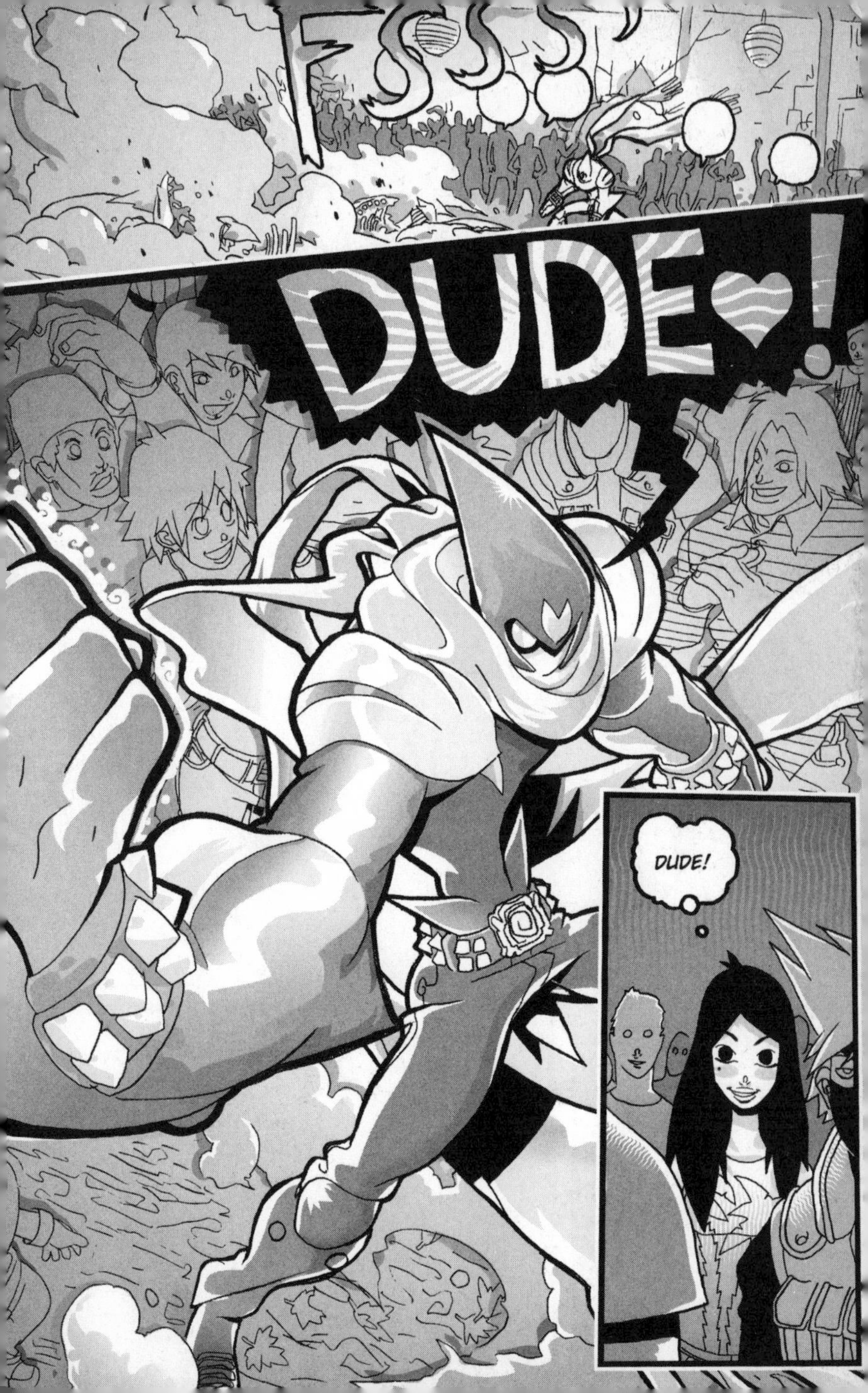
FSSS
DUDE♥!
DUDE!

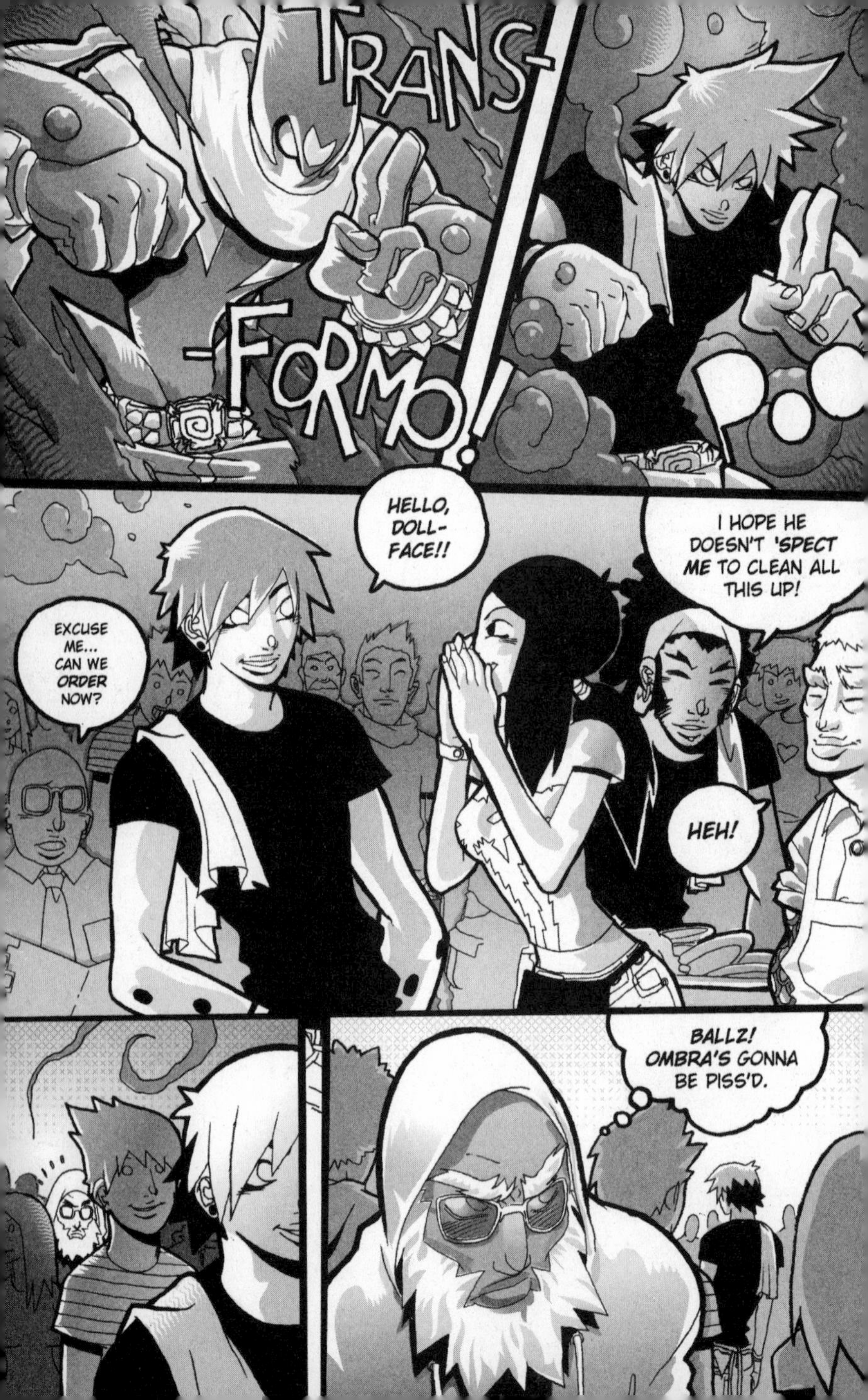
TRANS-
-FORMO!!
POOF
HELLO, DOLL-FACE!!
I HOPE HE DOESN'T 'SPECT ME TO CLEAN ALL THIS UP!
EXCUSE ME... CAN WE ORDER NOW?
HEH!
BALLZ! OMBRA'S GONNA BE PISS'D.

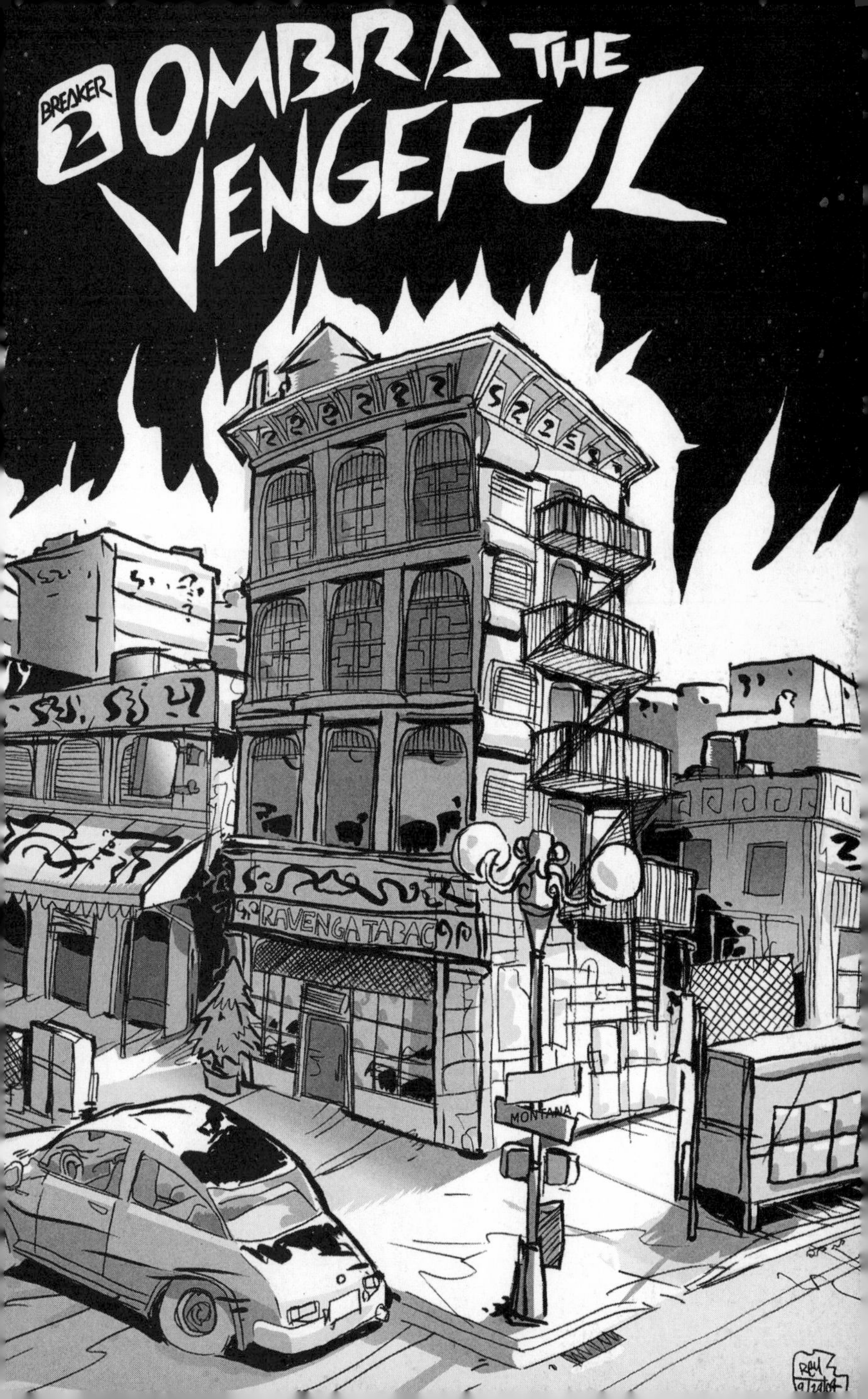
BREAKER 2
OMBRA THE VENGEFUL
RAVENGA TABAC
MONTANA

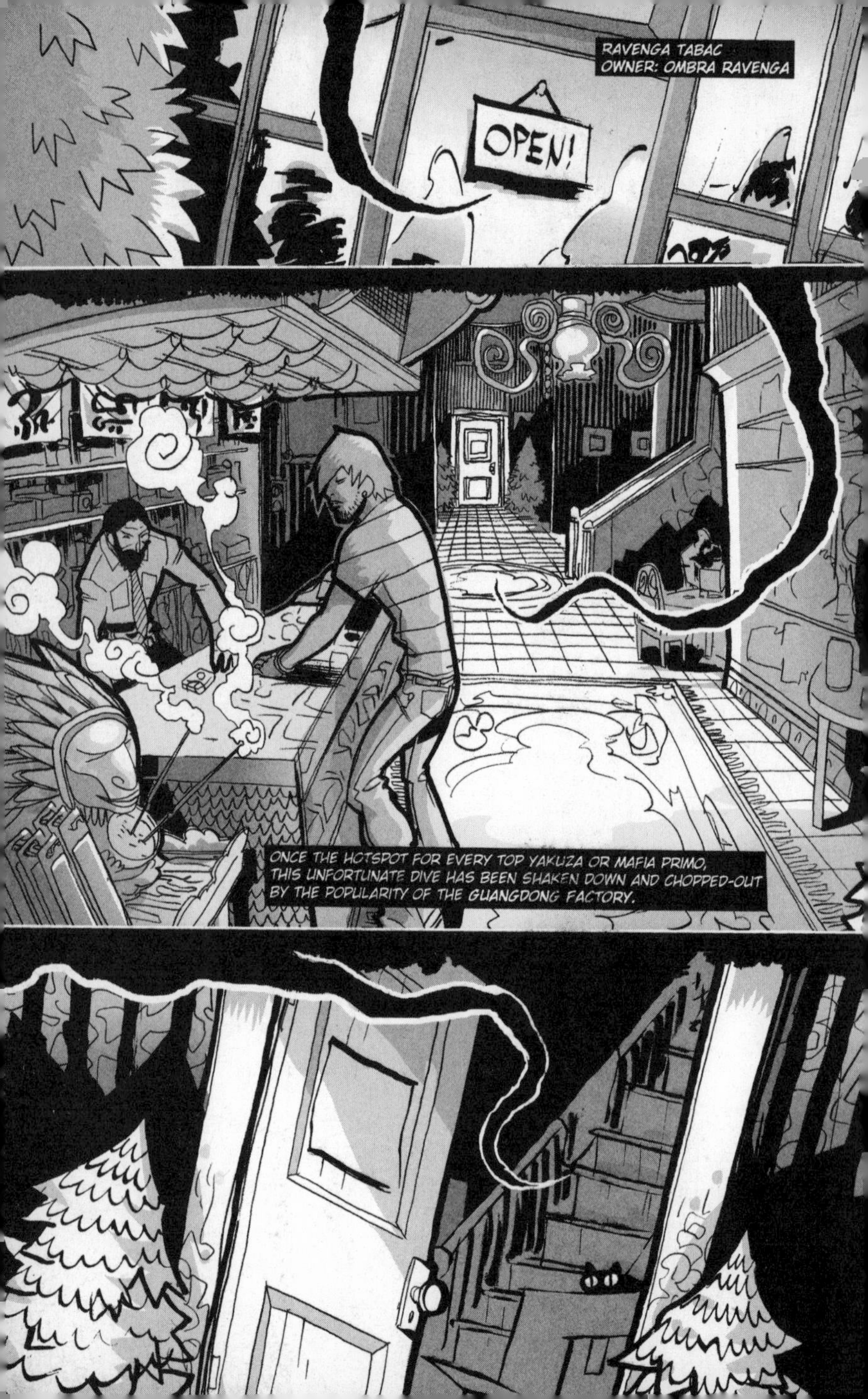
RAVENGA TABAC
OWNER: OMBRA RAVENGA
OPEN!
ONCE THE HOTSPOT FOR EVERY TOP YAKUZA OR MAFIA PRIMO, THIS UNFORTUNATE DIVE HAS BEEN SHAKEN DOWN AND CHOPPED-OUT BY THE POPULARITY OF THE GUANGDONG FACTORY.

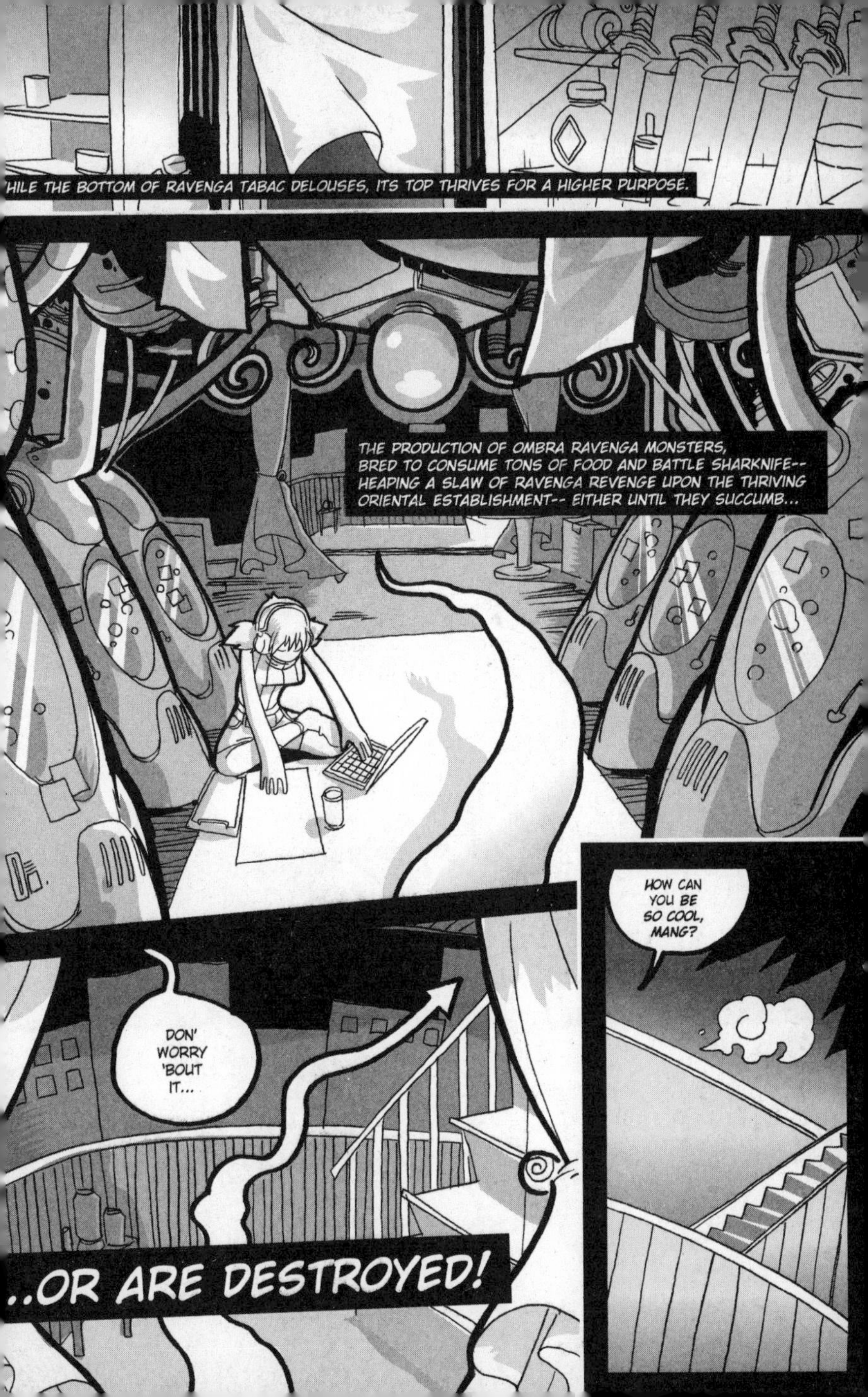
HILE THE BOTTOM OF RAVENGA TABAC DELOUSES, ITS TOP THRIVES FOR A HIGHER PURPOSE.
THE PRODUCTION OF OMBRA RAVENGA MONSTERS, BRED TO CONSUME TONS OF FOOD AND BATTLE SHARKNIFE-- HEAPING A SLAW OF RAVENGA REVENGE UPON THE THRIVING ORIENTAL ESTABLISHMENT-- EITHER UNTIL THEY SUCCUMB...
HOW CAN YOU BE SO COOL, MANG?
DON' WORRY 'BOUT IT...
..OR ARE DESTROYED!

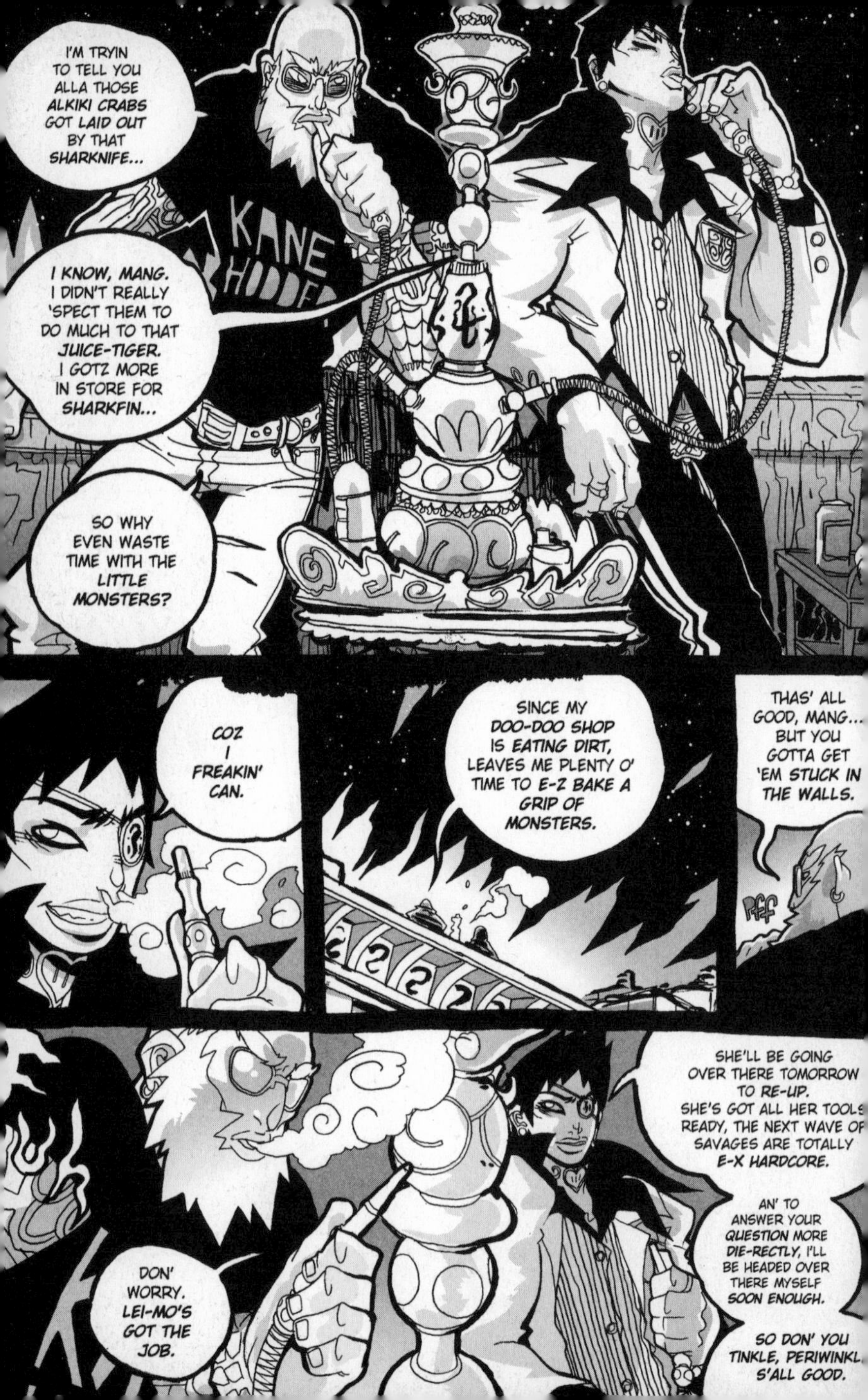
I'M TRYIN TO TELL YOU ALLA THOSE ALKIKI CRABS GOT LAID OUT BY THAT SHARKNIFE...
KANE HODDER
I KNOW, MANG. I DIDN'T REALLY 'SPECT THEM TO DO MUCH TO THAT JUICE-TIGER. I GOTZ MORE IN STORE FOR SHARKFIN...
SO WHY EVEN WASTE TIME WITH THE LITTLE MONSTERS?
COZ I FREAKIN' CAN.
SINCE MY DOO-DOO SHOP IS EATING DIRT, LEAVES ME PLENTY O' TIME TO E-Z BAKE A GRIP OF MONSTERS.
THAS' ALL GOOD, MANG... BUT YOU GOTTA GET 'EM STUCK IN THE WALLS.
Pff
DON' WORRY. LEI-MO'S GOT THE JOB.
SHE'LL BE GOING OVER THERE TOMORROW TO RE-UP. SHE'S GOT ALL HER TOOLS READY, THE NEXT WAVE OF SAVAGES ARE TOTALLY E-X HARDCORE.
AN' TO ANSWER YOUR QUESTION MORE DIE-RECTLY, I'LL BE HEADED OVER THERE MYSELF SOON ENOUGH.
SO DON' YOU TINKLE, PERIWINKL S'ALL GOOD.

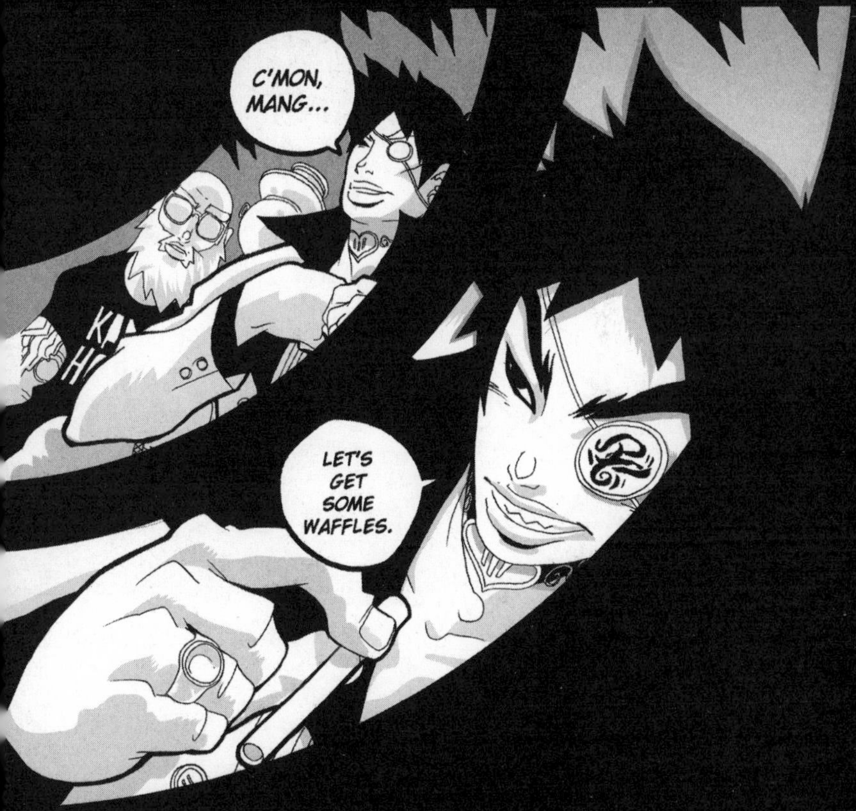
C'MON, MANG...
LET'S GET SOME WAFFLES.

At least one person has said...

"The lifespan of a gangster can be told through the suits he has worn."

Ombra Ravenga has worn many suits.

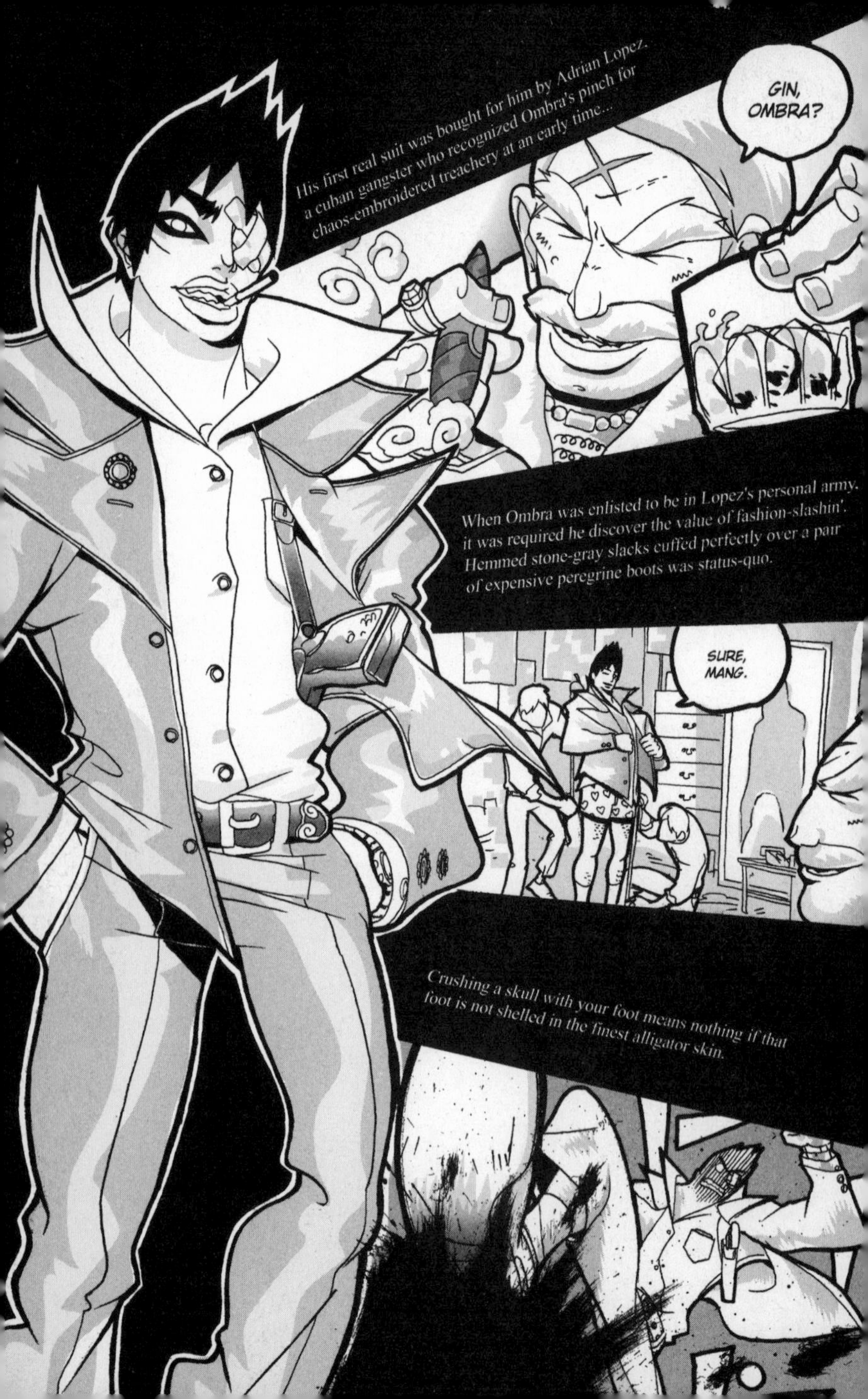
His first real suit was bought for him by Adrian Lopez, a cuban gangster who recognized Ombra's pinch for chaos-embroidered treachery at an early time...
GIN, OMBRA?
When Ombra was enlisted to be in Lopez's personal army, it was required he discover the value of fashion-slashin'. Hemmed stone-gray slacks cuffed perfectly over a pair of expensive peregrine boots was status-quo.
SURE, MANG.
Crushing a skull with your foot means nothing if that foot is not shelled in the finest alligator skin.

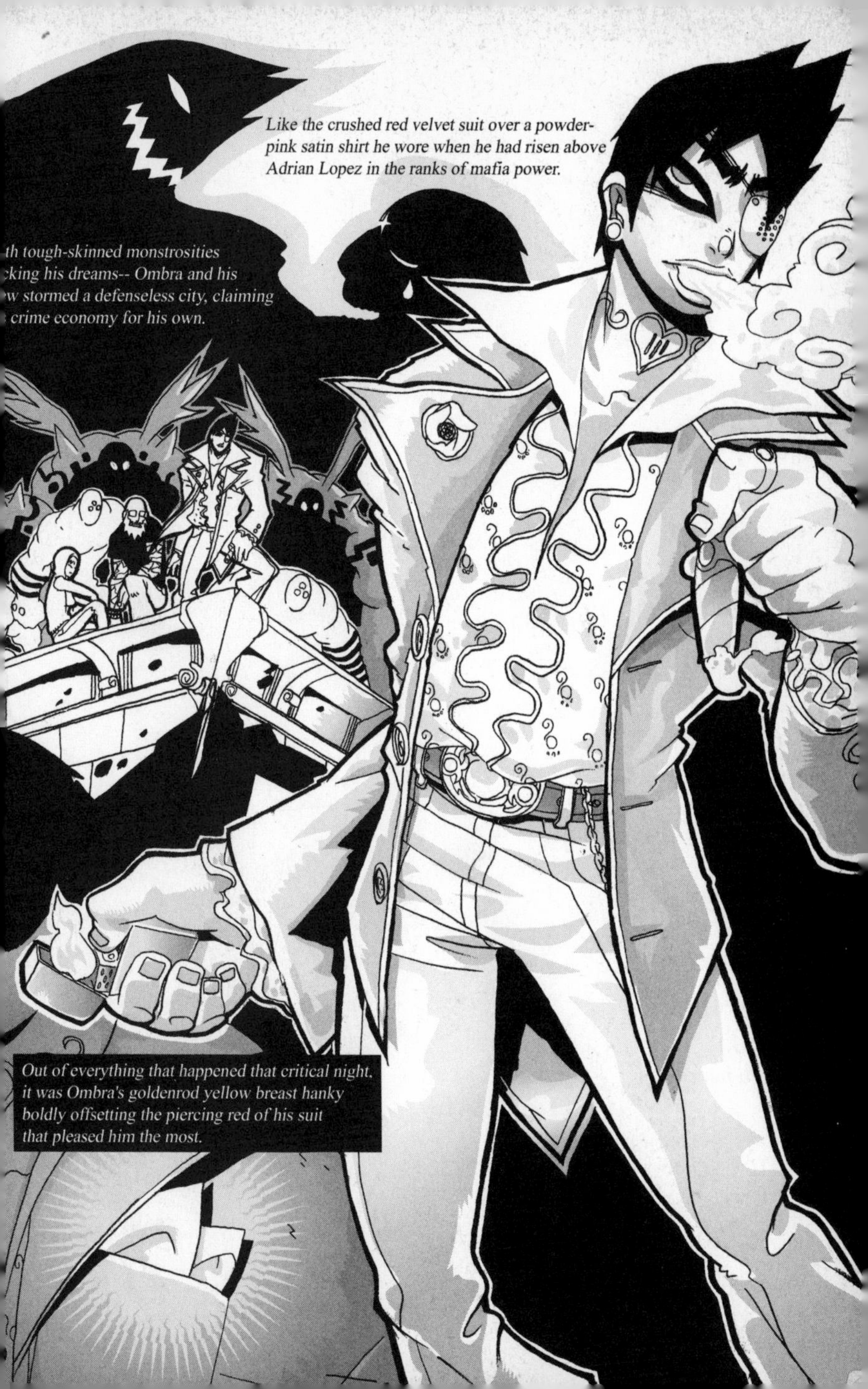
Like the crushed red velvet suit over a powder-pink satin shirt he wore when he had risen above Adrian Lopez in the ranks of mafia power.
th tough-skinned monstrosities
cking his dreams-- Ombra and his
w stormed a defenseless city, claiming
crime economy for his own.
Out of everything that happened that critical night, it was Ombra's goldenrod yellow breast hanky boldly offsetting the piercing red of his suit that pleased him the most.

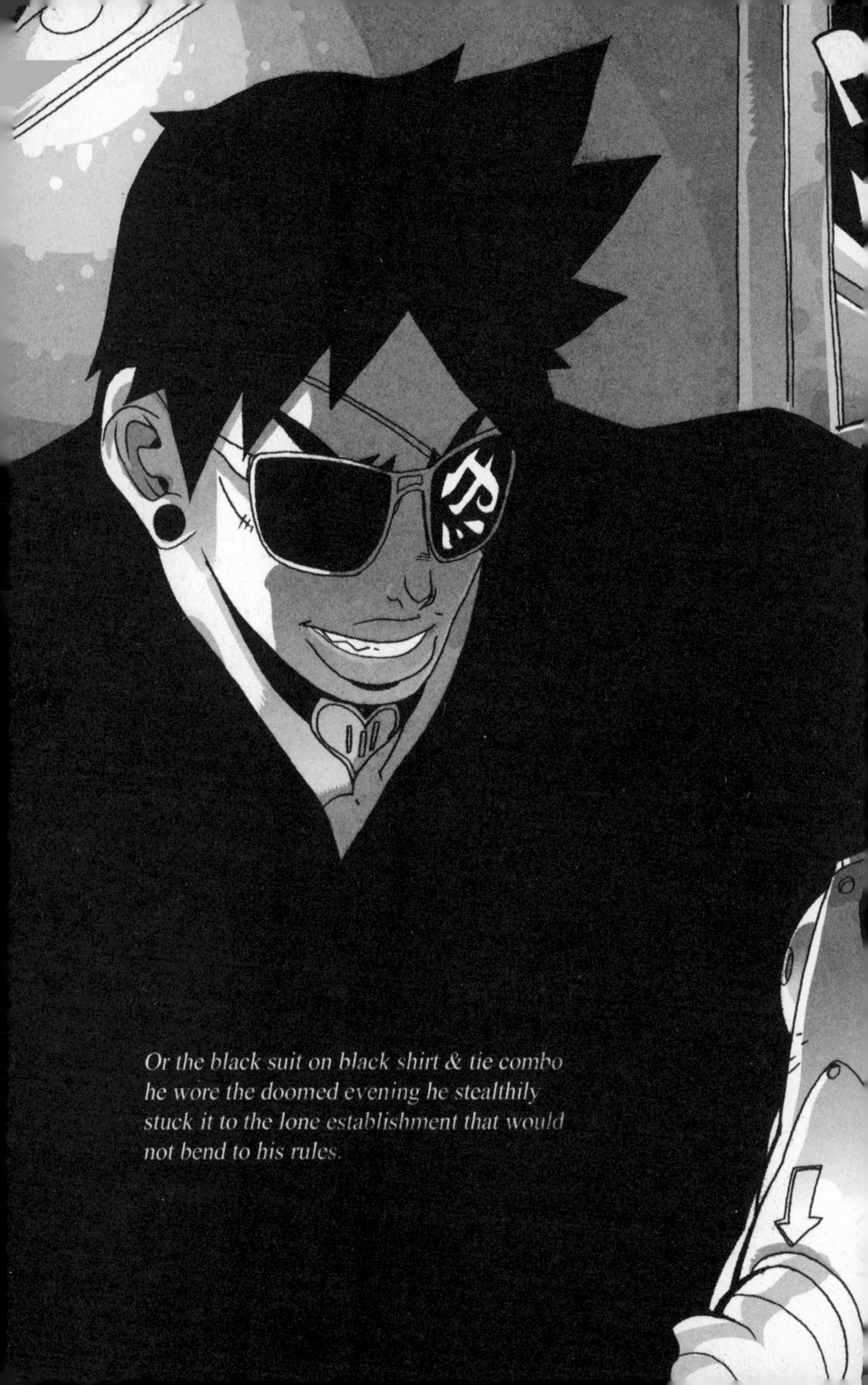
Or the black suit on black shirt & tie combo he wore the doomed evening he stealthily stuck it to the lone establishment that would not bend to his rules.

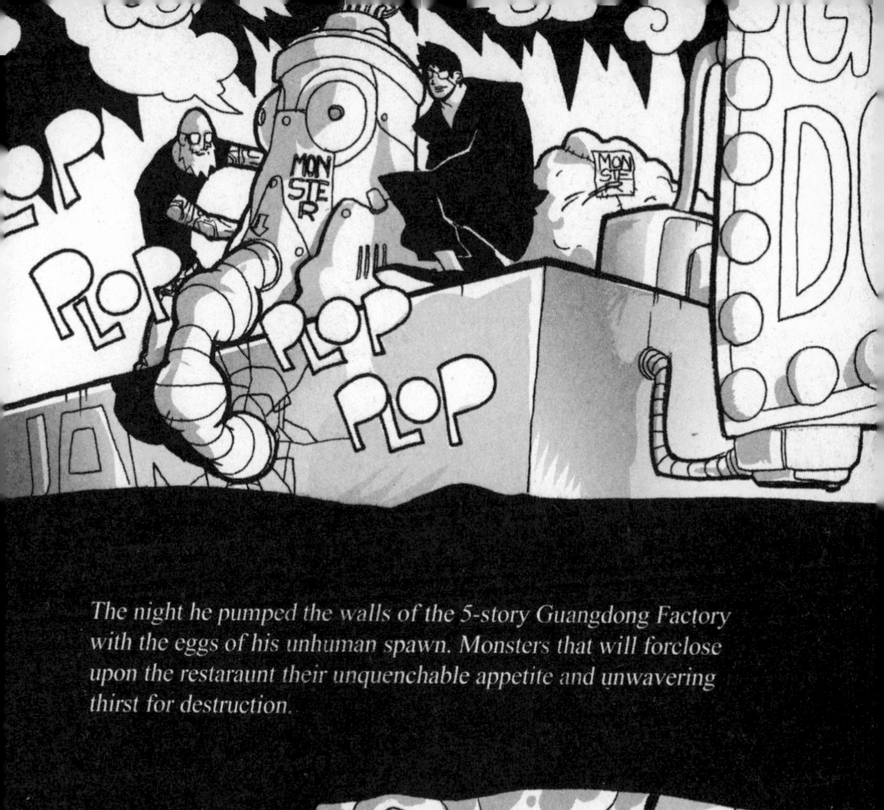
MON
STE
R
MON
STE
R
PLOP
PLOP
PLOP

The night he pumped the walls of the 5-story Guangdong Factory with the eggs of his unhuman spawn. Monsters that will forclose upon the restaraunt their unquenchable appetite and unwavering thirst for destruction.

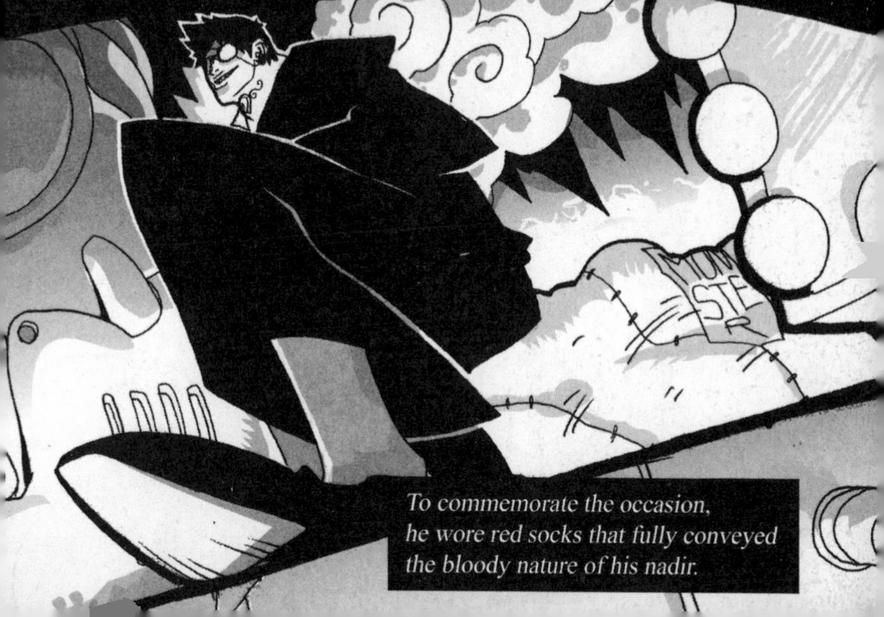
MON
STE
R
To commemorate the occasion,
he wore red socks that fully conveyed
the bloody nature of his nadir.

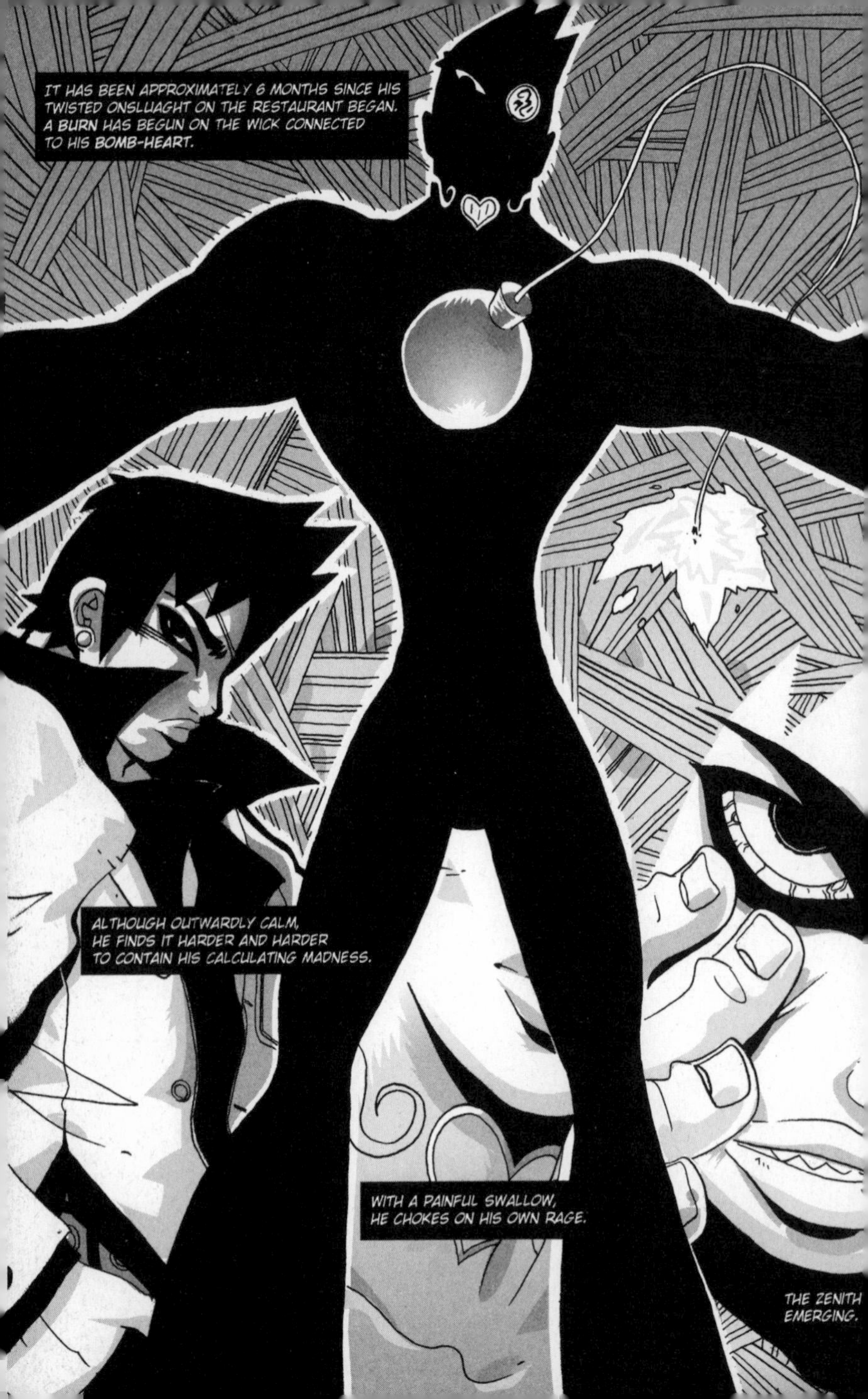
IT HAS BEEN APPROXIMATELY 6 MONTHS SINCE HIS TWISTED ONSLUAGHT ON THE RESTAURANT BEGAN. A BURN HAS BEGUN ON THE WICK CONNECTED TO HIS BOMB-HEART.
ALTHOUGH OUTWARDLY CALM, HE FINDS IT HARDER AND HARDER TO CONTAIN HIS CALCULATING MADNESS.
WITH A PAINFUL SWALLOW, HE CHOKES ON HIS OWN RAGE.
THE ZENITH EMERGING.

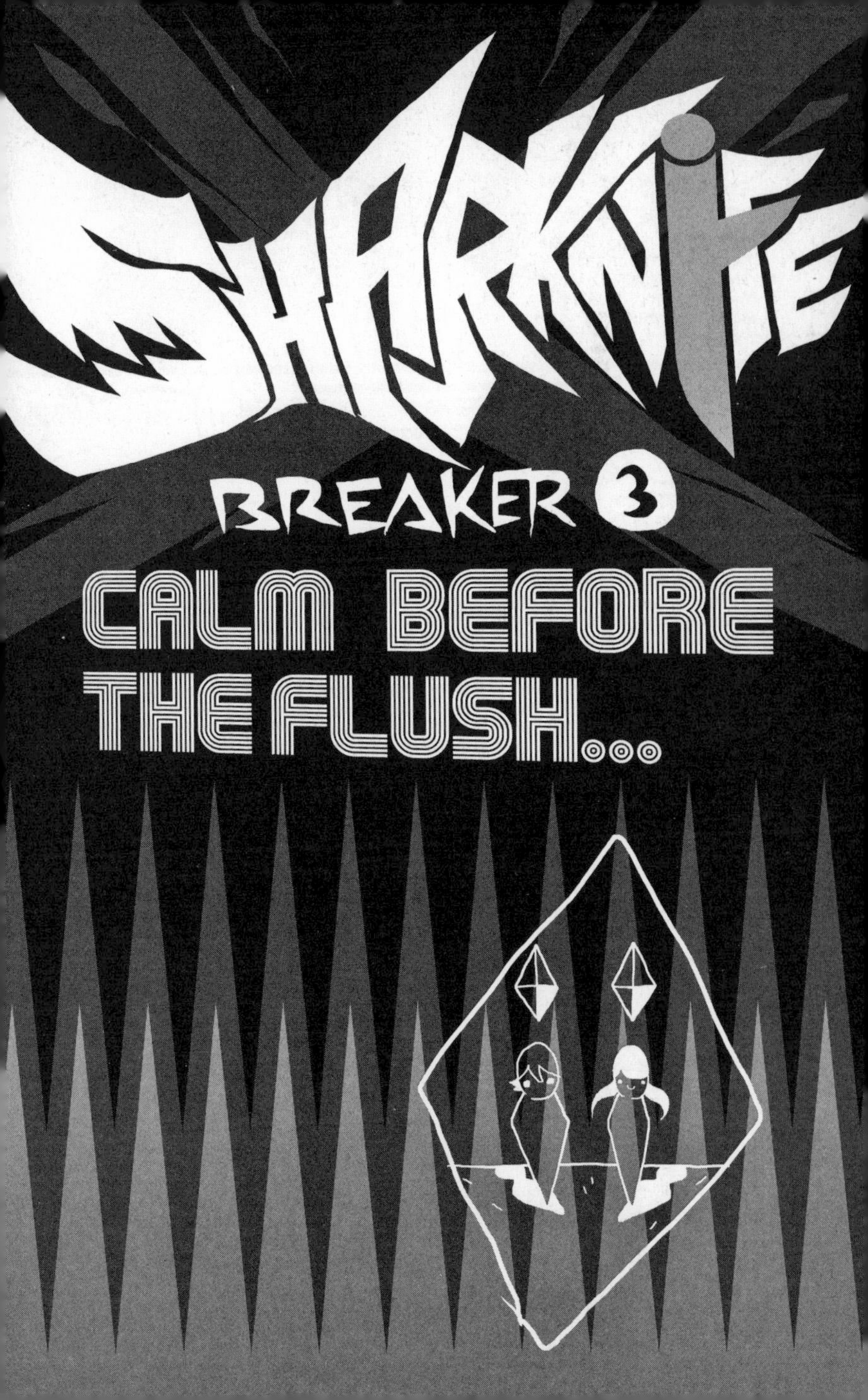
SHARKNIFE
BREAKER 3
CALM BEFORE THE FLUSH...

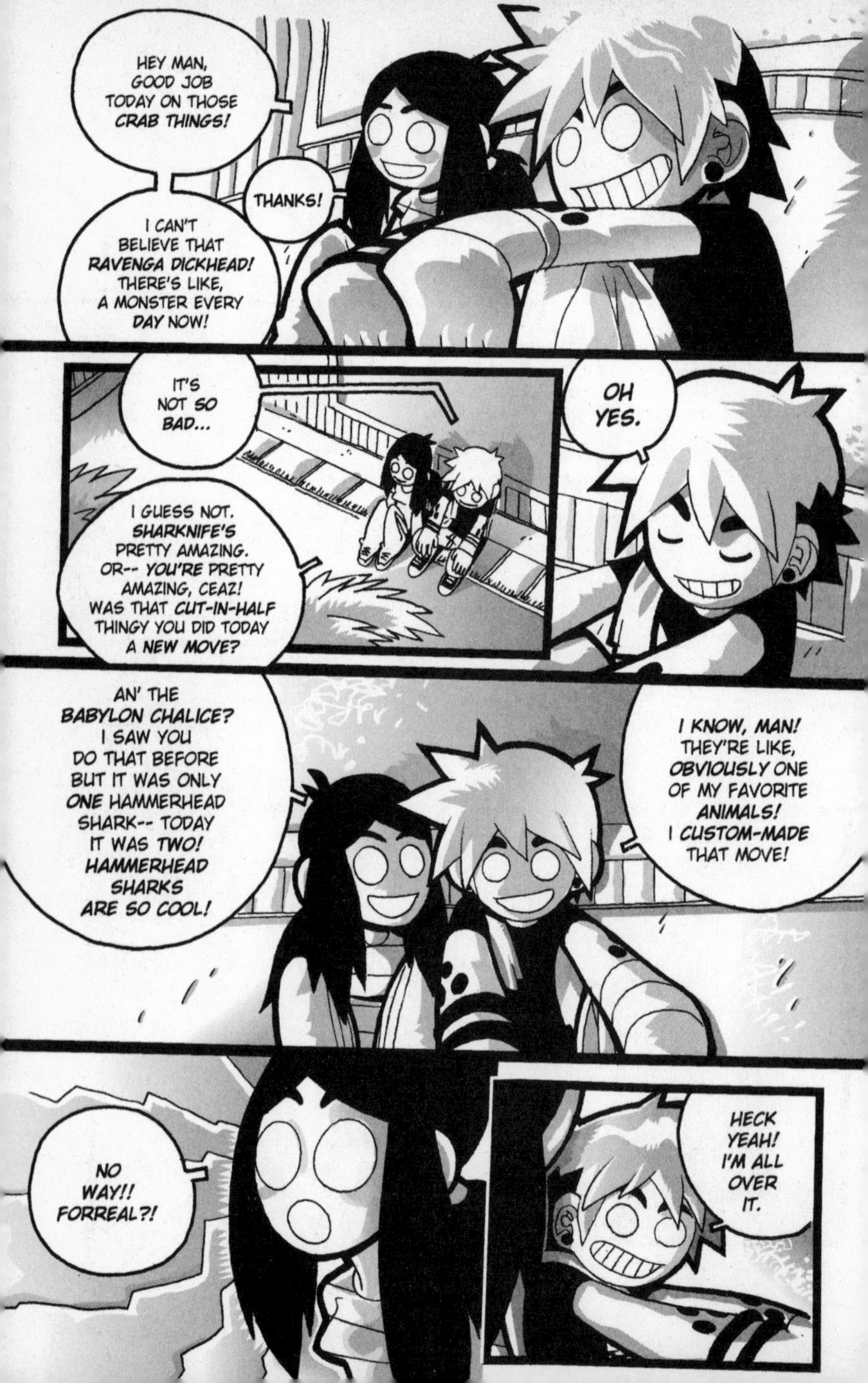
HEY MAN, GOOD JOB TODAY ON THOSE CRAB THINGS!
THANKS!
I CAN'T BELIEVE THAT RAVENGA DICKHEAD! THERE'S LIKE, A MONSTER EVERY DAY NOW!
IT'S NOT SO BAD...
OH YES.
I GUESS NOT. SHARKNIFE'S PRETTY AMAZING. OR-- YOU'RE PRETTY AMAZING, CEAZ! WAS THAT CUT-IN-HALF THINGY YOU DID TODAY A NEW MOVE?
AN' THE BABYLON CHALICE? I SAW YOU DO THAT BEFORE BUT IT WAS ONLY ONE HAMMERHEAD SHARK-- TODAY IT WAS TWO! HAMMERHEAD SHARKS ARE SO COOL!
I KNOW, MAN! THEY'RE LIKE, OBVIOUSLY ONE OF MY FAVORITE ANIMALS! I CUSTOM-MADE THAT MOVE!
NO WAY!! FORREAL?!
HECK YEAH! I'M ALL OVER IT.

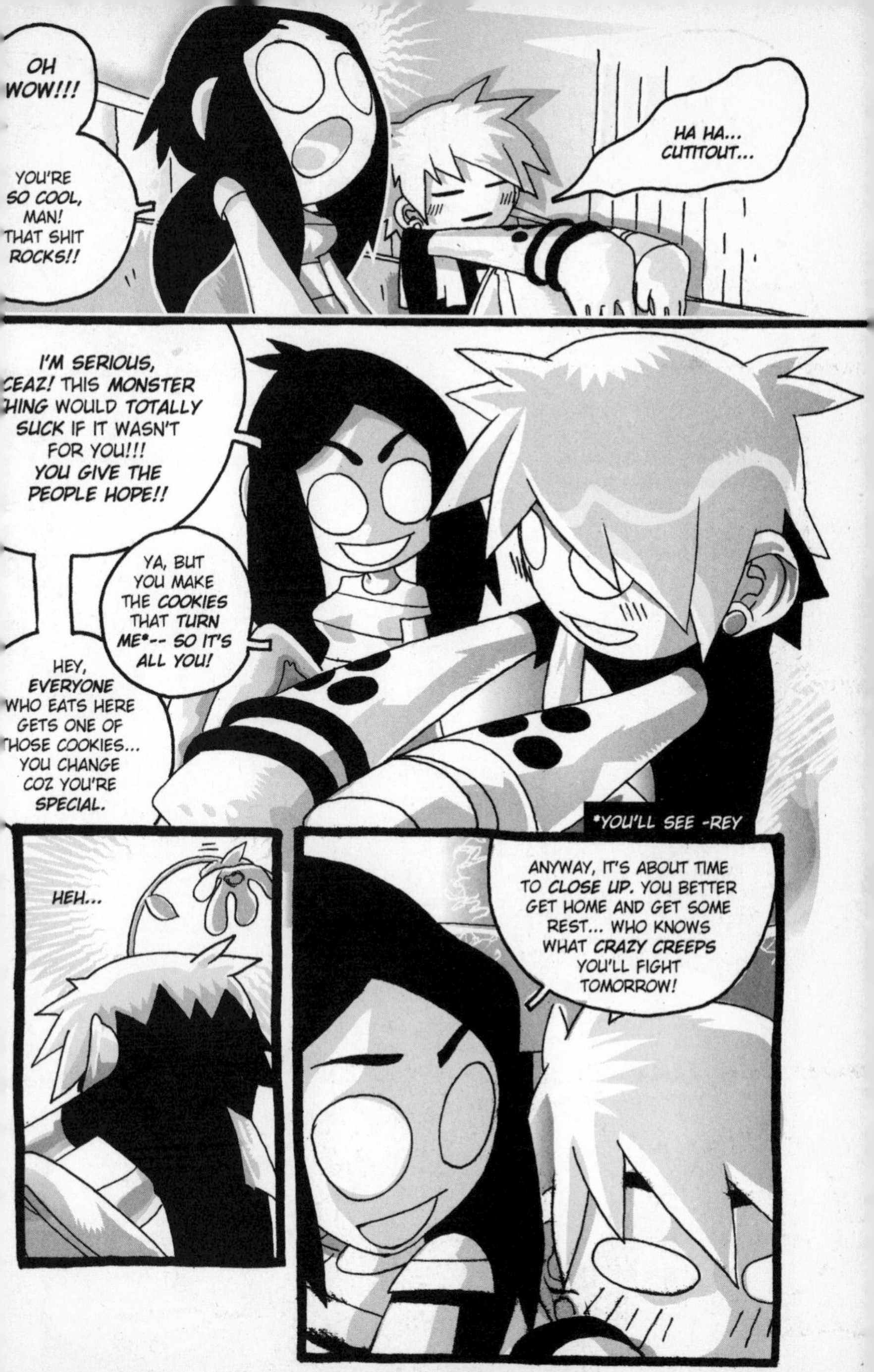
OH WOW!!!
YOU'RE SO COOL, MAN! THAT SHIT ROCKS!!
HA HA... CUTITOUT...
I'M SERIOUS, CEAZ! THIS MONSTER THING WOULD TOTALLY SUCK IF IT WASN'T FOR YOU!!! YOU GIVE THE PEOPLE HOPE!!
YA, BUT YOU MAKE THE COOKIES THAT TURN ME*-- SO IT'S ALL YOU!
HEY, EVERYONE WHO EATS HERE GETS ONE OF THOSE COOKIES... YOU CHANGE COZ YOU'RE SPECIAL.
*YOU'LL SEE -REY
HEH...
ANYWAY, IT'S ABOUT TIME TO CLOSE UP. YOU BETTER GET HOME AND GET SOME REST... WHO KNOWS WHAT CRAZY CREEPS YOU'LL FIGHT TOMORROW!

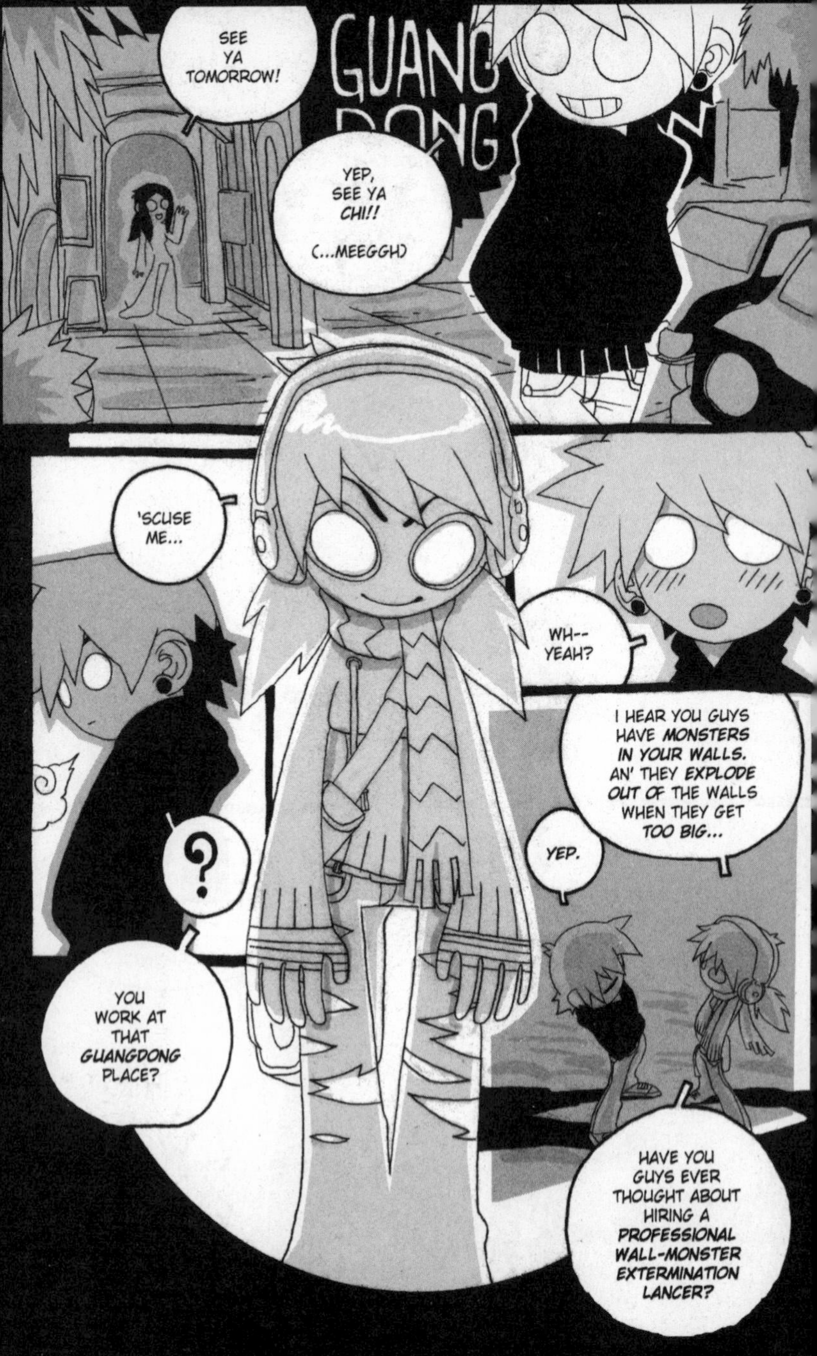
SEE YA TOMORROW!
GUANGDONG
YEP, SEE YA CHI!!
(...MEEGGH)
'SCUSE ME...
WH-- YEAH?
?
YOU WORK AT THAT GUANGDONG PLACE?
I HEAR YOU GUYS HAVE MONSTERS IN YOUR WALLS. AN' THEY EXPLODE OUT OF THE WALLS WHEN THEY GET TOO BIG...
YEP.
HAVE YOU GUYS EVER THOUGHT ABOUT HIRING A PROFESSIONAL WALL-MONSTER EXTERMINATION LANCER?

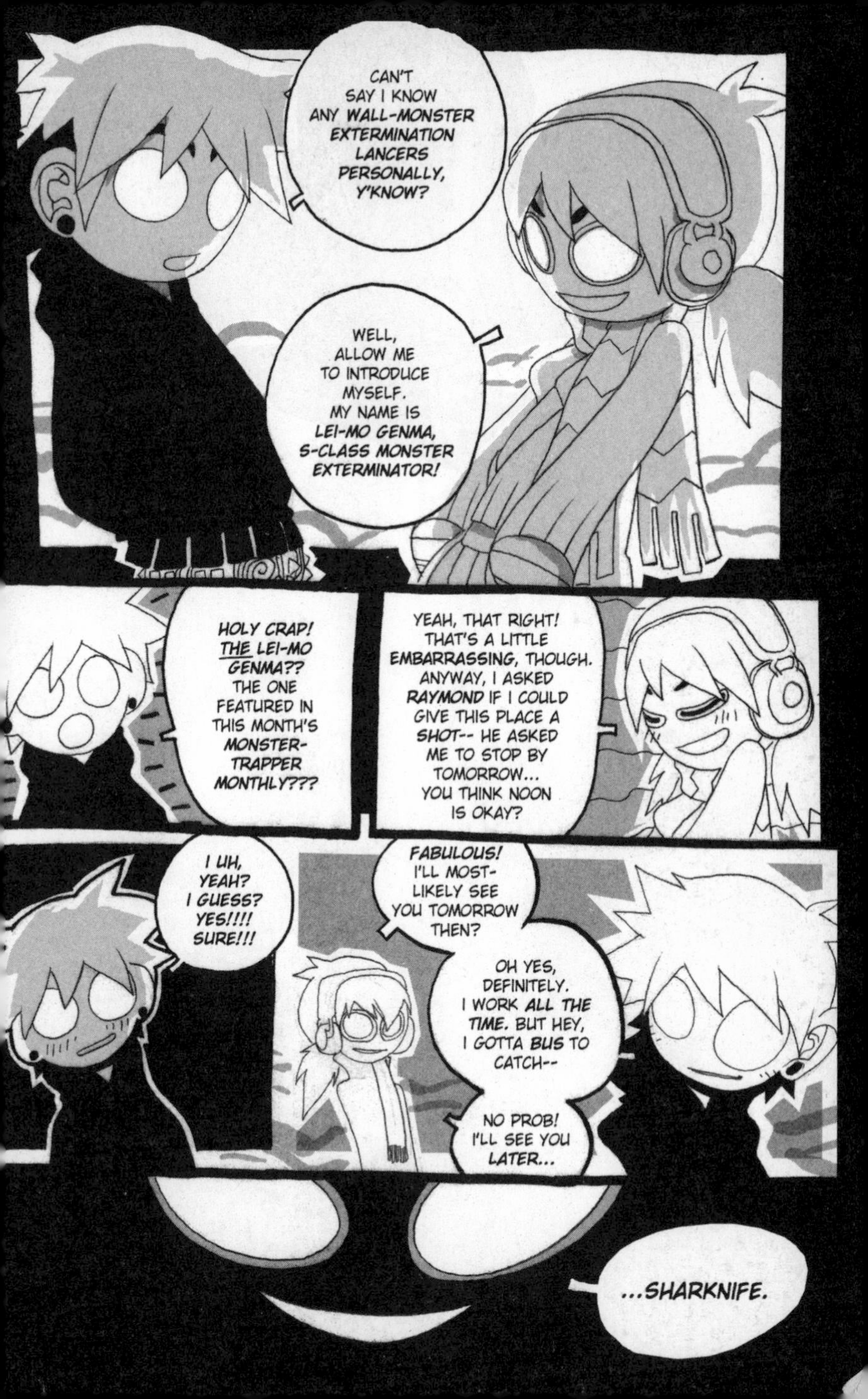
CAN'T SAY I KNOW ANY WALL-MONSTER EXTERMINATION LANCERS PERSONALLY, Y'KNOW?
WELL, ALLOW ME TO INTRODUCE MYSELF. MY NAME IS LEI-MO GENMA, S-CLASS MONSTER EXTERMINATOR!
HOLY CRAP! THE LEI-MO GENMA?? THE ONE FEATURED IN THIS MONTH'S MONSTER-TRAPPER MONTHLY???
YEAH, THAT RIGHT! THAT'S A LITTLE EMBARRASSING, THOUGH. ANYWAY, I ASKED RAYMOND IF I COULD GIVE THIS PLACE A SHOT-- HE ASKED ME TO STOP BY TOMORROW... YOU THINK NOON IS OKAY?
I UH, YEAH? I GUESS? YES!!!! SURE!!!
FABULOUS! I'LL MOST-LIKELY SEE YOU TOMORROW THEN?
OH YES, DEFINITELY. I WORK ALL THE TIME. BUT HEY, I GOTTA BUS TO CATCH--
NO PROB! I'LL SEE YOU LATER...
...SHARKNIFE.

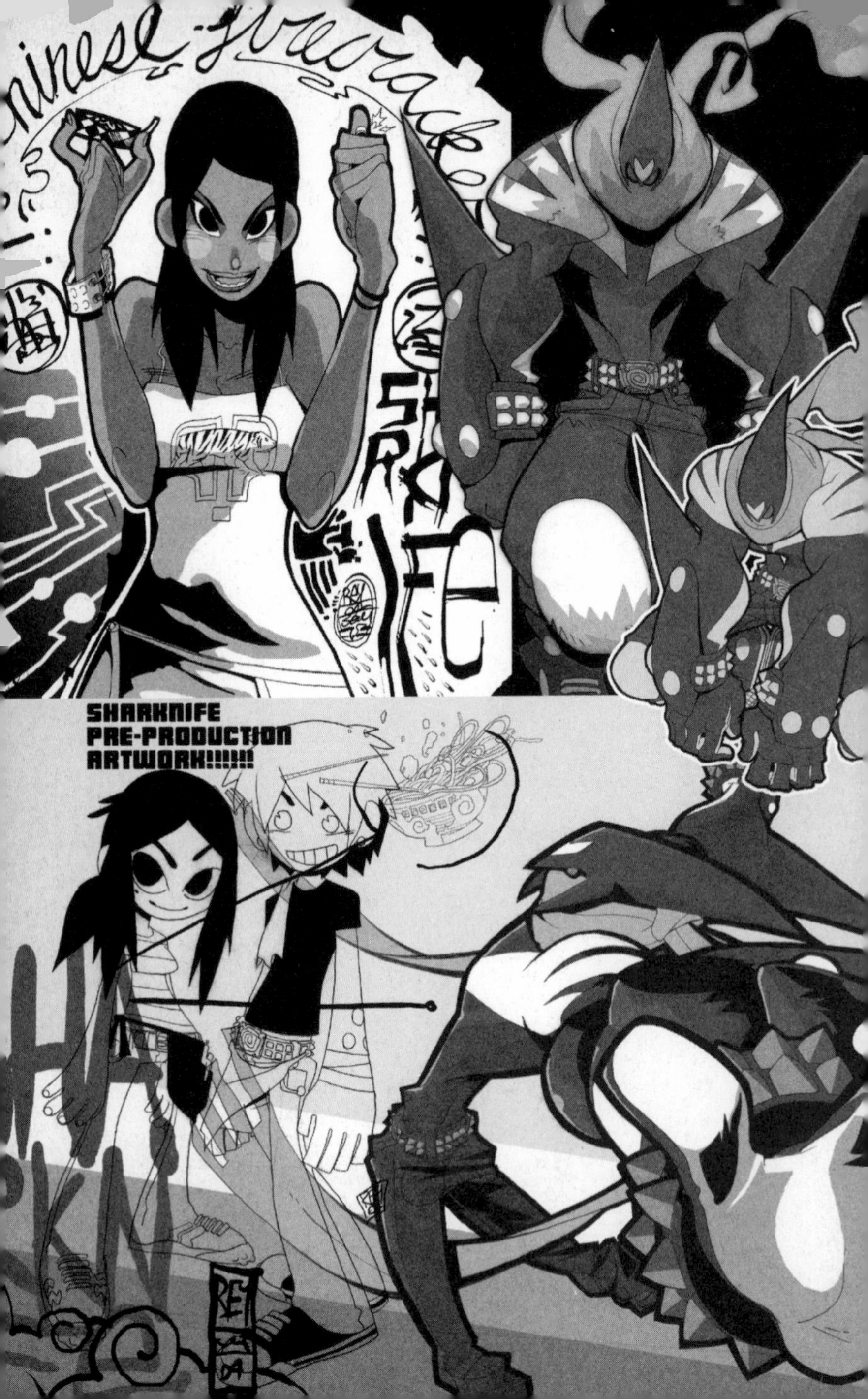

SHARKNIFE
PRE-PRODUCTION
ARTWORK!!!!!!

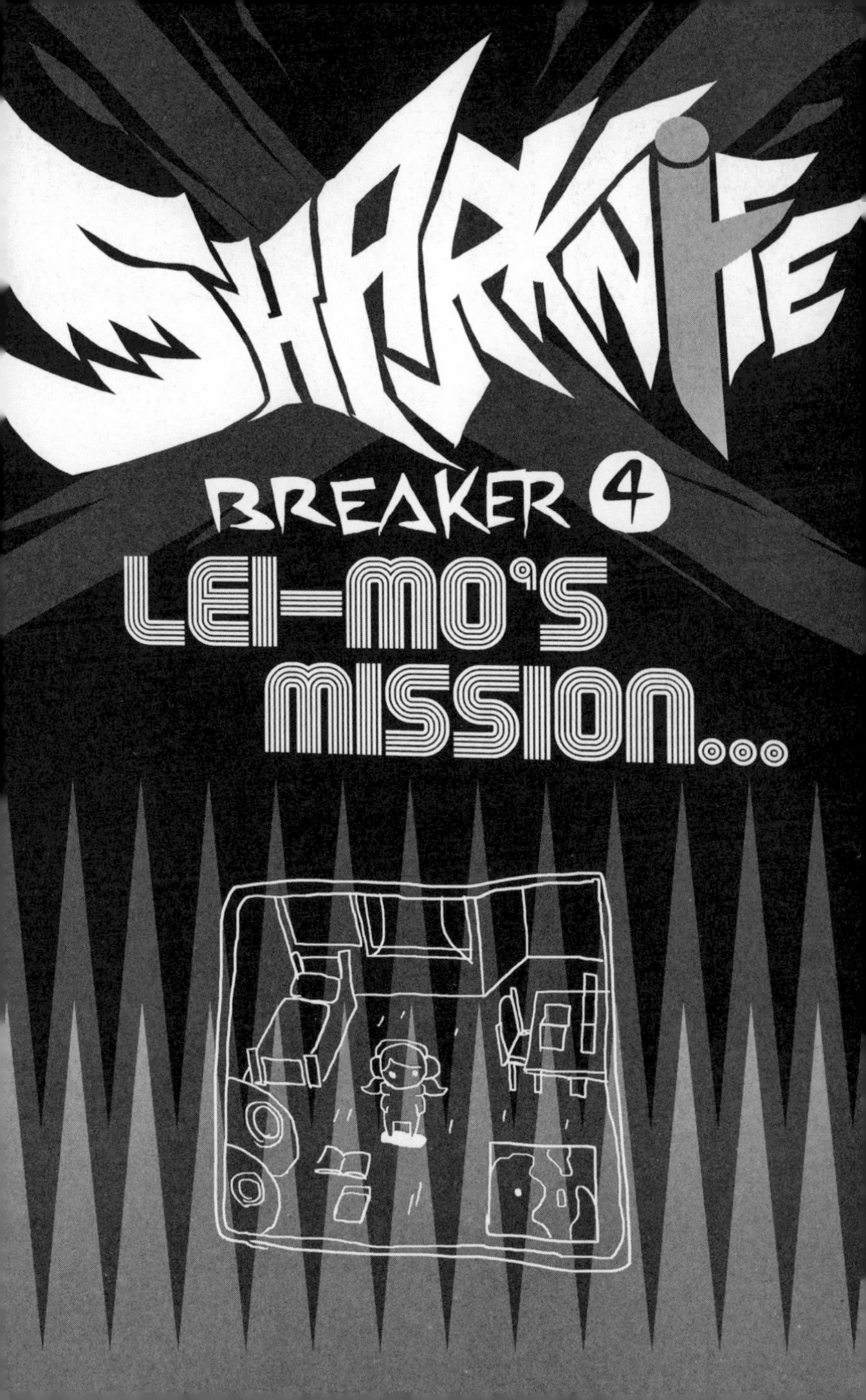
SHARKNIFE
BREAKER 4
LEI-MO'S MISSION...

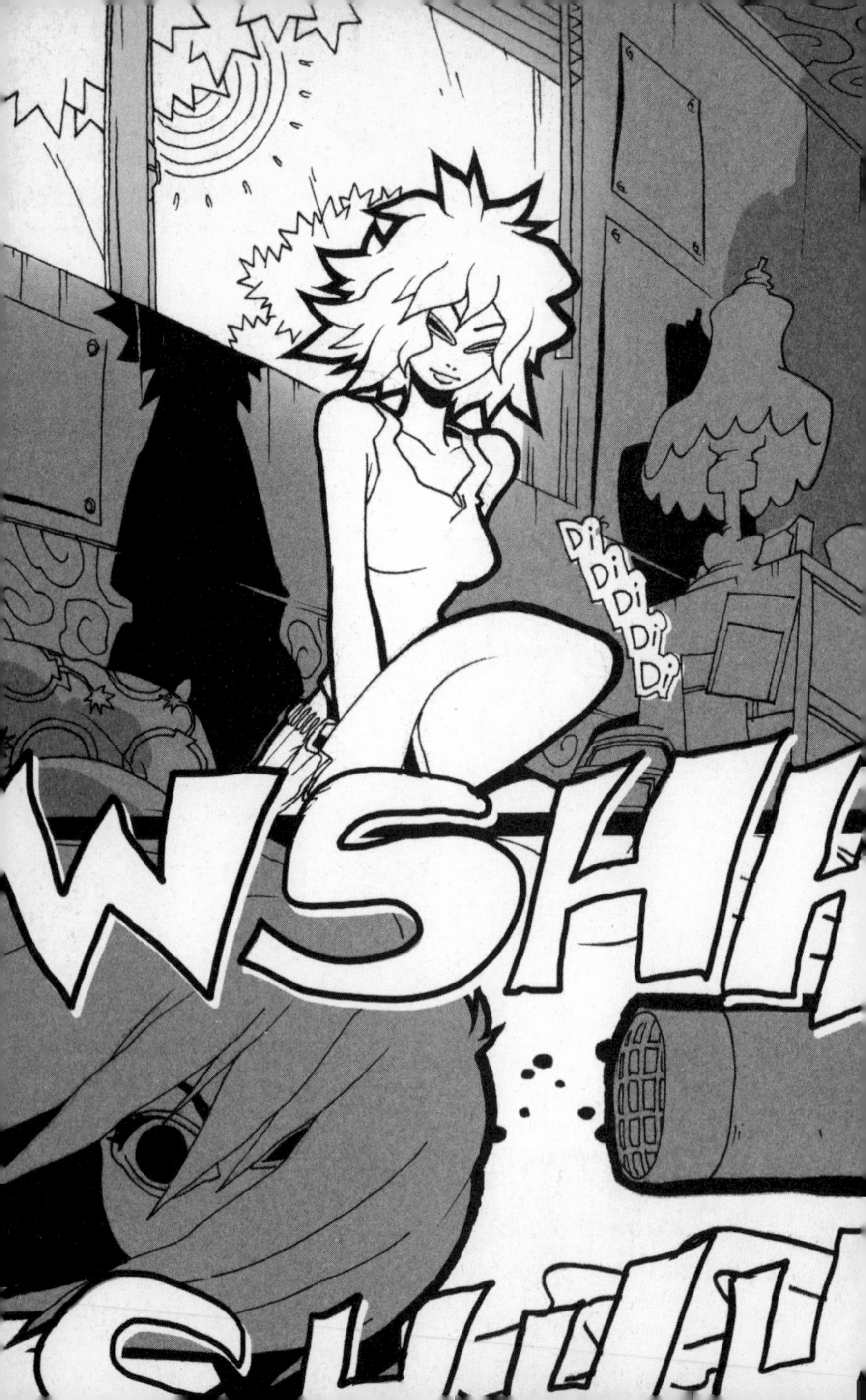
Di Di Di Di Di
WSH

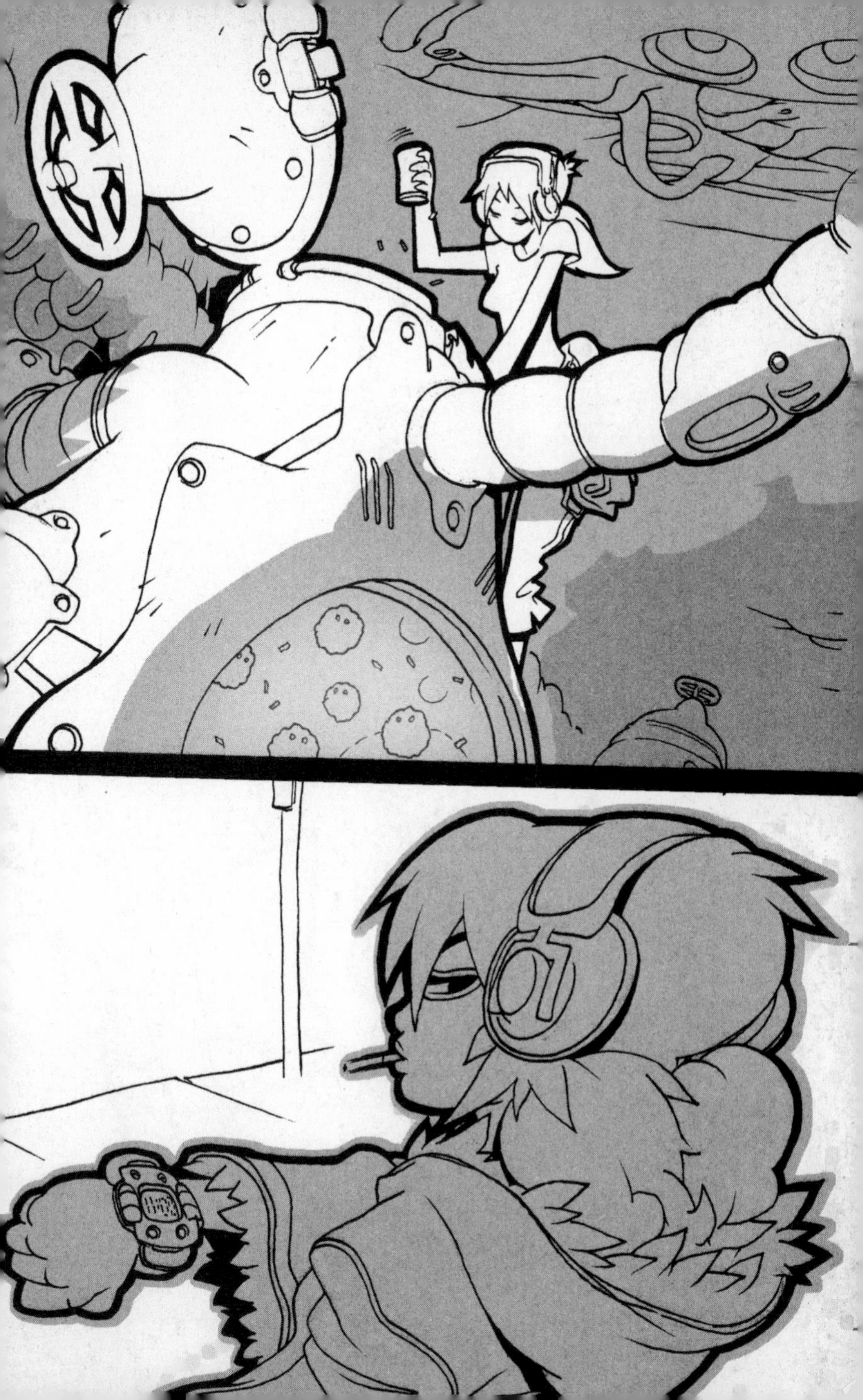

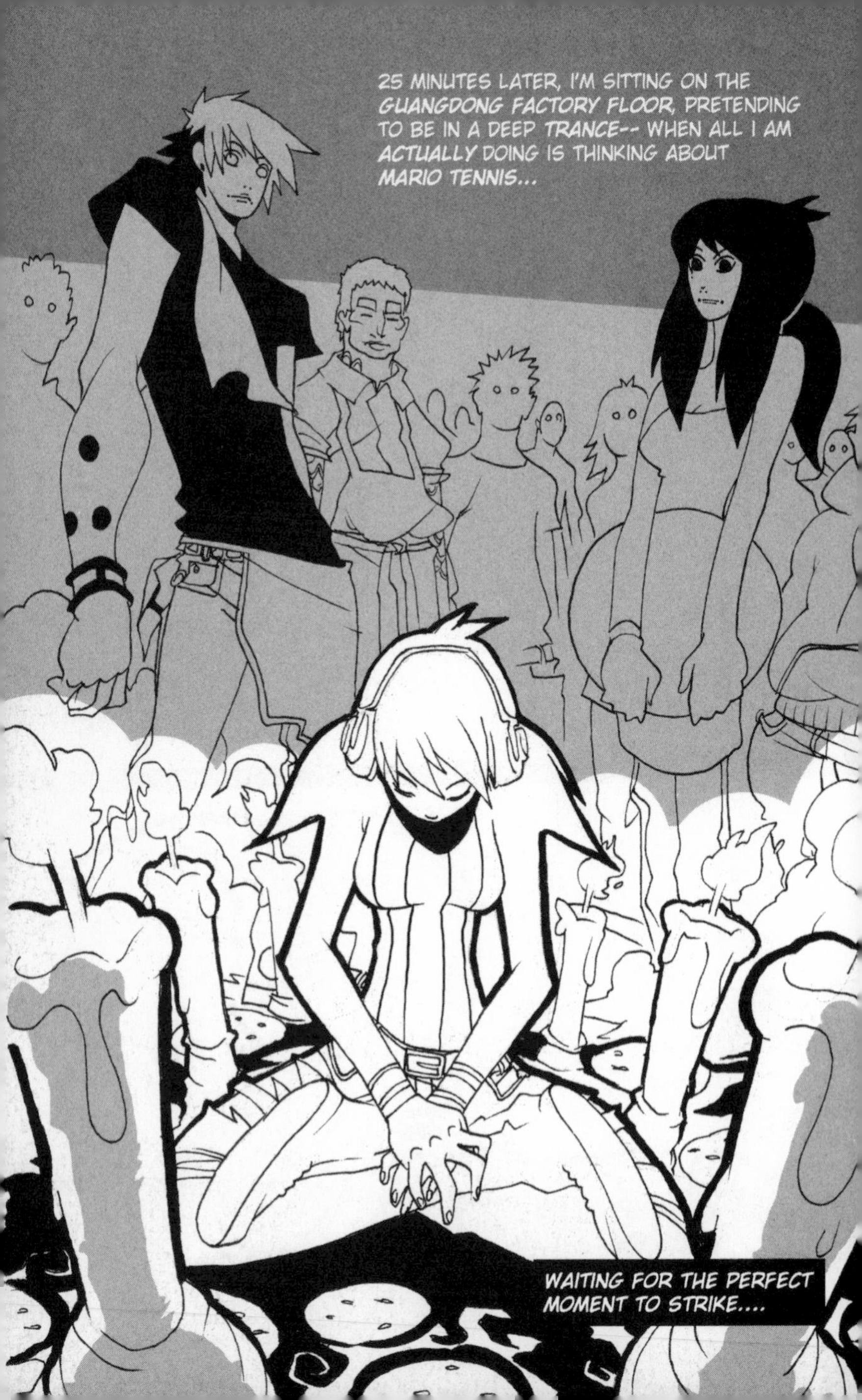
25 MINUTES LATER, I'M SITTING ON THE GUANGDONG FACTORY FLOOR, PRETENDING TO BE IN A DEEP TRANCE-- WHEN ALL I AM ACTUALLY DOING IS THINKING ABOUT MARIO TENNIS...
WAITING FOR THE PERFECT MOMENT TO STRIKE....

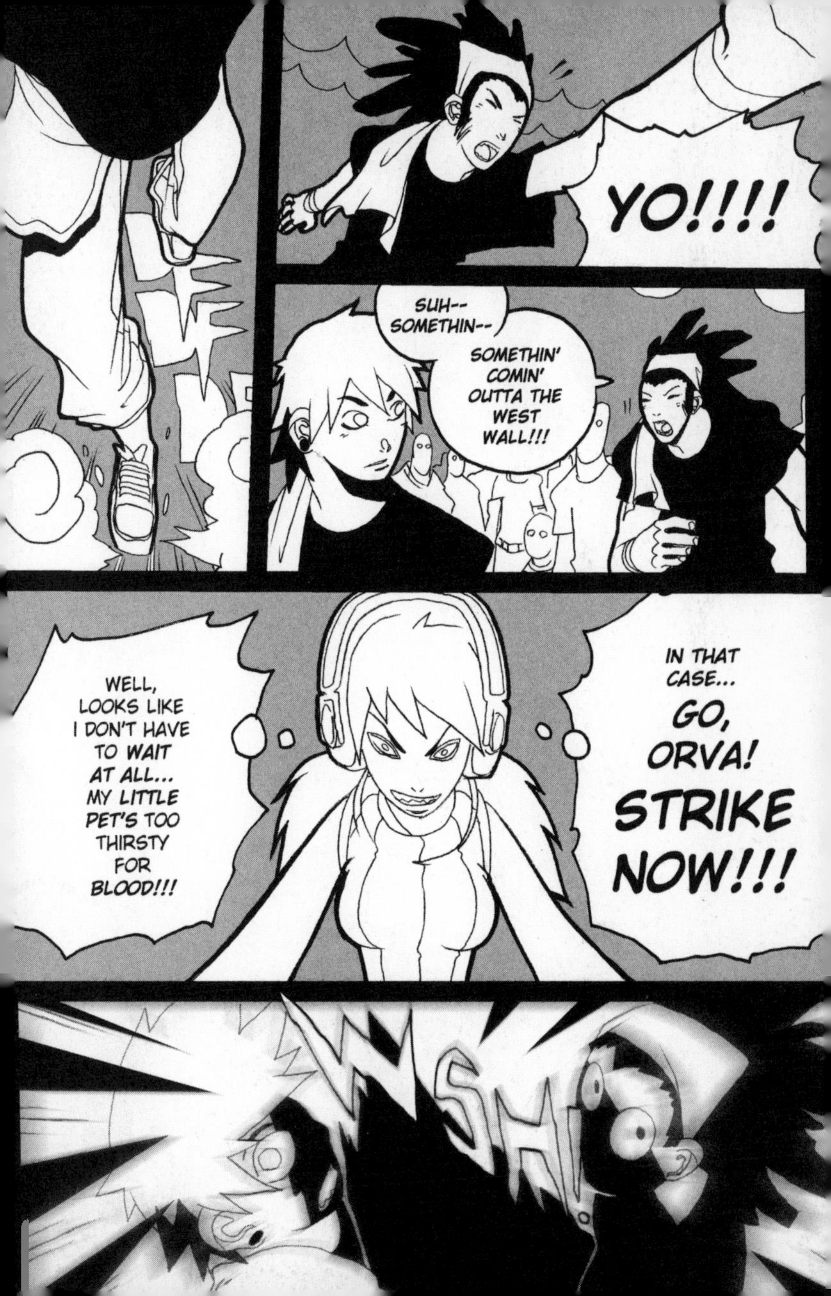
YO!!!!
SUH-- SOMETHIN--
SOMETHIN' COMIN' OUTTA THE WEST WALL!!!
WELL, LOOKS LIKE I DON'T HAVE TO WAIT AT ALL... MY LITTLE PET'S TOO THIRSTY FOR BLOOD!!!
IN THAT CASE... GO, ORVA! STRIKE NOW!!!

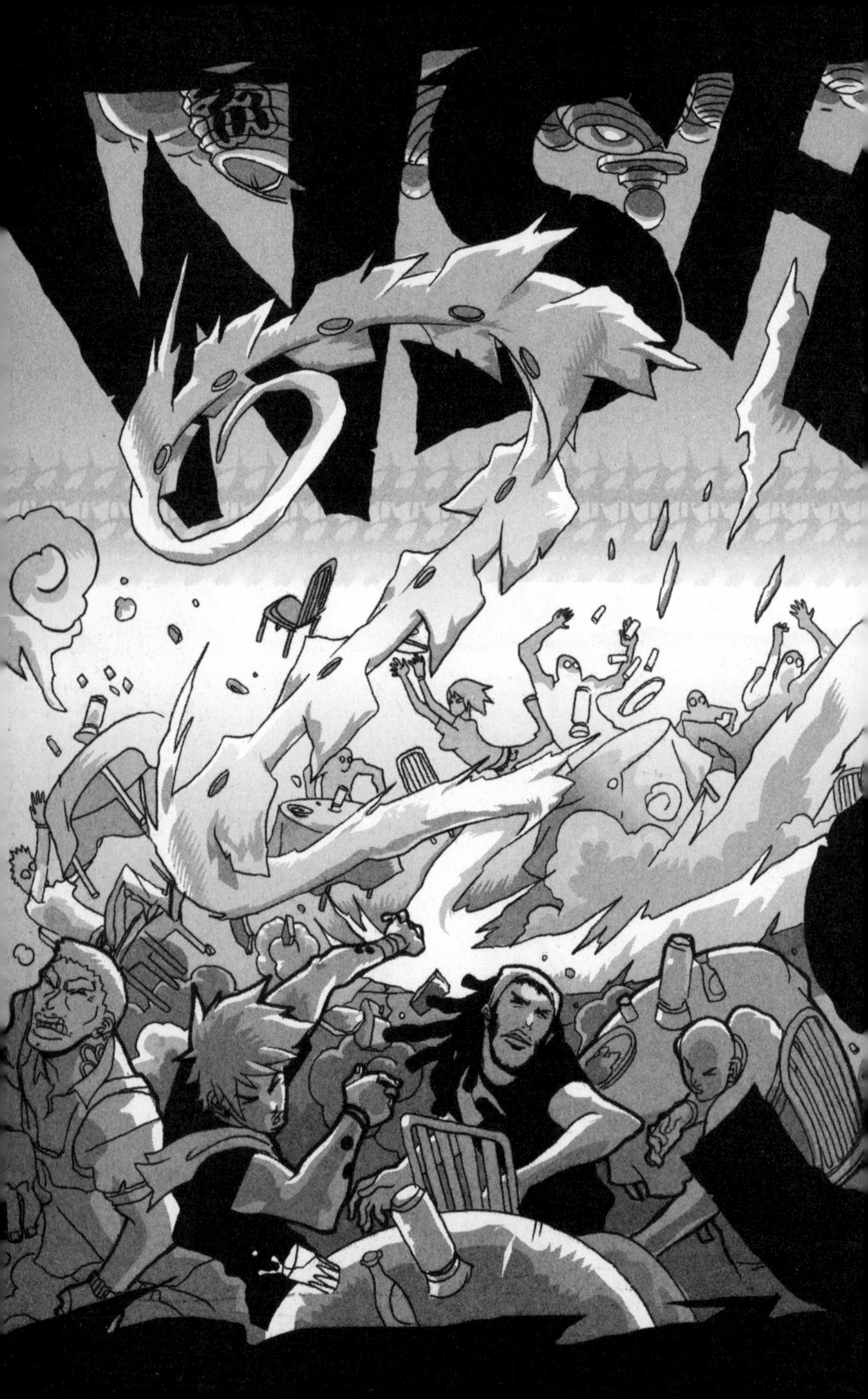

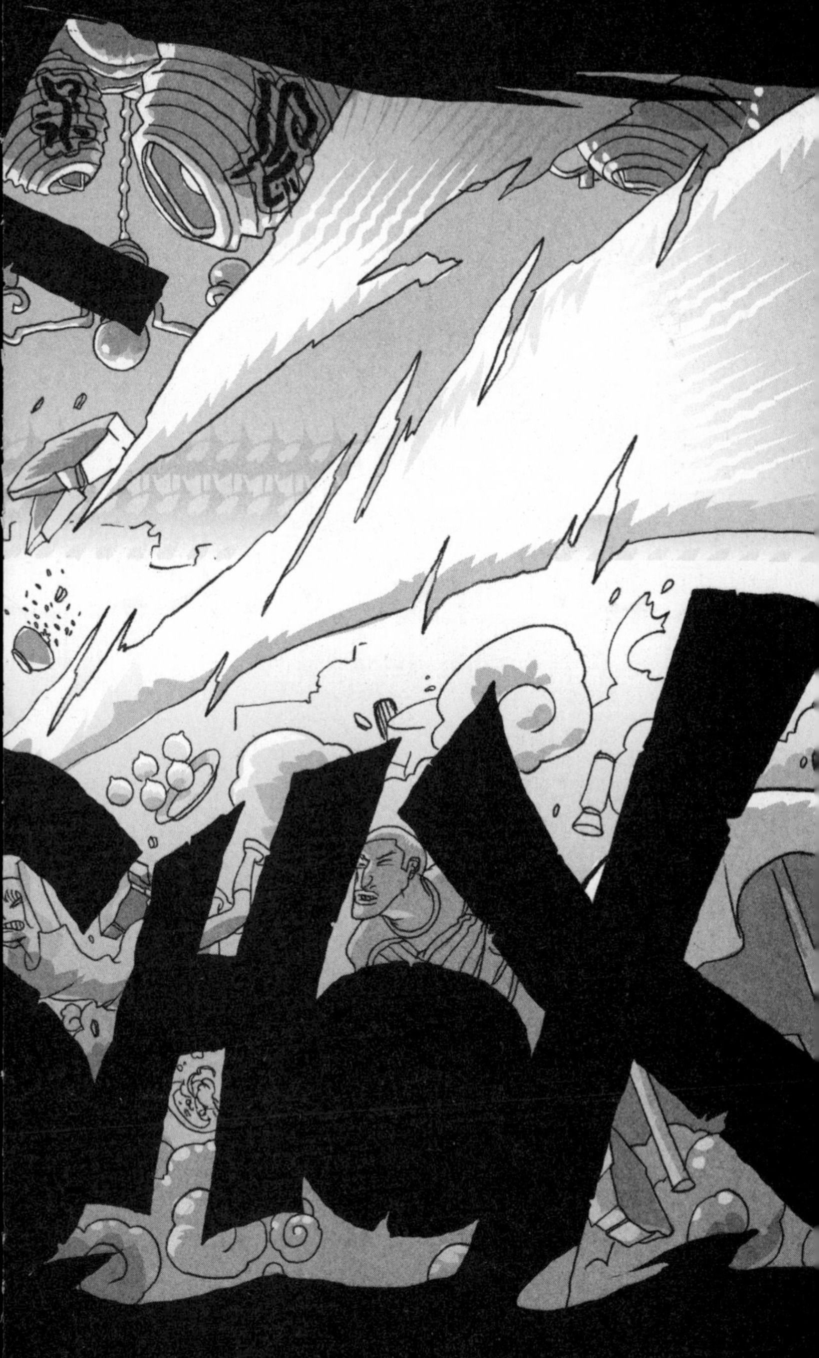

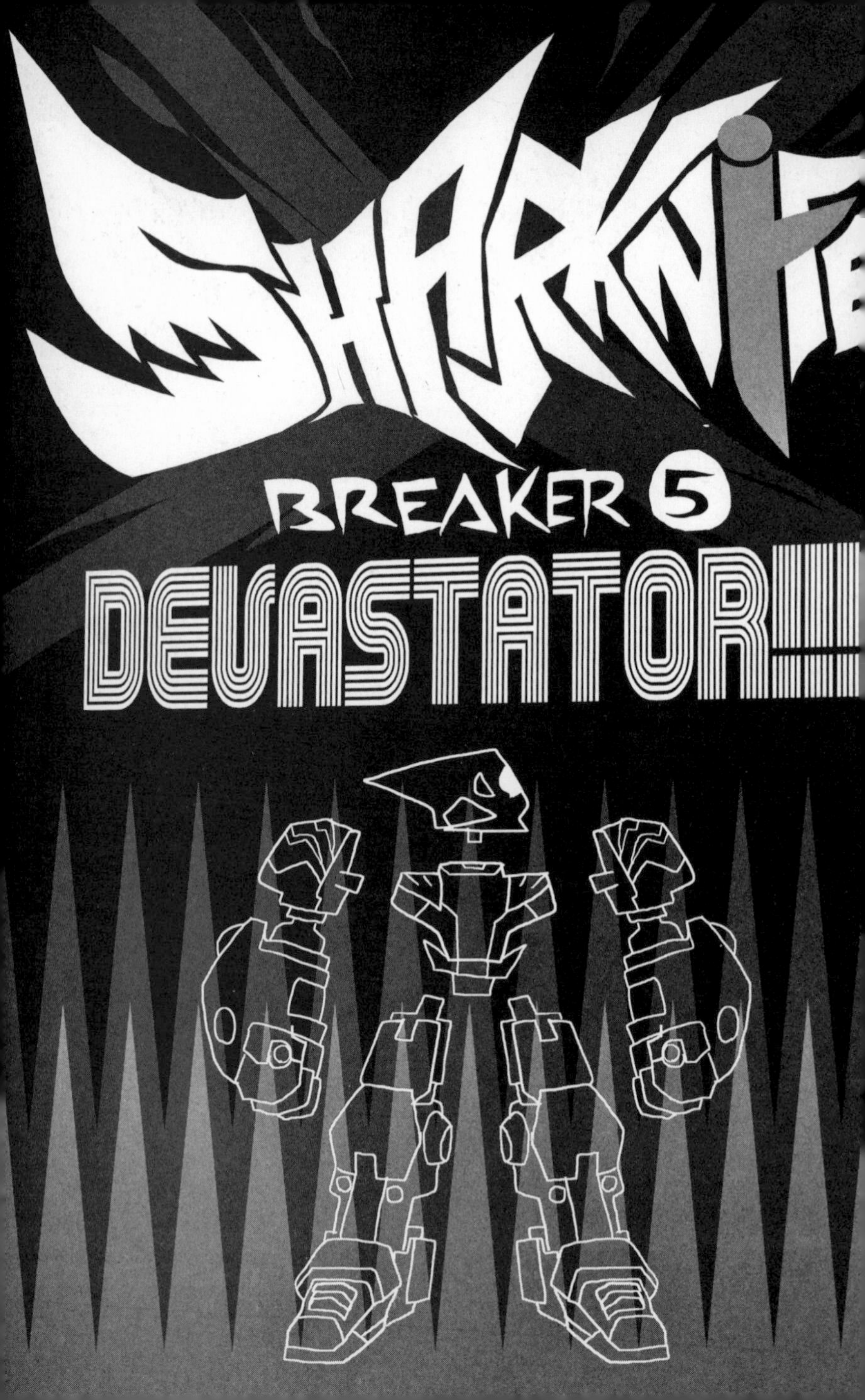
SHARKNIFE
BREAKER 5
DEVASTATOR!!!

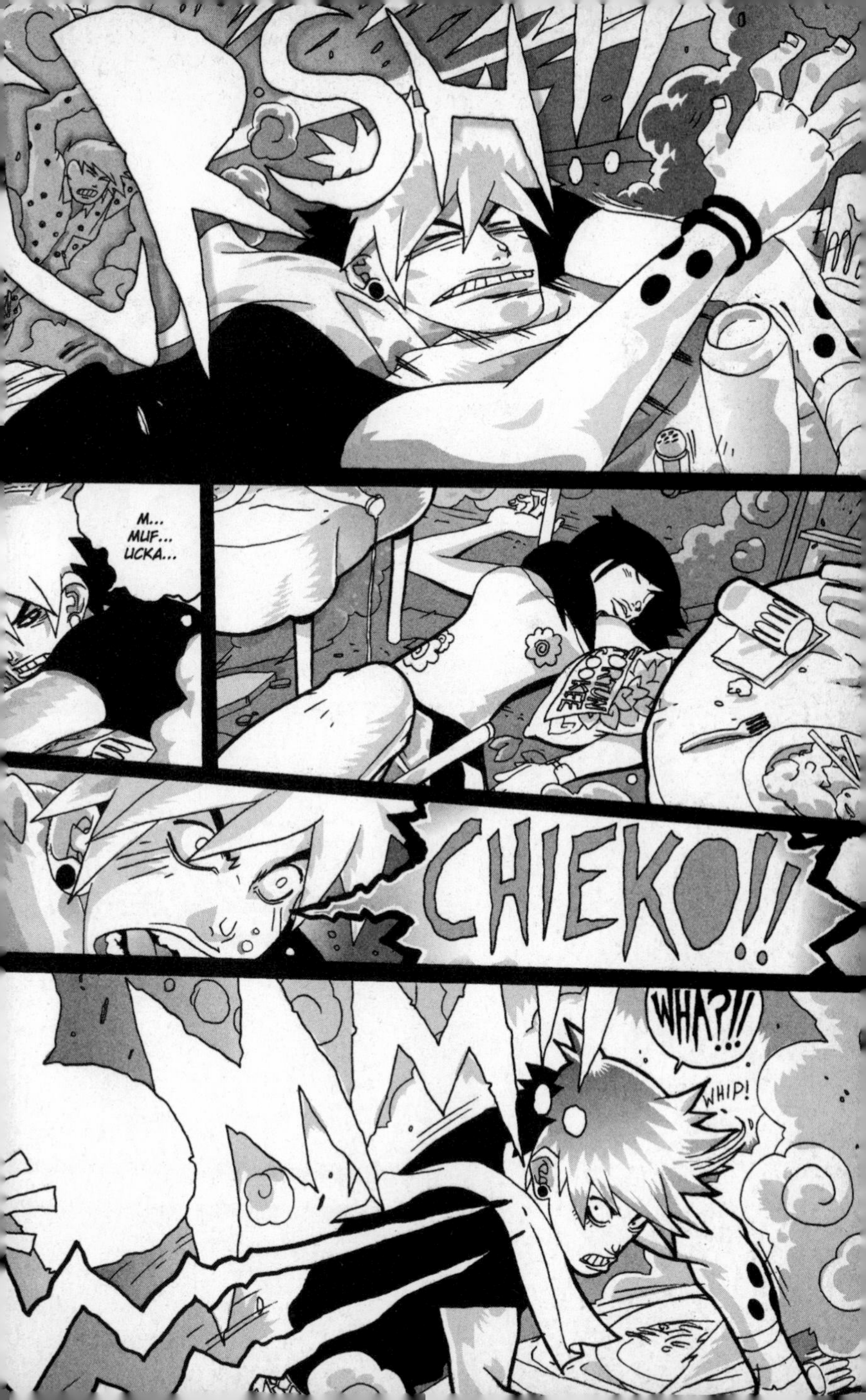
M... MUF... UCKA...
FORTUNE COOKEE
CHIEKO!!
WHA?!!
WHIP!

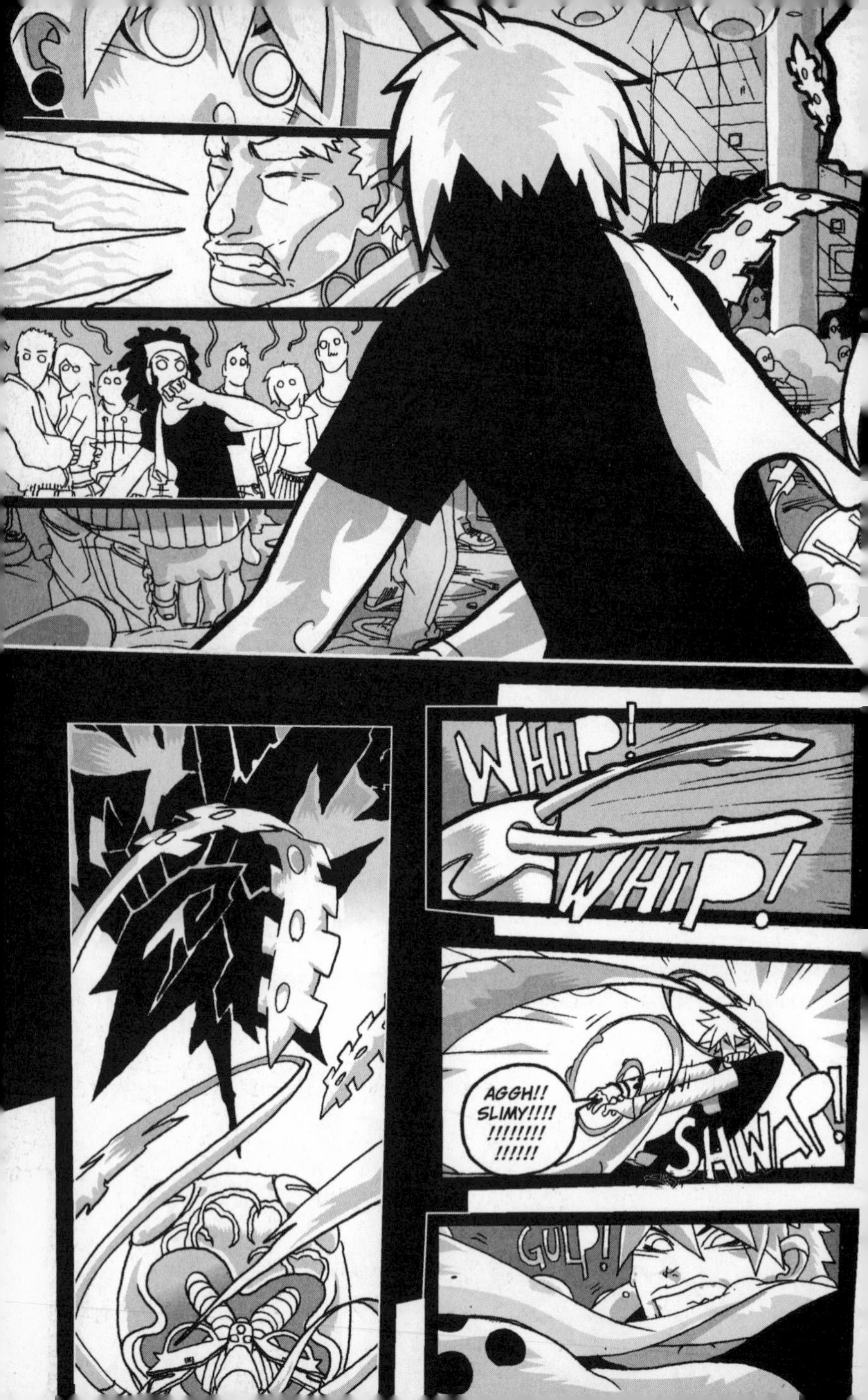
WHIP!
WHIP!
AGGH!! SLIMY!!!! !!!!!!!! !!!!!!
SHWAP!
GULP!

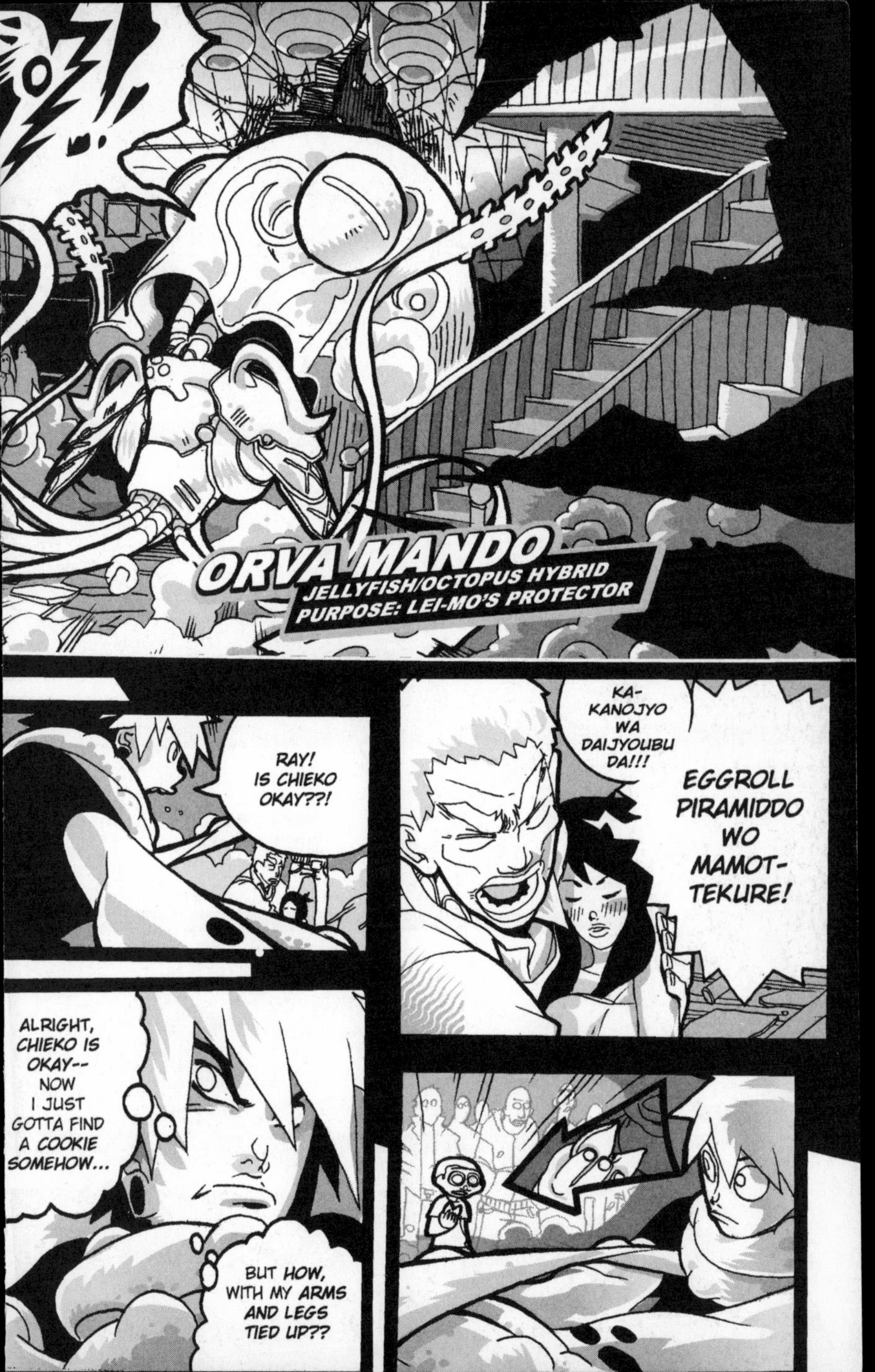
ORVA MANDO
JELLYFISH/OCTOPUS HYBRID
PURPOSE: LEI-MO'S PROTECTOR
RAY! IS CHIEKO OKAY??!
KA-KANOJYO WA DAIJYOUBU DA!!!
EGGROLL PIRAMIDDO WO MAMOT-TEKURE!
ALRIGHT, CHIEKO IS OKAY-- NOW I JUST GOTTA FIND A COOKIE SOMEHOW...
BUT HOW, WITH MY ARMS AND LEGS TIED UP??

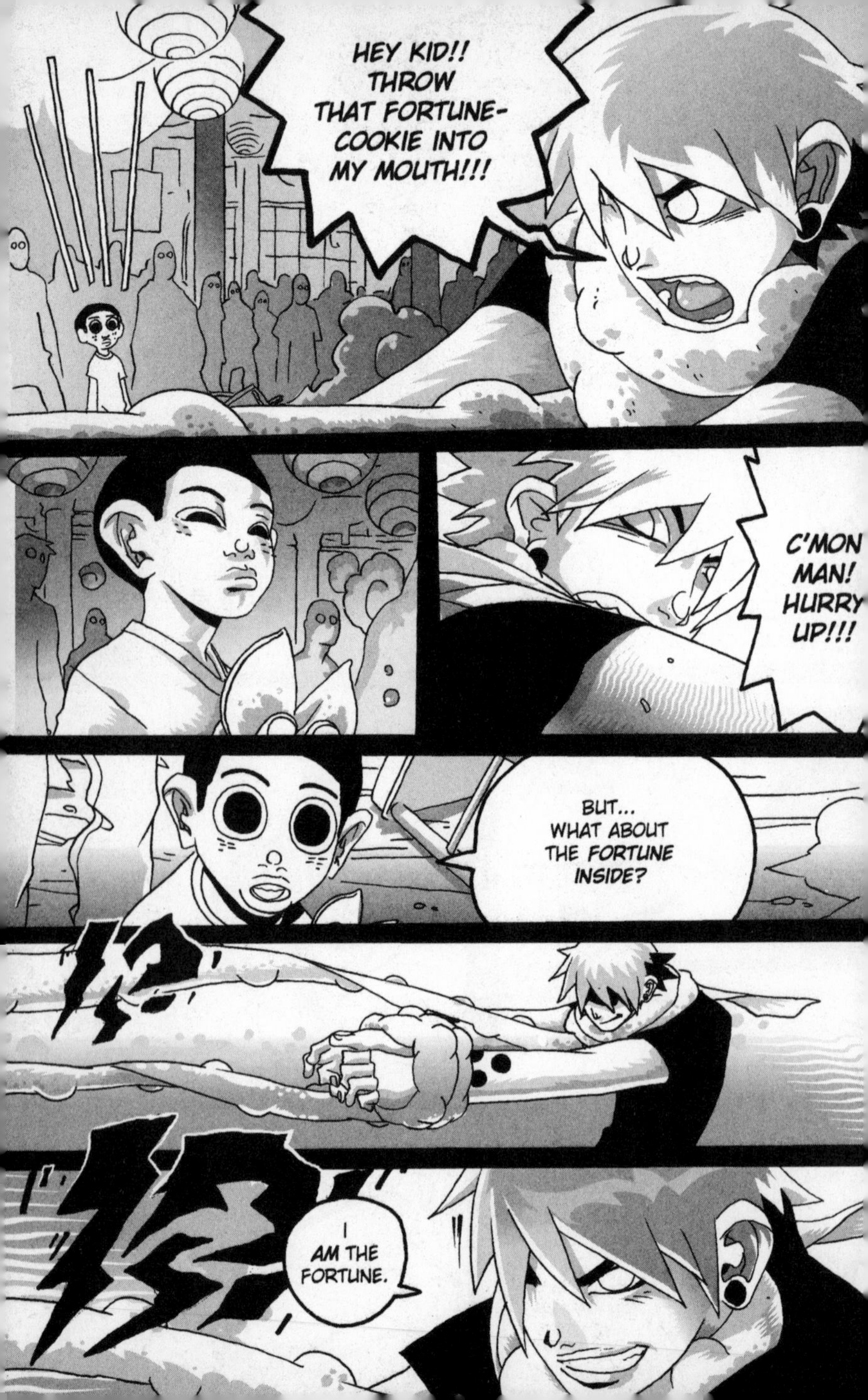
HEY KID!! THROW THAT FORTUNE-COOKIE INTO MY MOUTH!!!
C'MON MAN! HURRY UP!!!
BUT... WHAT ABOUT THE FORTUNE INSIDE?
I AM THE FORTUNE.

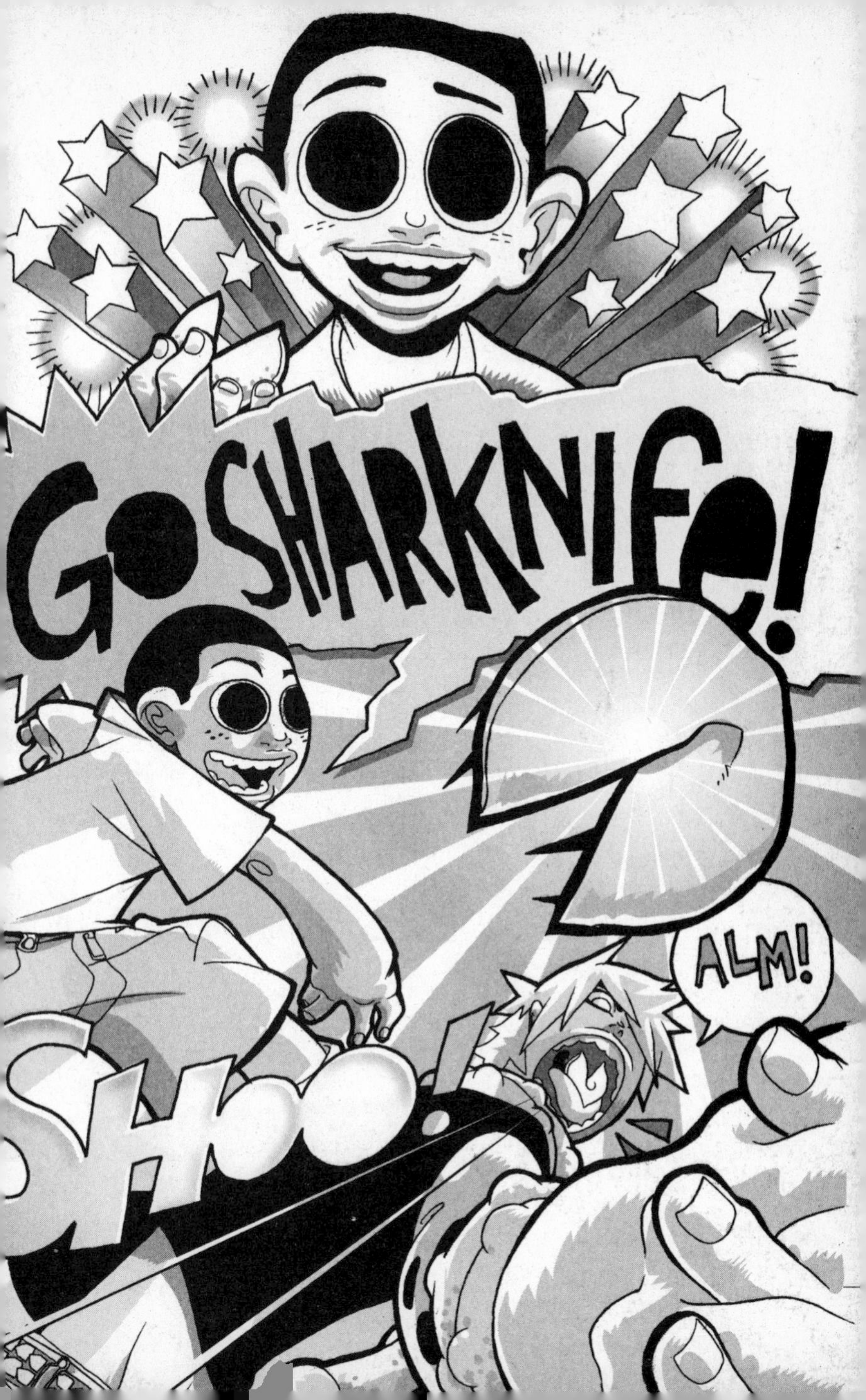
GO SHARKNIFE!
ALM!

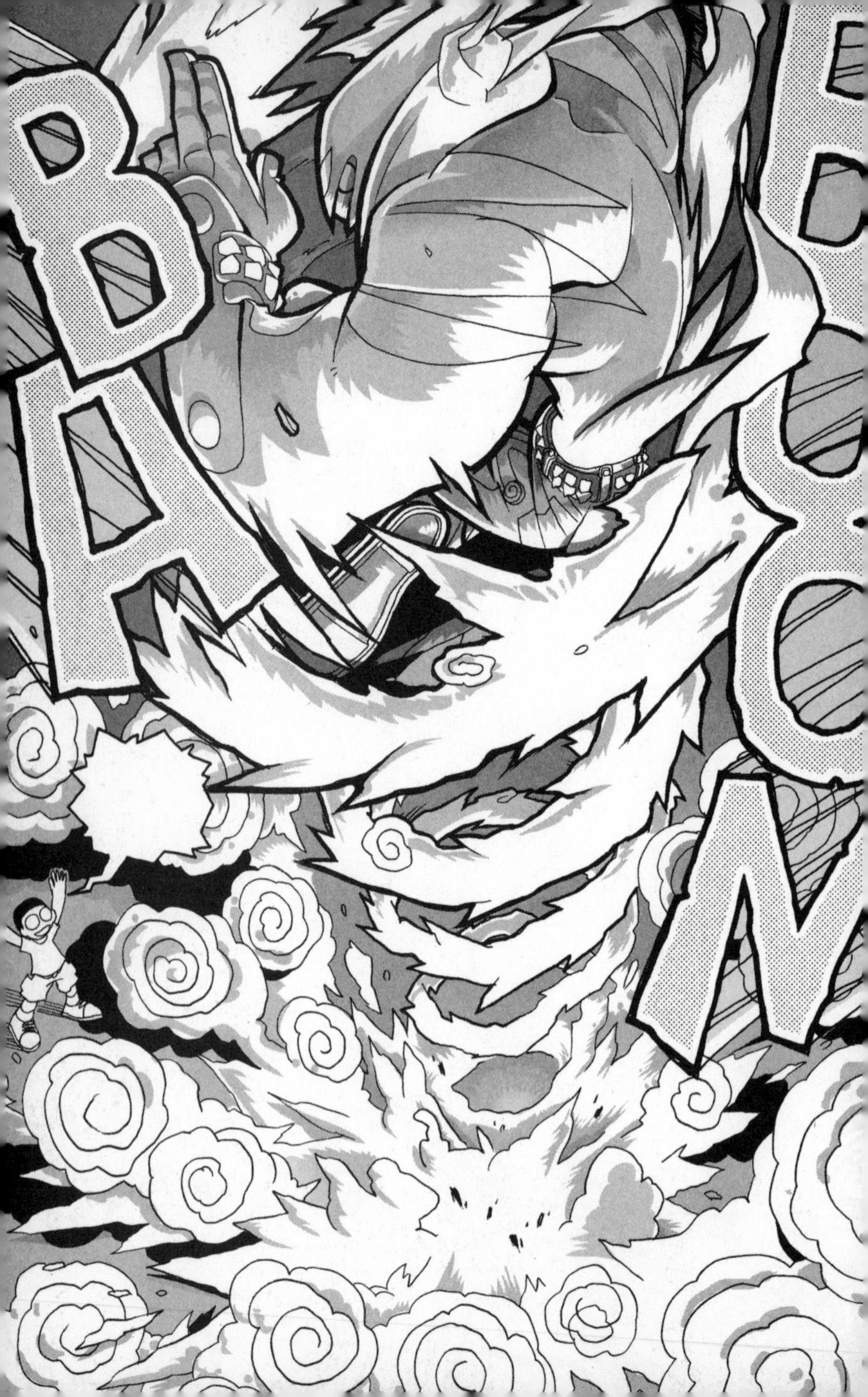

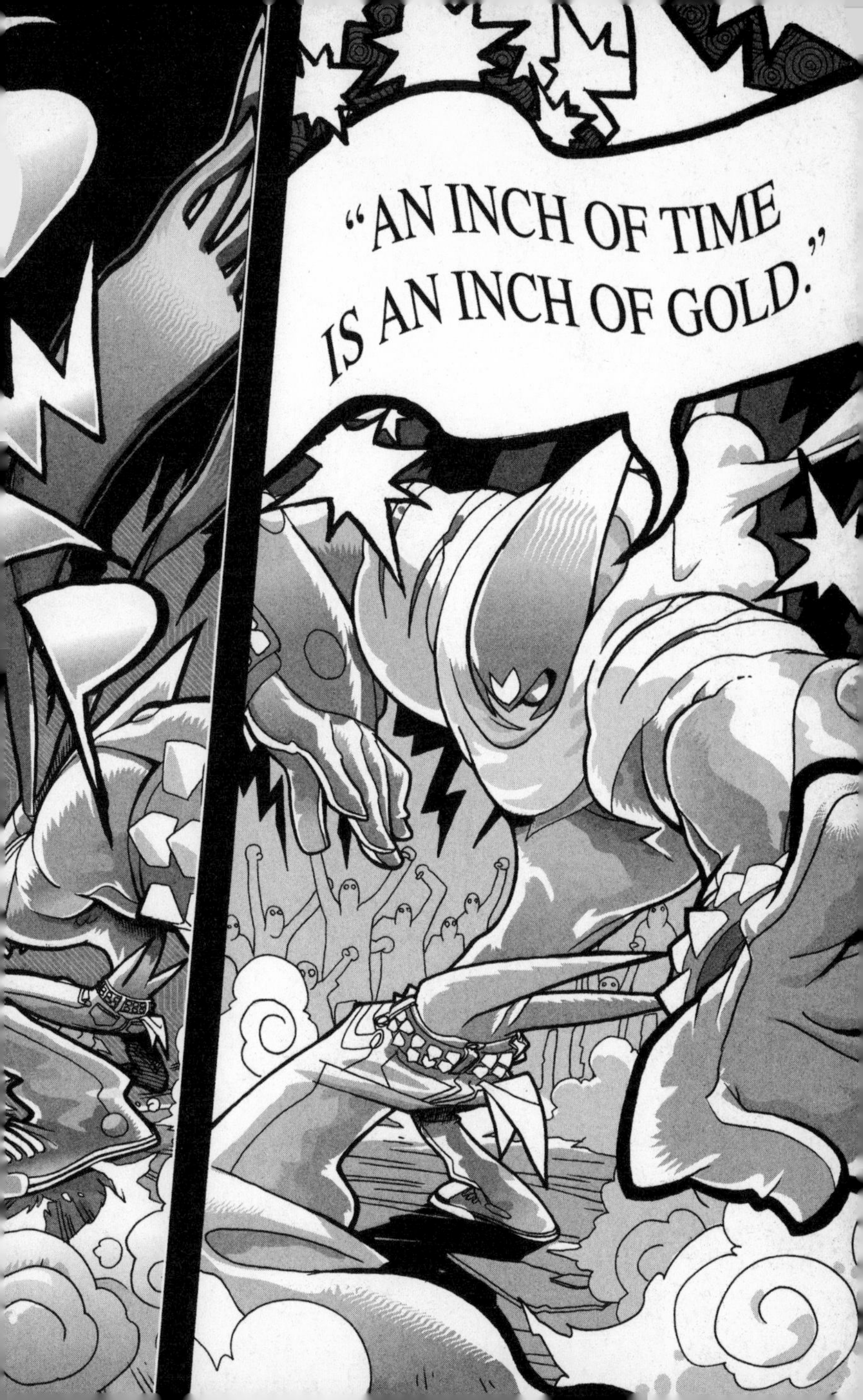
"AN INCH OF TIME IS AN INCH OF GOLD."

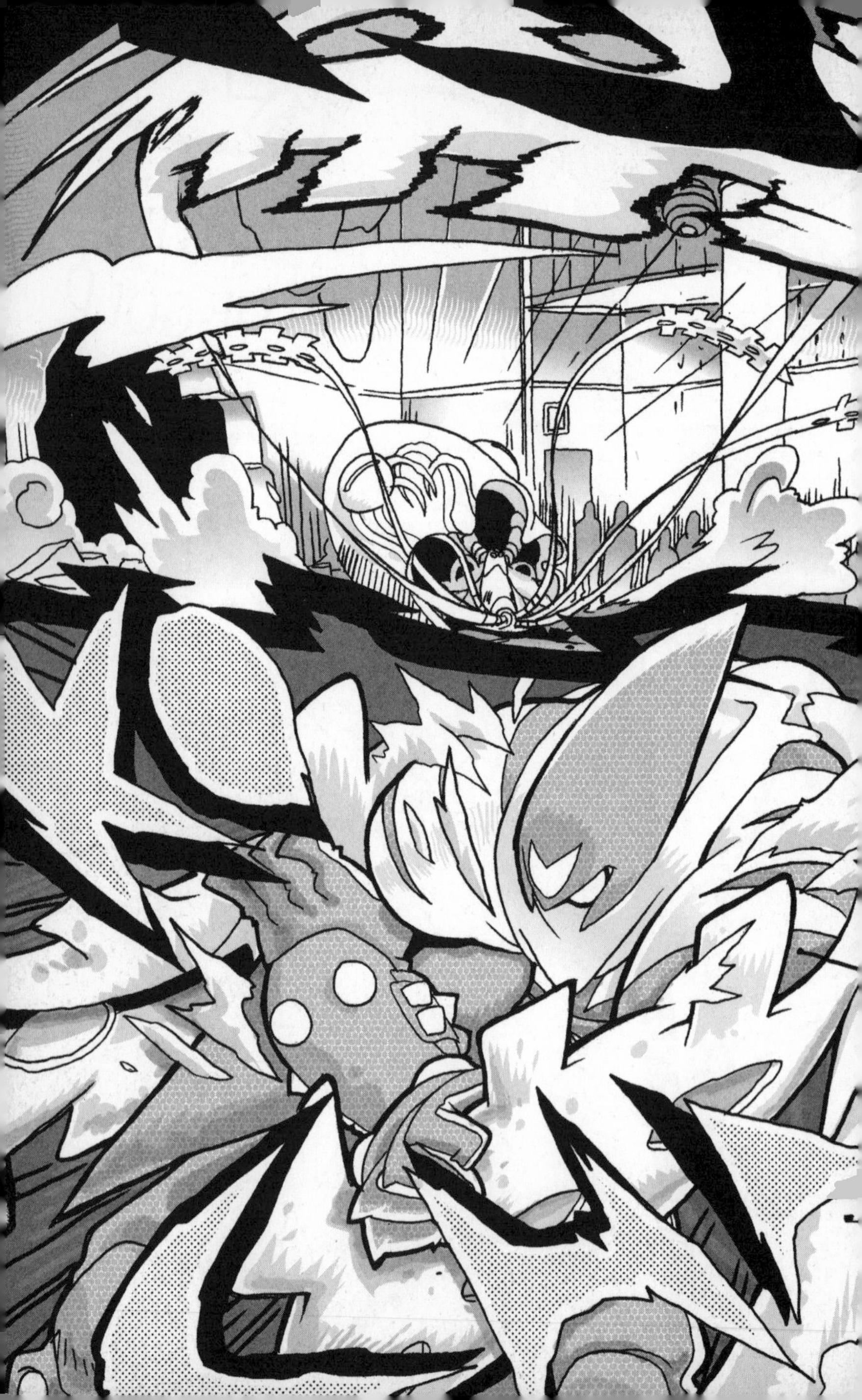

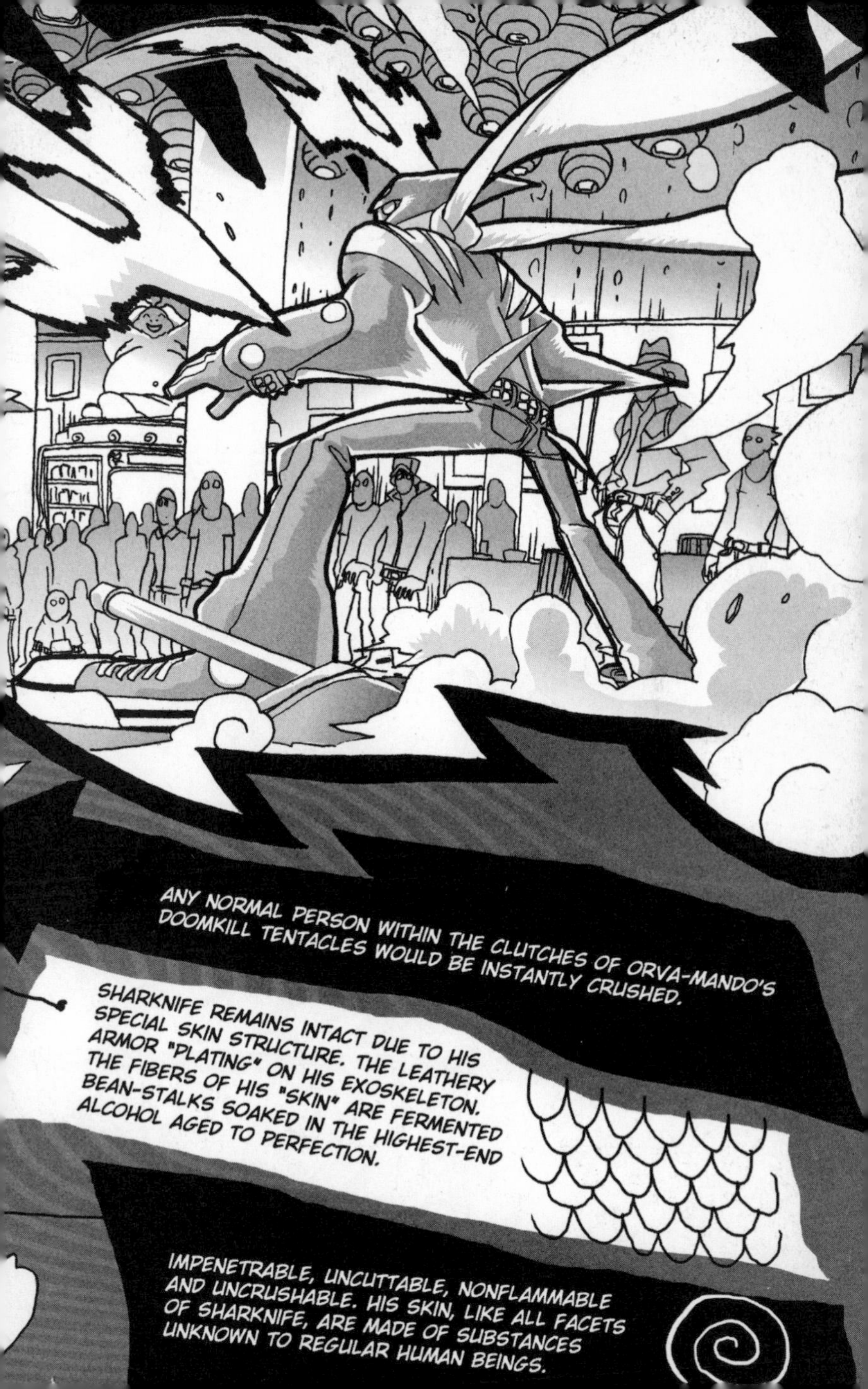
ANY NORMAL PERSON WITHIN THE CLUTCHES OF ORVA-MANDO'S DOOMKILL TENTACLES WOULD BE INSTANTLY CRUSHED.
SHARKNIFE REMAINS INTACT DUE TO HIS SPECIAL SKIN STRUCTURE. THE LEATHERY ARMOR "PLATING" ON HIS EXOSKELETON. THE FIBERS OF HIS "SKIN" ARE FERMENTED BEAN-STALKS SOAKED IN THE HIGHEST-END ALCOHOL AGED TO PERFECTION.
IMPENETRABLE, UNCUTTABLE, NONFLAMMABLE AND UNCRUSHABLE. HIS SKIN, LIKE ALL FACETS OF SHARKNIFE, ARE MADE OF SUBSTANCES UNKNOWN TO REGULAR HUMAN BEINGS.

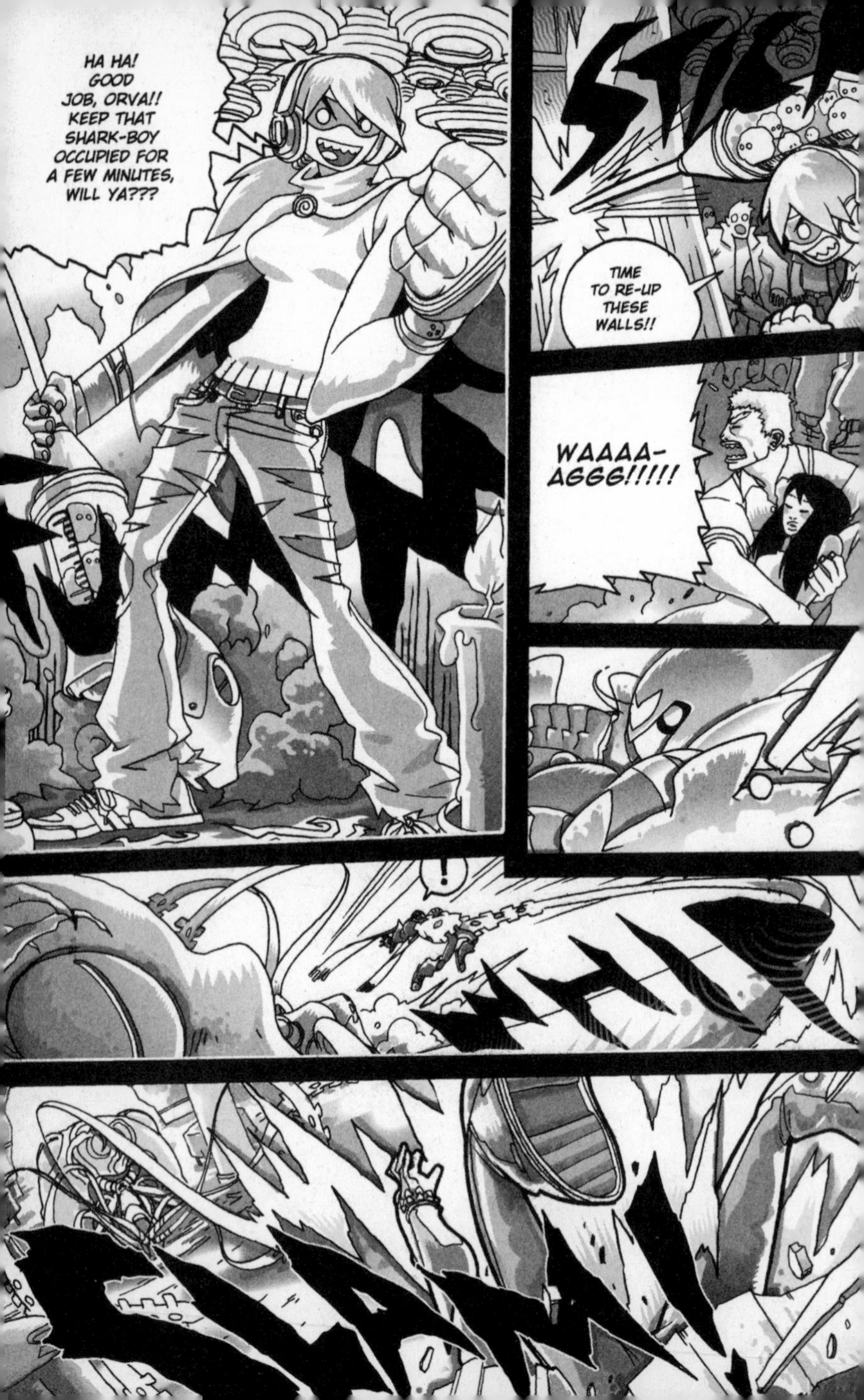
HA HA! GOOD JOB, ORVA!! KEEP THAT SHARK-BOY OCCUPIED FOR A FEW MINUTES, WILL YA???
TIME TO RE-UP THESE WALLS!!
WAAAA-AGGG!!!!!
!

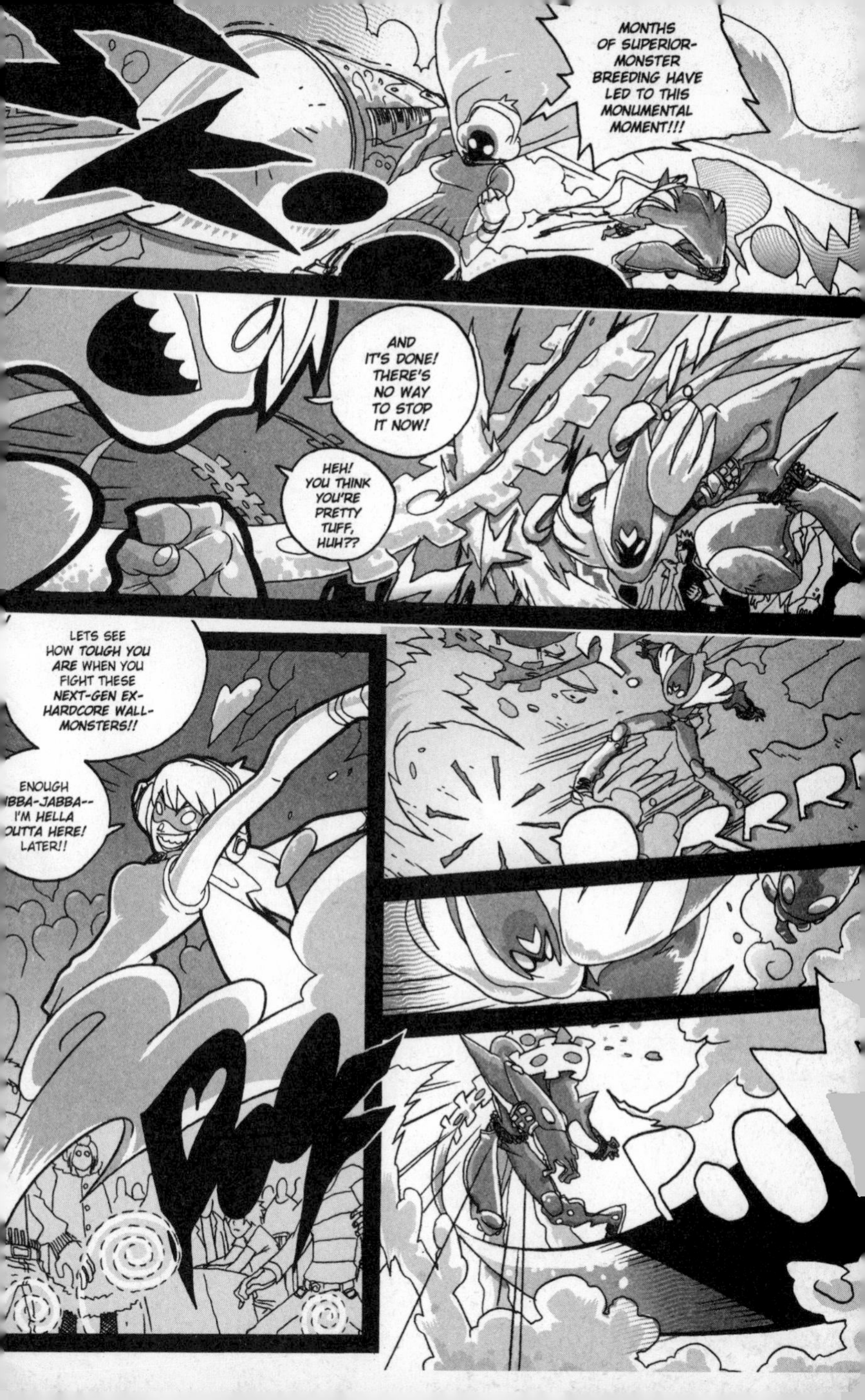
MONTHS OF SUPERIOR-MONSTER BREEDING HAVE LED TO THIS MONUMENTAL MOMENT!!!
AND IT'S DONE! THERE'S NO WAY TO STOP IT NOW!
HEH! YOU THINK YOU'RE PRETTY TUFF, HUH??
LETS SEE HOW TOUGH YOU ARE WHEN YOU FIGHT THESE NEXT-GEN EX-HARDCORE WALL-MONSTERS!!
ENOUGH IBBA-JABBA-- I'M HELLA UTTA HERE! LATER!!

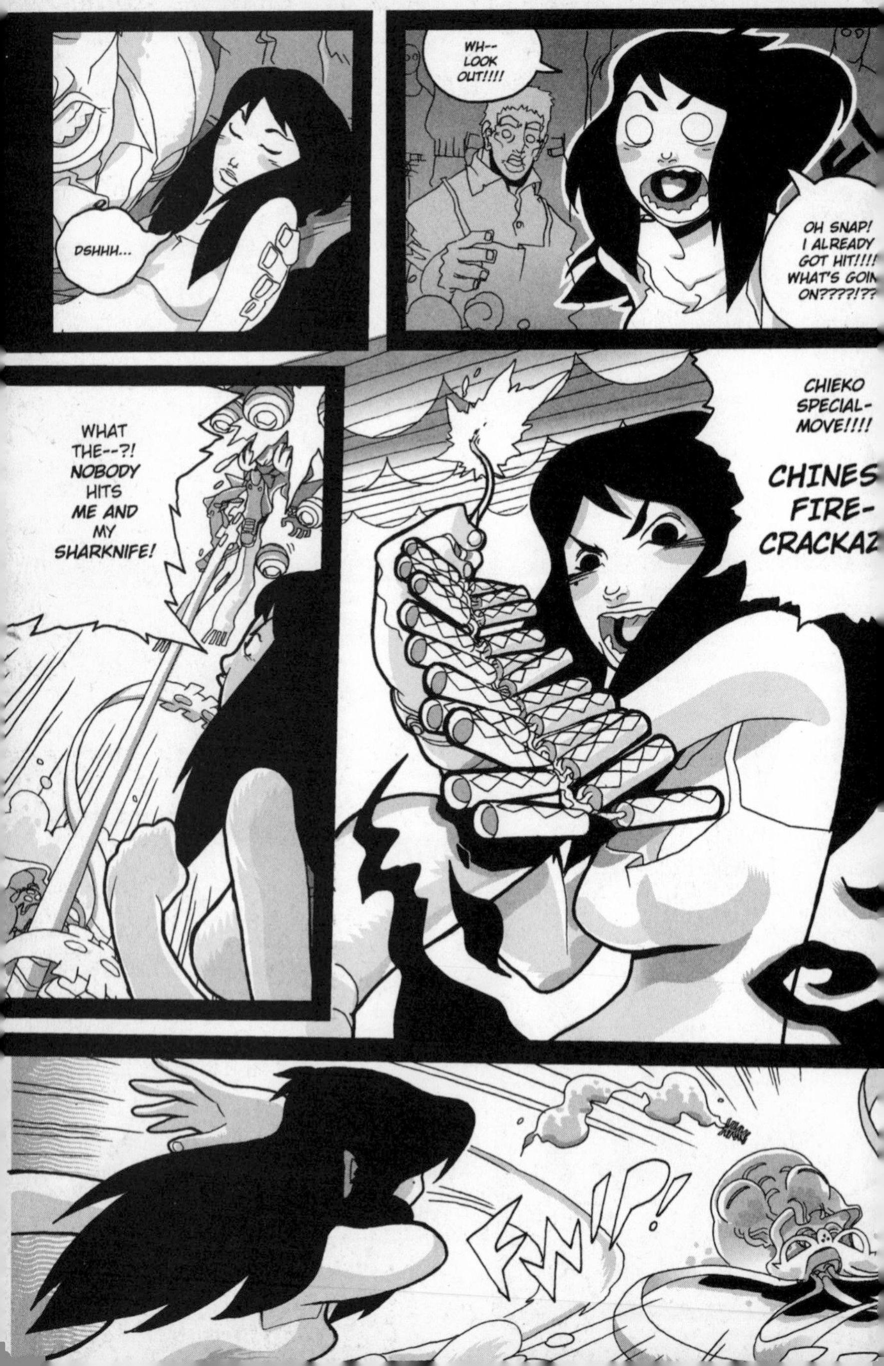
DSHHH...
WH-- LOOK OUT!!!!
OH SNAP! I ALREADY GOT HIT!!!! WHAT'S GOIN ON????!??
WHAT THE--?! NOBODY HITS ME AND MY SHARKNIFE!
CHIEKO SPECIAL-MOVE!!!!
CHINES FIRE-CRACKAZ
FWIP!

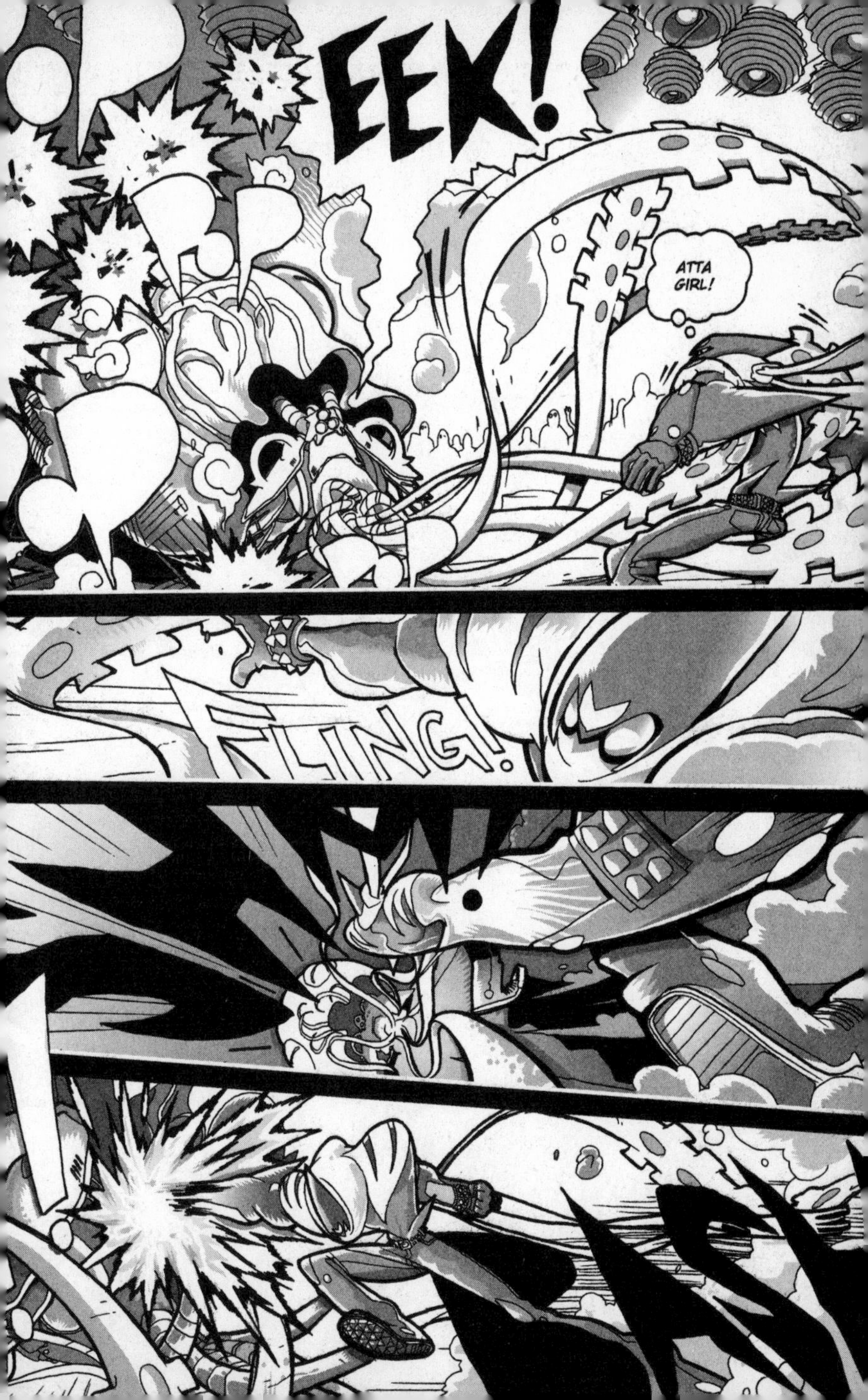
EEK!
ATTA GIRL!
FLING!

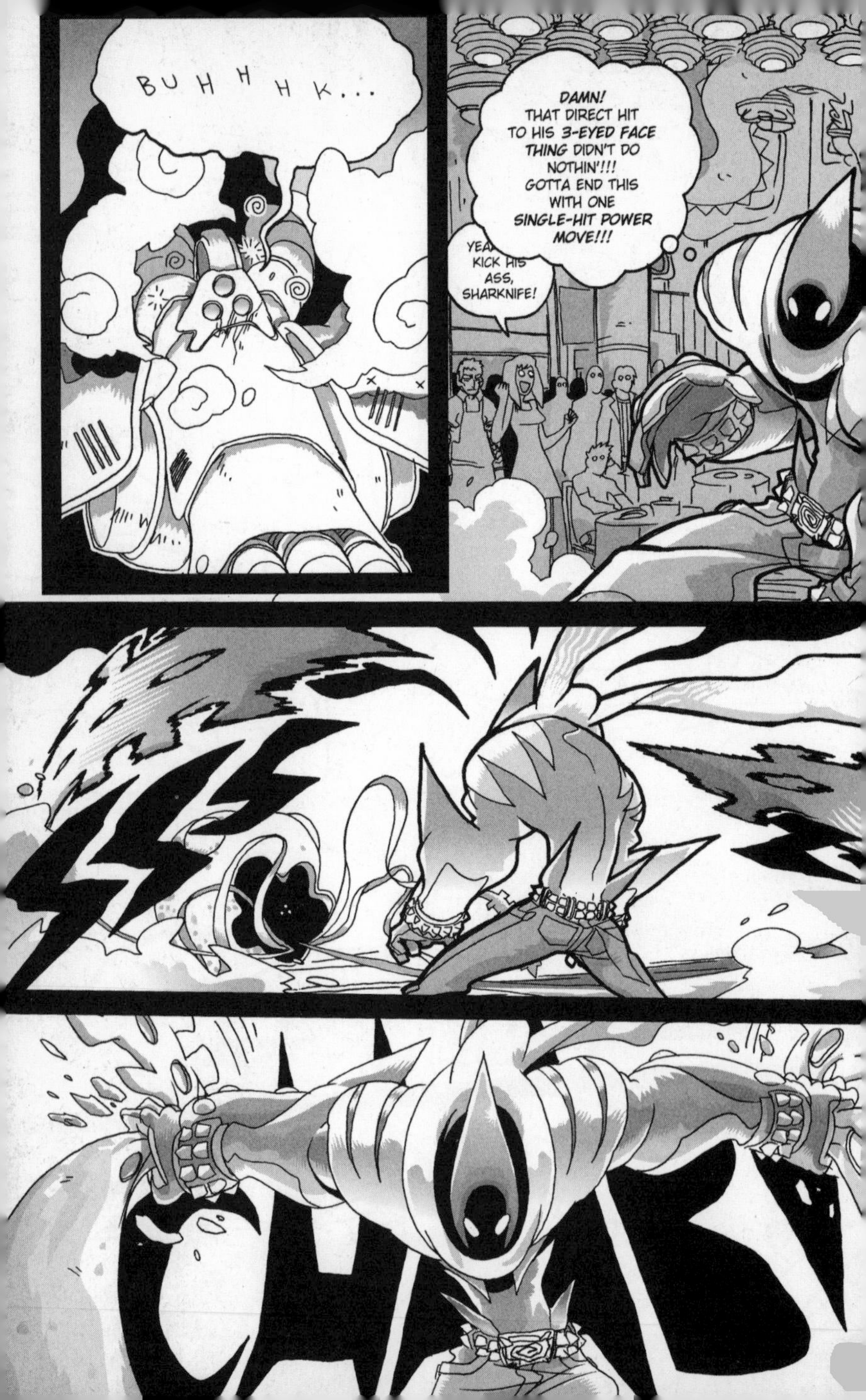
BUHHHK...
DAMN! THAT DIRECT HIT TO HIS 3-EYED FACE THING DIDN'T DO NOTHIN'!!! GOTTA END THIS WITH ONE SINGLE-HIT POWER MOVE!!!
KICK HIS ASS, SHARKNIFE!

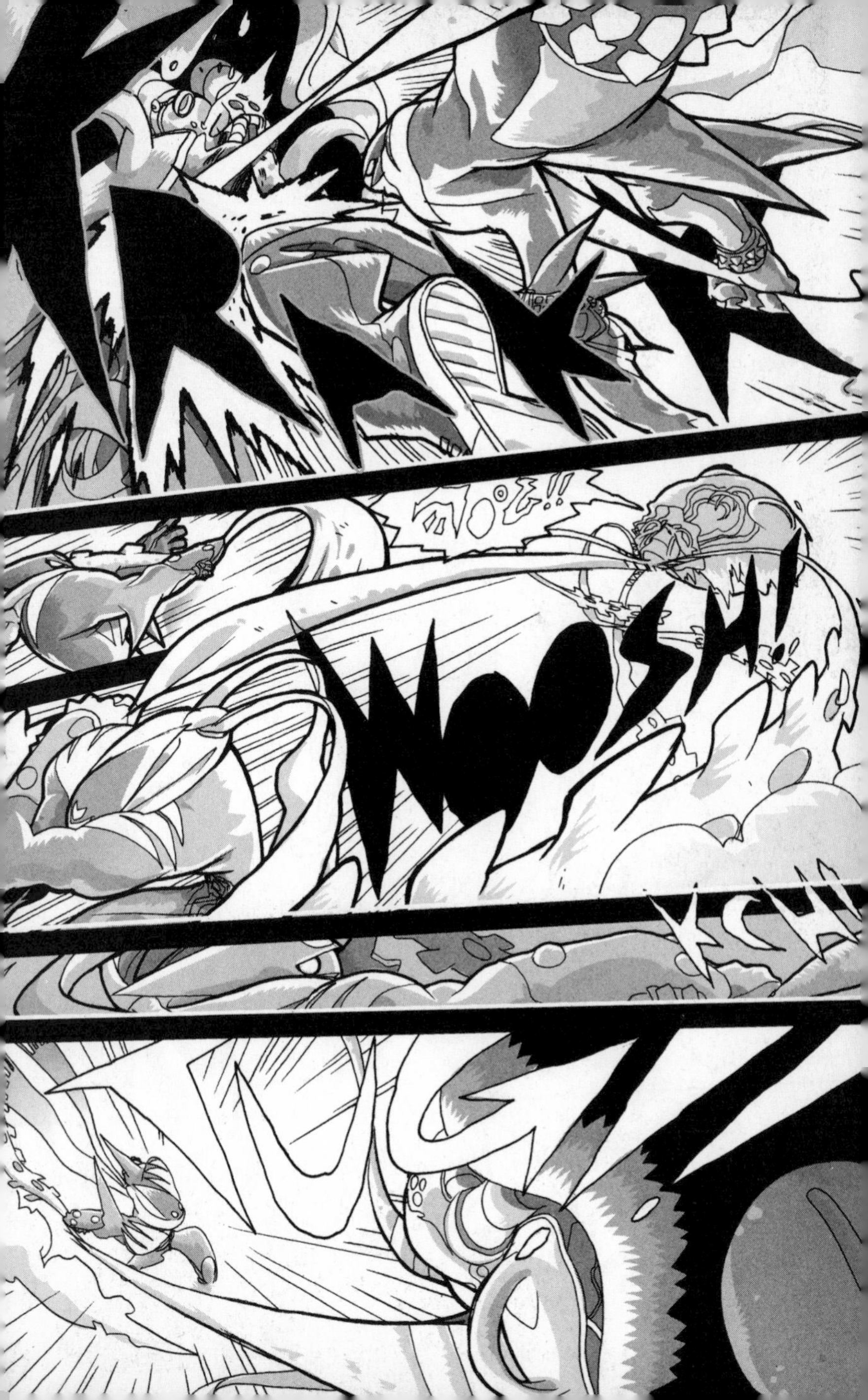
WOOSH!

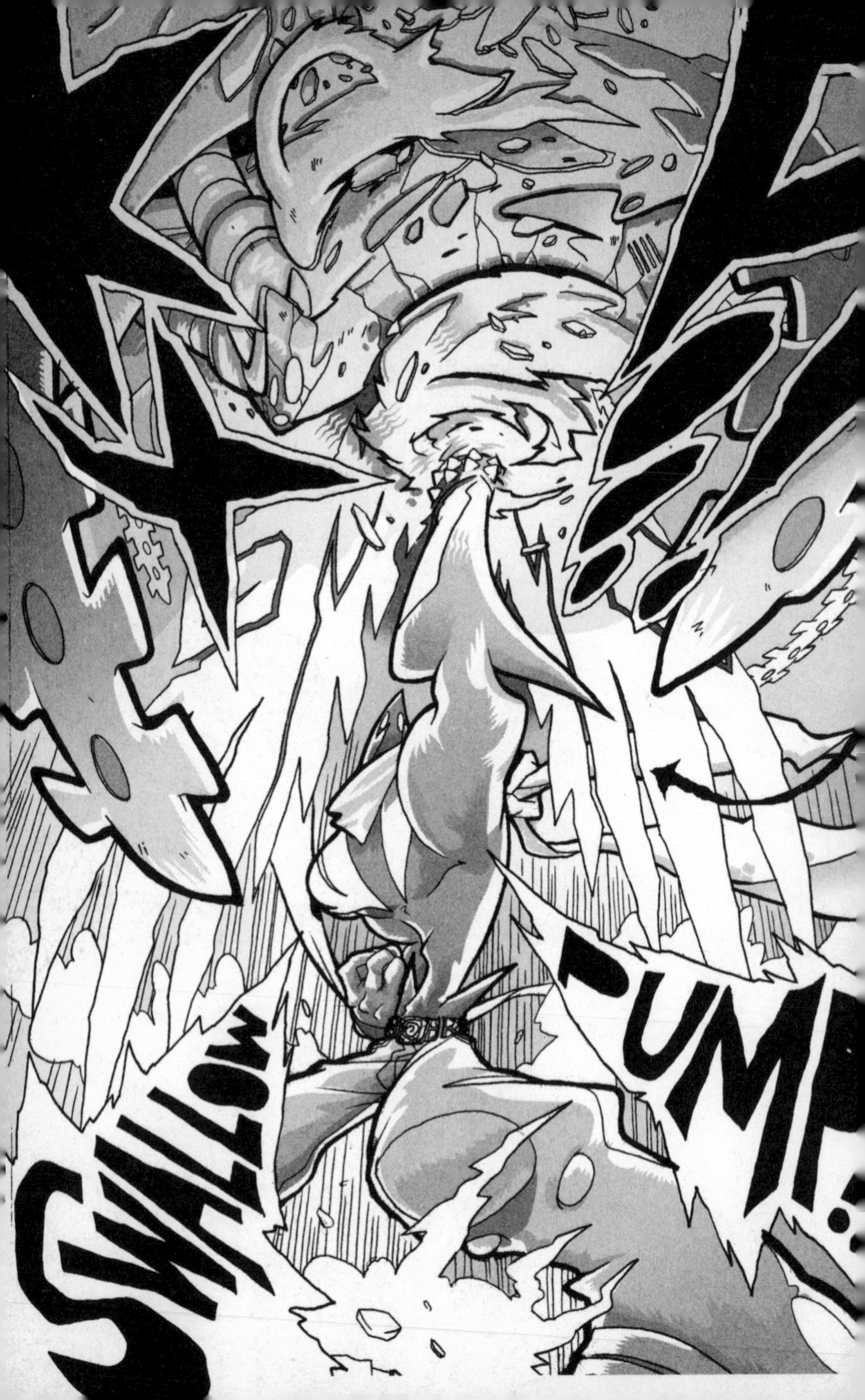
SWALLOW
PUMP!!

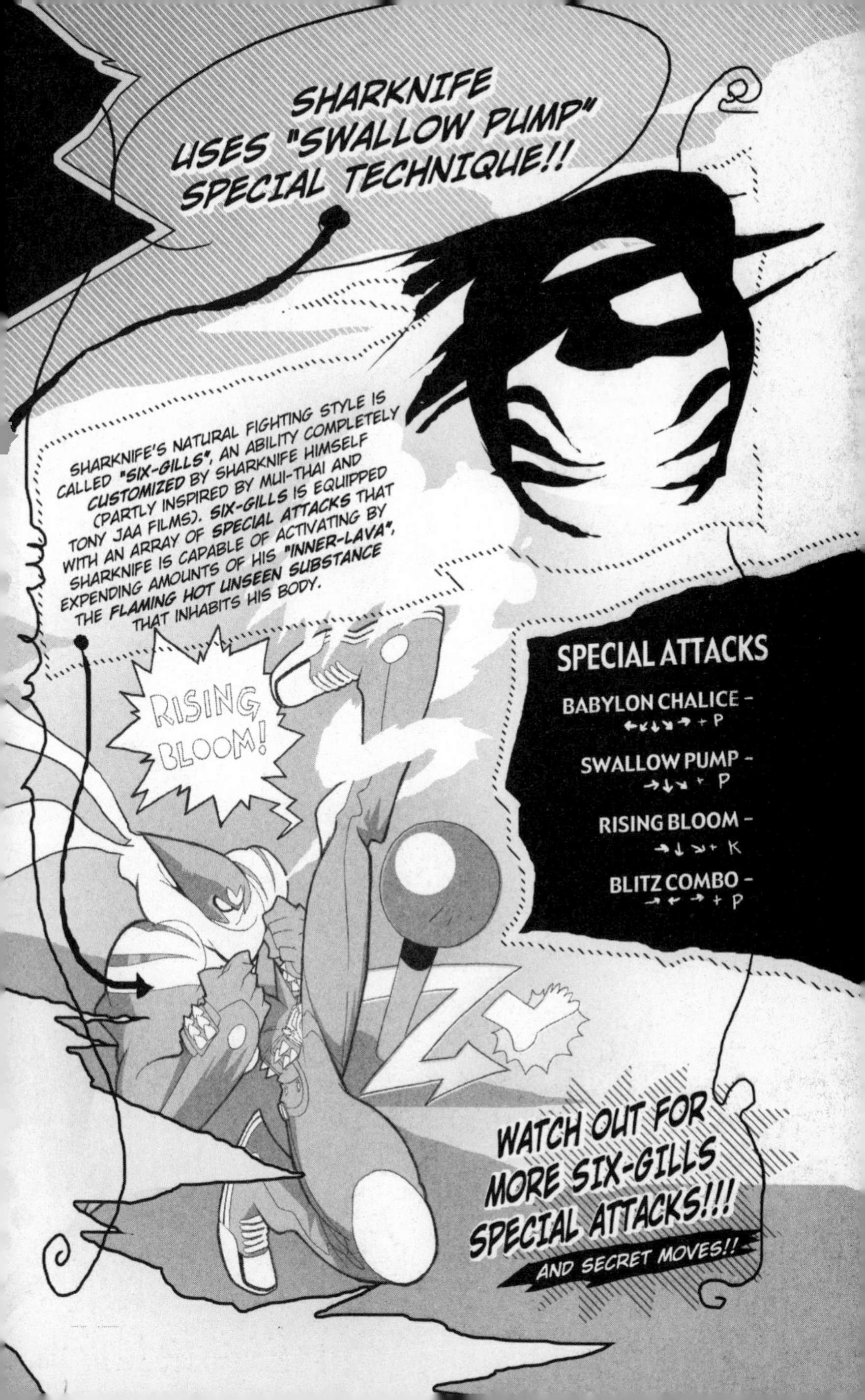
SHARKNIFE USES "SWALLOW PUMP" SPECIAL TECHNIQUE!!
SHARKNIFE'S NATURAL FIGHTING STYLE IS CALLED "SIX-GILLS", AN ABILITY COMPLETELY CUSTOMIZED BY SHARKNIFE HIMSELF (PARTLY INSPIRED BY MUI-THAI AND TONY JAA FILMS). SIX-GILLS IS EQUIPPED WITH AN ARRAY OF SPECIAL ATTACKS THAT SHARKNIFE IS CAPABLE OF ACTIVATING BY EXPENDING AMOUNTS OF HIS "INNER-LAVA", THE FLAMING HOT UNSEEN SUBSTANCE THAT INHABITS HIS BODY.
RISING BLOOM!
SPECIAL ATTACKS
BABYLON CHALICE – ←↙↓↘→ + P
SWALLOW PUMP – →↓↘ + P
RISING BLOOM – →↓↘ + K
BLITZ COMBO – →←→ + P
WATCH OUT FOR MORE SIX-GILLS SPECIAL ATTACKS!!!
AND SECRET MOVES!!

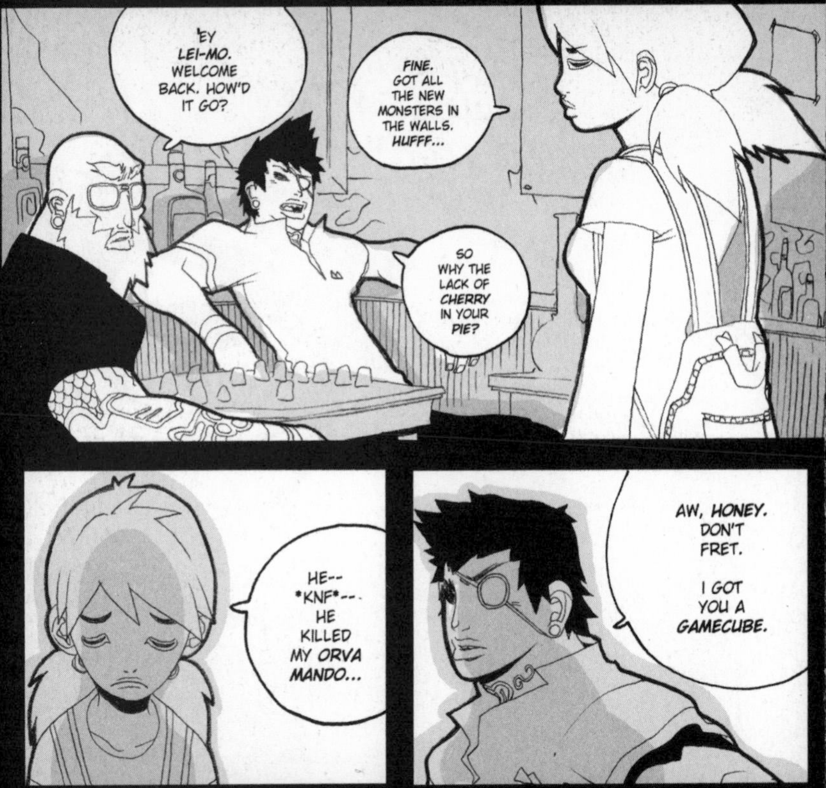
'EY LEI-MO. WELCOME BACK. HOW'D IT GO?
FINE. GOT ALL THE NEW MONSTERS IN THE WALLS. HUFFF...
SO WHY THE LACK OF CHERRY IN YOUR PIE?
HE-- *KNF*-- HE KILLED MY ORVA MANDO...
AW, HONEY. DON'T FRET.
I GOT YOU A GAMECUBE.

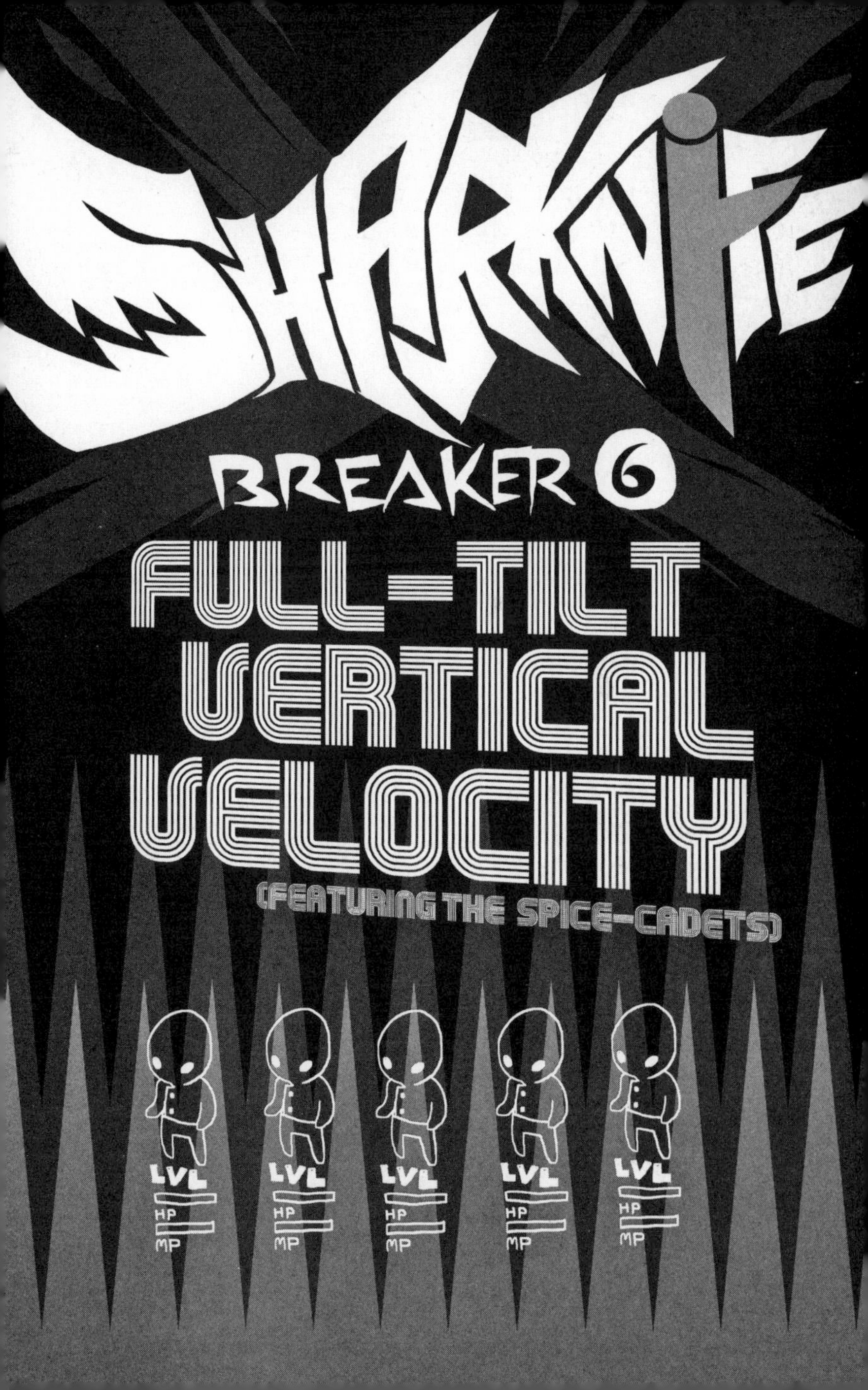
SHARKNIFE
BREAKER 6
FULL-TILT VERTICAL VELOCITY
(FEATURING THE SPICE-CADETS)
LVL
HP
MP
LVL
HP
MP
LVL
HP
MP
LVL
HP
MP
LVL
HP
MP

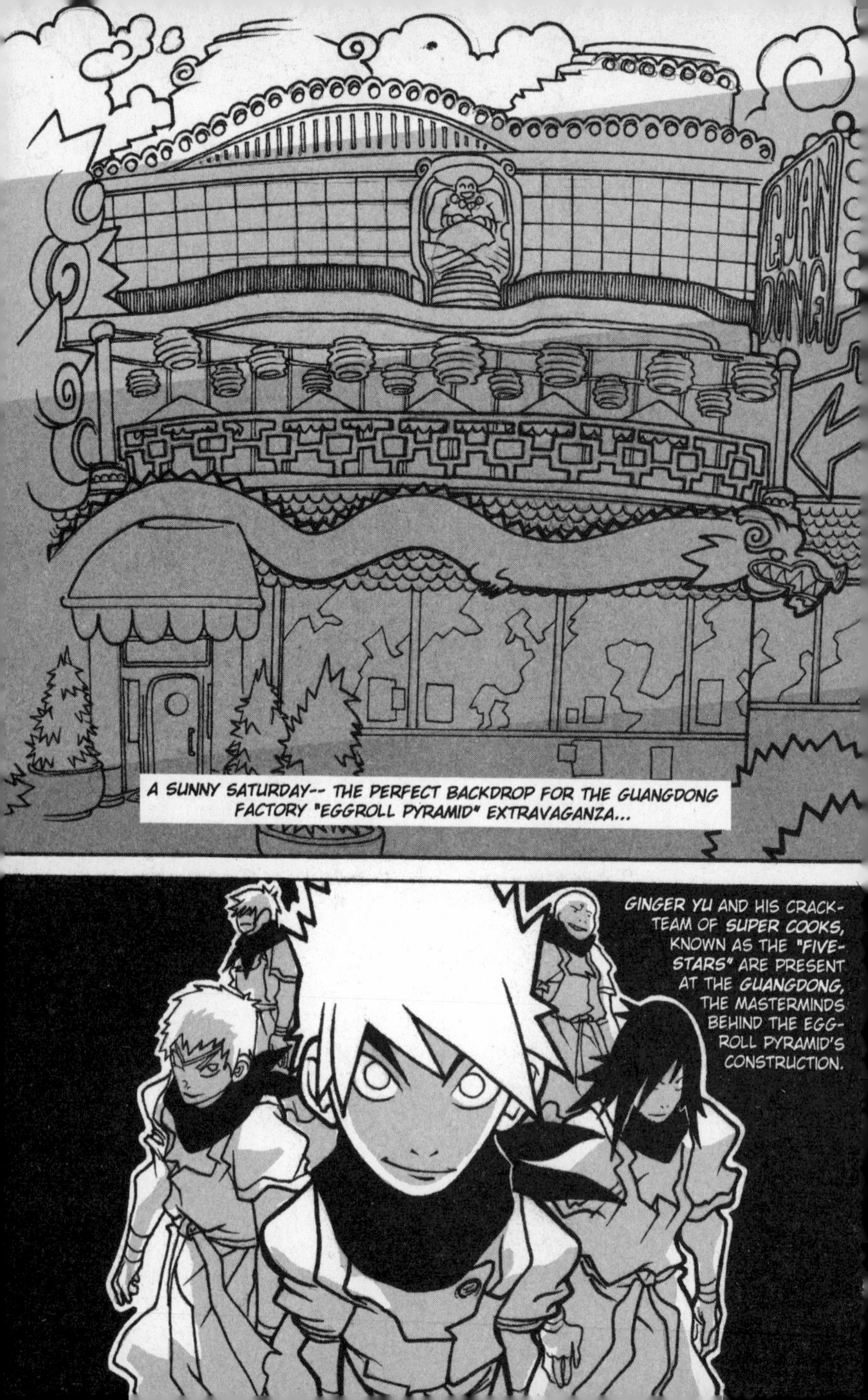
GUANGDONG
A SUNNY SATURDAY-- THE PERFECT BACKDROP FOR THE GUANGDONG FACTORY "EGGROLL PYRAMID" EXTRAVAGANZA...
GINGER YU AND HIS CRACK-TEAM OF SUPER COOKS, KNOWN AS THE "FIVE-STARS" ARE PRESENT AT THE GUANGDONG, THE MASTERMINDS BEHIND THE EGG-ROLL PYRAMID'S CONSTRUCTION.

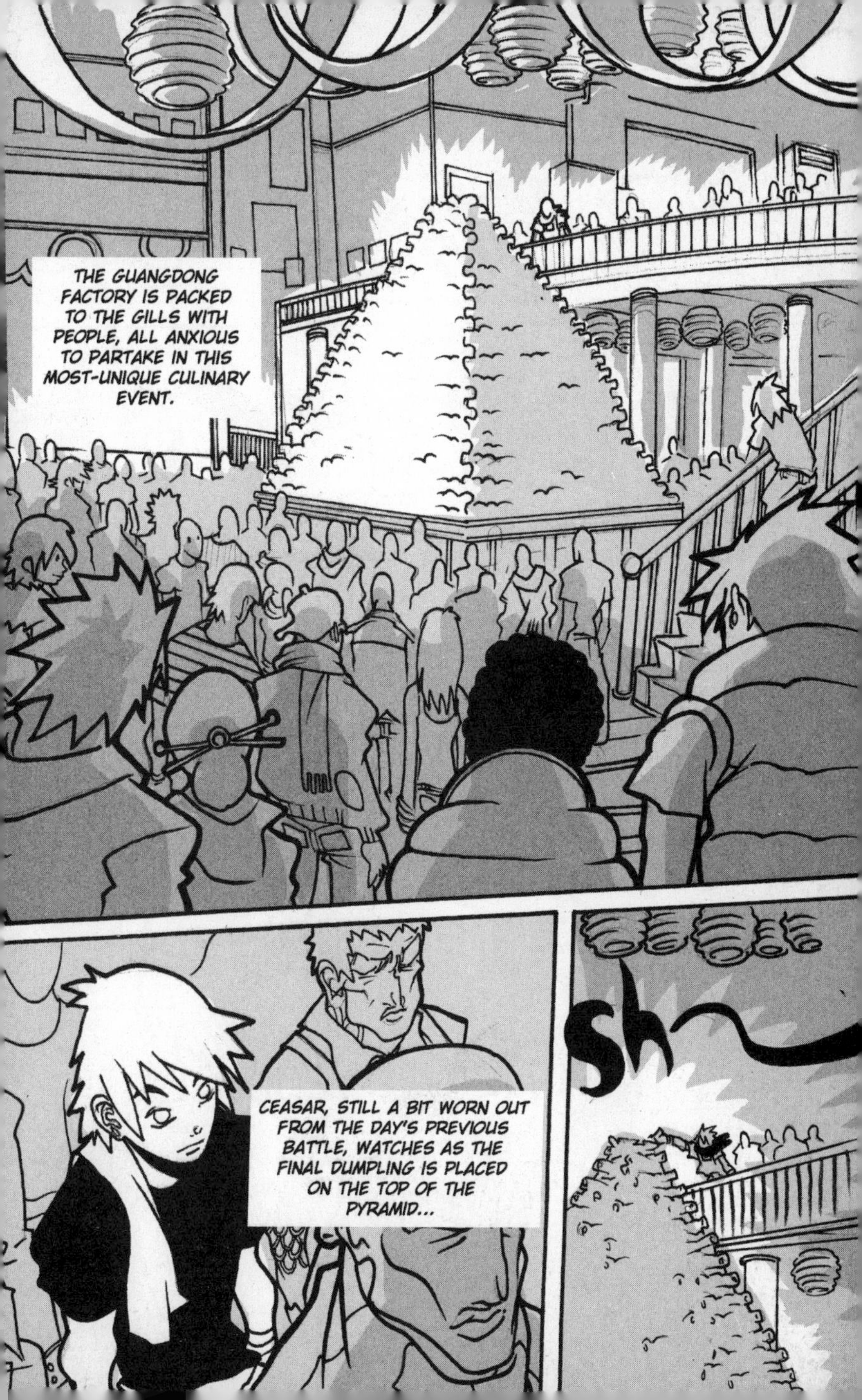
THE GUANGDONG FACTORY IS PACKED TO THE GILLS WITH PEOPLE, ALL ANXIOUS TO PARTAKE IN THIS MOST-UNIQUE CULINARY EVENT.
CEASAR, STILL A BIT WORN OUT FROM THE DAY'S PREVIOUS BATTLE, WATCHES AS THE FINAL DUMPLING IS PLACED ON THE TOP OF THE PYRAMID...
Sh

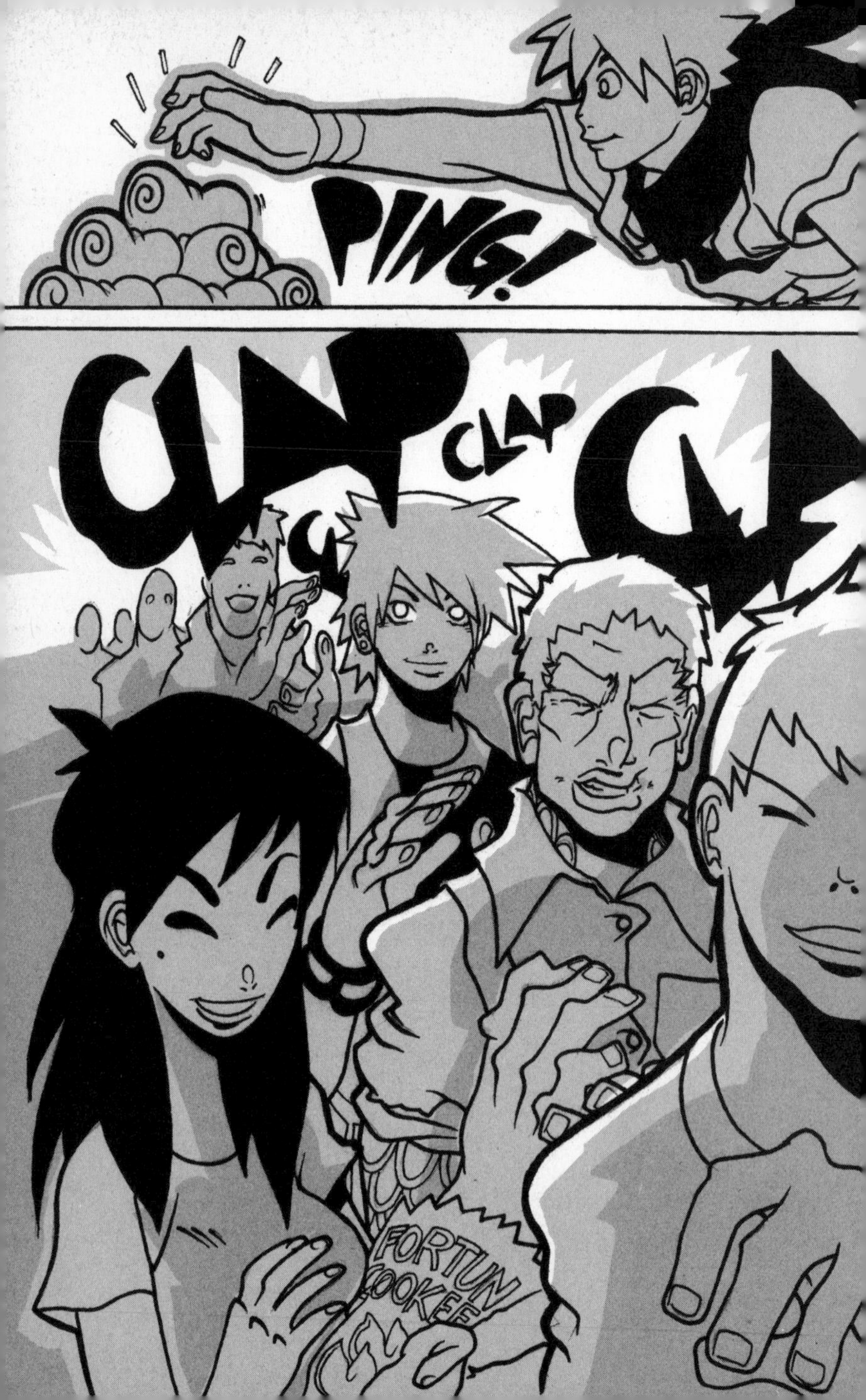
PING!
CLAP
CLAP
FORTUN COOKEE

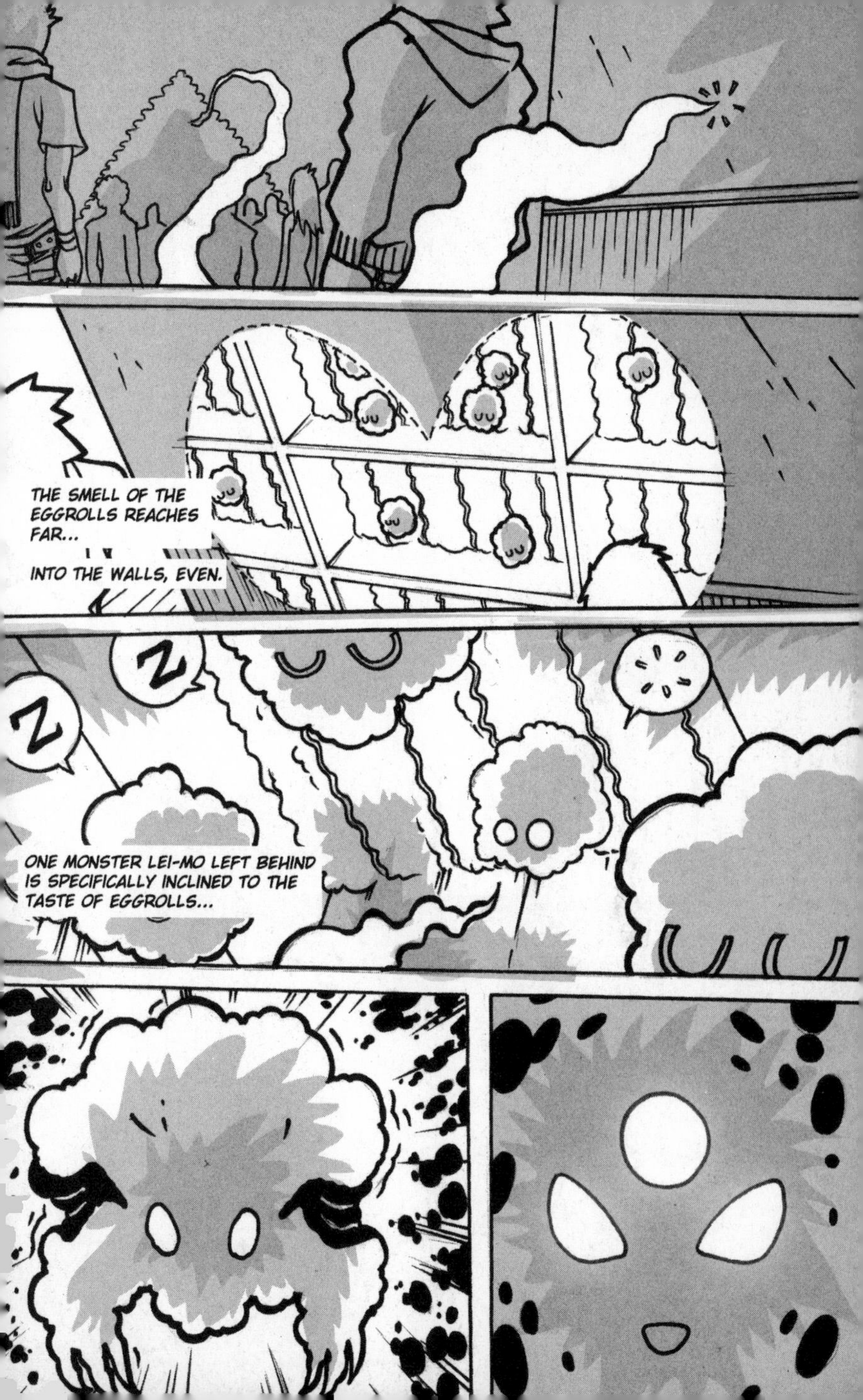
THE SMELL OF THE EGGROLLS REACHES FAR...
INTO THE WALLS, EVEN.
Z
Z
ONE MONSTER LEI-MO LEFT BEHIND IS SPECIFICALLY INCLINED TO THE TASTE OF EGGROLLS...

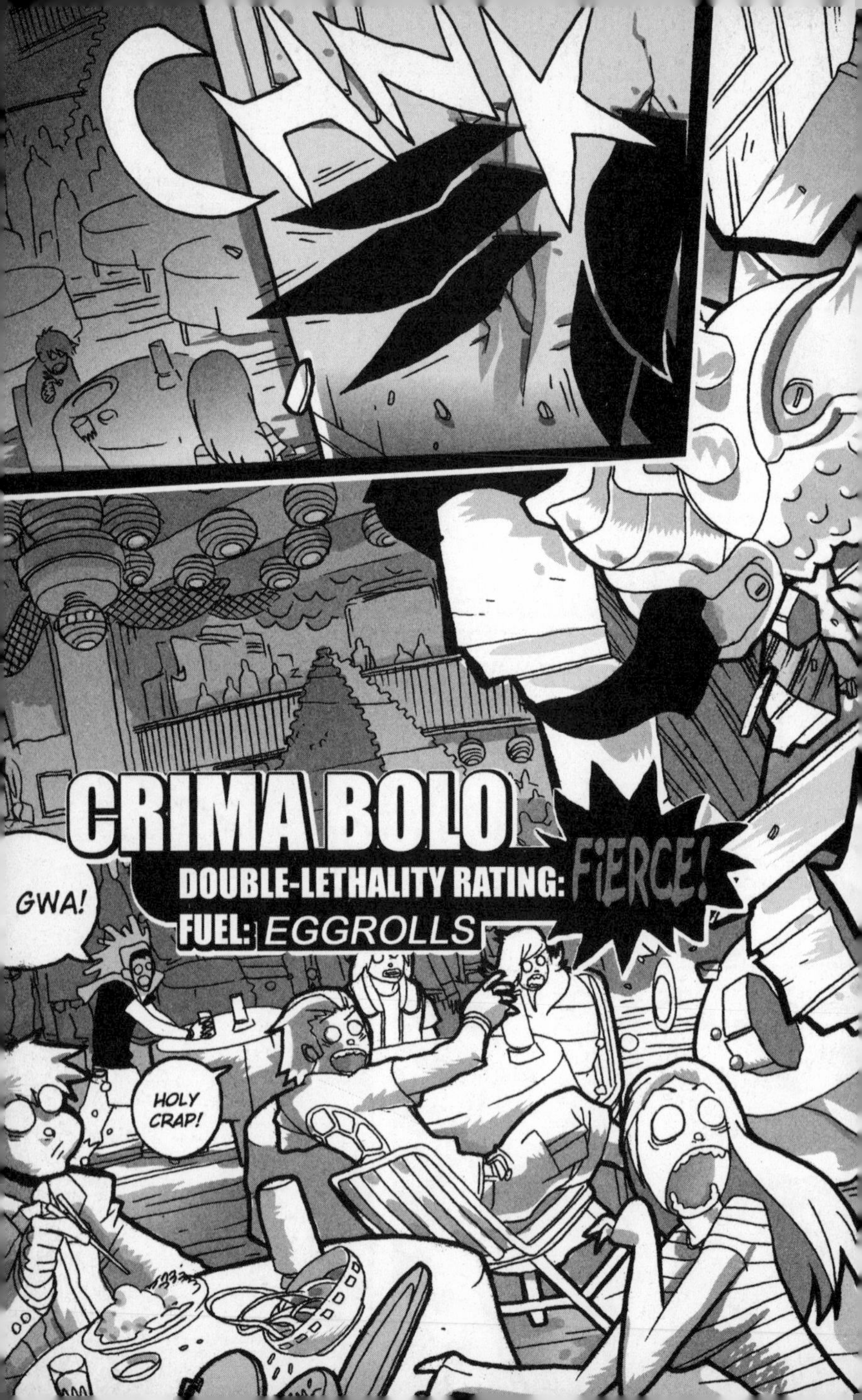

CRIMA BOLO
DOUBLE-LETHALITY RATING: FiERCE!
FUEL: EGGROLLS
GWA!
HOLY CRAP!

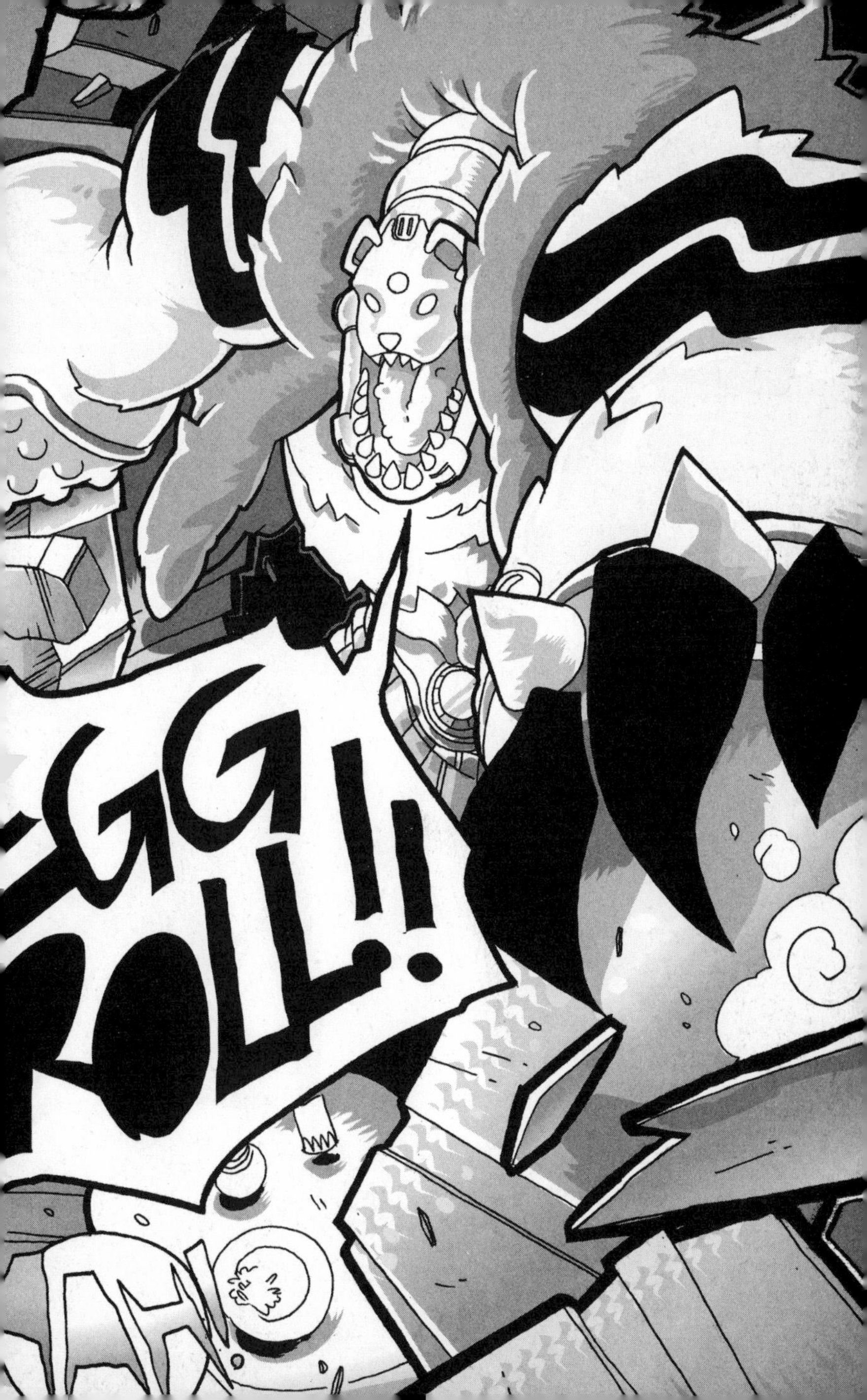
GG
OLL!!

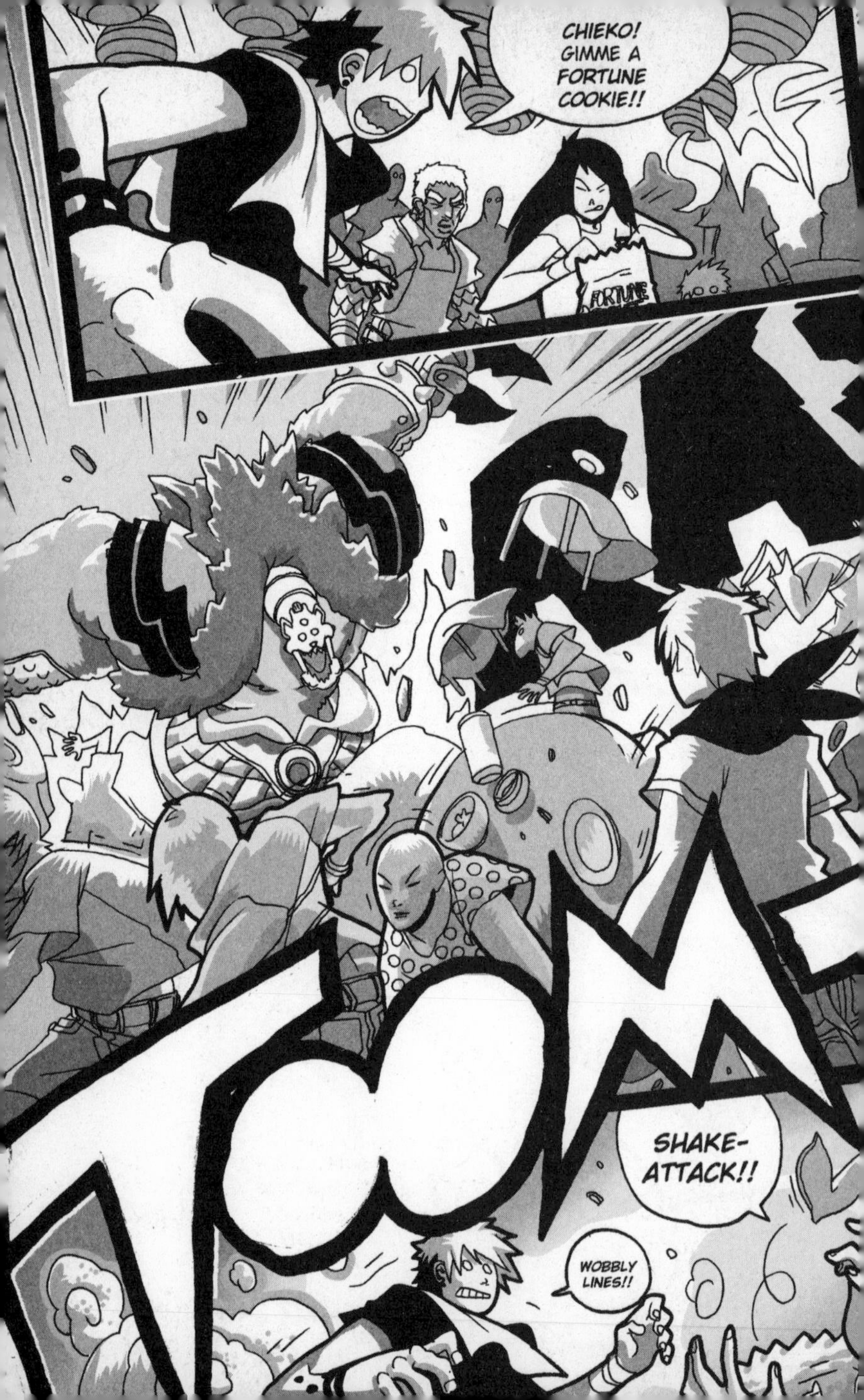
CHIEKO! GIMME A FORTUNE COOKIE!!
FORTUNE
SHAKE-ATTACK!!
WOBBLY LINES!!

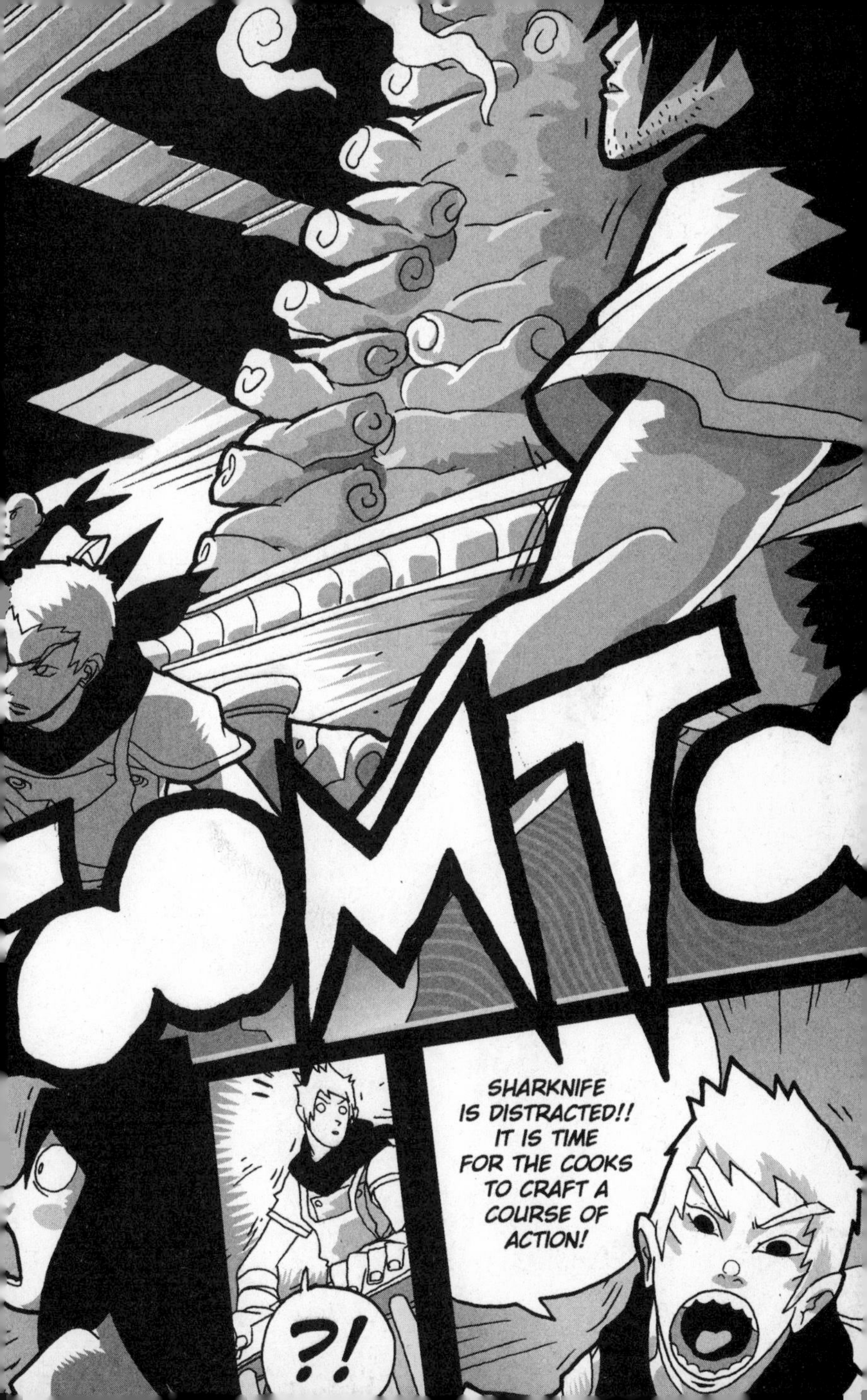

SHARKNIFE IS DISTRACTED!! IT IS TIME FOR THE COOKS TO CRAFT A COURSE OF ACTION!
?!

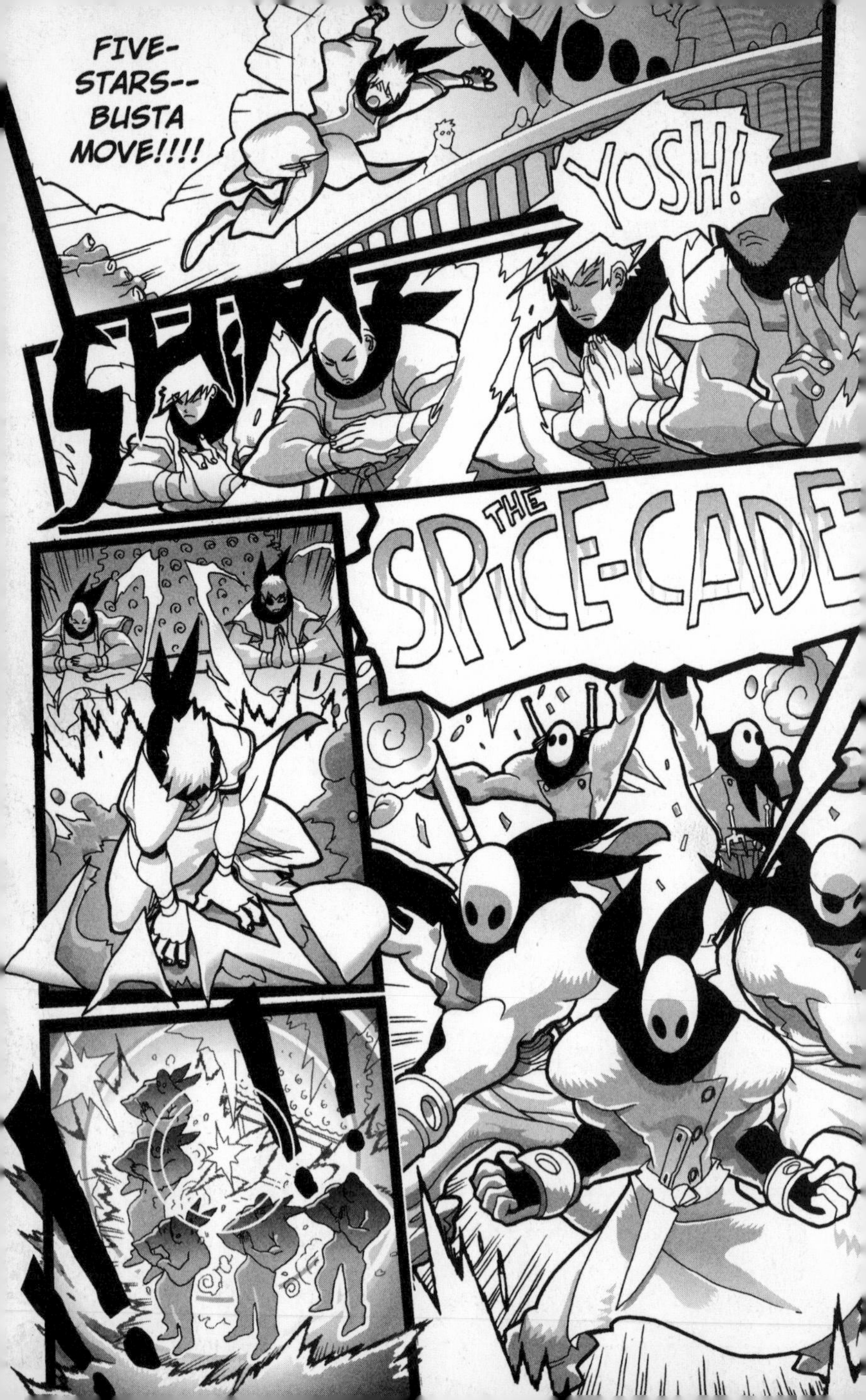

FIVE-
STARS--
BUSTA
MOVE!!!!
WO...
YOSH!
THE
SPICE-CADE

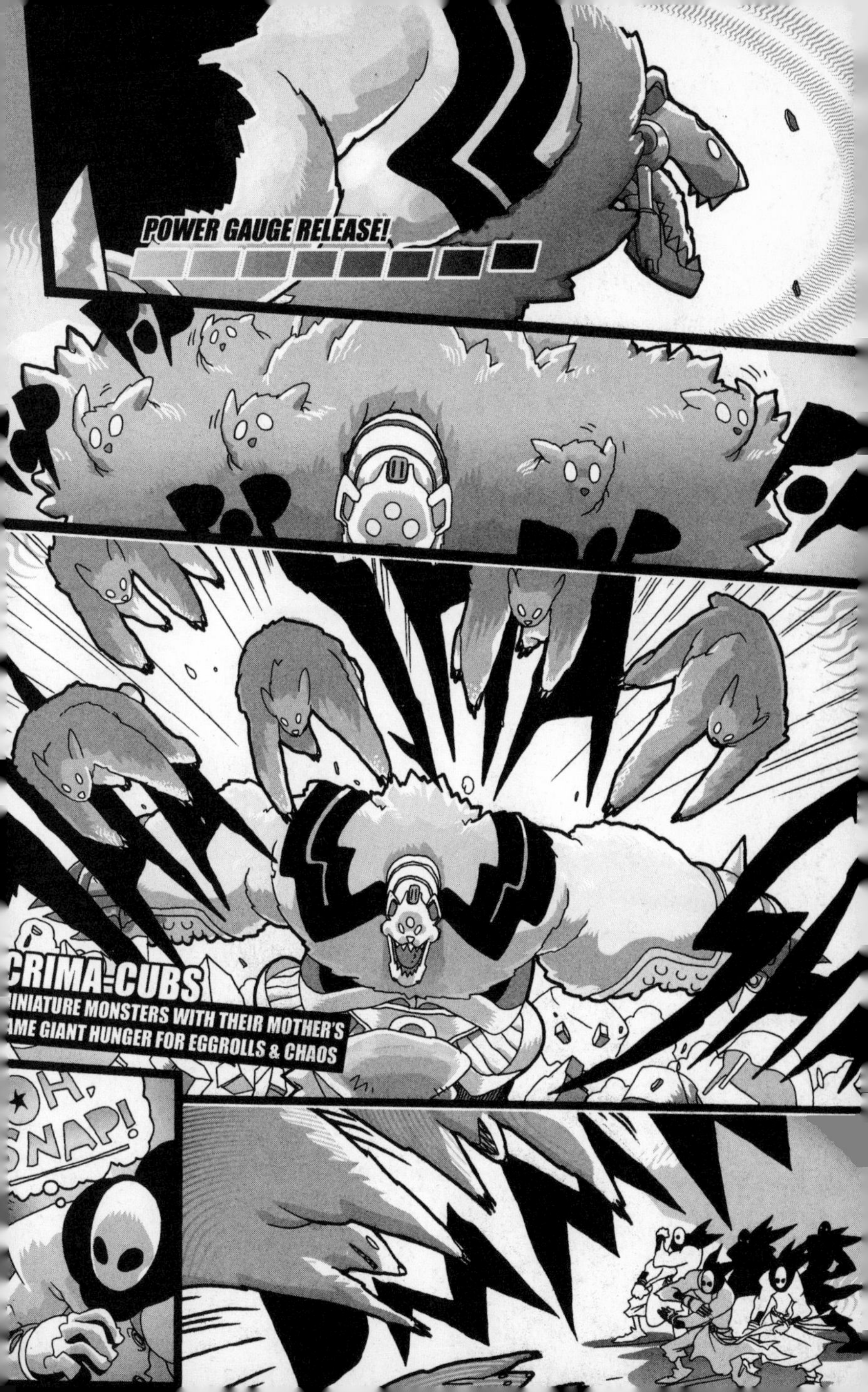
POWER GAUGE RELEASE!
CRIMA-CUBS
INIATURE MONSTERS WITH THEIR MOTHER'S
AME GIANT HUNGER FOR EGGROLLS & CHAOS
OH, SNAP!

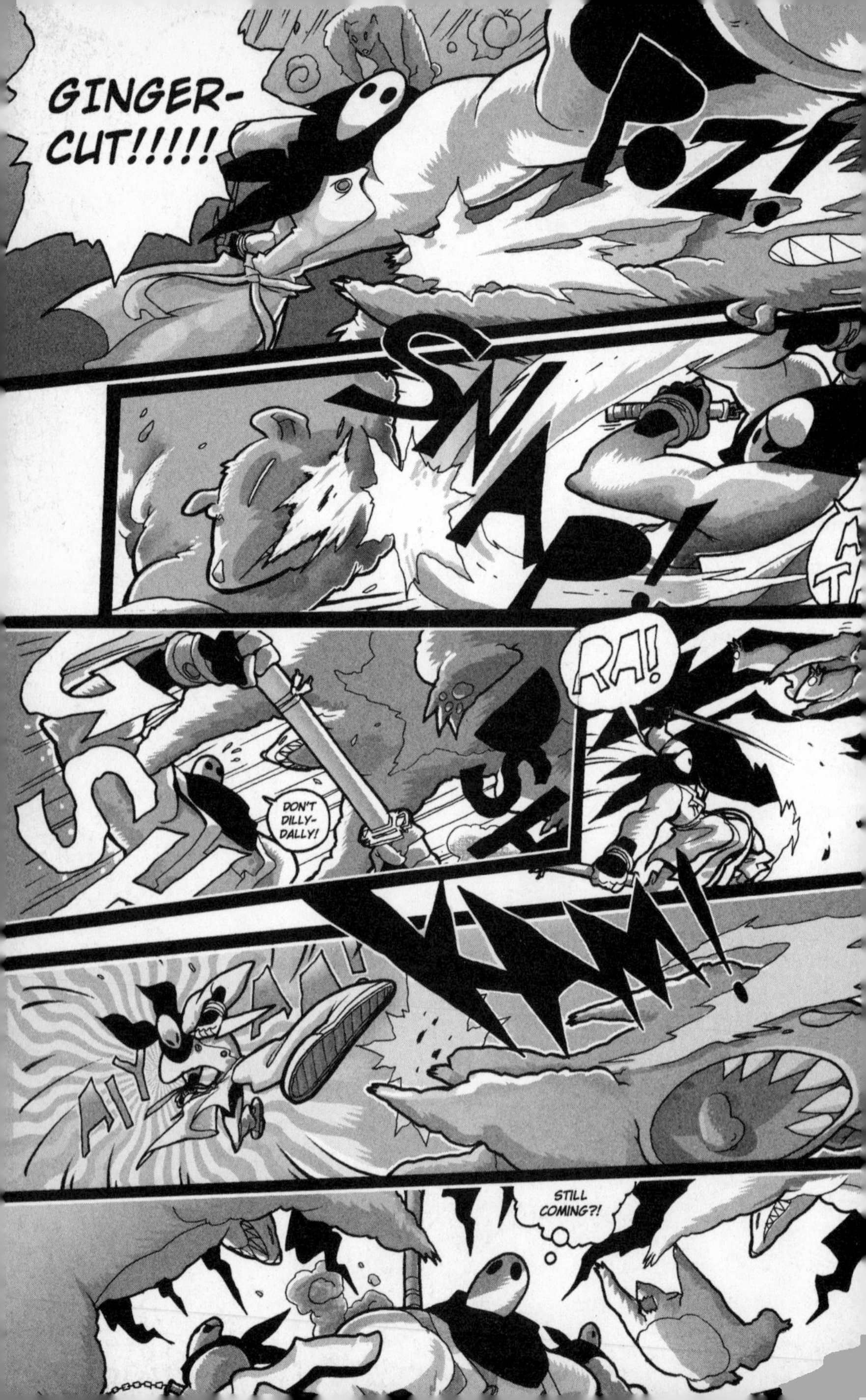
GINGER-CUT!!!!!!
DOZ!
SNAP!
RA!
DON'T DILLY-DALLY!
SPSH
STILL COMING?!

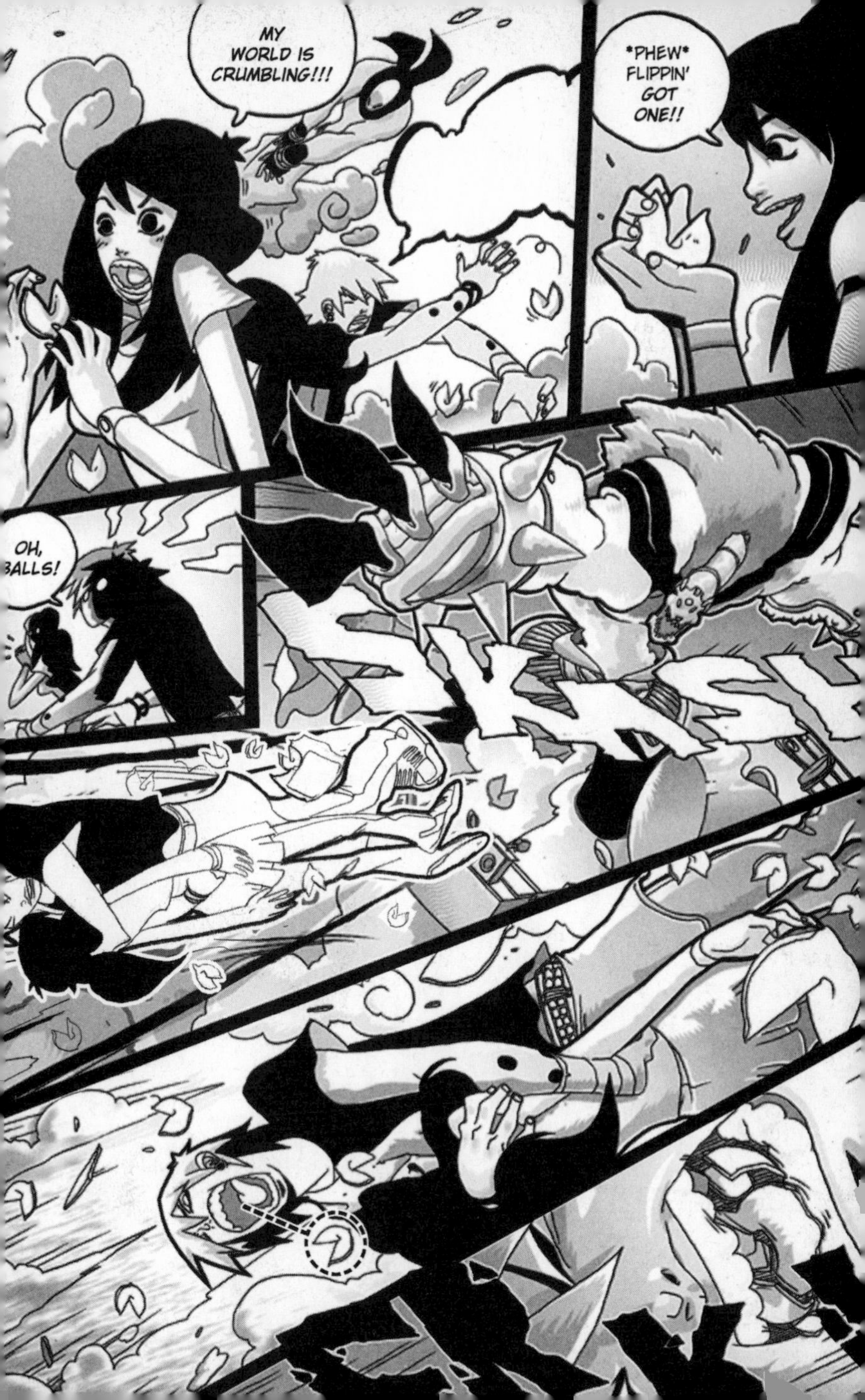
MY WORLD IS CRUMBLING!!!
PHEW FLIPPIN' GOT ONE!!
OH, BALLS!

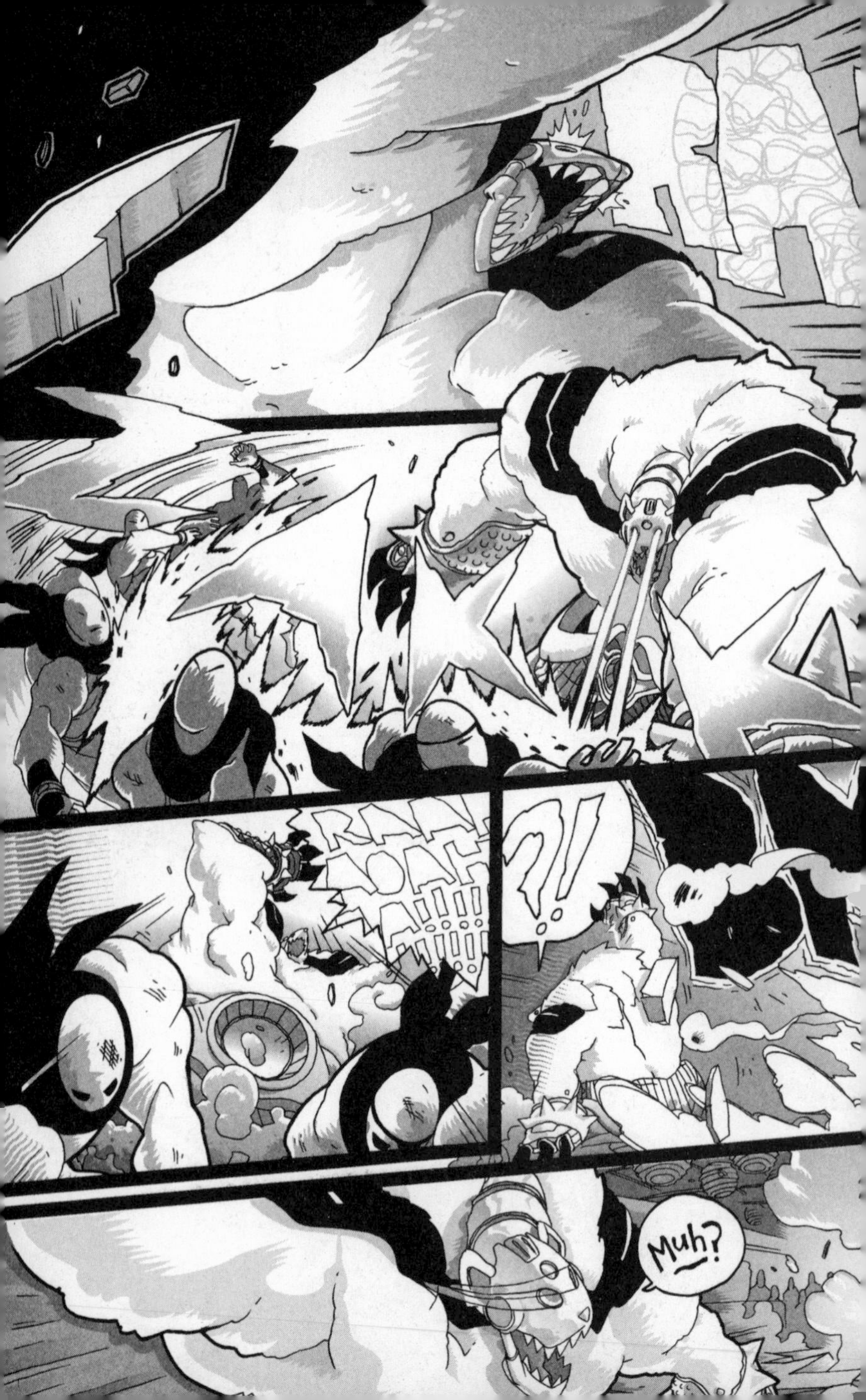
RAA
OAH
A!!!
A!!!!
?!
Muh?

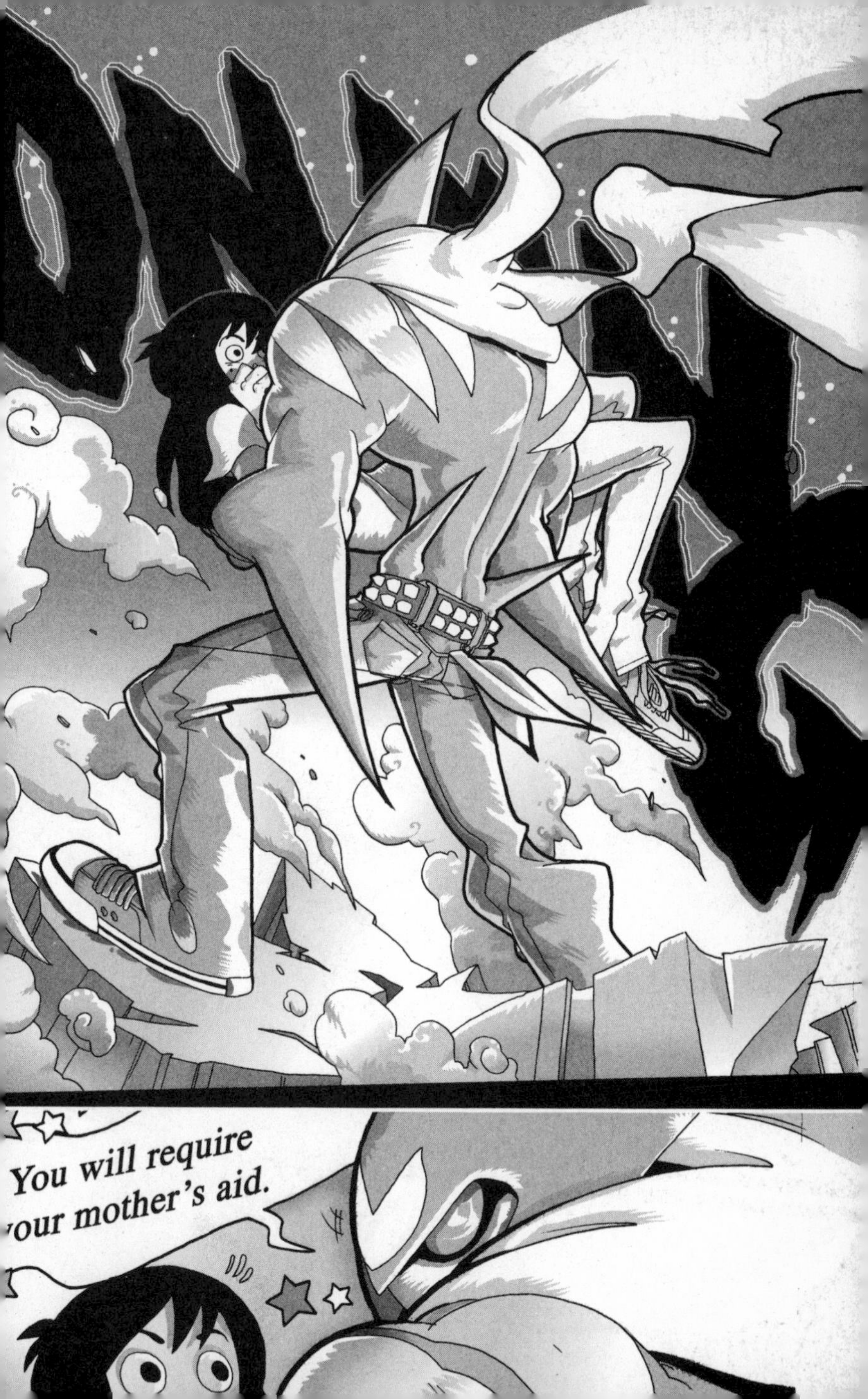
You will require
your mother's aid.

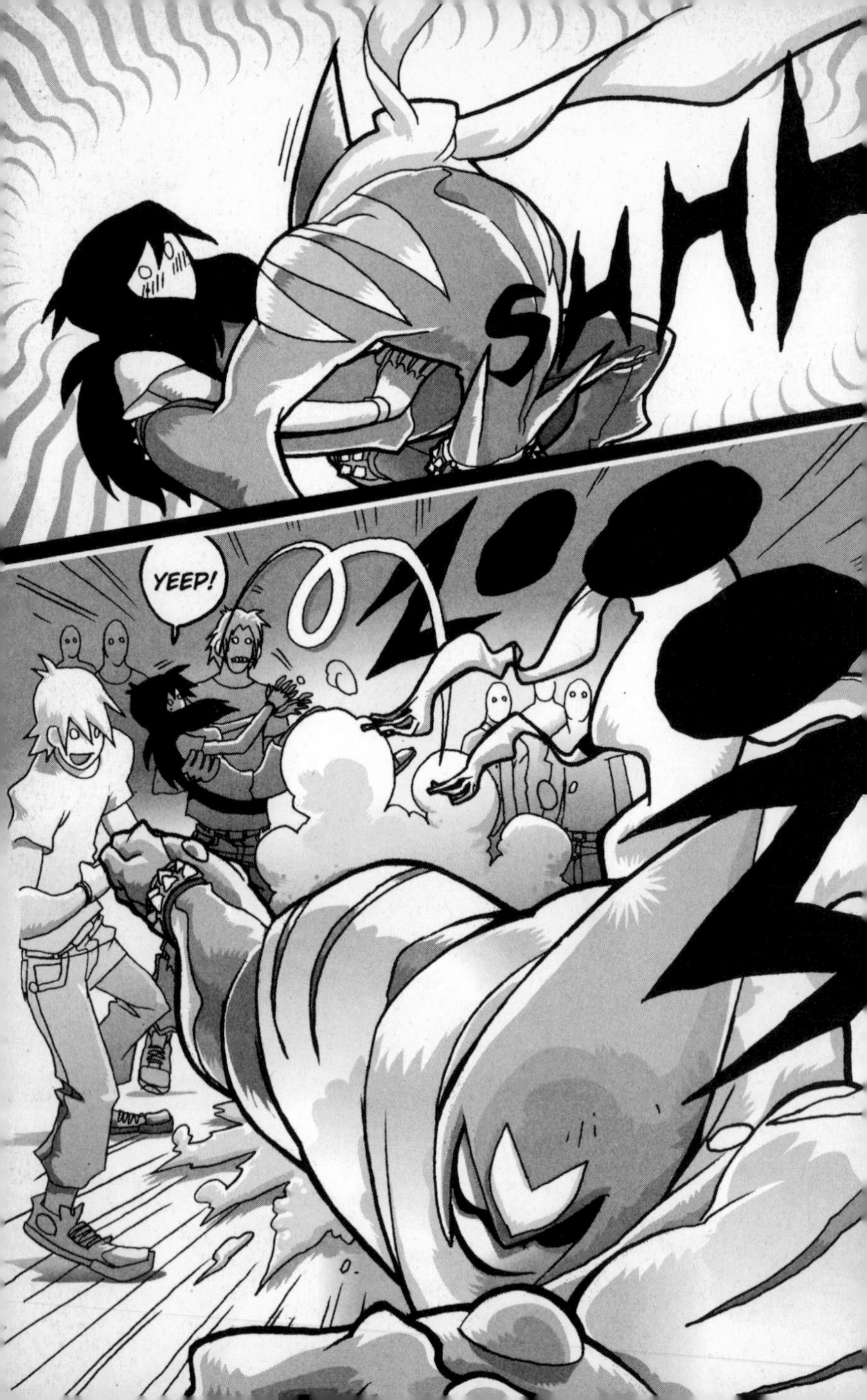
YEEP!

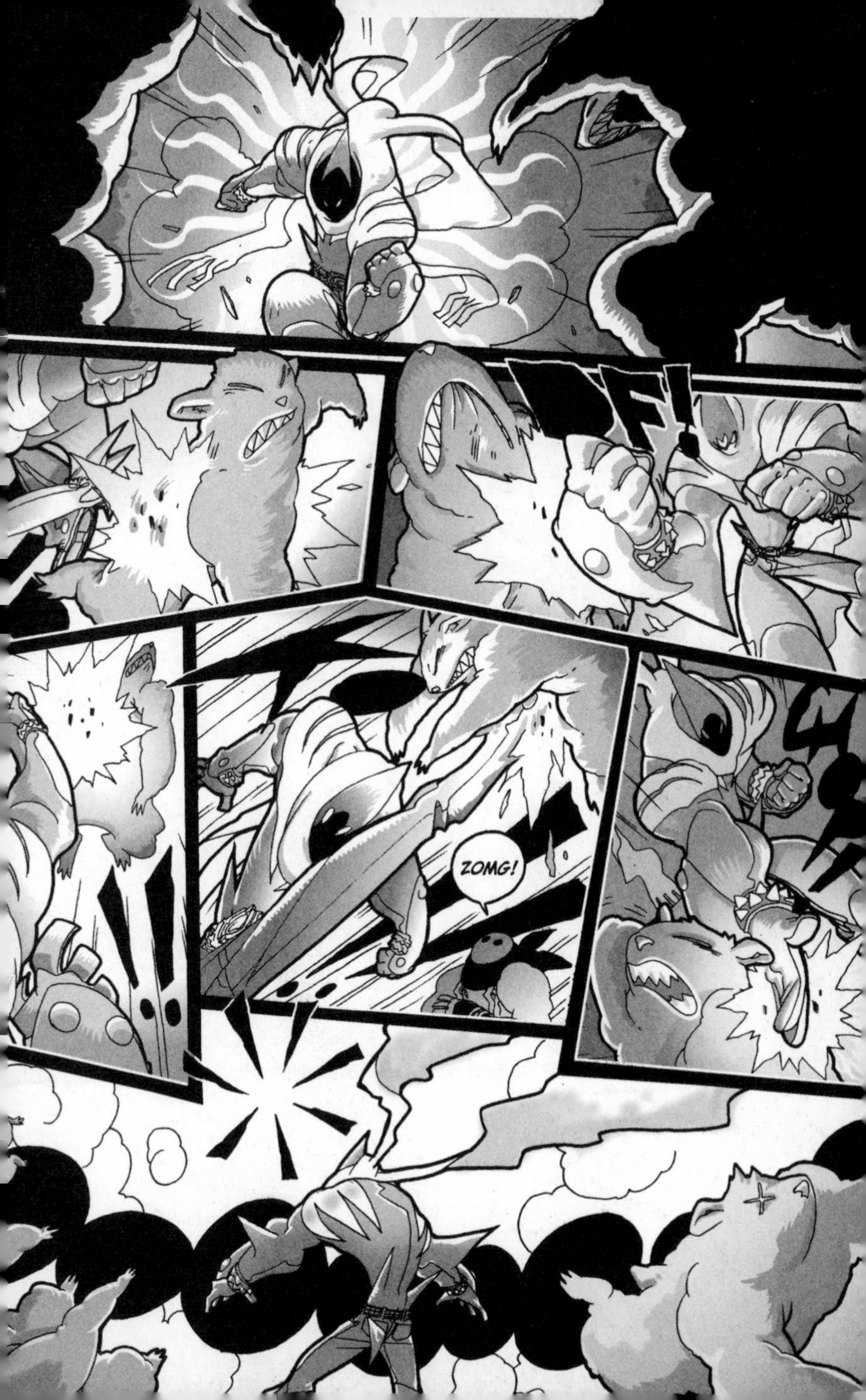
ZOMG!

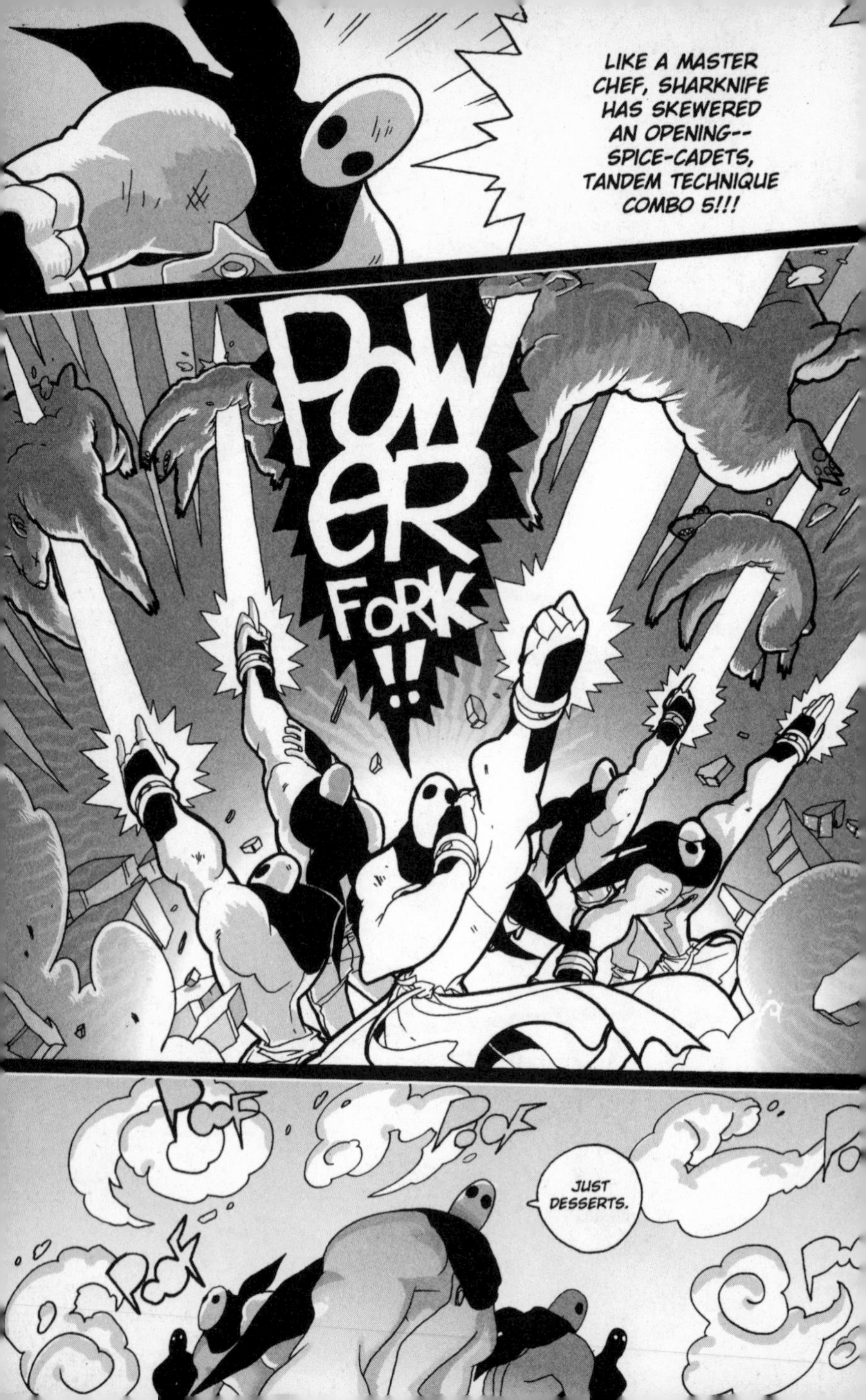
LIKE A MASTER CHEF, SHARKNIFE HAS SKEWERED AN OPENING-- SPICE-CADETS, TANDEM TECHNIQUE COMBO 5!!!
POWER FORK!!
POOF
POOF
JUST DESSERTS.
POOF

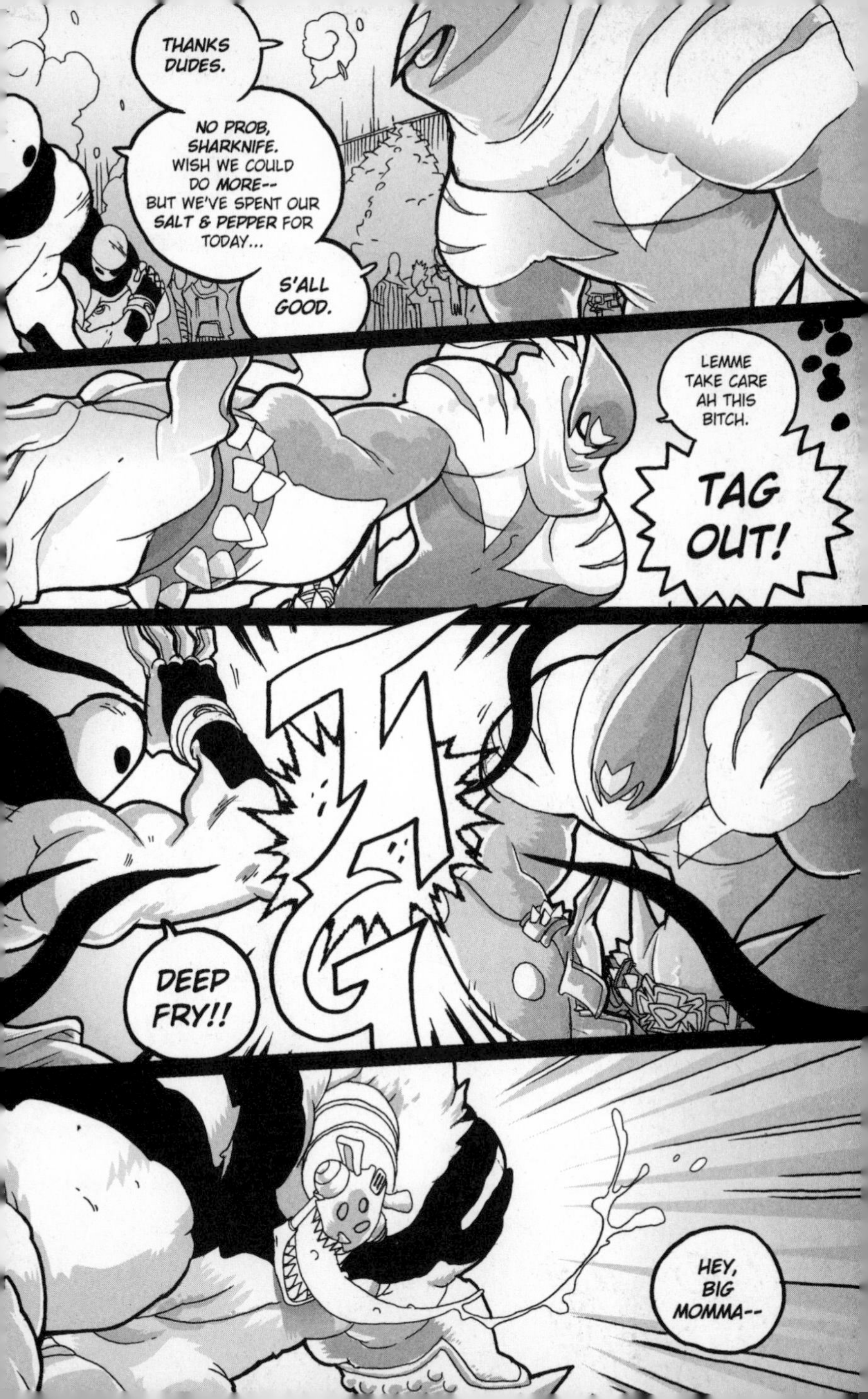
THANKS DUDES.
NO PROB, SHARKNIFE. WISH WE COULD DO MORE-- BUT WE'VE SPENT OUR SALT & PEPPER FOR TODAY...
S'ALL GOOD.
LEMME TAKE CARE AH THIS BITCH.
TAG OUT!
DEEP FRY!!
HEY, BIG MOMMA--

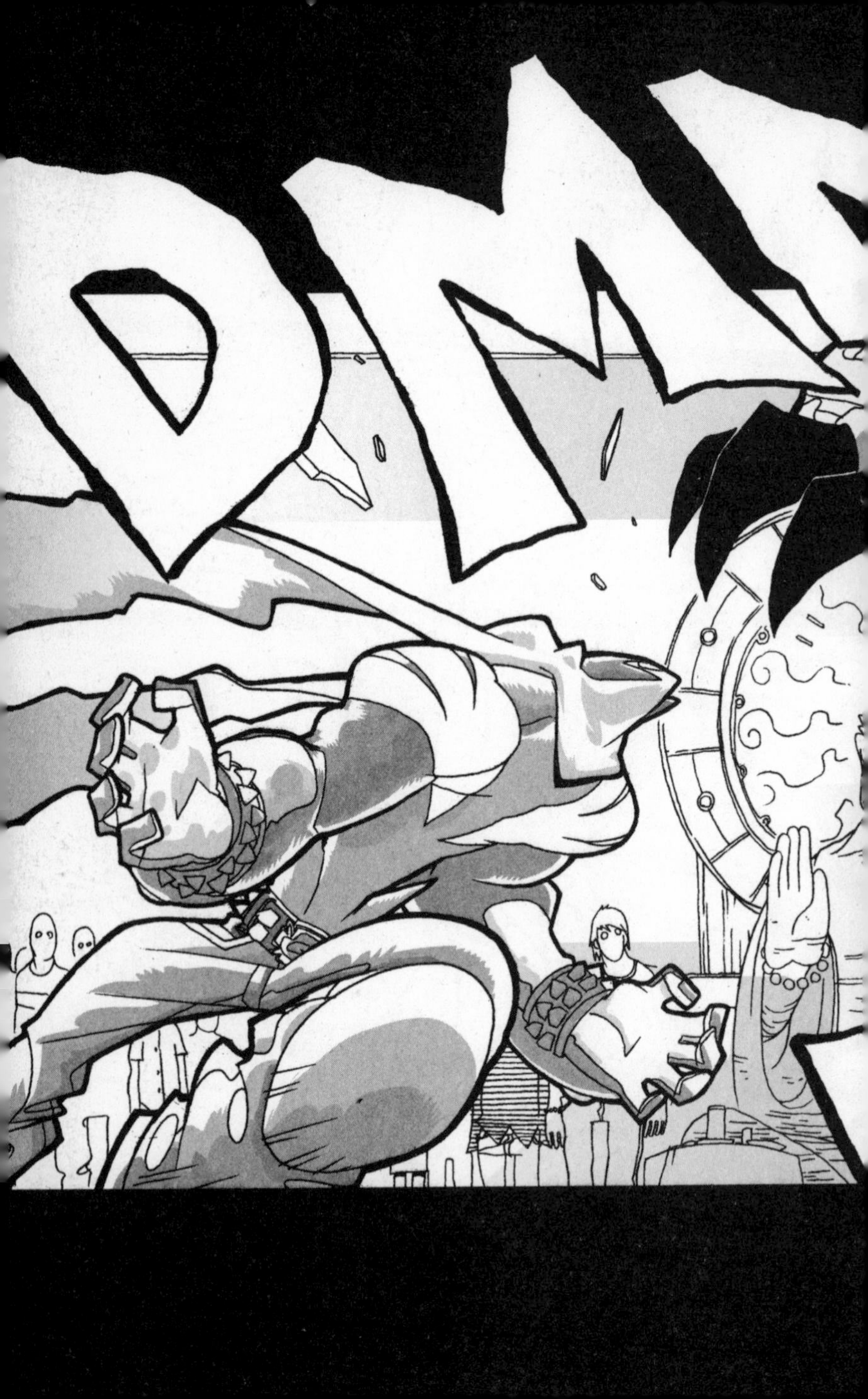

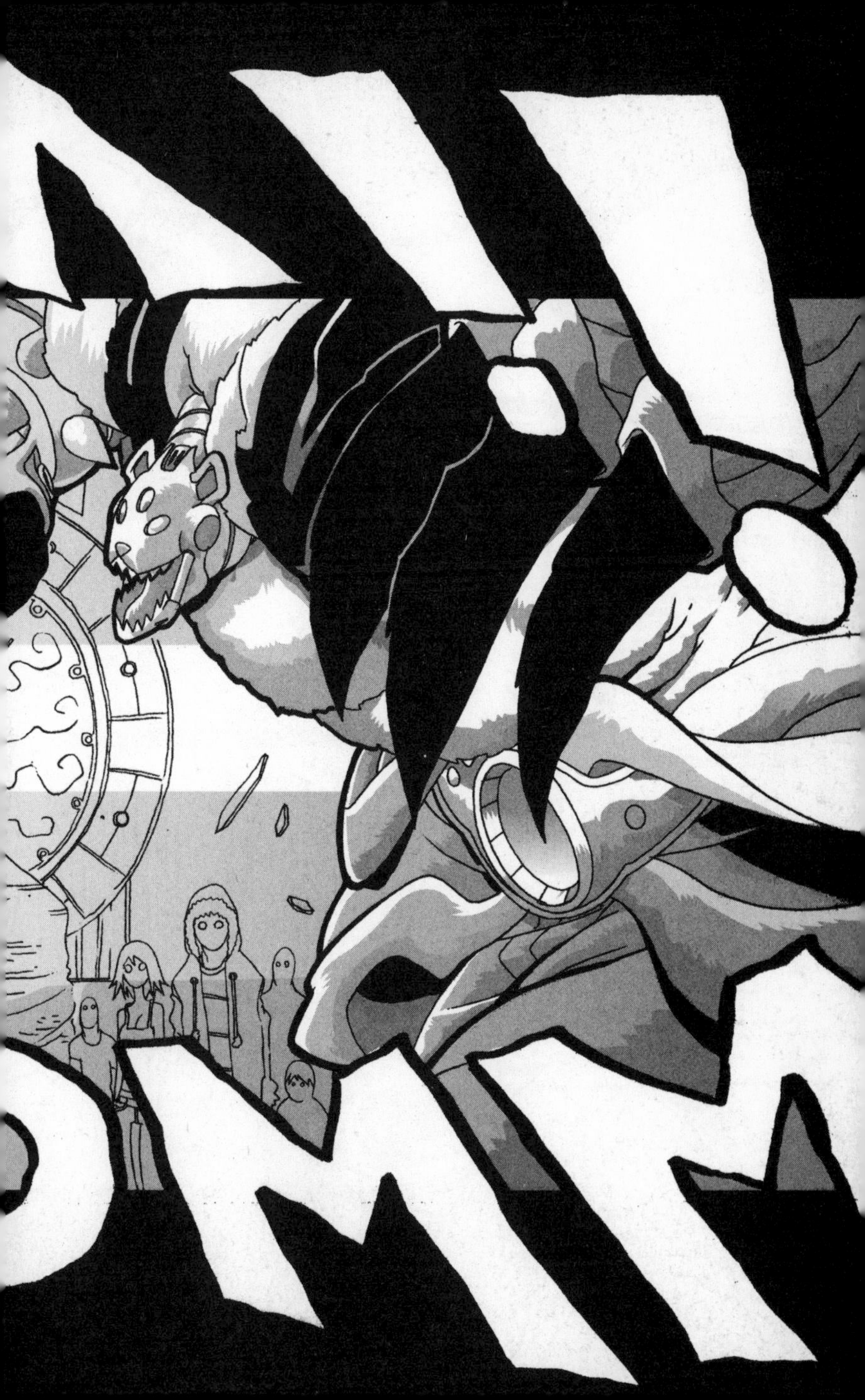

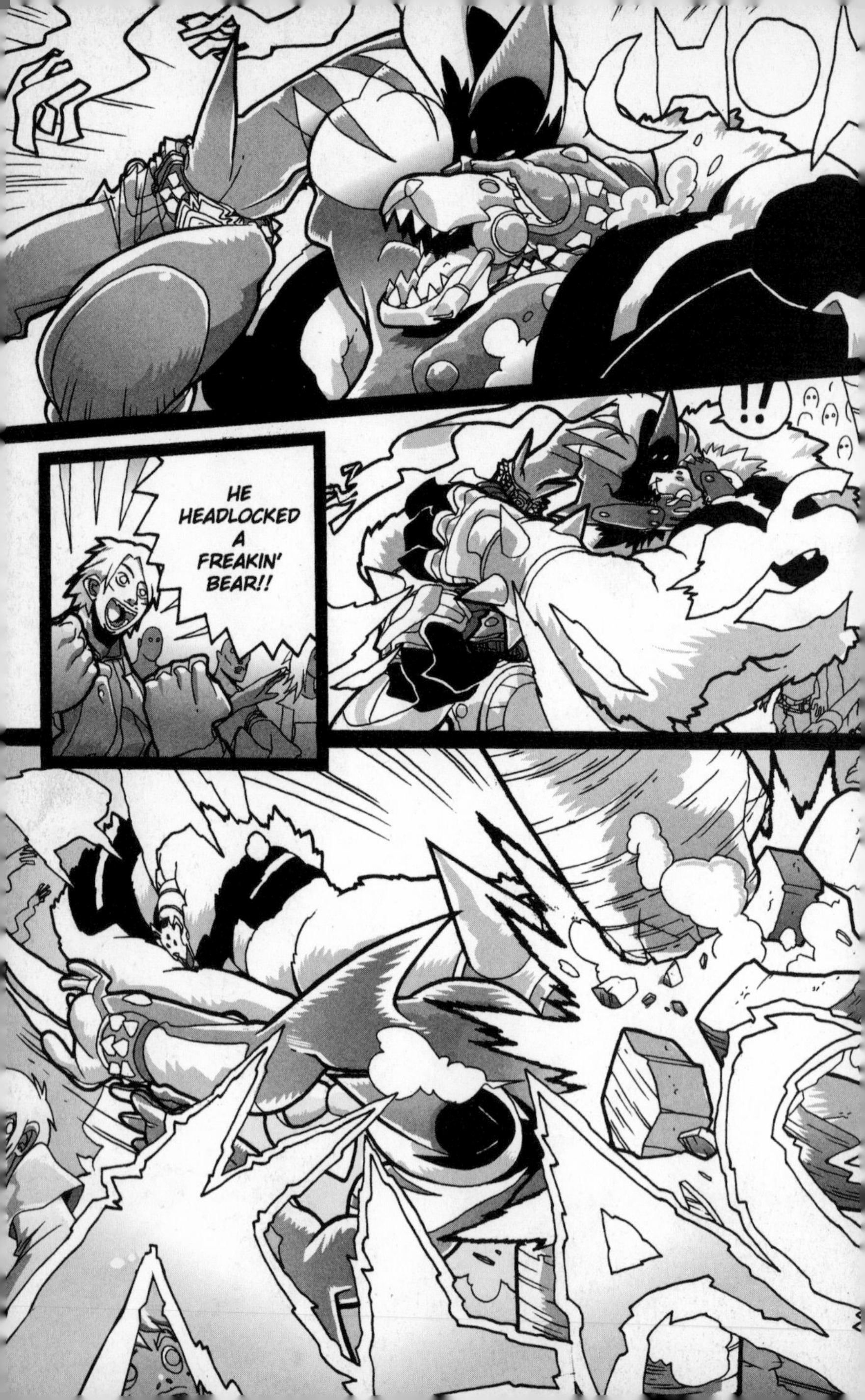
!!
HE HEADLOCKED A FREAKIN' BEAR!!

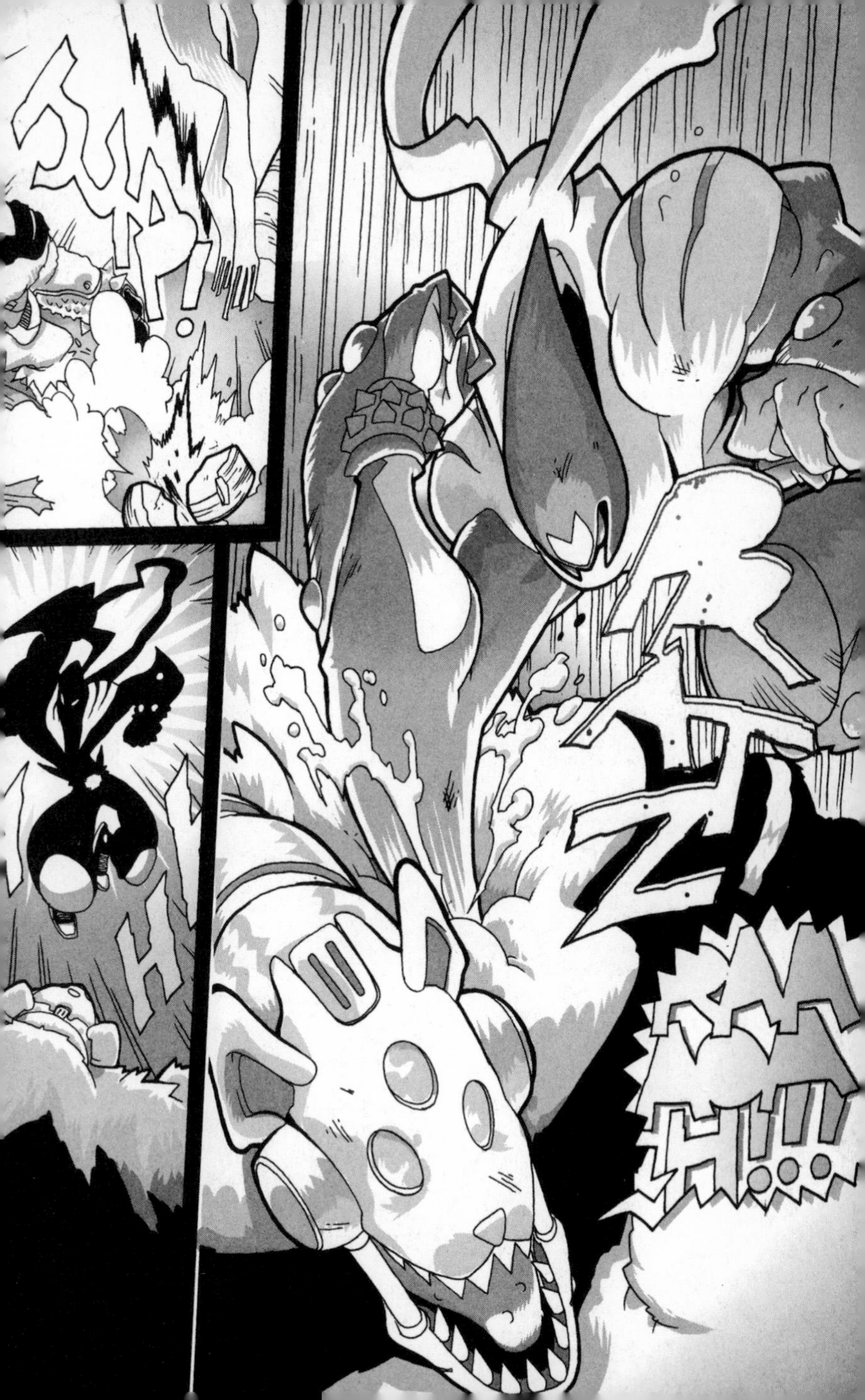

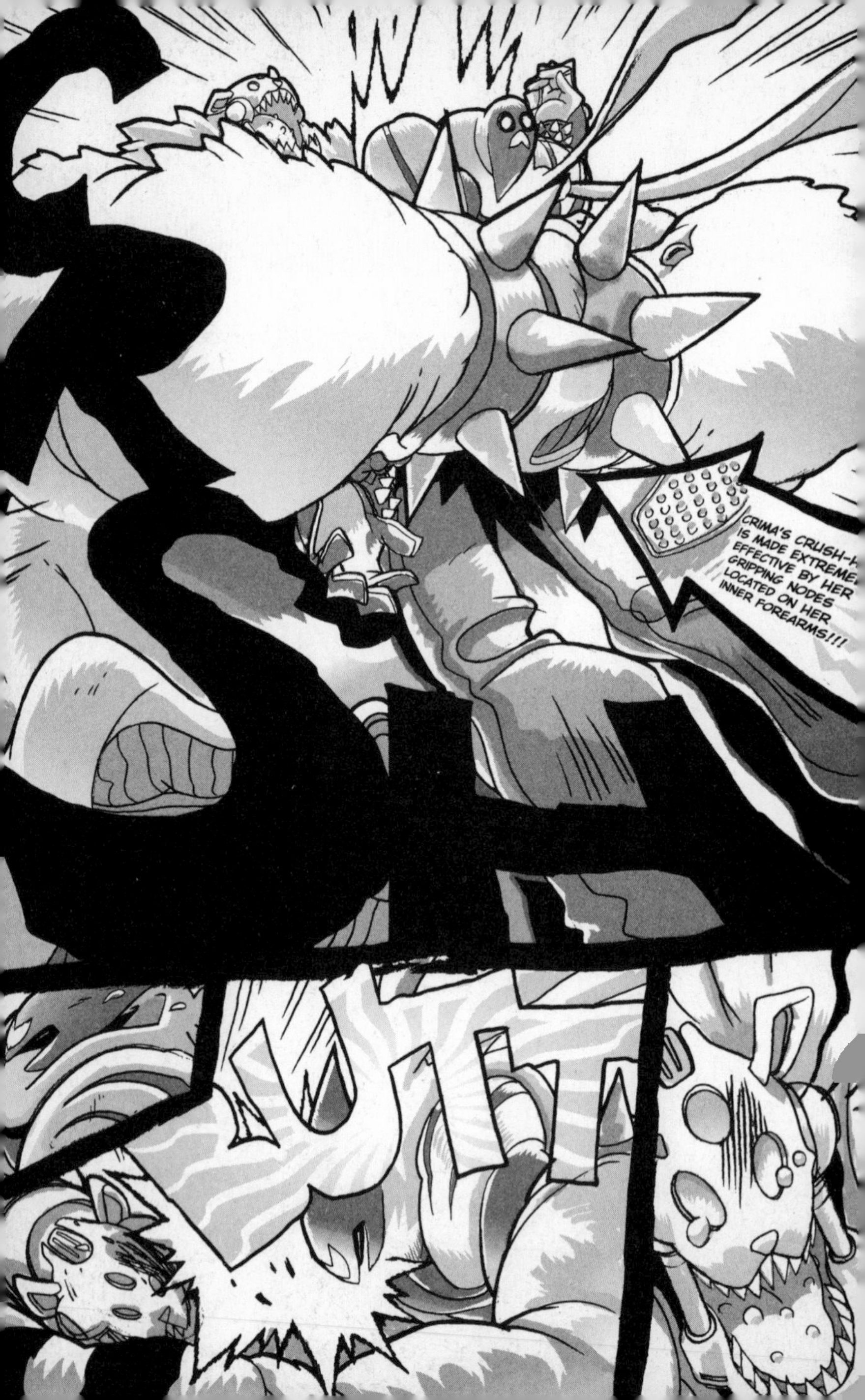
CRIMA'S CRUSH-
IS MADE EXTREME
EFFECTIVE BY HER
GRIPPING NODES
LOCATED ON HER
INNER FOREARMS!!!

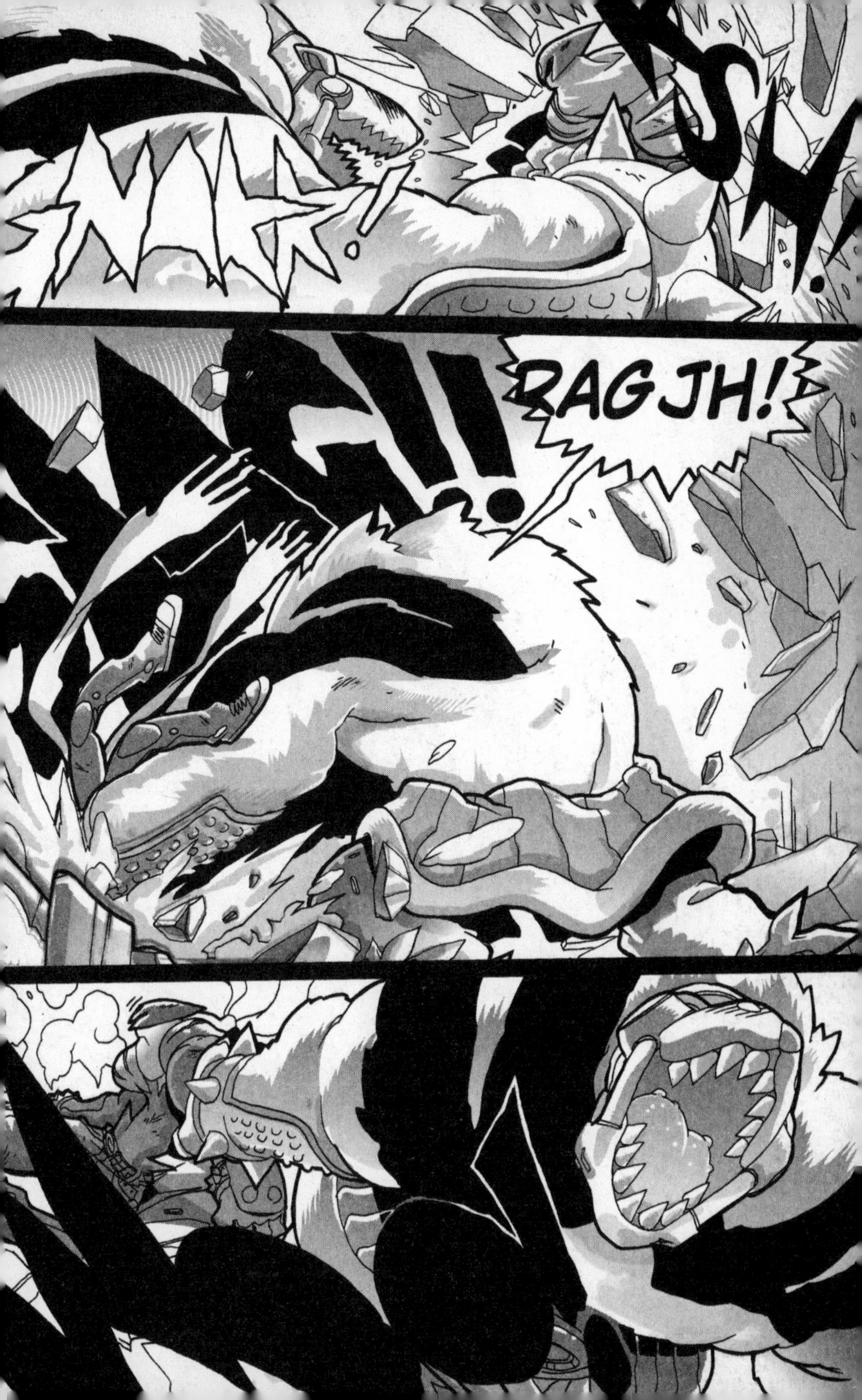
NAK!
RAGJH!

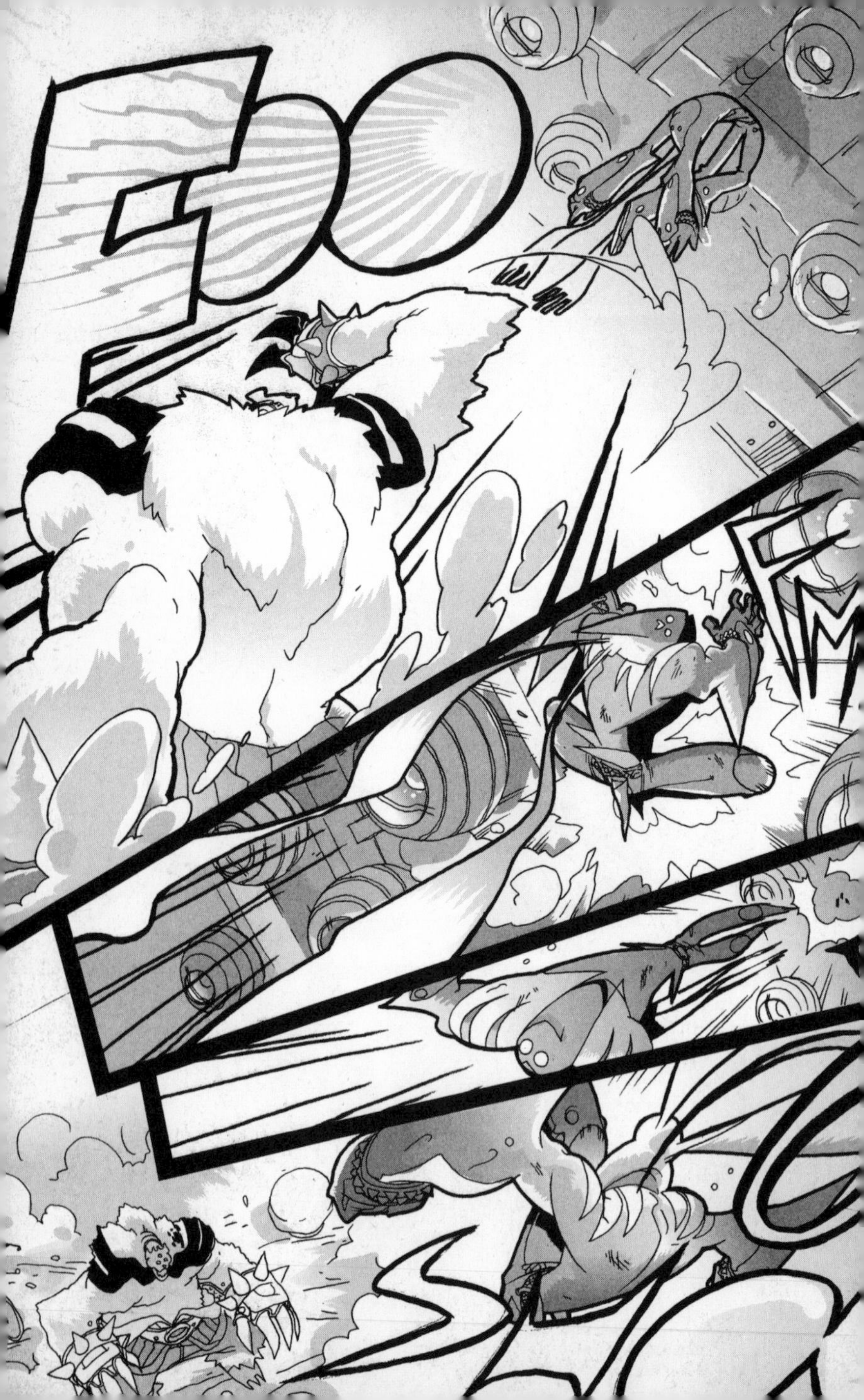

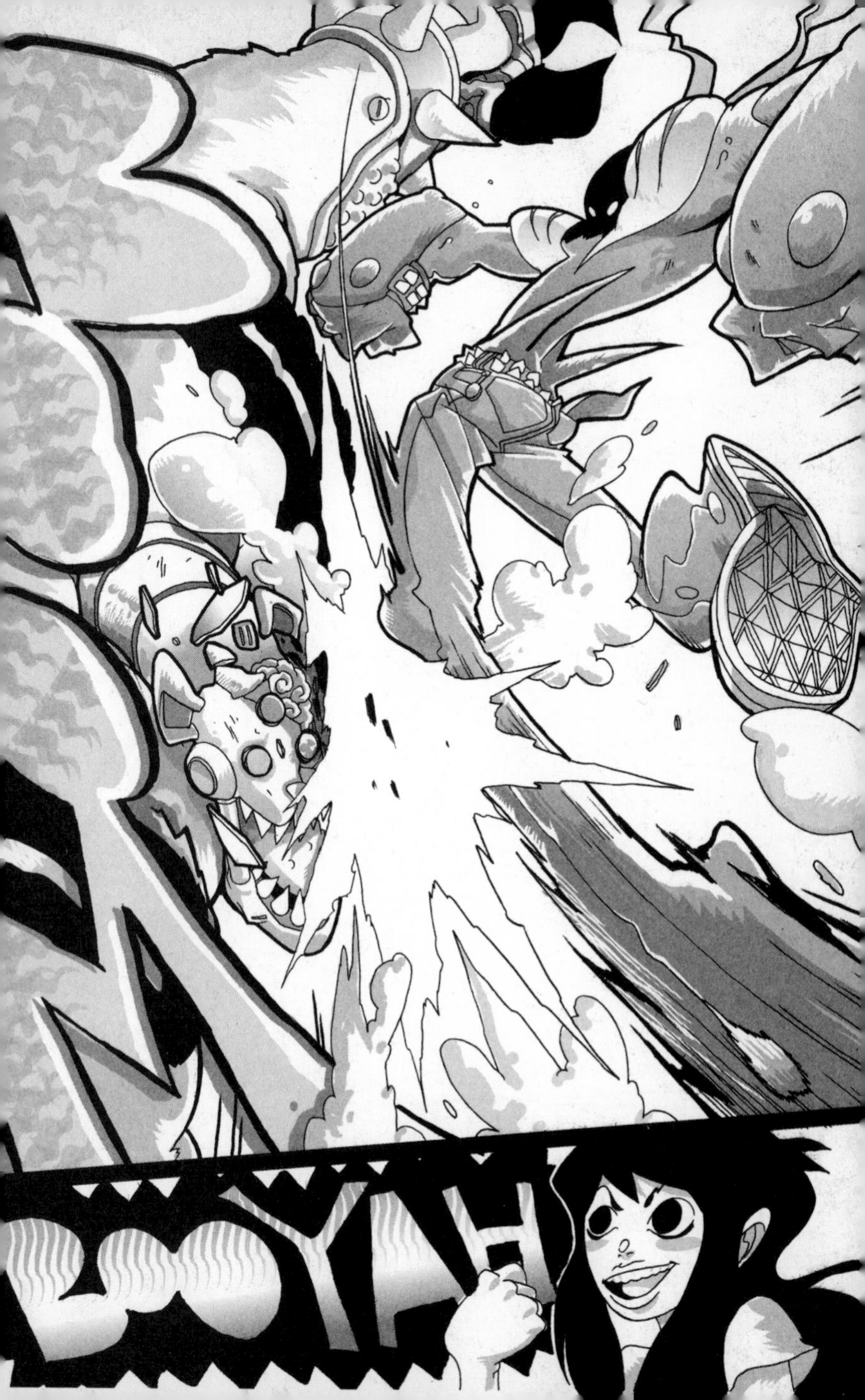
BOOYAH

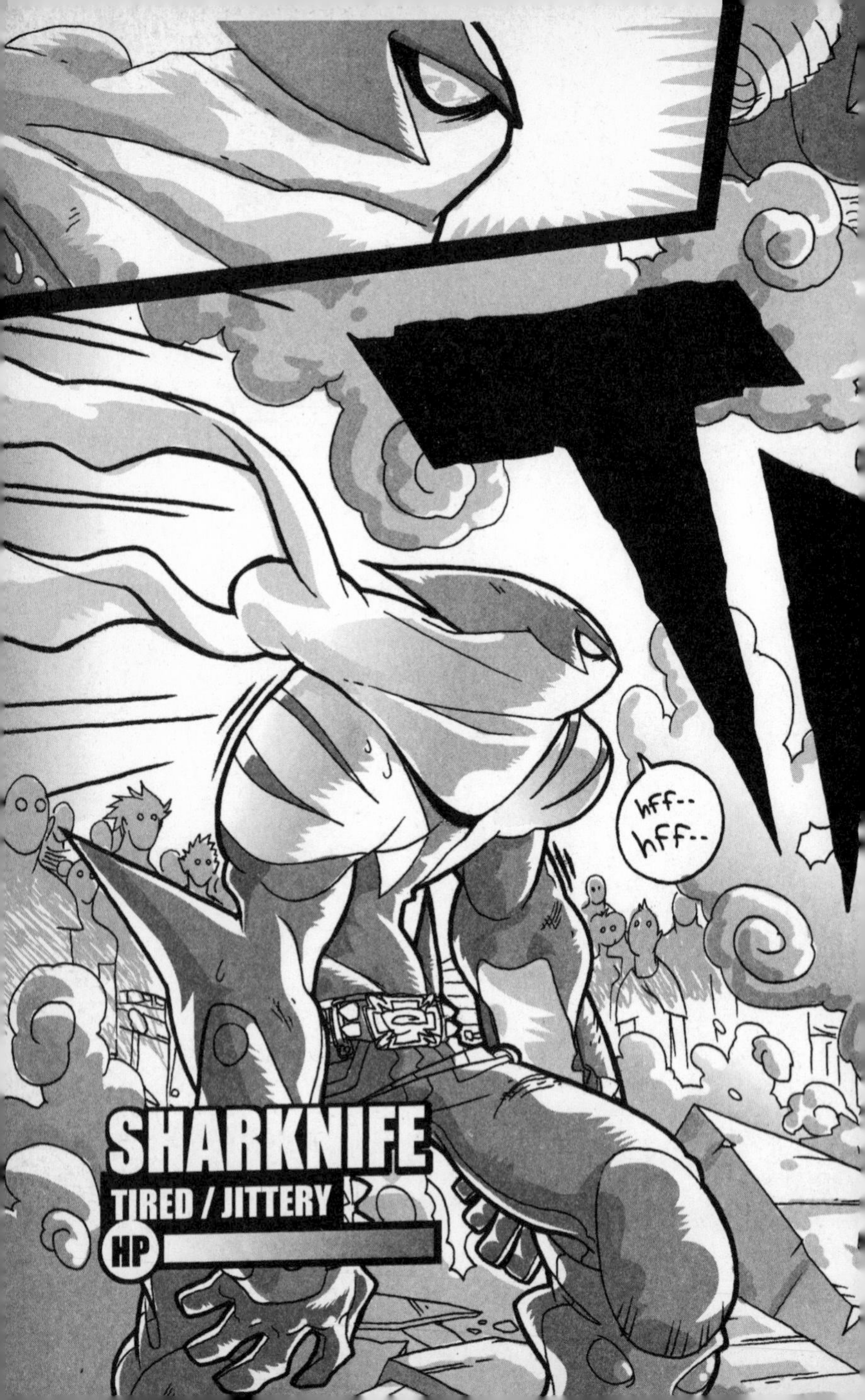
hff--
hff--
SHARKNIFE
TIRED / JITTERY
HP

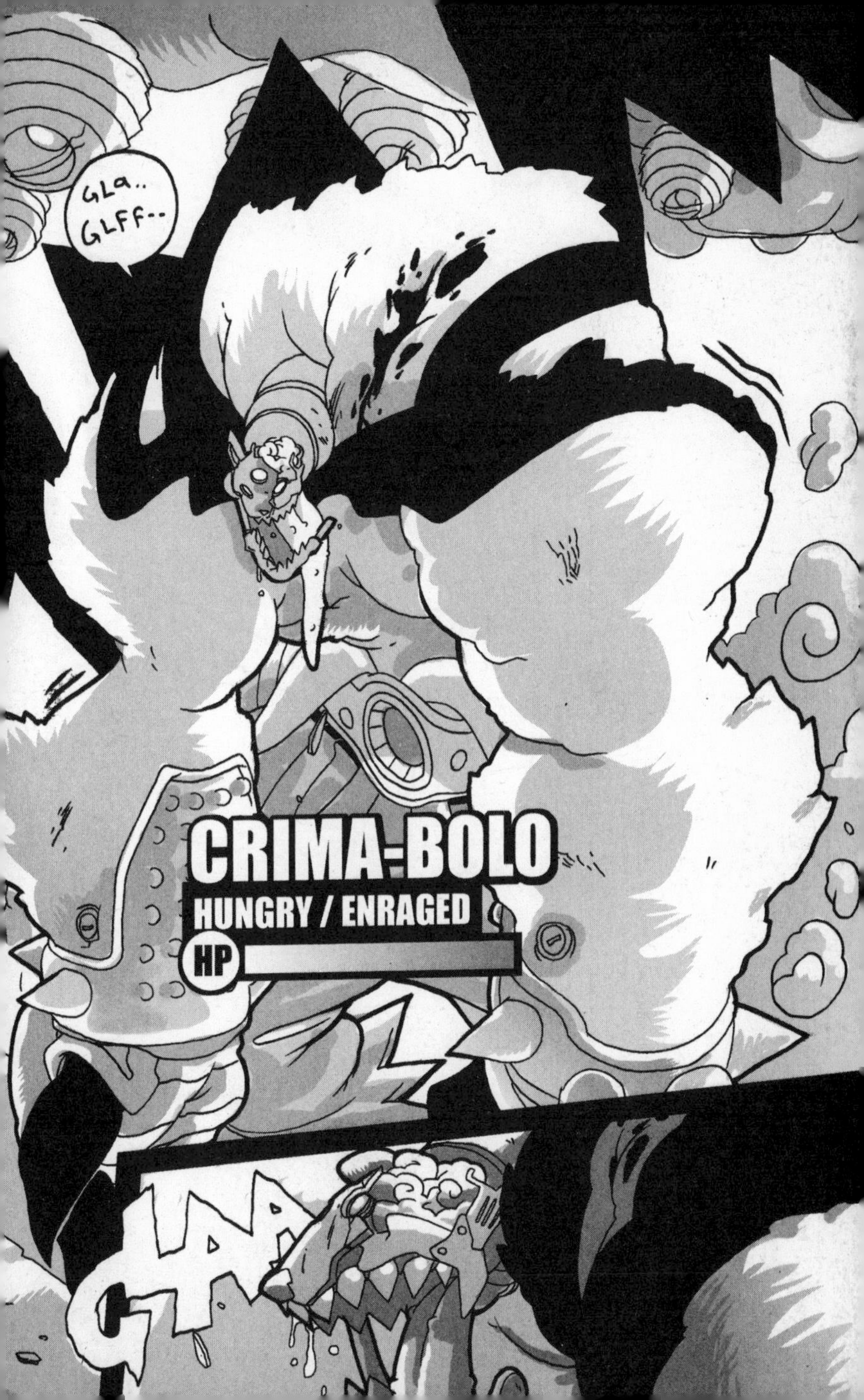

GLa.. GLFF--
CRIMA-BOLO
HUNGRY / ENRAGED
HP

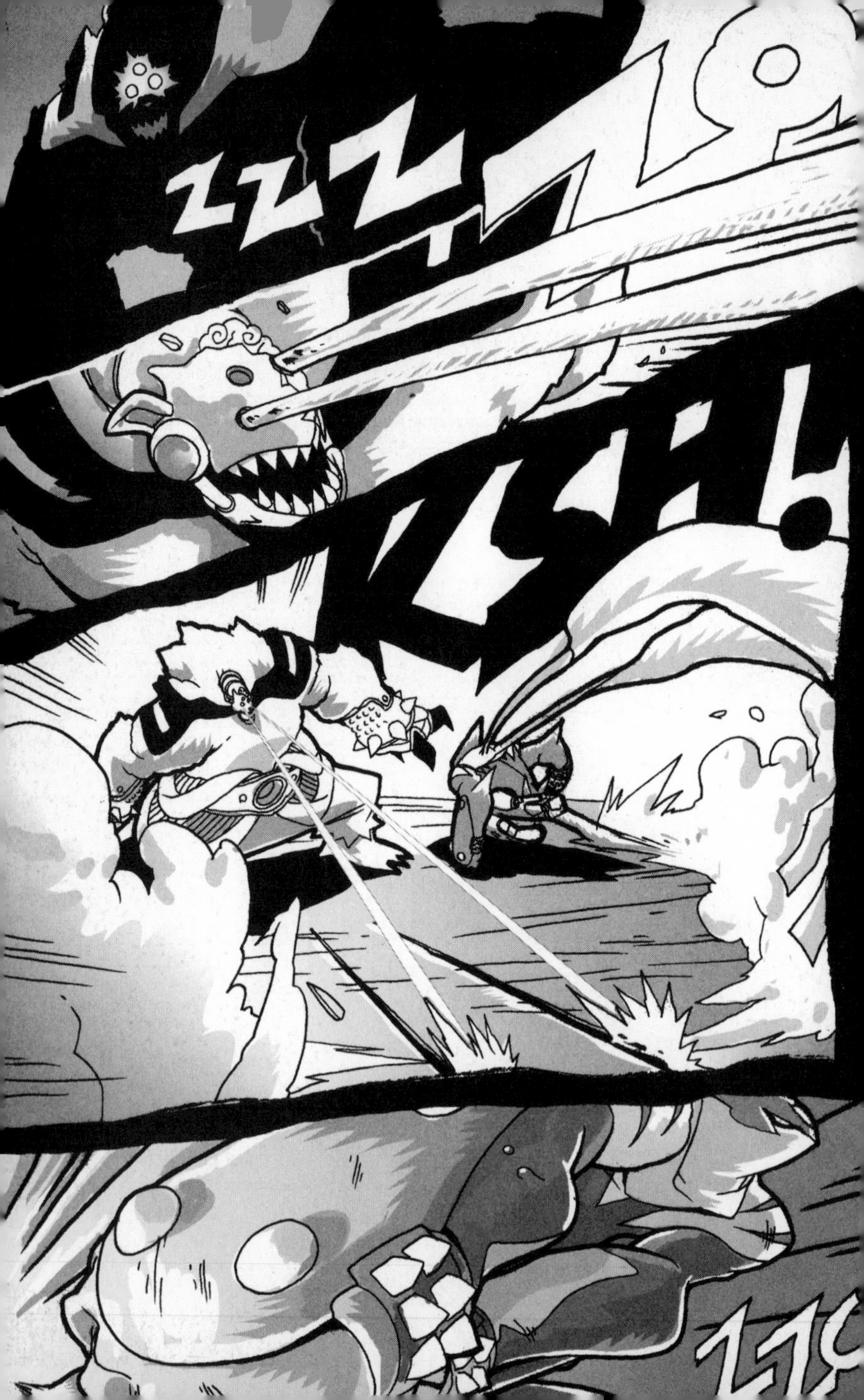

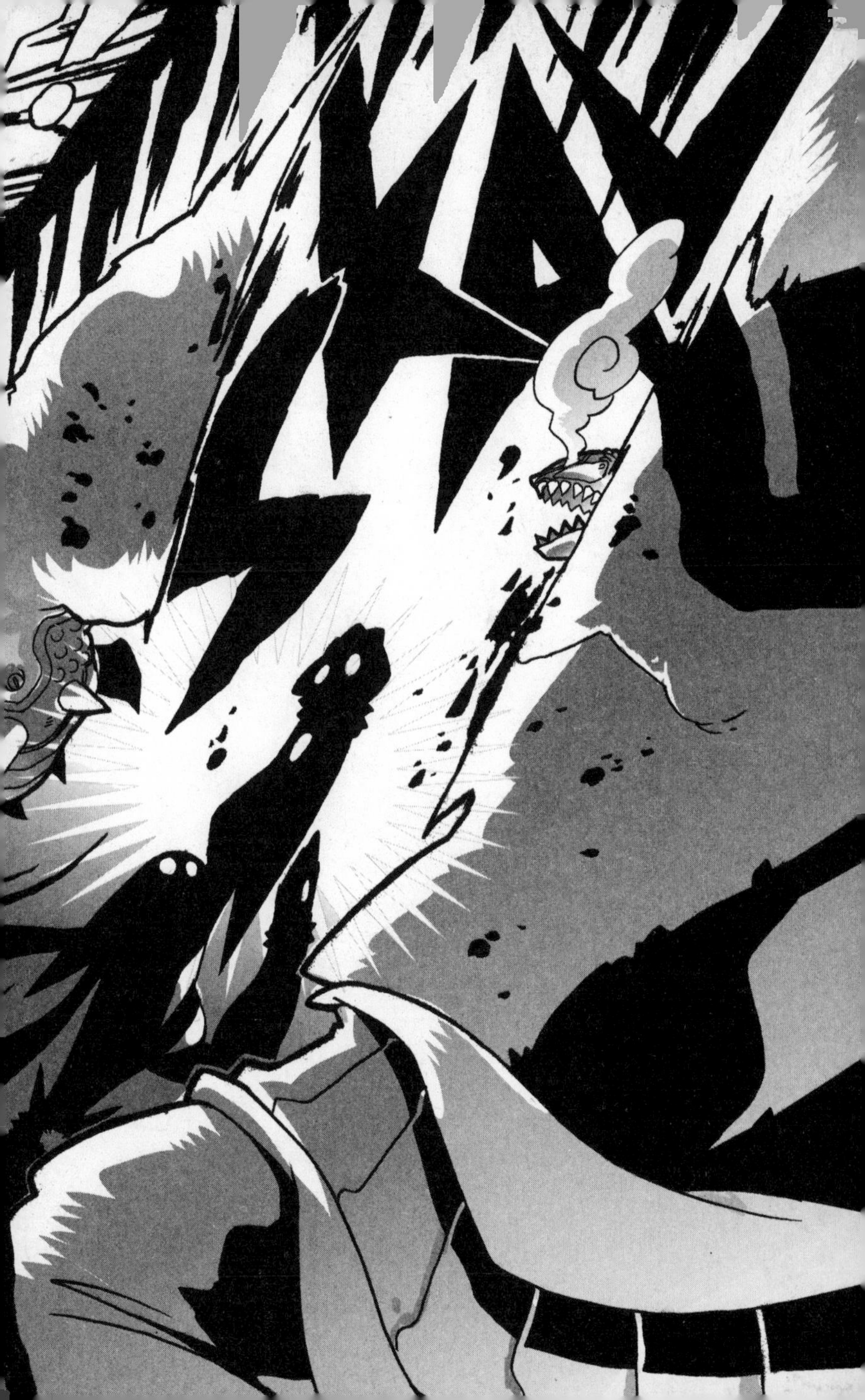

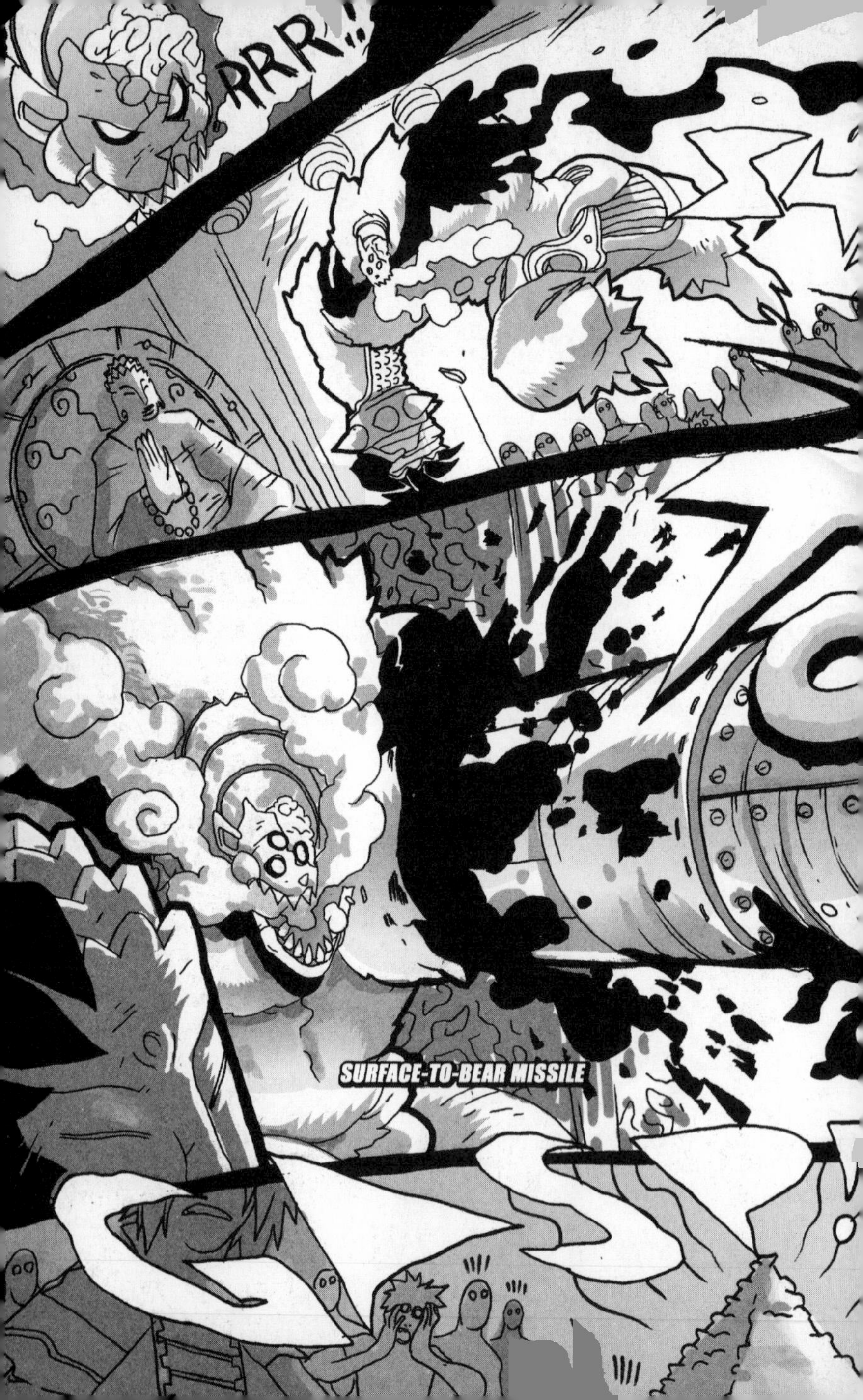
RRR!!
SURFACE-TO-BEAR MISSILE

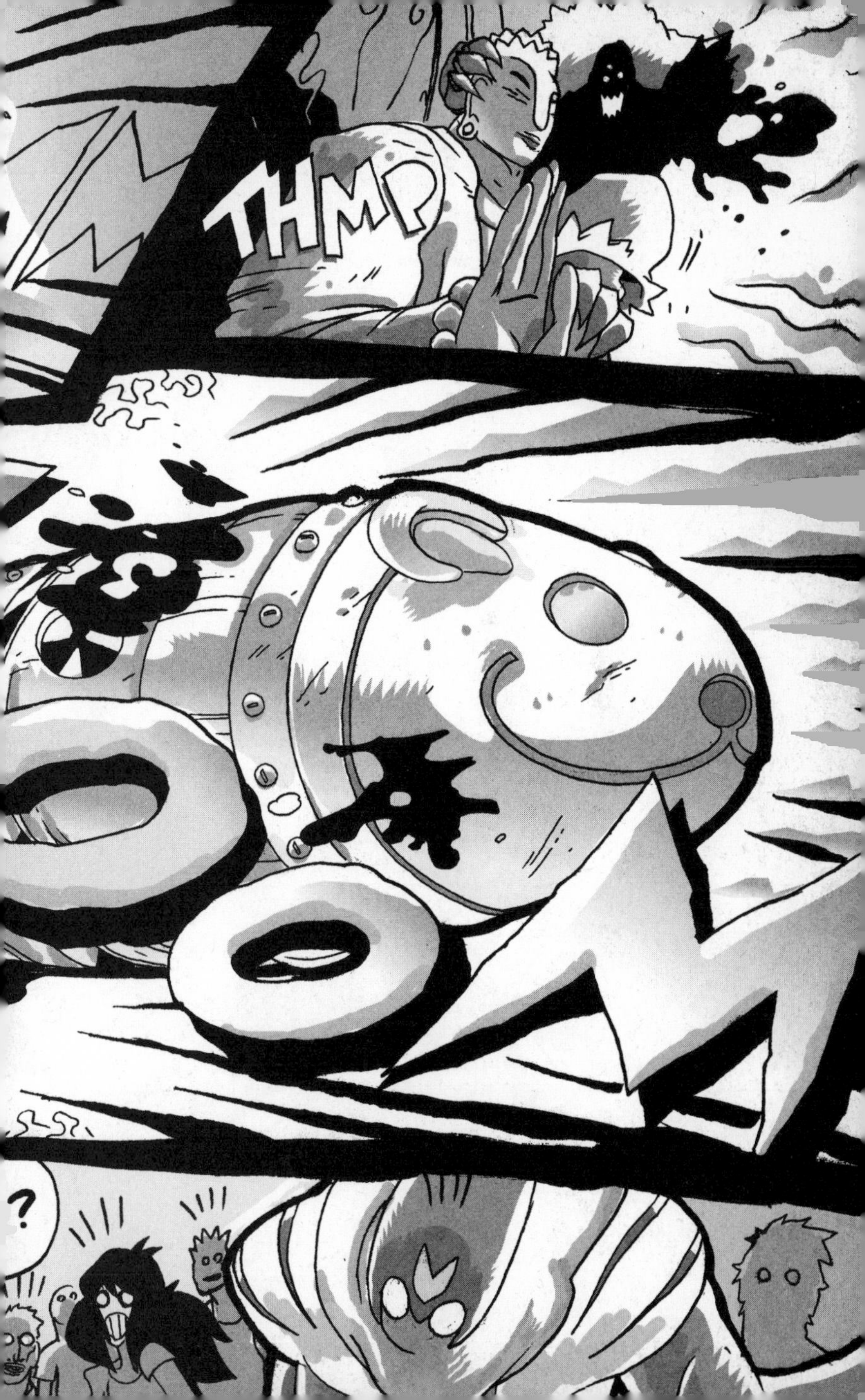
THMP
?

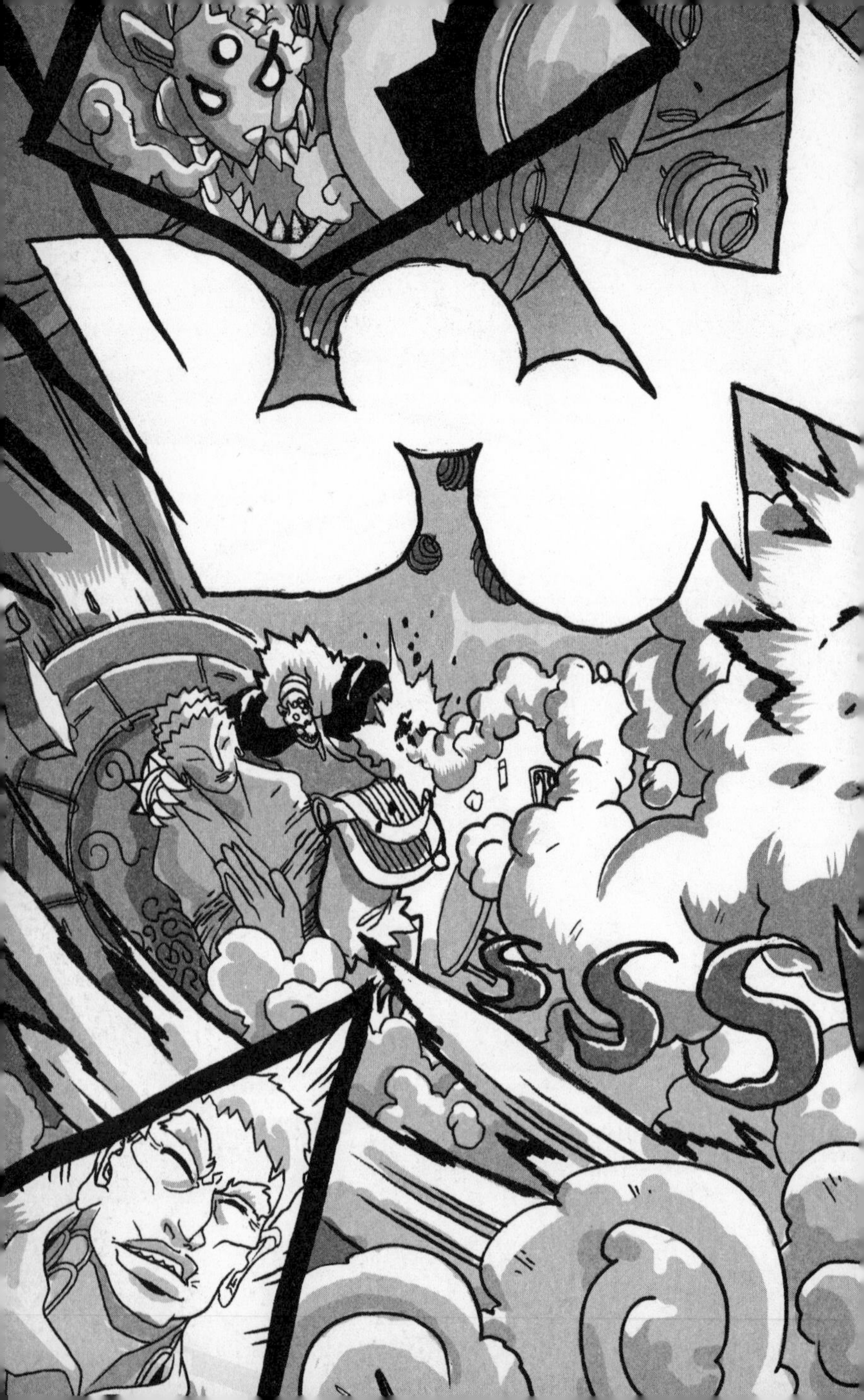

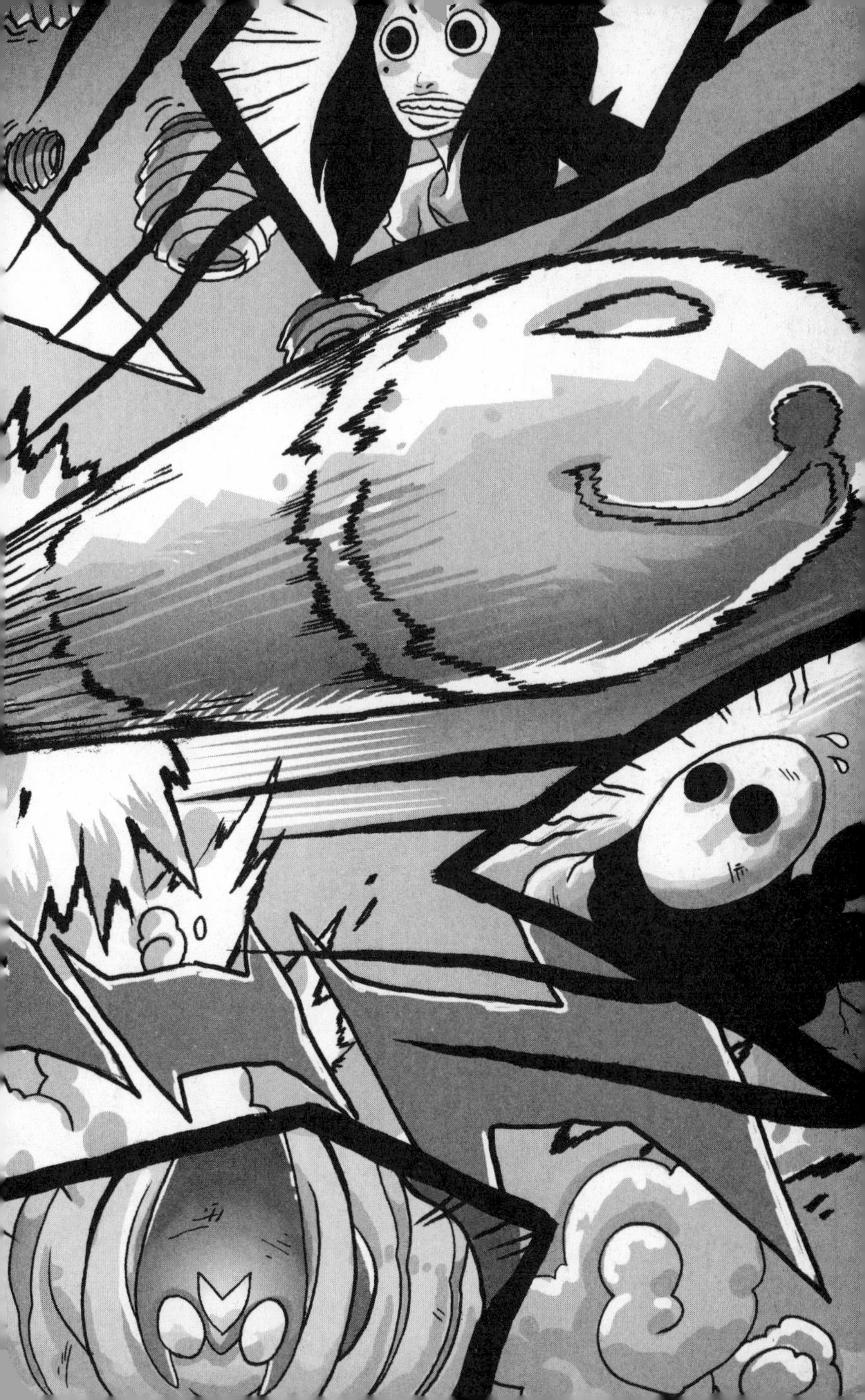

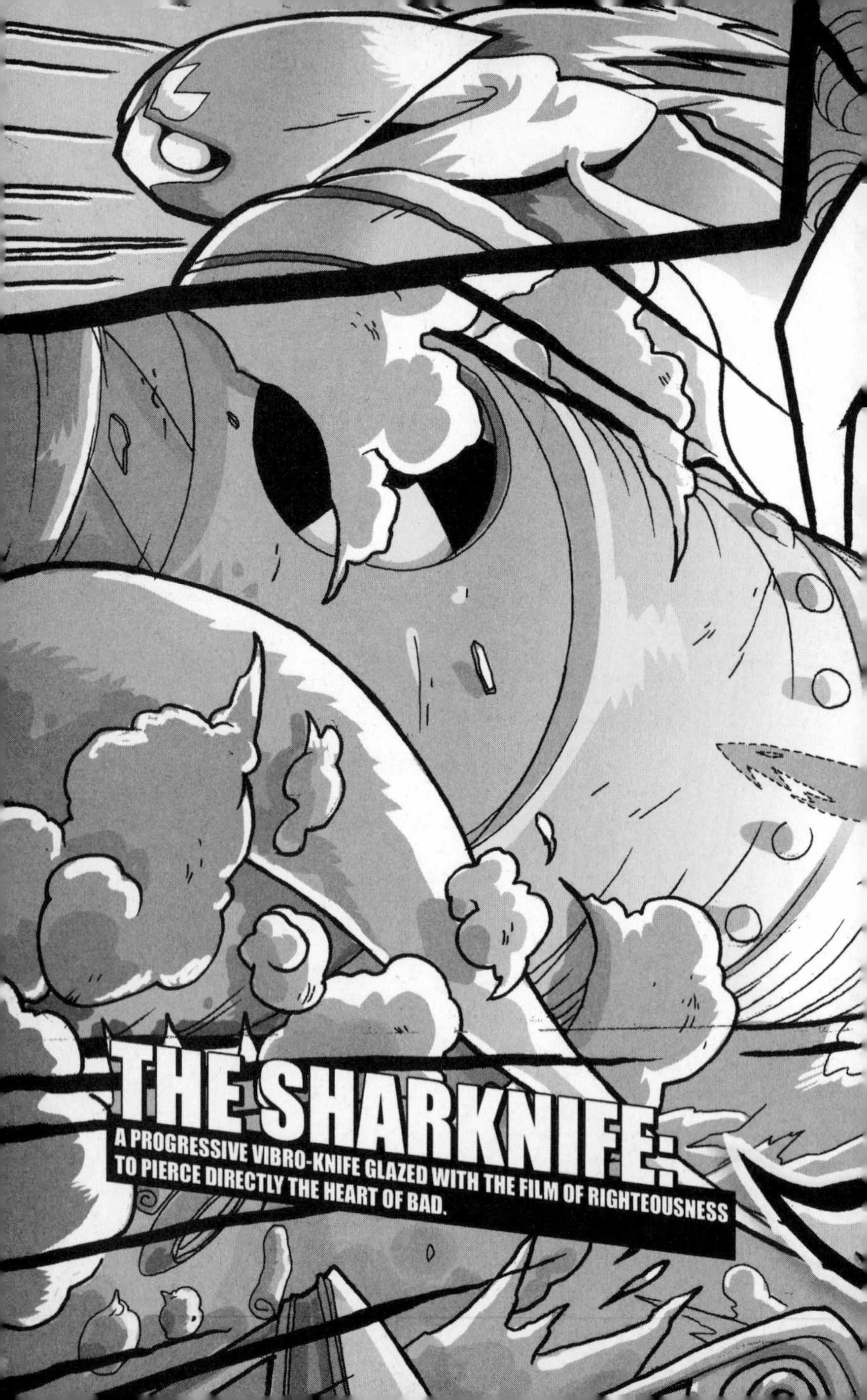
THE SHARKNIFE:
A PROGRESSIVE VIBRO-KNIFE GLAZED WITH THE FILM OF RIGHTEOUSNESS
TO PIERCE DIRECTLY THE HEART OF BAD.

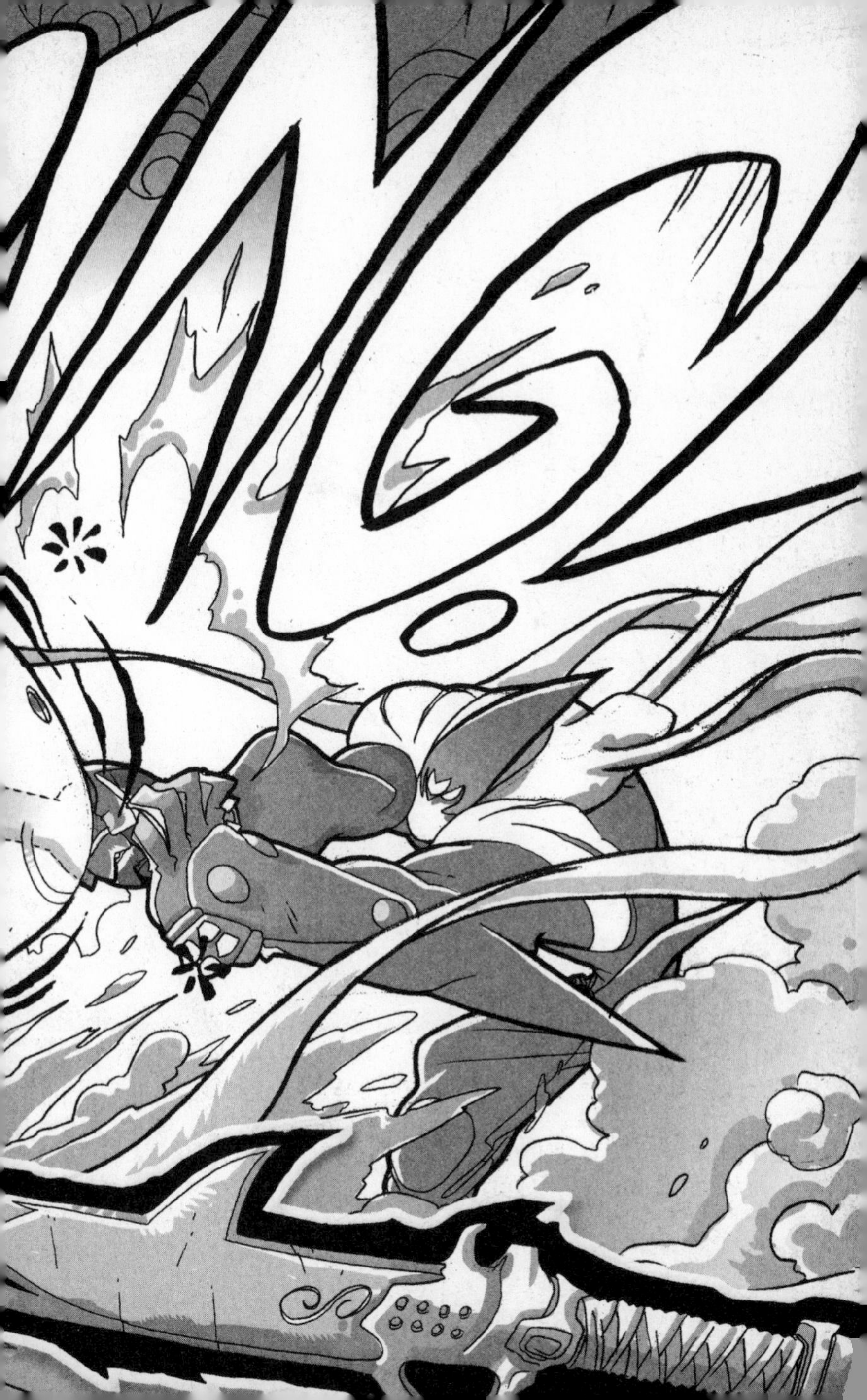

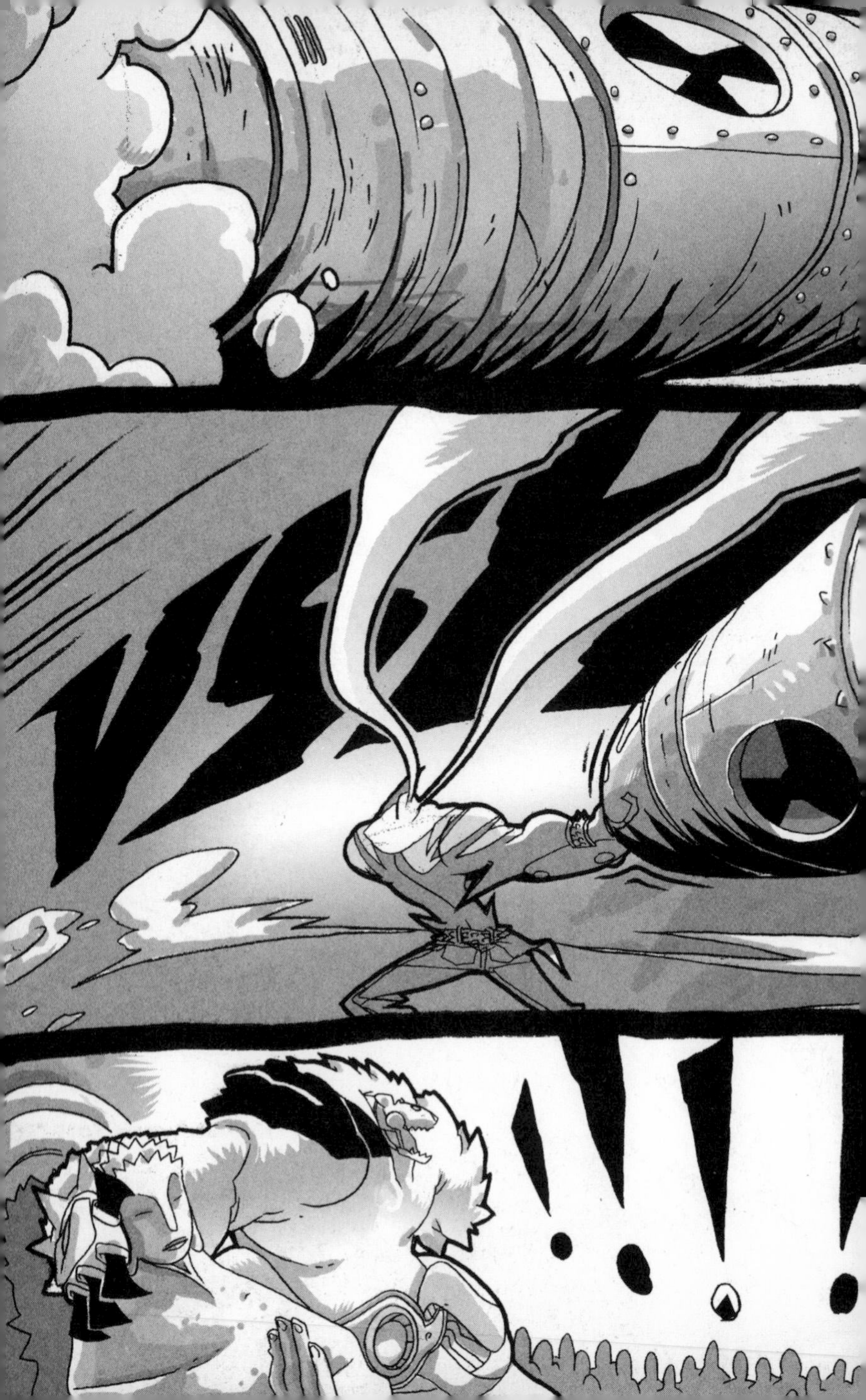

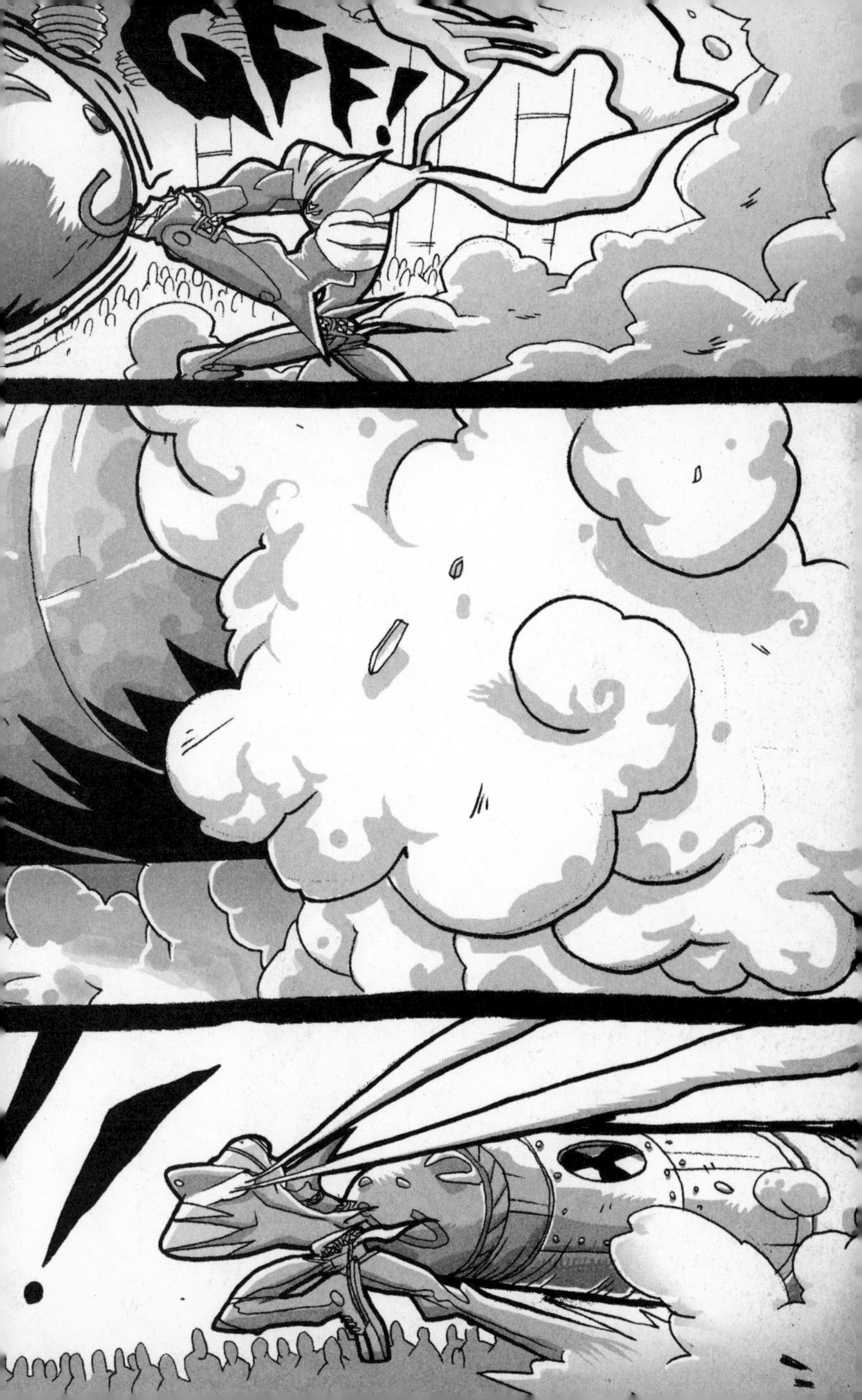
OFF!
!

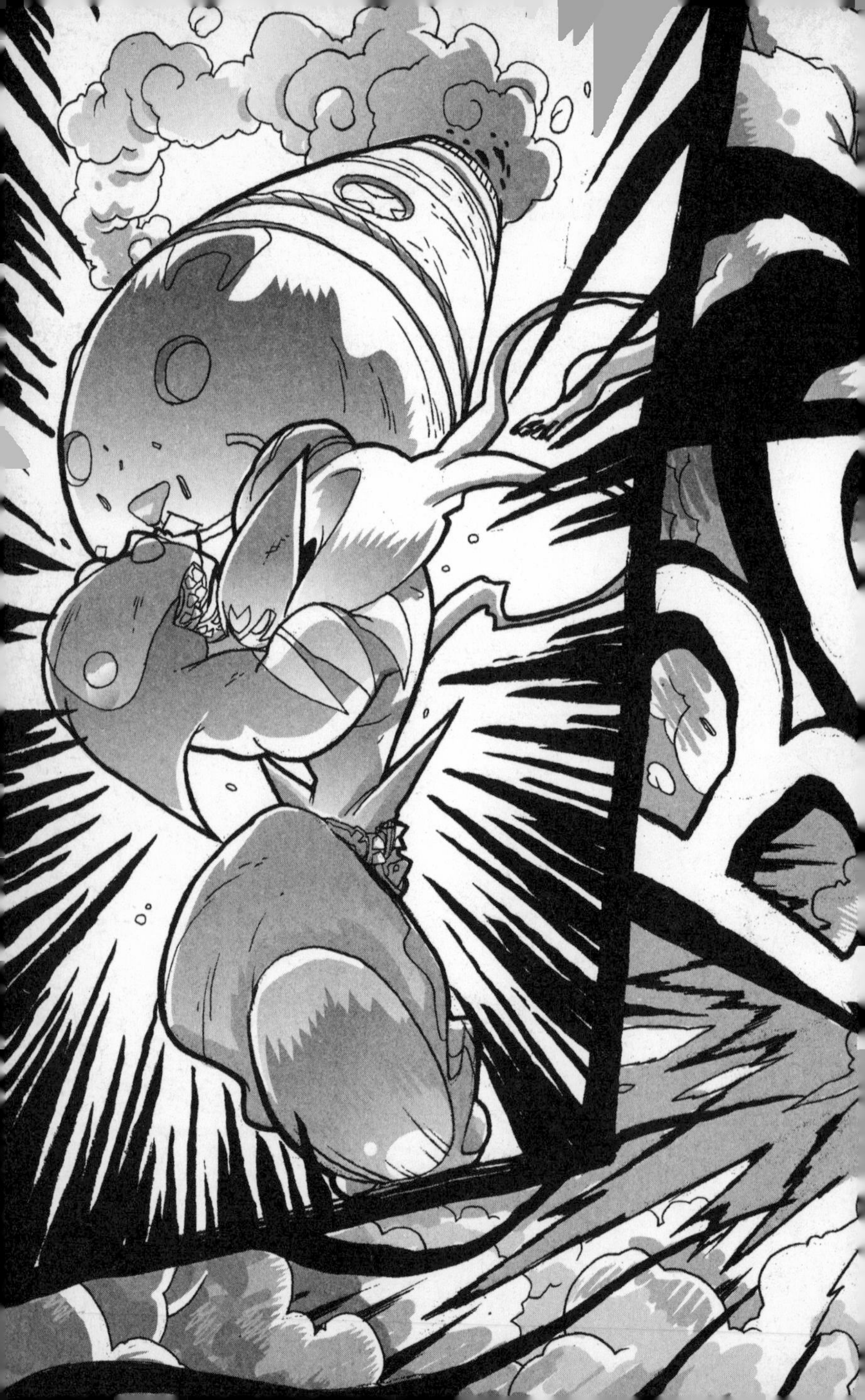

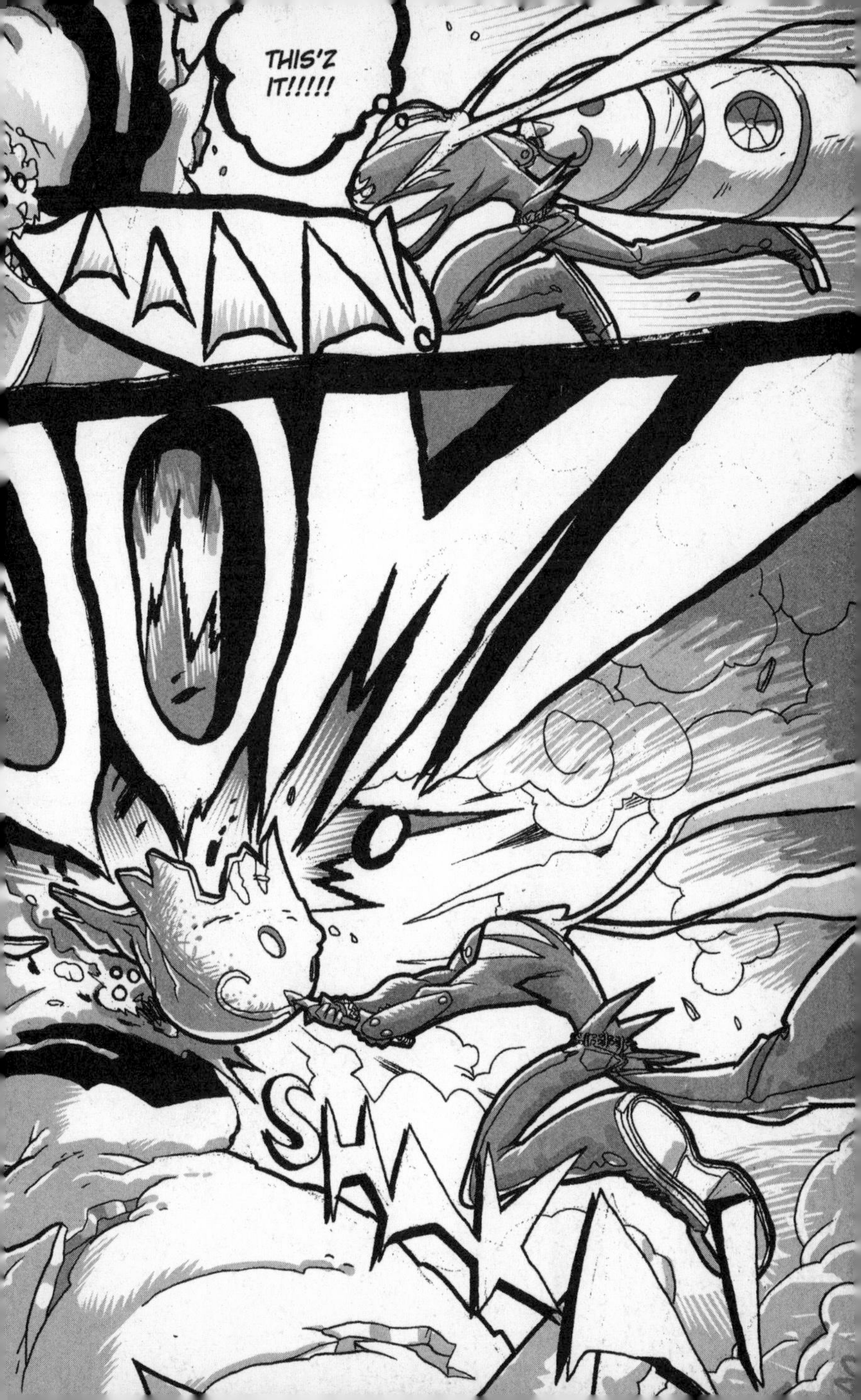
THIS'Z IT!!!!!

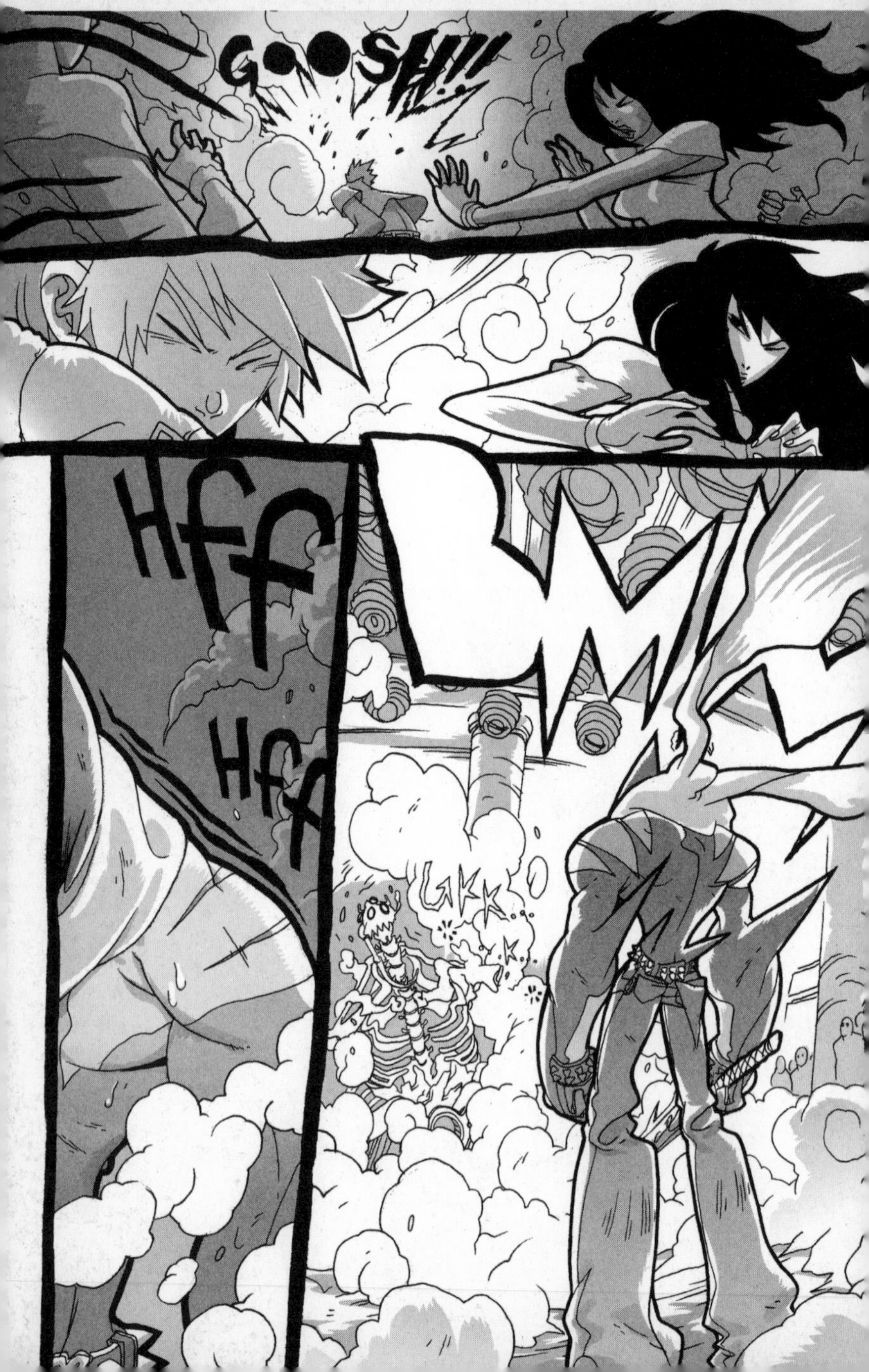
GOOSH!!
Hff
Hff
GKK

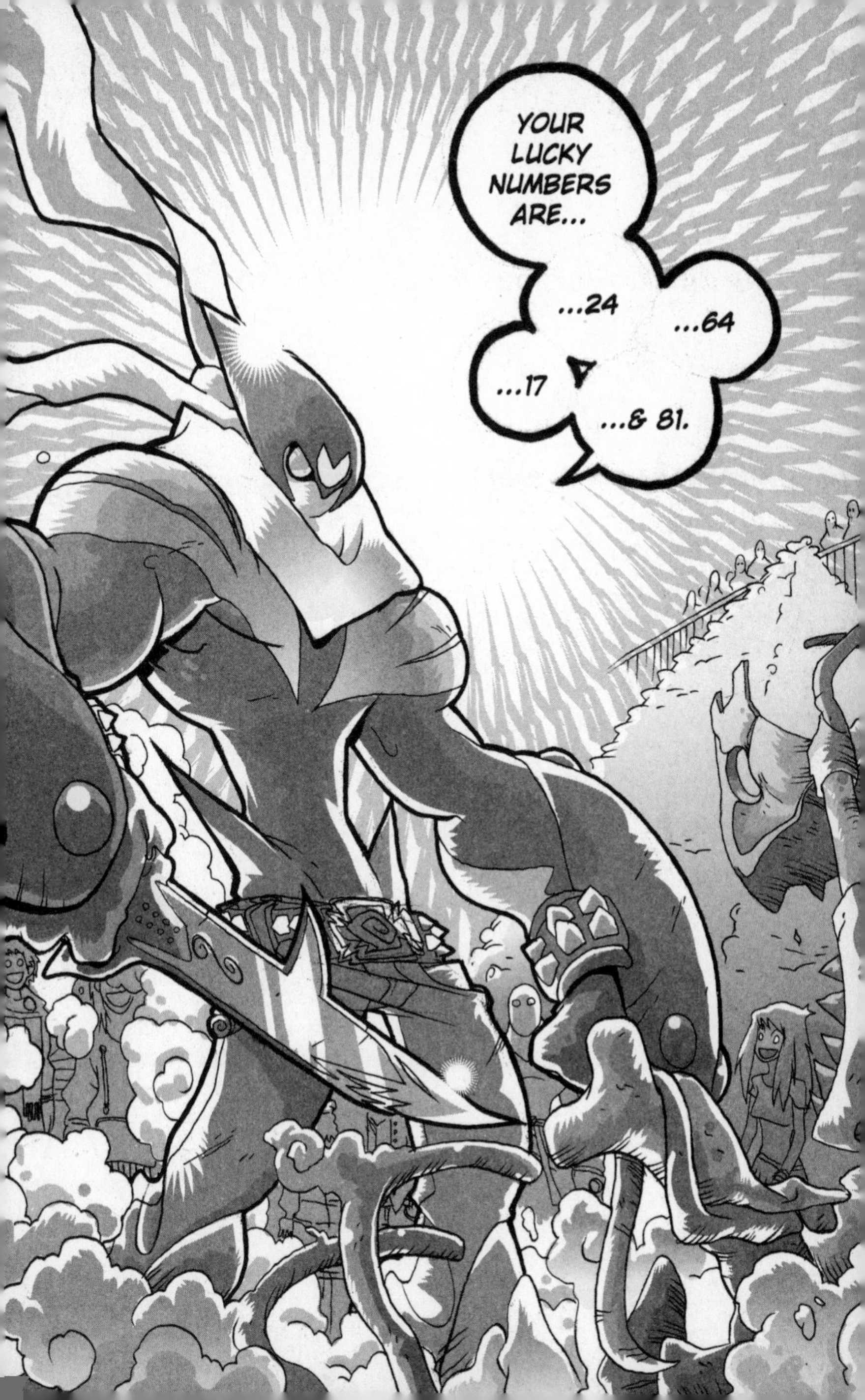
YOUR LUCKY NUMBERS ARE...
...24
...64
...17
...& 81.

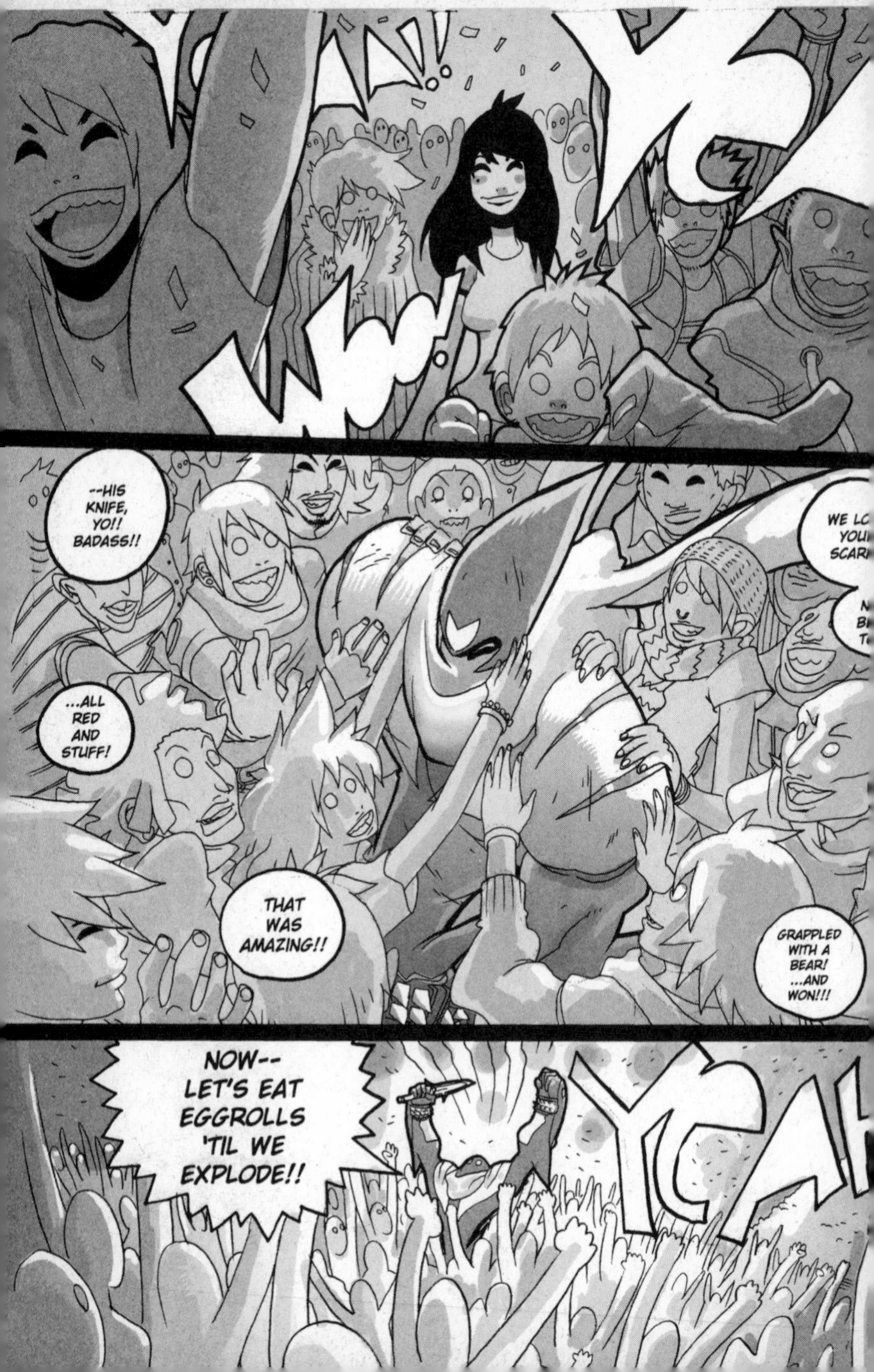
YAY!!
YAY!!
WOO!
--HIS KNIFE, YO!! BADASS!!
...ALL RED AND STUFF!
THAT WAS AMAZING!!
GRAPPLED WITH A BEAR! ...AND WON!!!
NOW-- LET'S EAT EGGROLLS 'TIL WE EXPLODE!!
YEAH

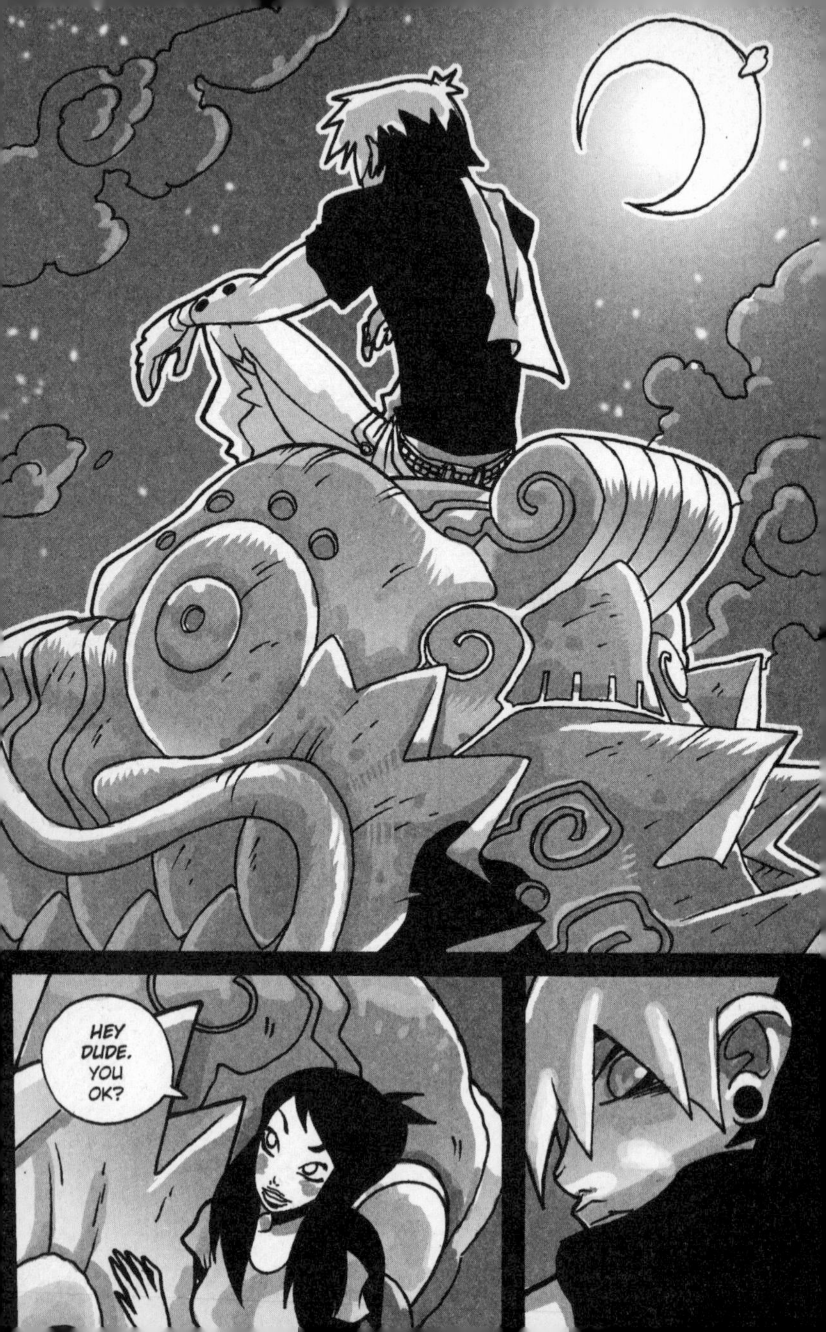
HEY DUDE. YOU OK?

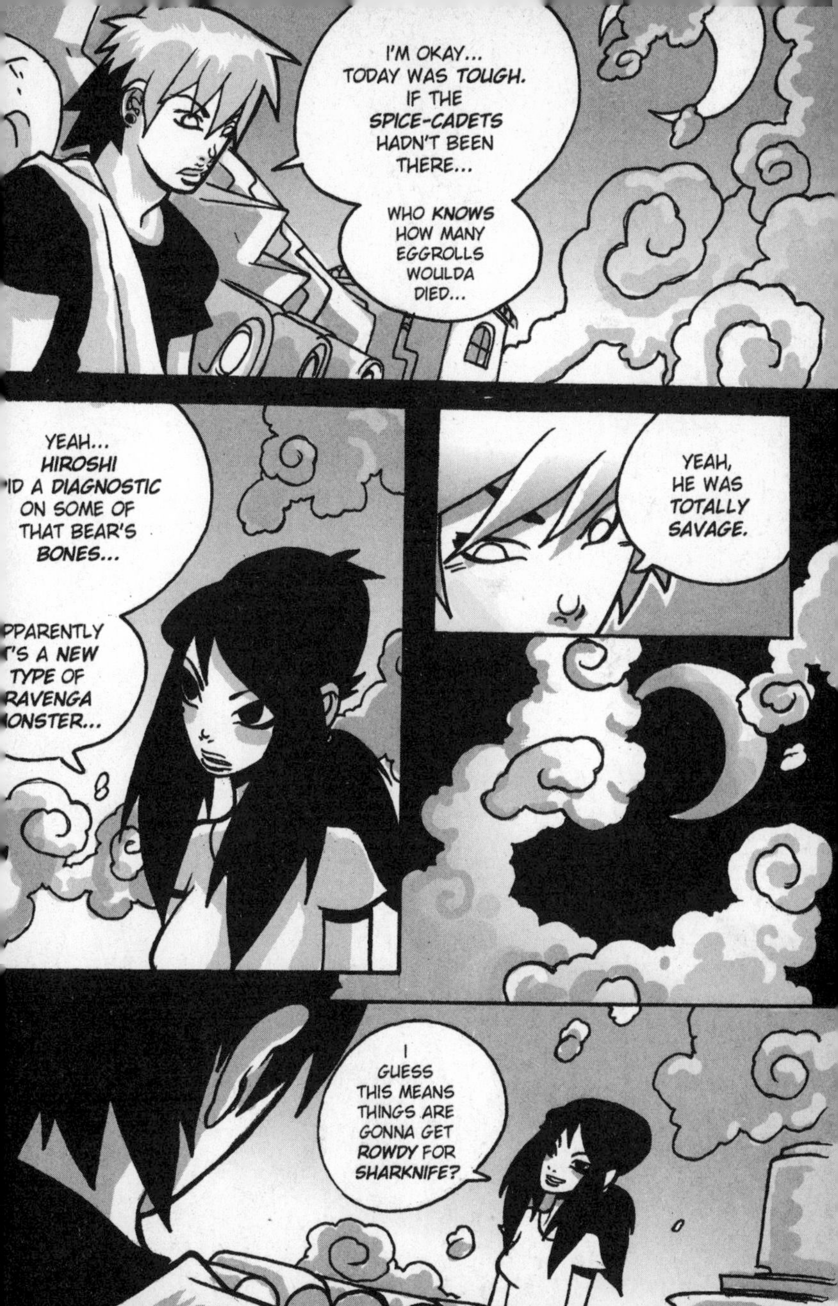
I'M OKAY... TODAY WAS TOUGH. IF THE SPICE-CADETS HADN'T BEEN THERE...
WHO KNOWS HOW MANY EGGROLLS WOULDA DIED...
YEAH... HIROSHI 'ID A DIAGNOSTIC ON SOME OF THAT BEAR'S BONES...
PPARENTLY T'S A NEW TYPE OF RAVENGA IONSTER...
YEAH, HE WAS TOTALLY SAVAGE.
I GUESS THIS MEANS THINGS ARE GONNA GET ROWDY FOR SHARKNIFE?

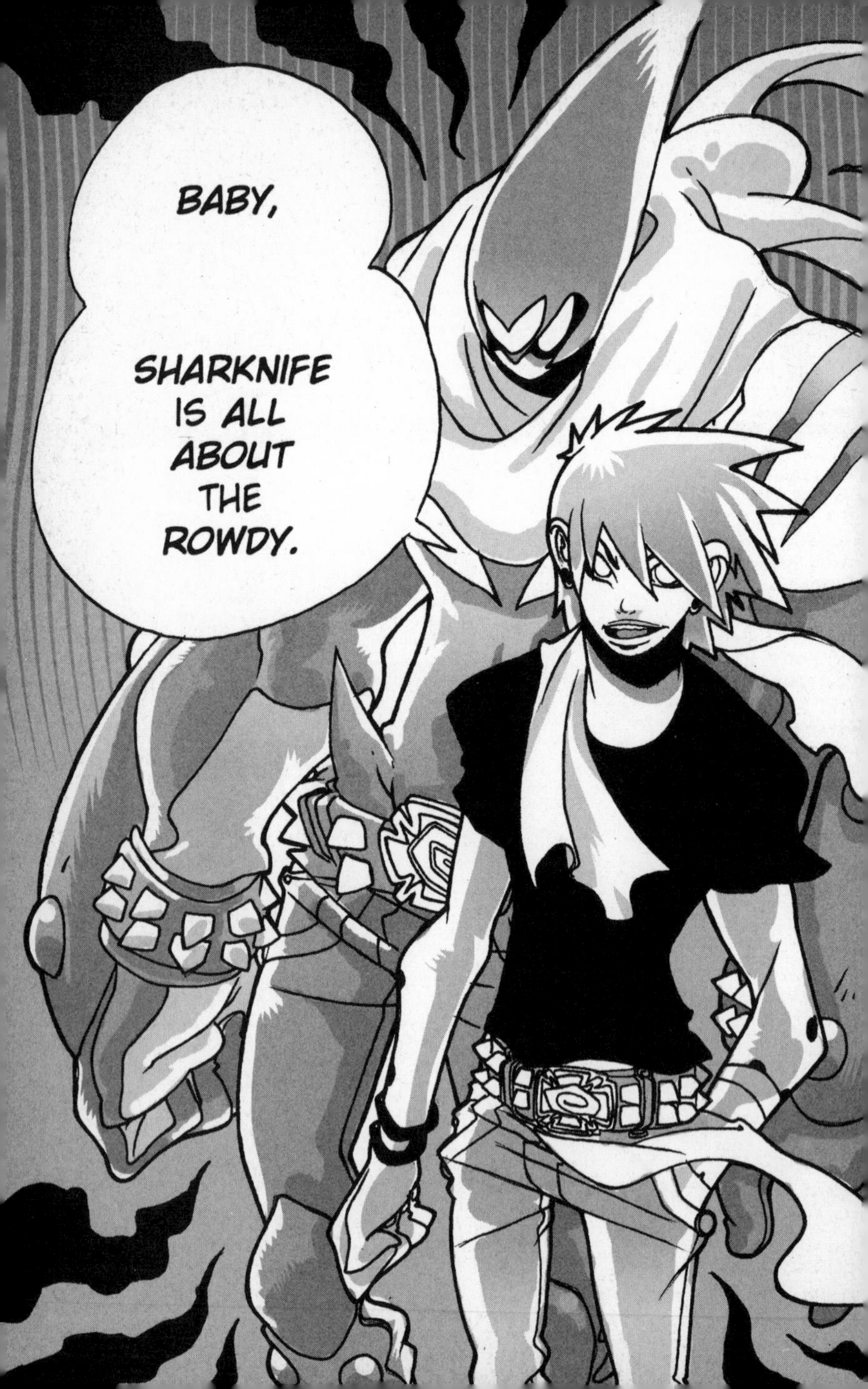
BABY,
SHARKNIFE IS ALL ABOUT THE ROWDY.

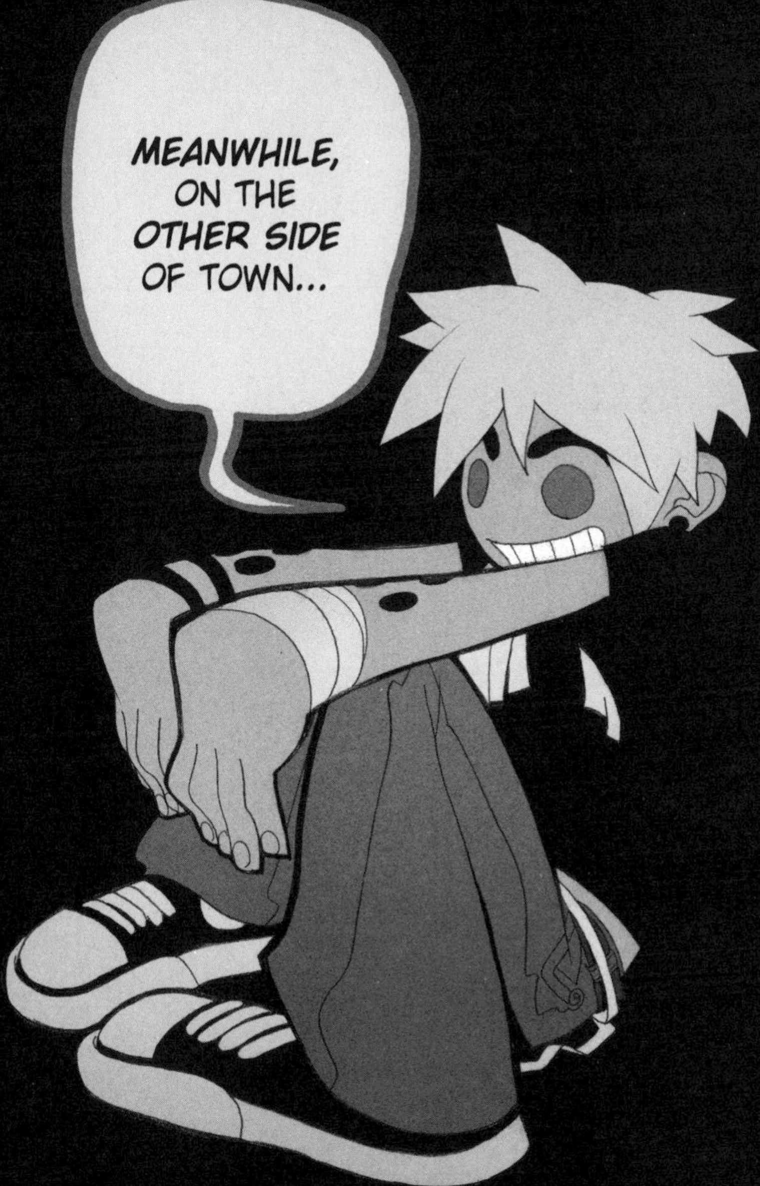
MEANWHILE, ON THE OTHER SIDE OF TOWN...

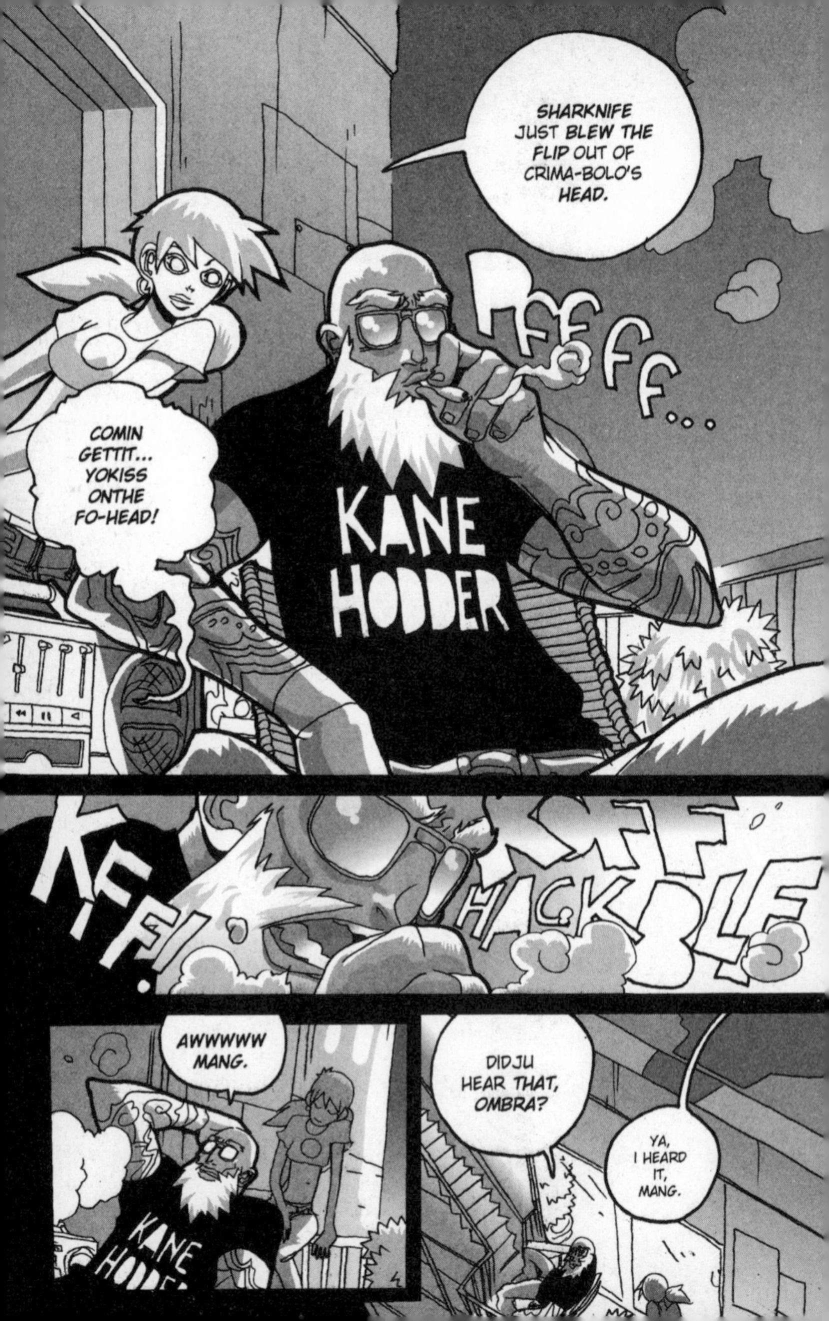
SHARKNIFE JUST BLEW THE FLIP OUT OF CRIMA-BOLO'S HEAD.
COMIN GETTIT... YOKISS ONTHE FO-HEAD!
KANE HODDER
FFFFF...
KFF! HACK
AWWWWW MANG.
DIDJU HEAR THAT, OMBRA?
YA, I HEARD IT, MANG.
KANE

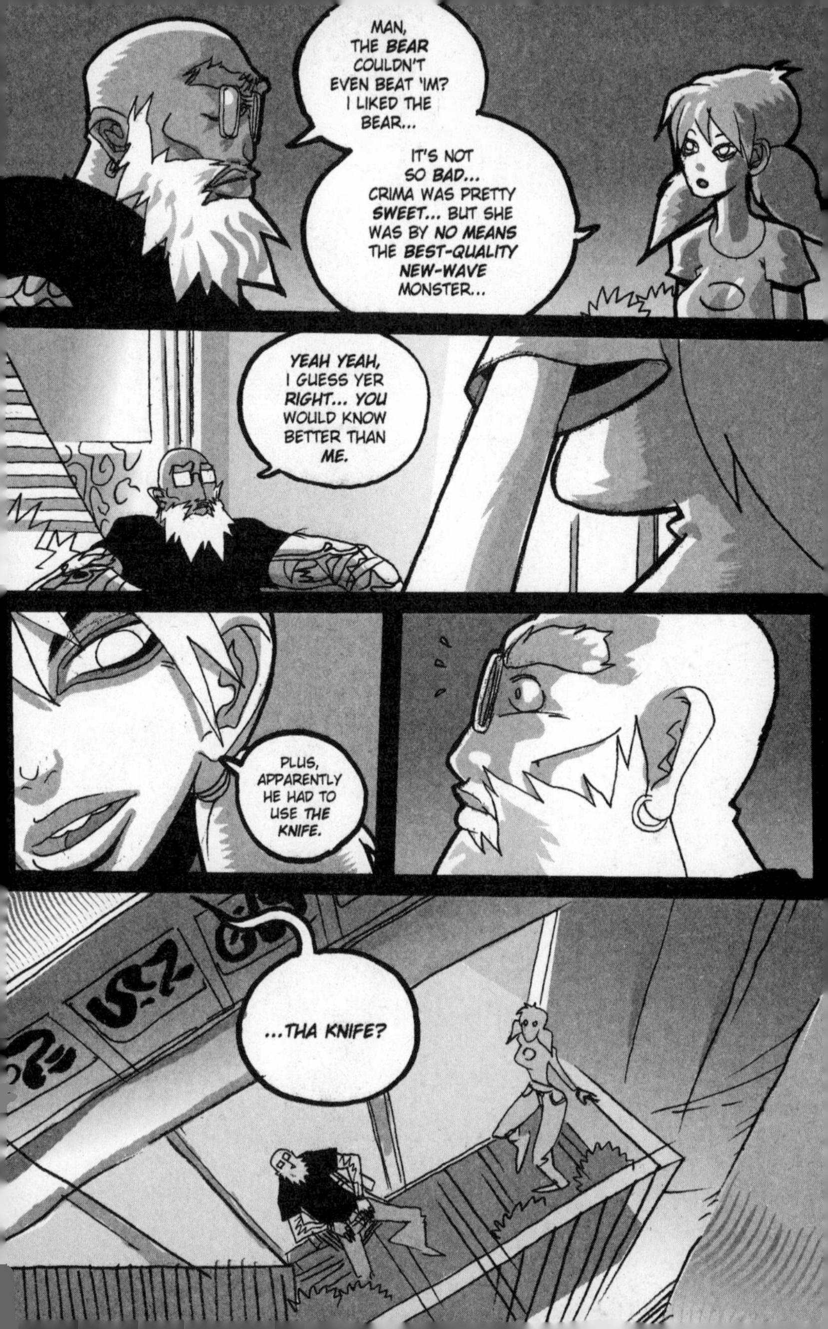
MAN, THE BEAR COULDN'T EVEN BEAT 'IM? I LIKED THE BEAR...
IT'S NOT SO BAD... CRIMA WAS PRETTY SWEET... BUT SHE WAS BY NO MEANS THE BEST-QUALITY NEW-WAVE MONSTER...
YEAH YEAH, I GUESS YER RIGHT... YOU WOULD KNOW BETTER THAN ME.
PLUS, APPARENTLY HE HAD TO USE THE KNIFE.
...THA KNIFE?

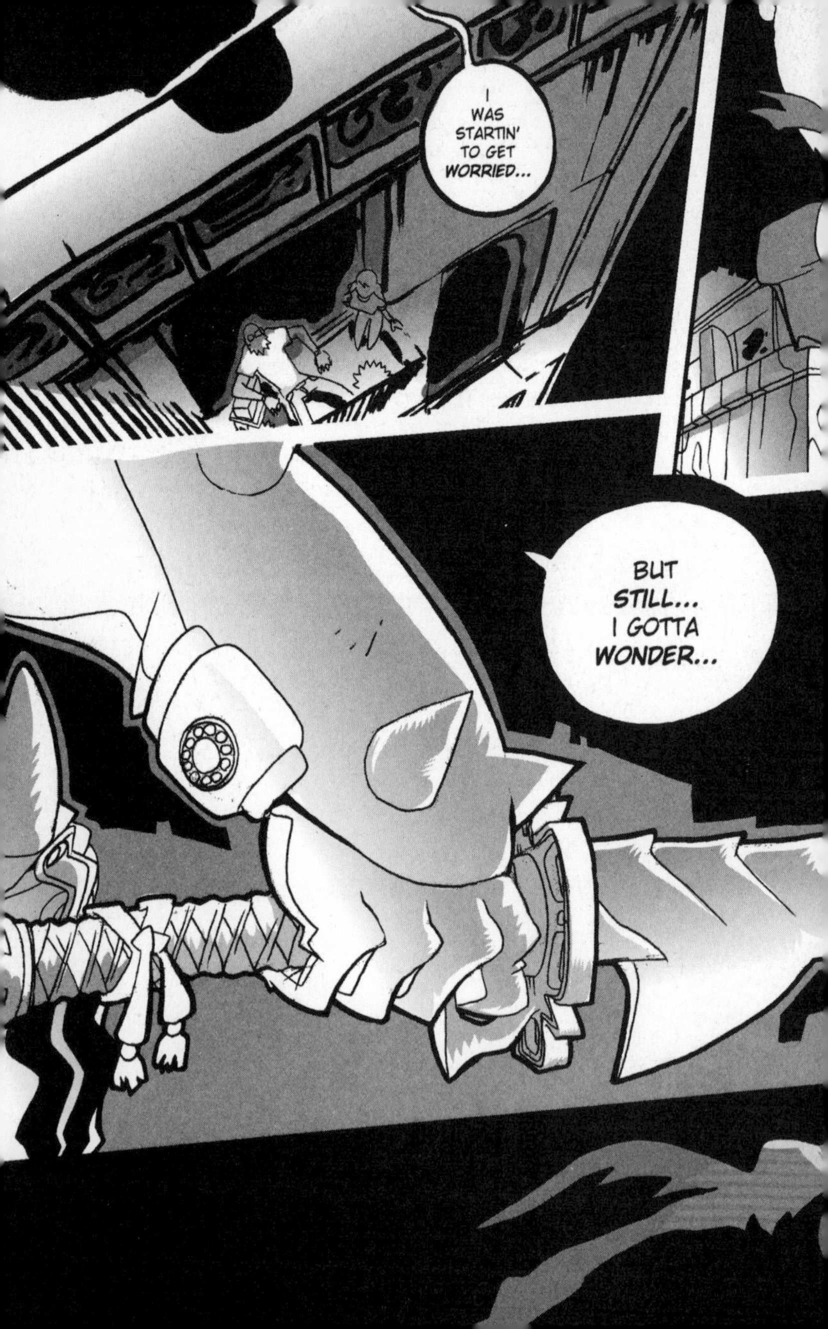
I WAS STARTIN' TO GET WORRIED...
BUT STILL... I GOTTA WONDER...

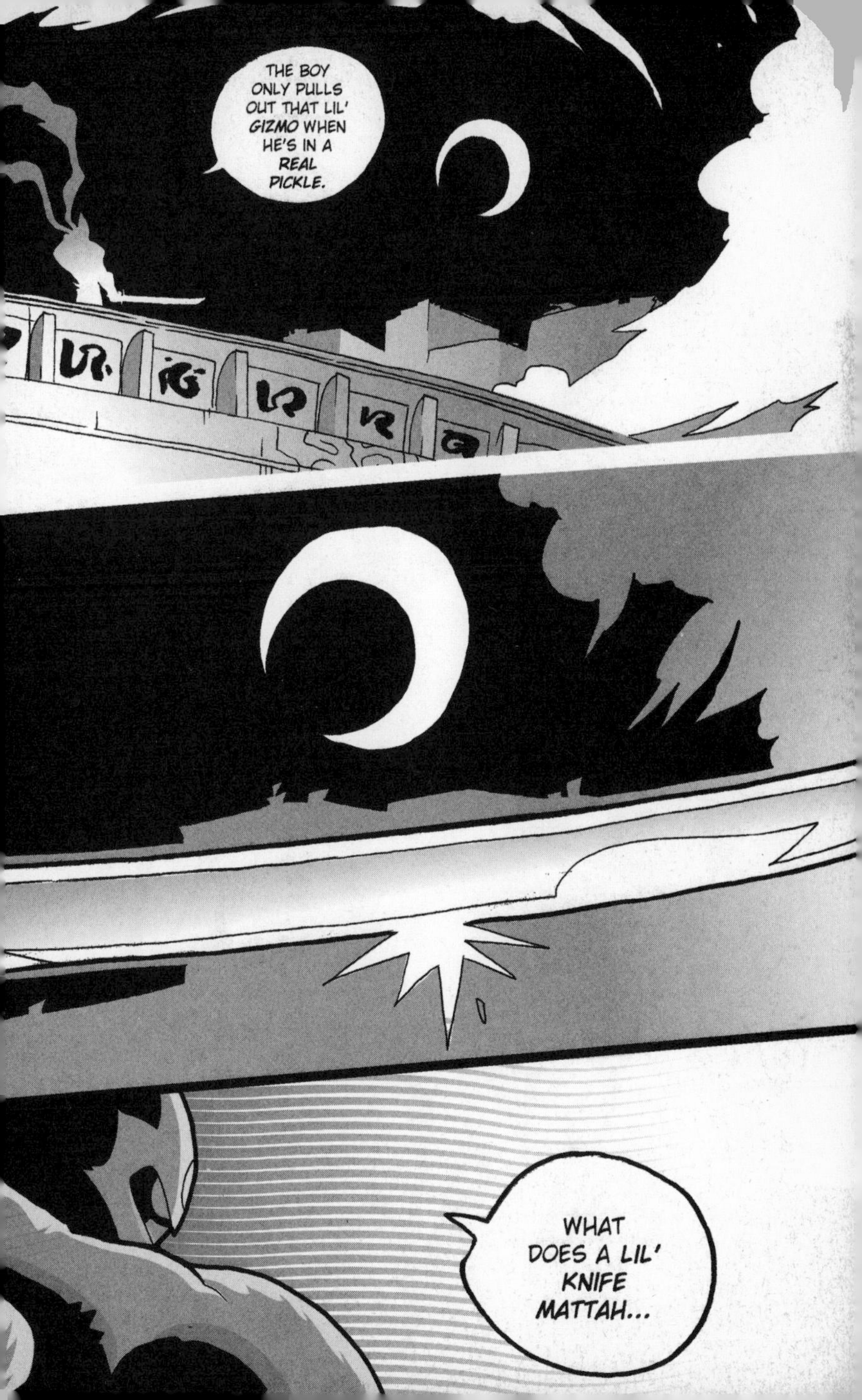
THE BOY ONLY PULLS OUT THAT LIL' GIZMO WHEN HE'S IN A REAL PICKLE.
WHAT DOES A LIL' KNIFE MATTAH...

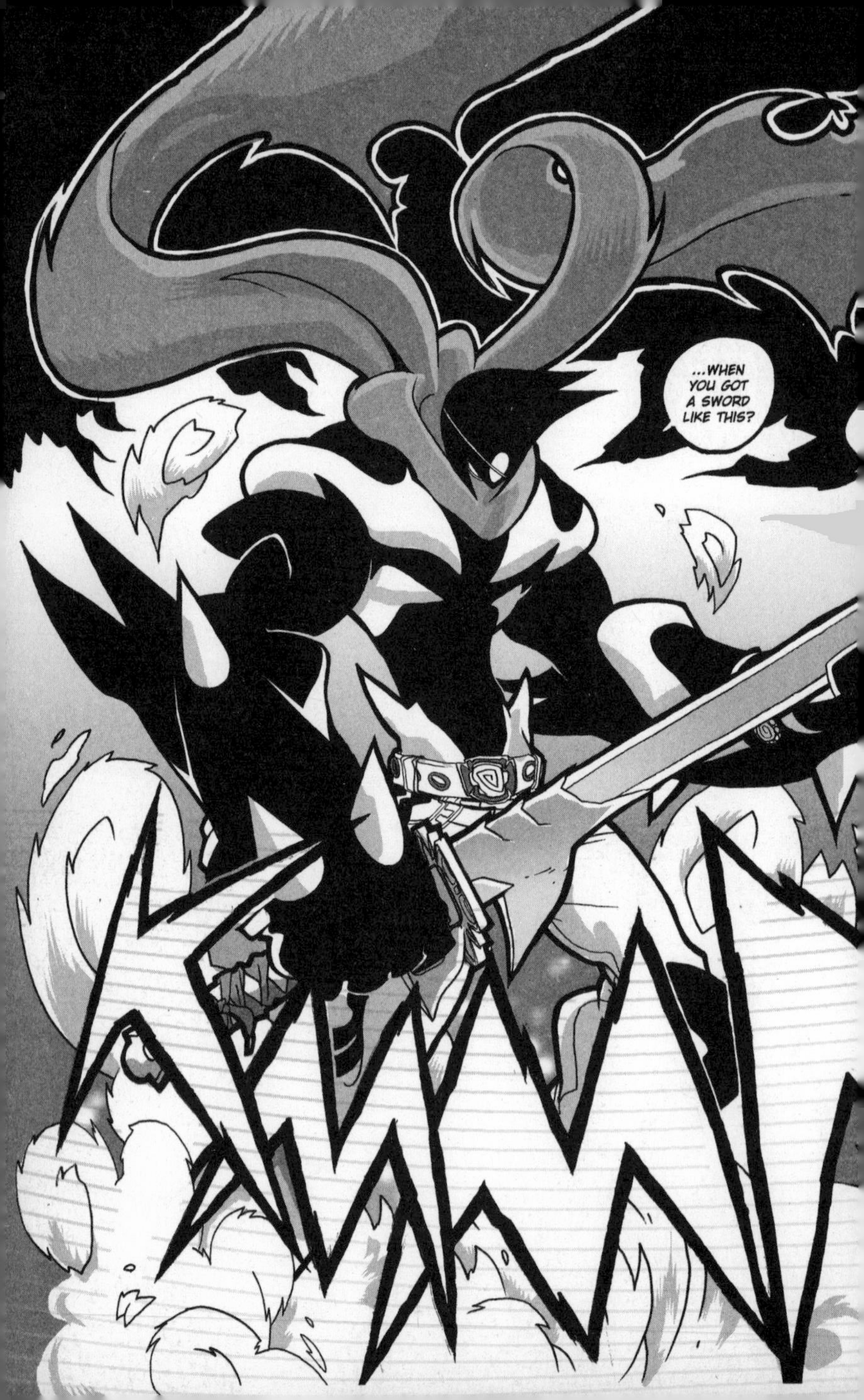
...WHEN YOU GOT A SWORD LIKE THIS?

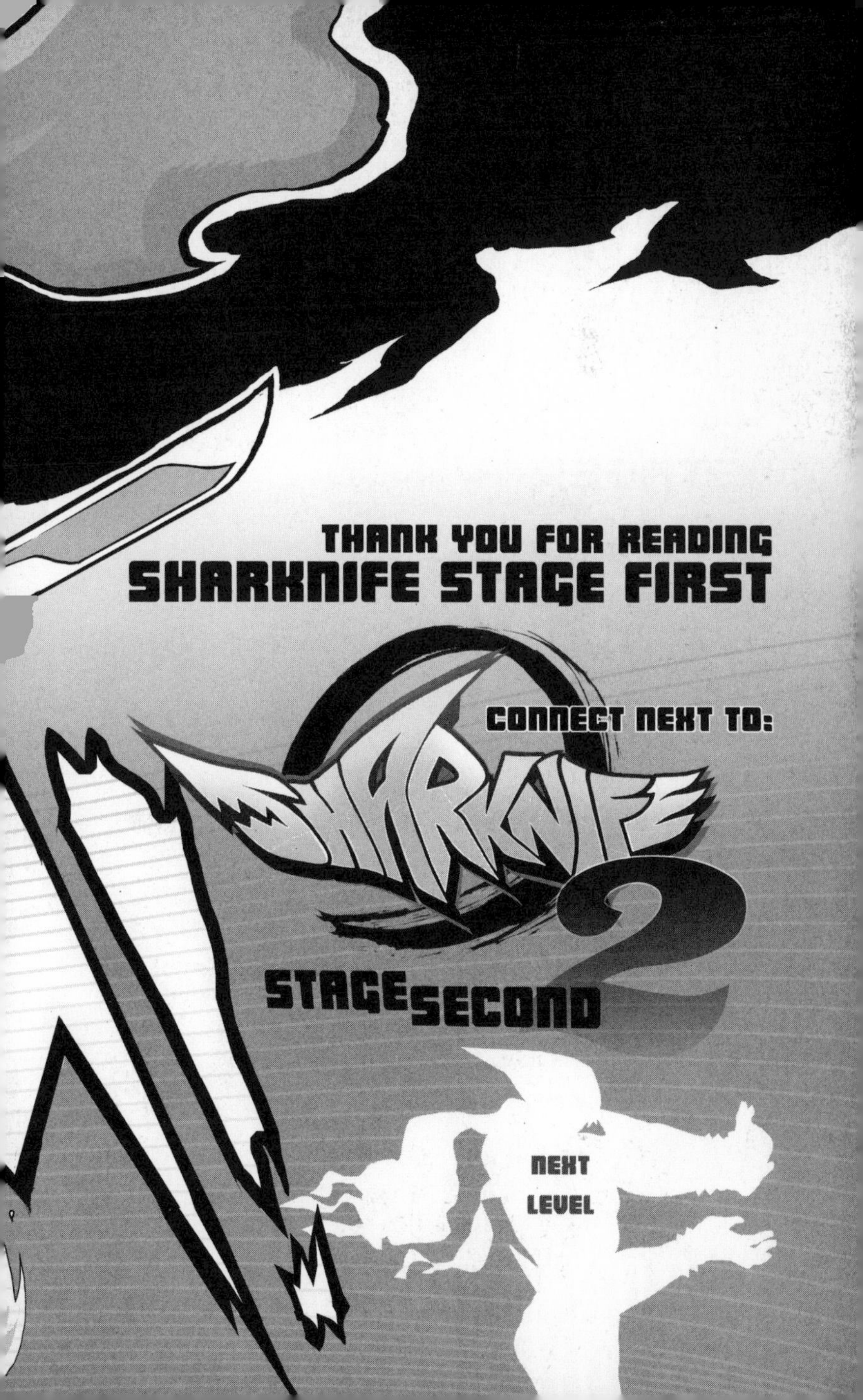
THANK YOU FOR READING
SHARKNIFE STAGE FIRST
CONNECT NEXT TO:
SHARKNIFE 2
STAGE SECOND
NEXT
LEVEL

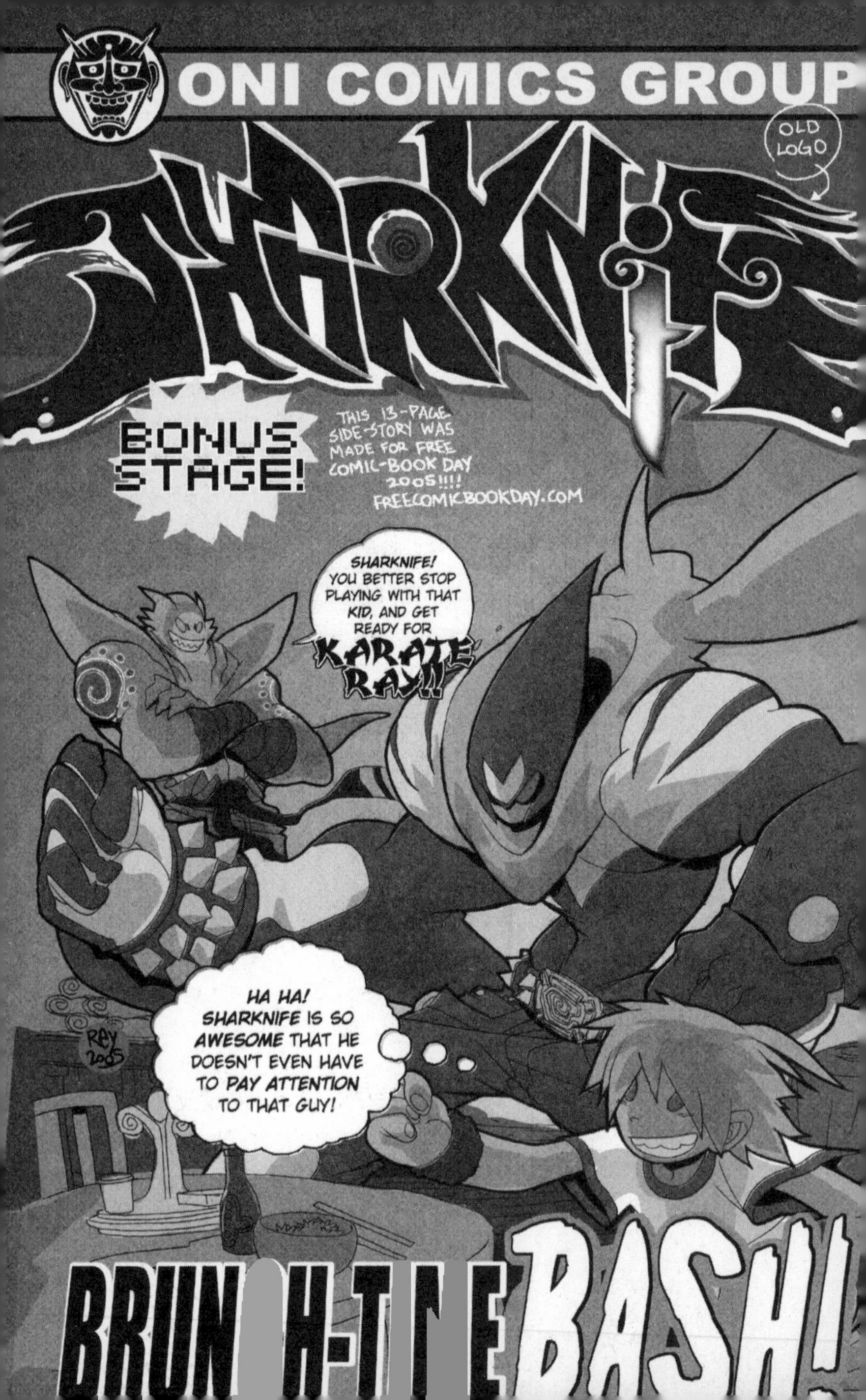
ONI COMICS GROUP
OLD LOGO
SHARKNIFE
BONUS STAGE!
THIS 13-PAGE SIDE-STORY WAS MADE FOR FREE COMIC-BOOK DAY 2005!!!!
FREECOMICBOOKDAY.COM
SHARKNIFE! YOU BETTER STOP PLAYING WITH THAT KID, AND GET READY FOR KARATE RAY!!
HA HA! SHARKNIFE IS SO AWESOME THAT HE DOESN'T EVEN HAVE TO PAY ATTENTION TO THAT GUY!
REY 2005
BASH!

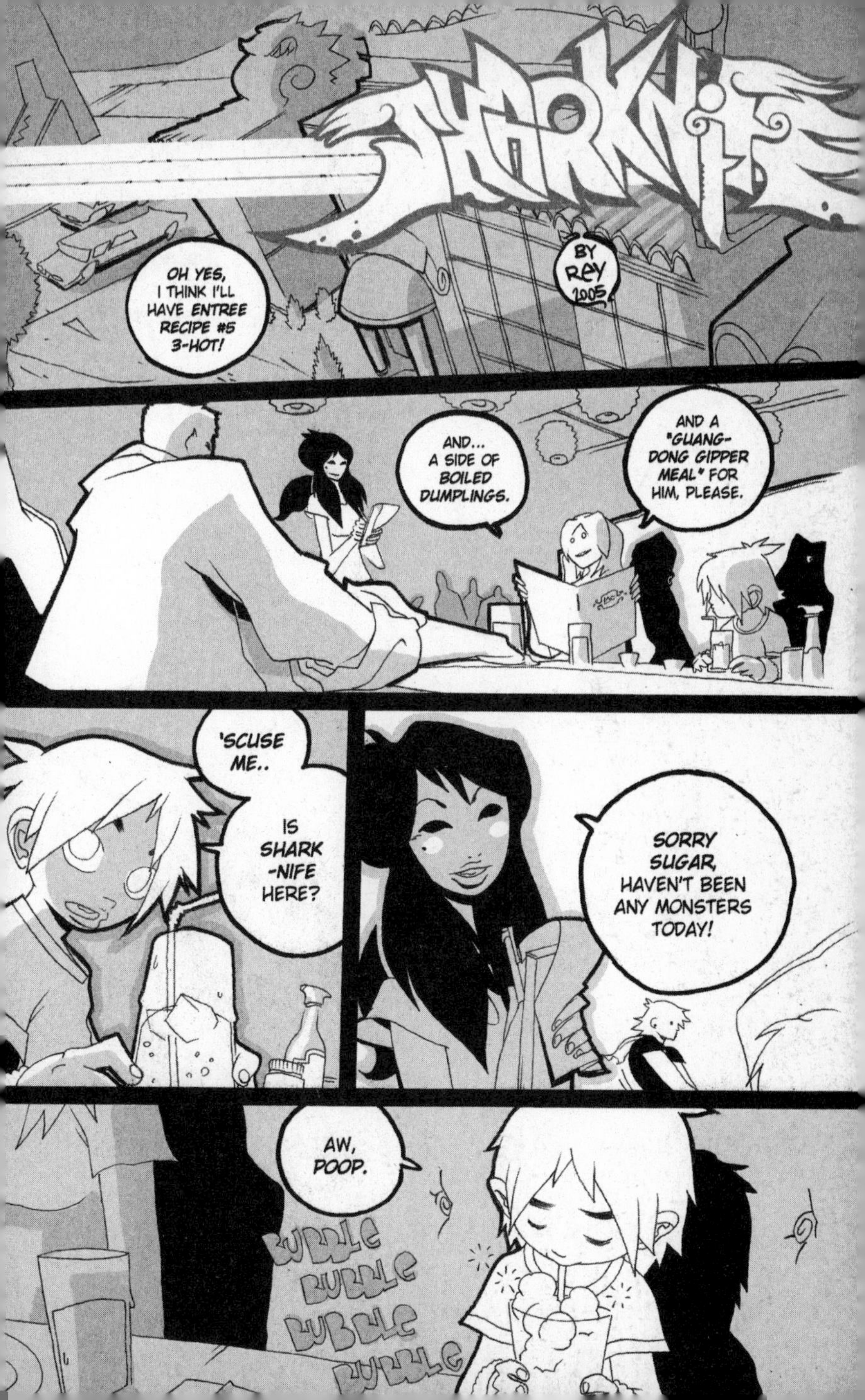
SHARKNIFE
BY Rey 2005
OH YES, I THINK I'LL HAVE ENTREE RECIPE #5 3-HOT!
AND... A SIDE OF BOILED DUMPLINGS.
AND A "GUANG-DONG GIPPER MEAL" FOR HIM, PLEASE.
'SCUSE ME..
IS SHARK-NIFE HERE?
SORRY SUGAR, HAVEN'T BEEN ANY MONSTERS TODAY!
AW, POOP.
BUBBLE BUBBLE BUBBLE BUBBLE

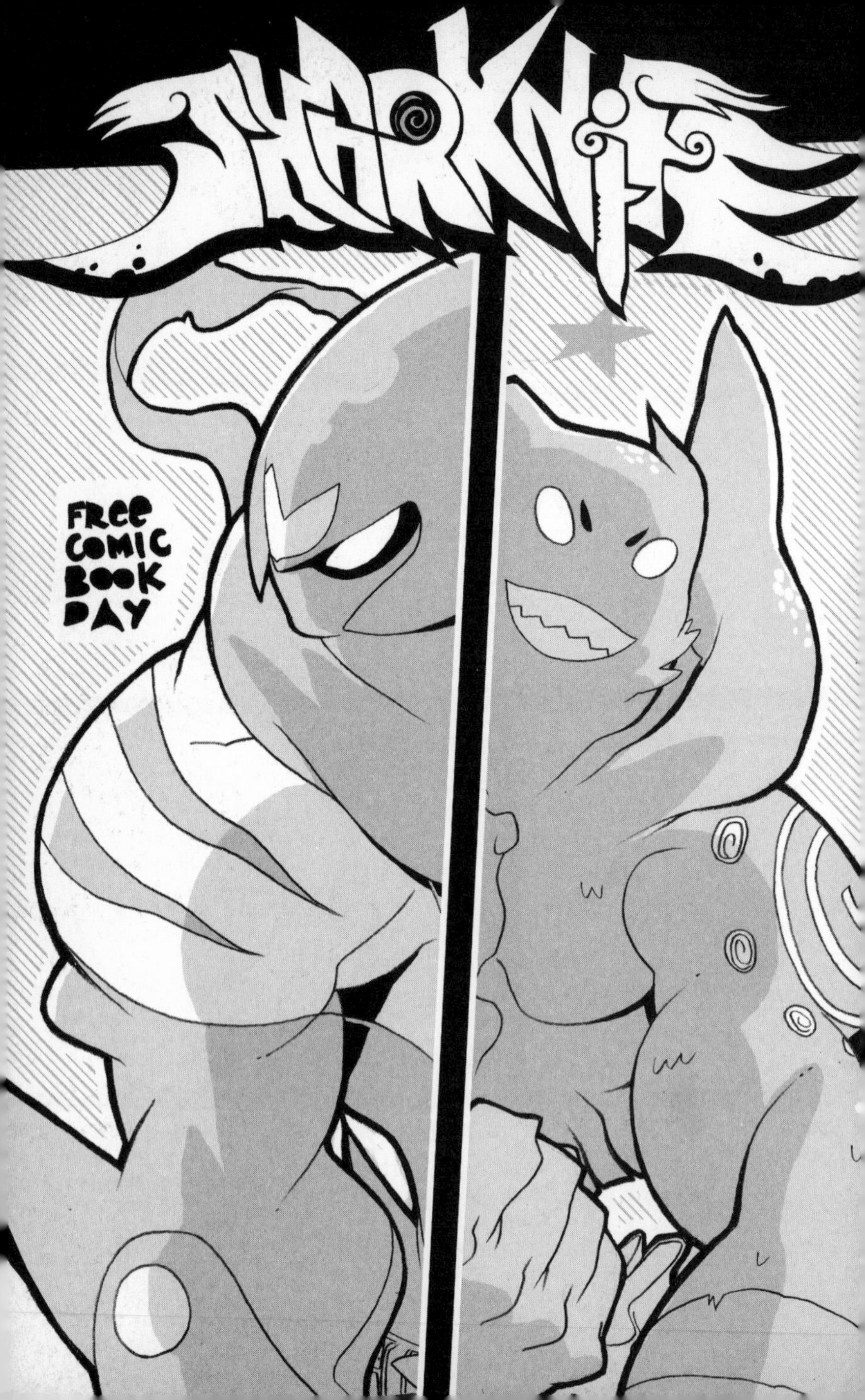
FREE
COMIC
BOOK
DAY

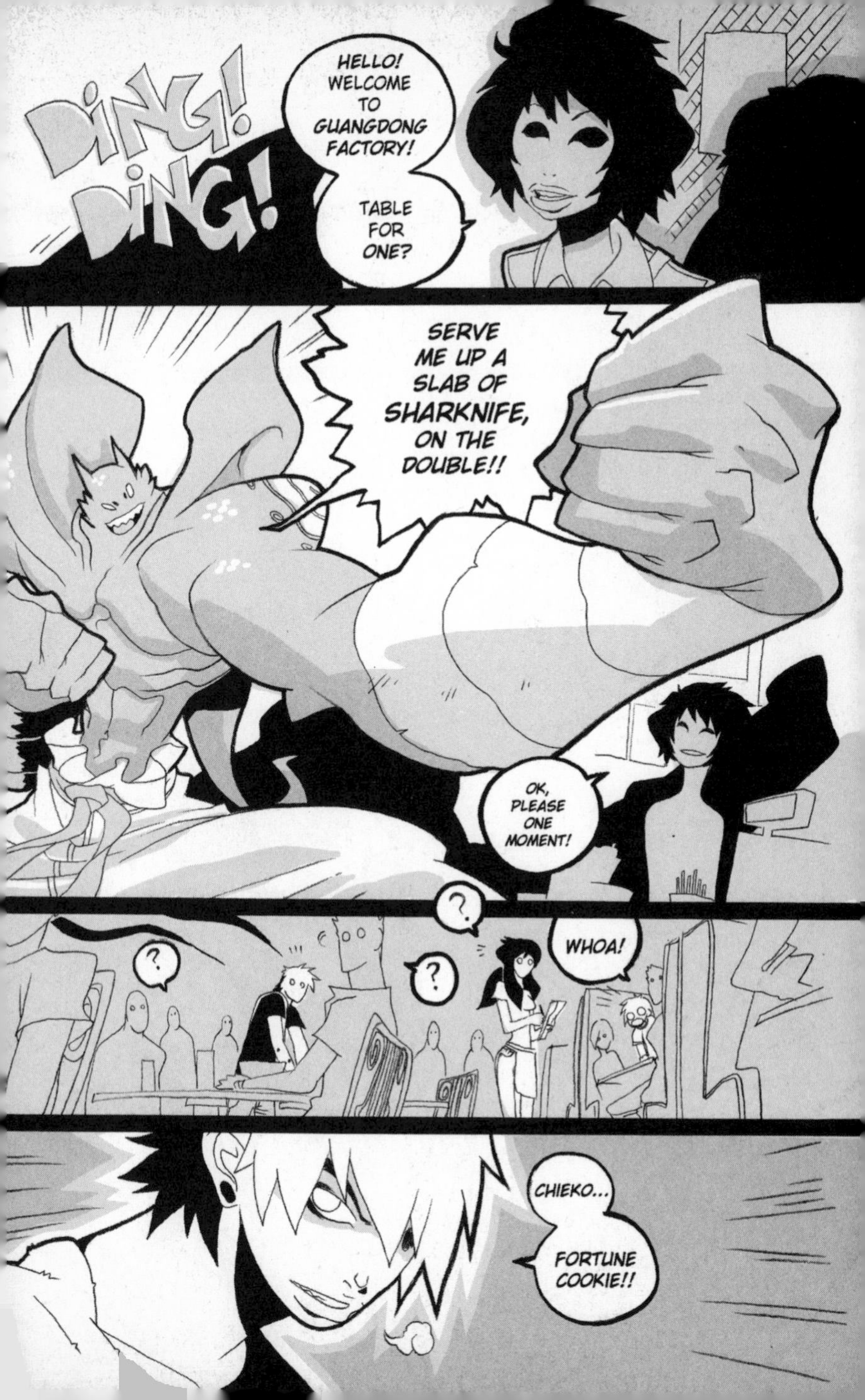
DING! DING!
HELLO! WELCOME TO GUANGDONG FACTORY!
TABLE FOR ONE?
SERVE ME UP A SLAB OF SHARKNIFE, ON THE DOUBLE!!
OK, PLEASE ONE MOMENT!
?
?
?
WHOA!
CHIEKO...
FORTUNE COOKIE!!

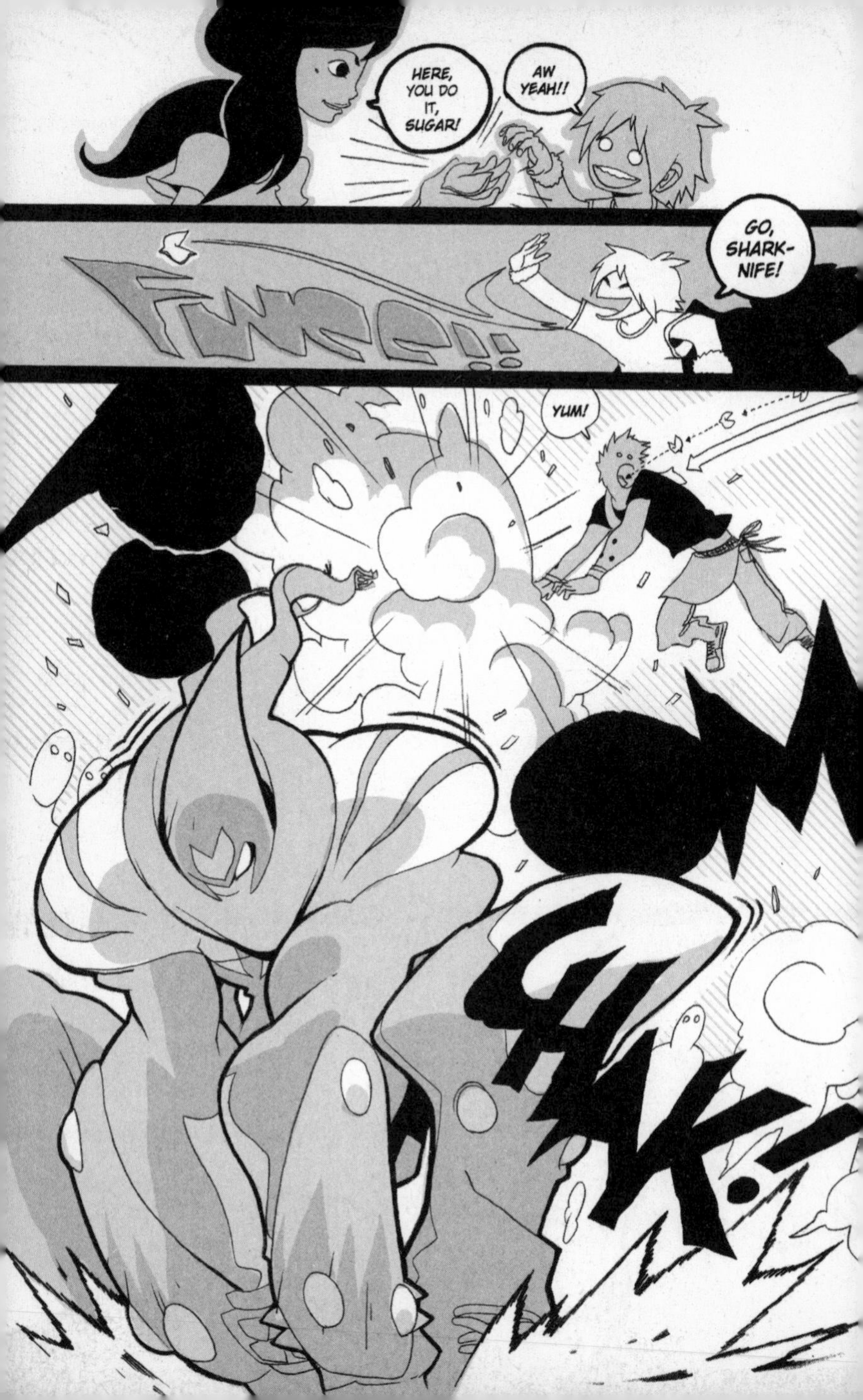
HERE, YOU DO IT, SUGAR!
AW YEAH!!
GO, SHARK-NIFE!
YUM!

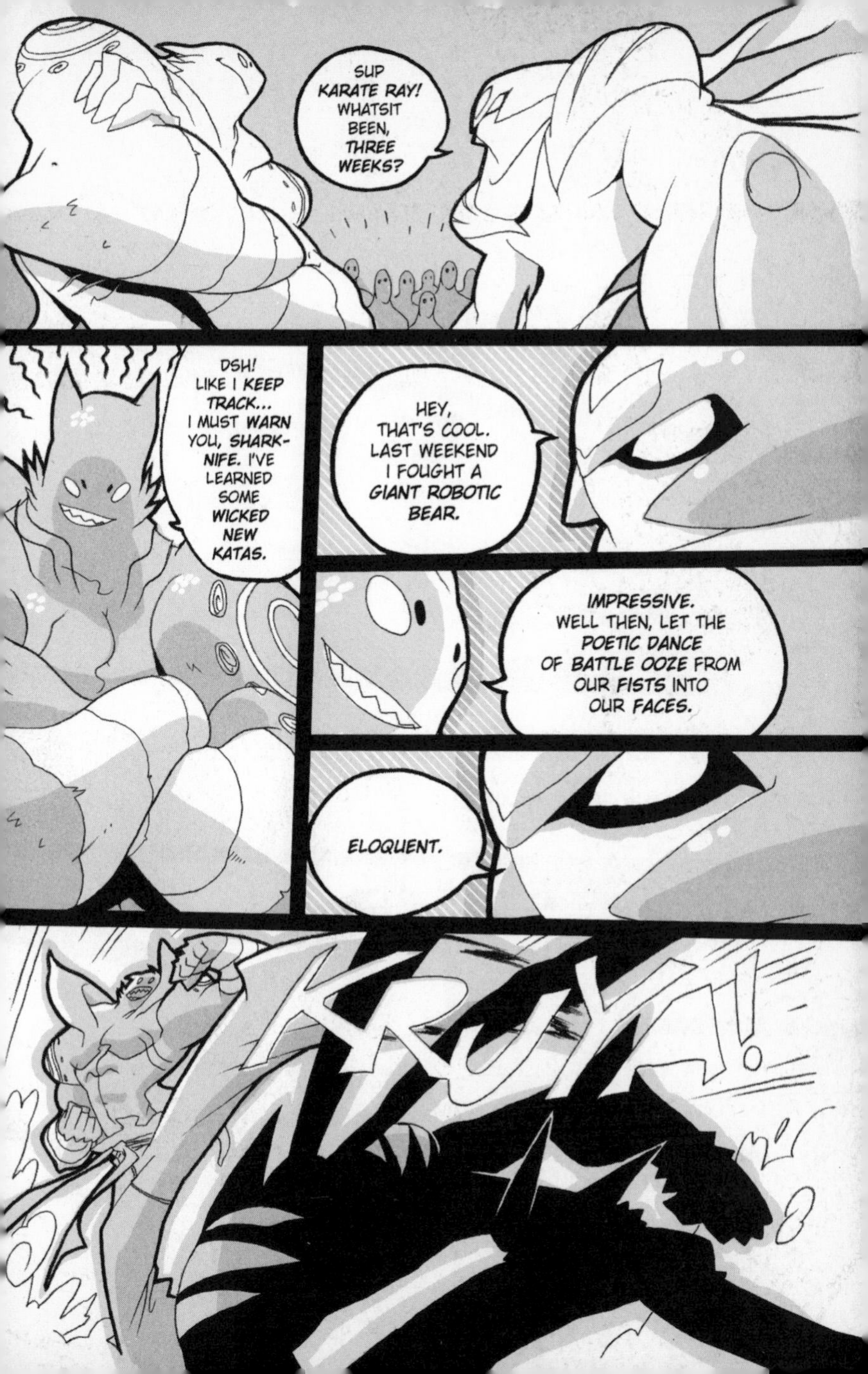
SUP KARATE RAY! WHATSIT BEEN, THREE WEEKS?
DSH! LIKE I KEEP TRACK... I MUST WARN YOU, SHARK-NIFE. I'VE LEARNED SOME WICKED NEW KATAS.
HEY, THAT'S COOL. LAST WEEKEND I FOUGHT A GIANT ROBOTIC BEAR.
IMPRESSIVE. WELL THEN, LET THE POETIC DANCE OF BATTLE OOZE FROM OUR FISTS INTO OUR FACES.
ELOQUENT.
KRUYT!

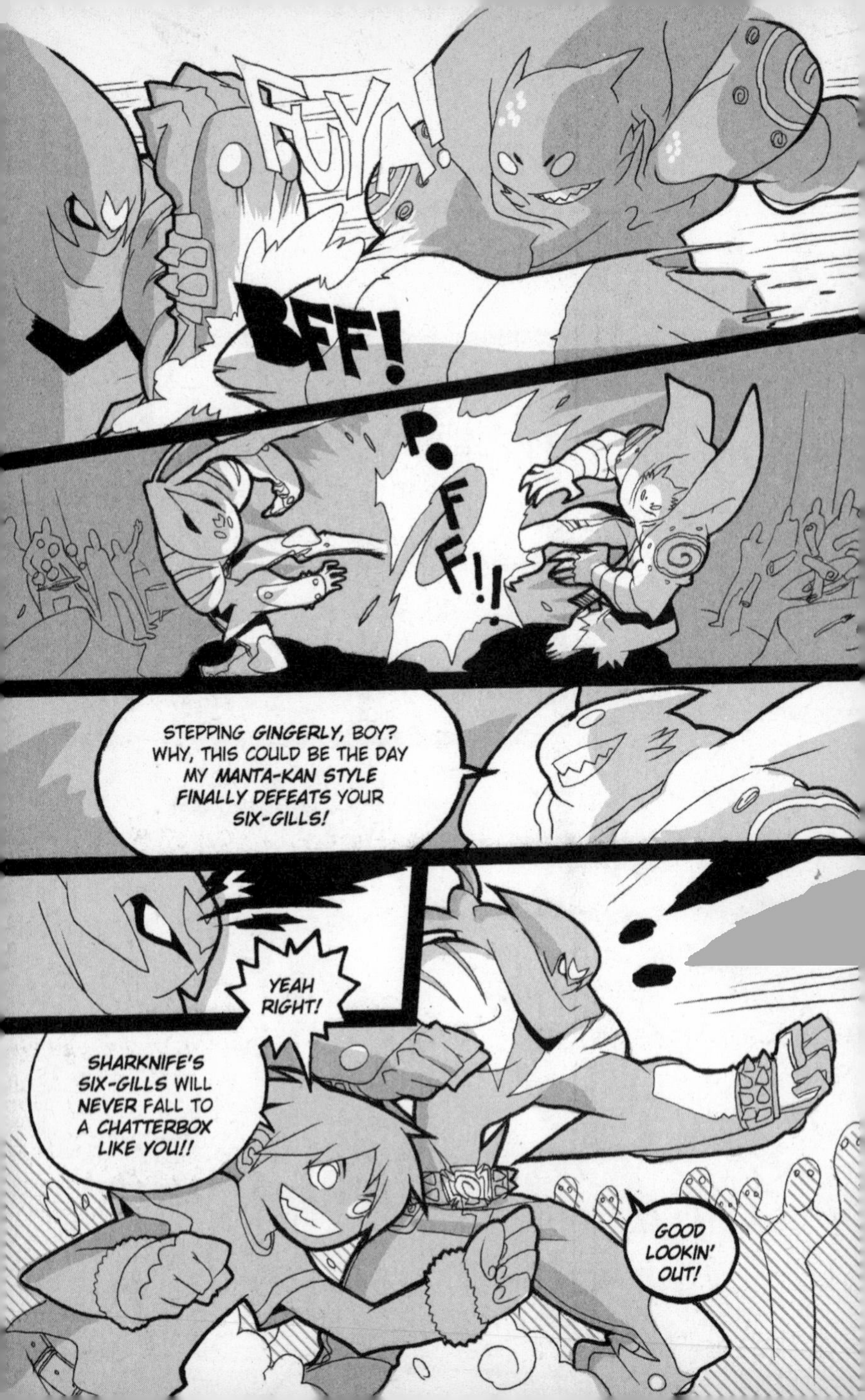
FUYA!
BFF!
POFF!!
STEPPING GINGERLY, BOY? WHY, THIS COULD BE THE DAY MY MANTA-KAN STYLE FINALLY DEFEATS YOUR SIX-GILLS!
YEAH RIGHT!
SHARKNIFE'S SIX-GILLS WILL NEVER FALL TO A CHATTERBOX LIKE YOU!!
GOOD LOOKIN' OUT!

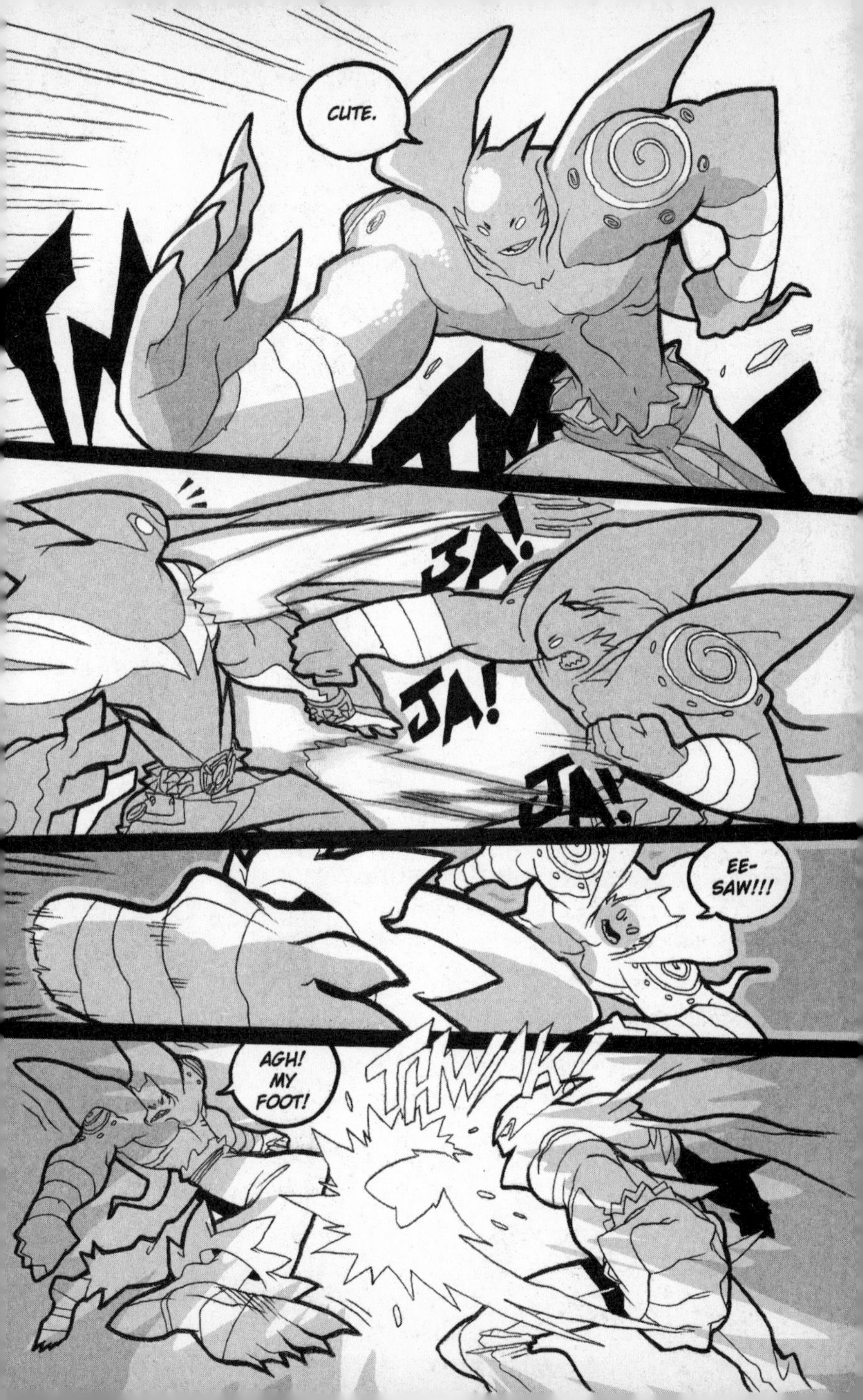
CUTE.
EE-SAW!!!
AGH! MY FOOT!
THWAK!

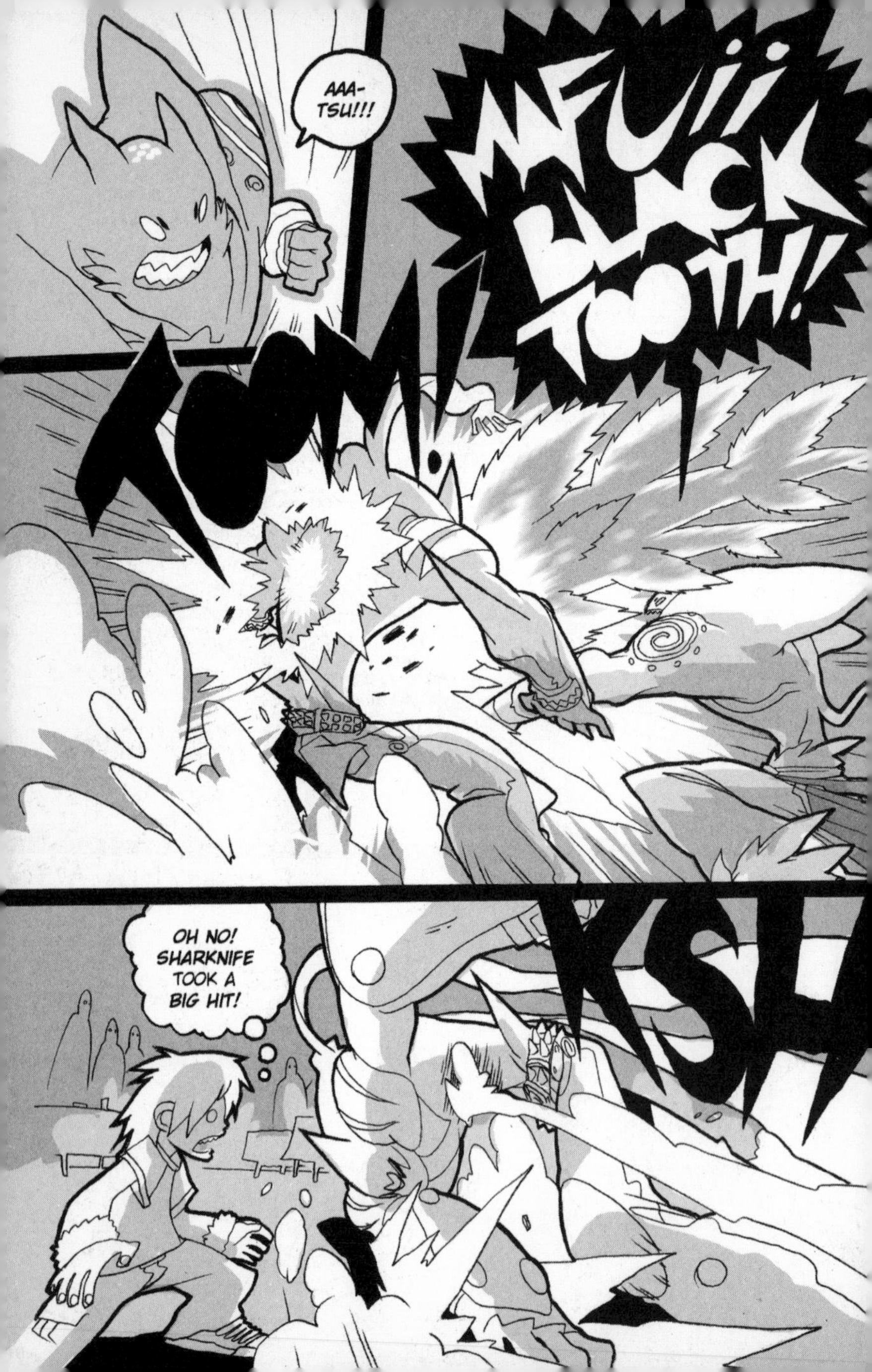
AAA-TSU!!!
AAAAA BLACK TOOTH!!
TOOM!
OH NO! SHARKNIFE TOOK A BIG HIT!
KSH

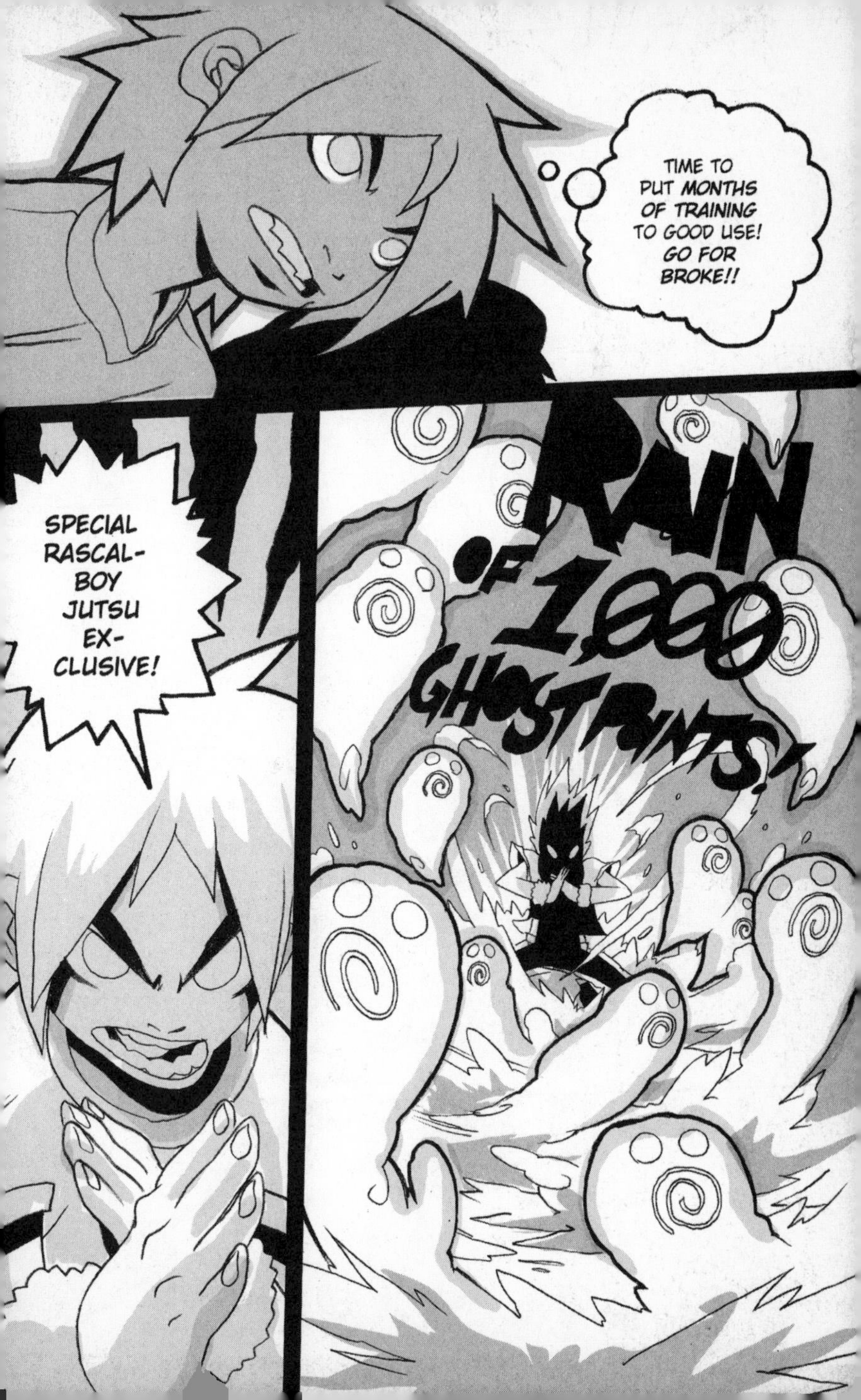
TIME TO PUT MONTHS OF TRAINING TO GOOD USE! GO FOR BROKE!!
SPECIAL RASCAL-BOY JUTSU EX-CLUSIVE!
RAIN OF 1,000 GHOSTPRINTS!

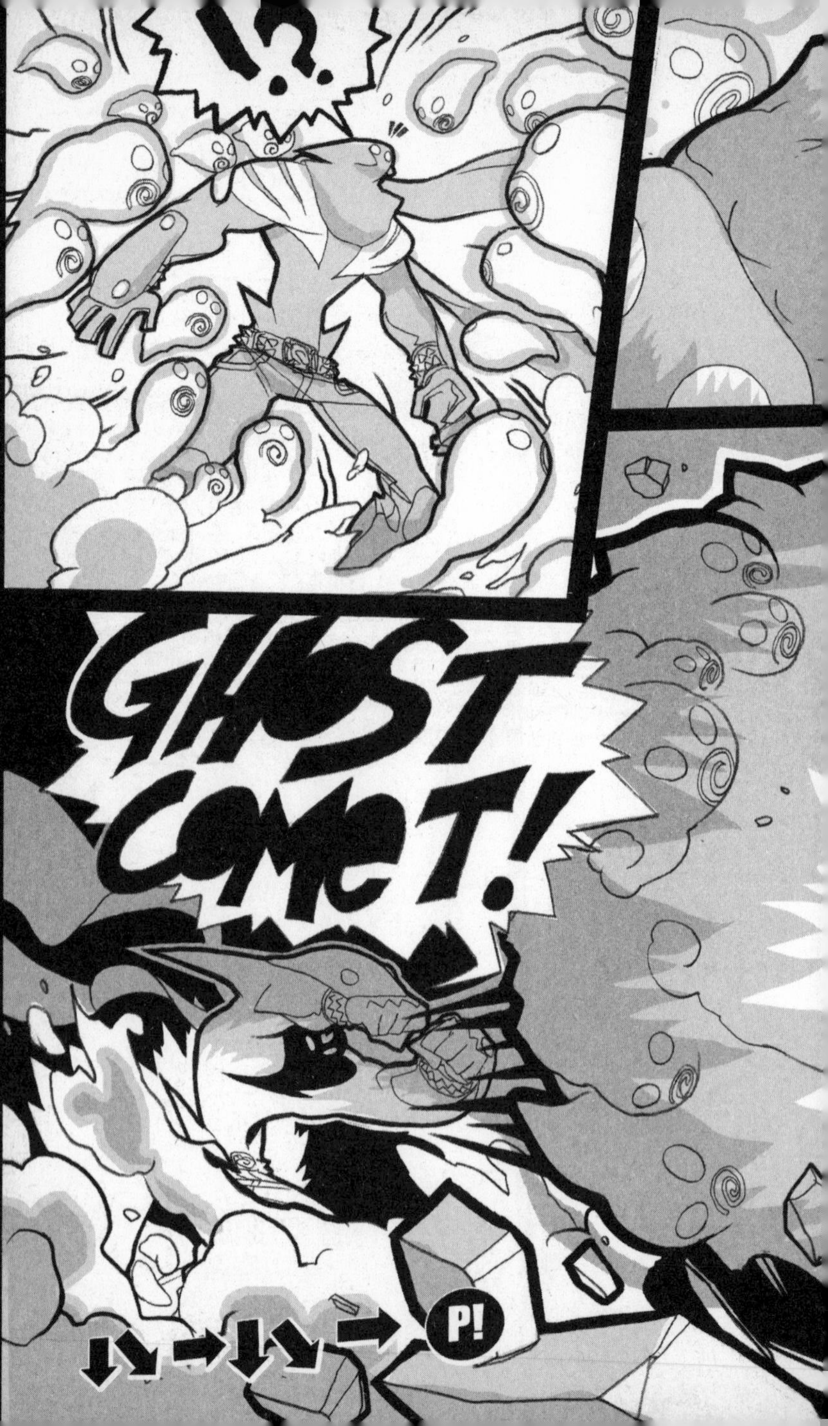
!?
GHOST COMET!
P!

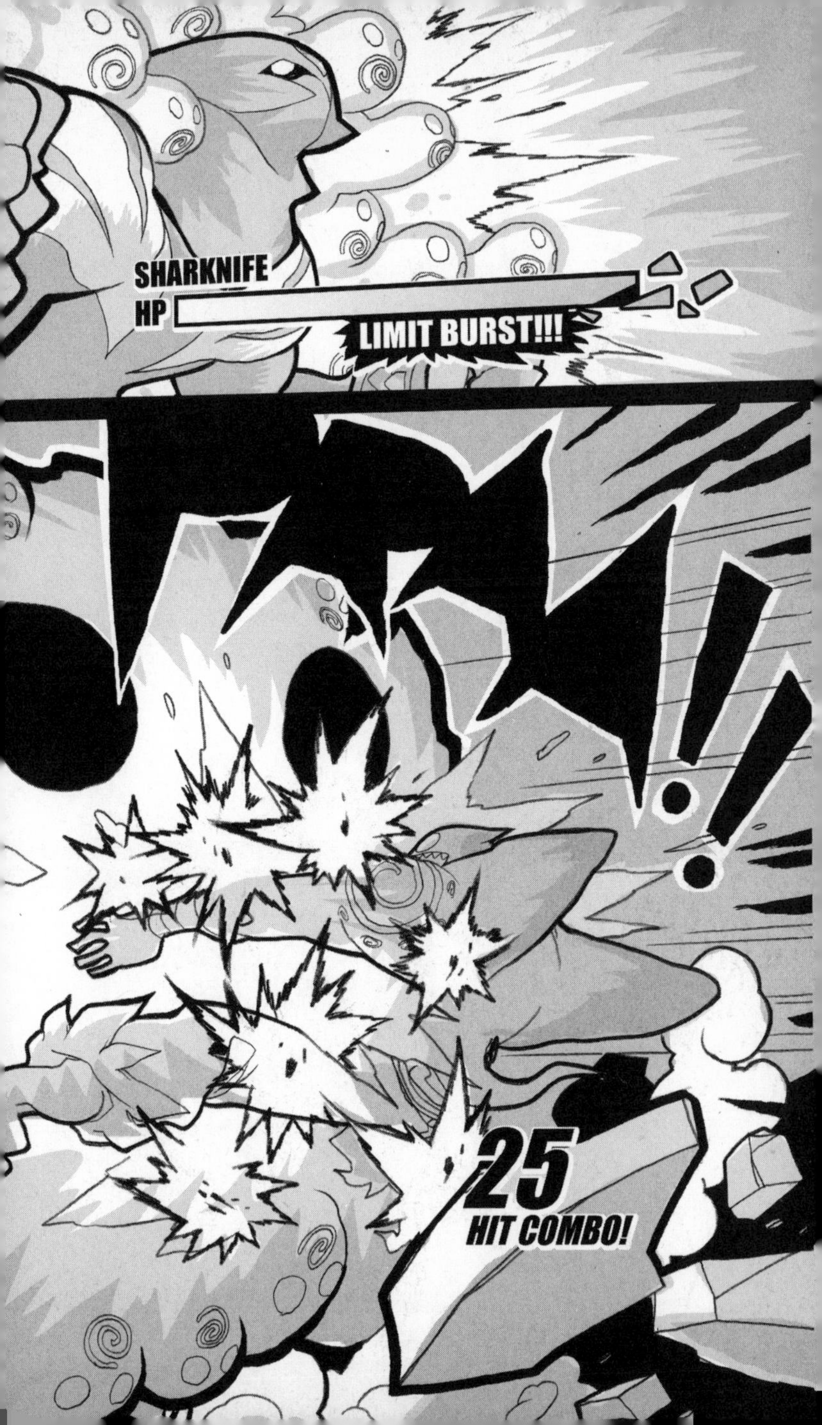
SHARKNIFE
HP
LIMIT BURST!!!
25
HIT COMBO!

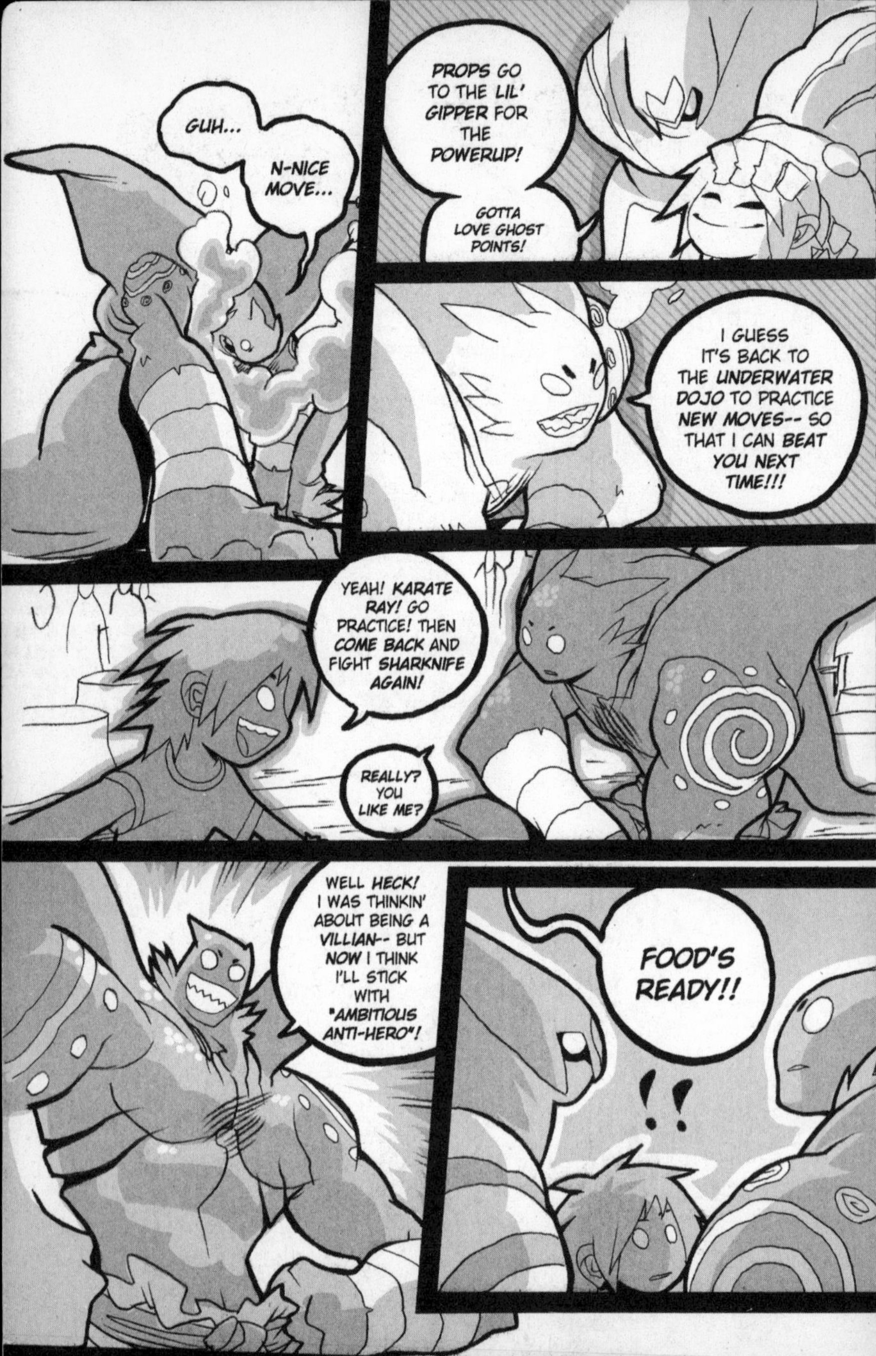
GUH...
N-NICE MOVE...
PROPS GO TO THE LIL' GIPPER FOR THE POWERUP!
GOTTA LOVE GHOST POINTS!
I GUESS IT'S BACK TO THE UNDERWATER DOJO TO PRACTICE NEW MOVES-- SO THAT I CAN BEAT YOU NEXT TIME!!!
YEAH! KARATE RAY! GO PRACTICE! THEN COME BACK AND FIGHT SHARKNIFE AGAIN!
REALLY? YOU LIKE ME?
WELL HECK! I WAS THINKIN' ABOUT BEING A VILLIAN-- BUT NOW I THINK I'LL STICK WITH "AMBITIOUS ANTI-HERO"!
FOOD'S READY!!
!!

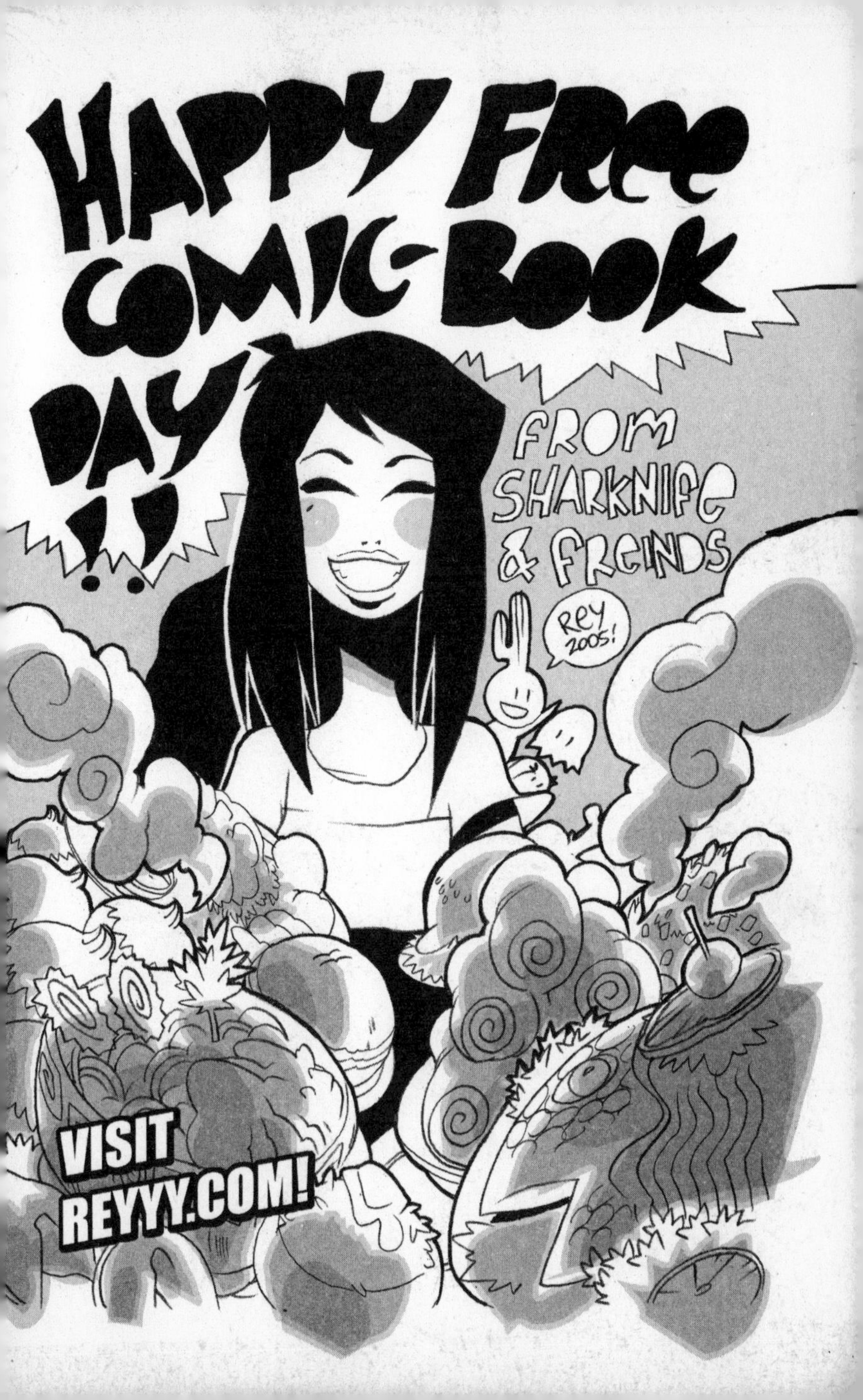
HAPPY FREE COMIC-BOOK DAY!!
FROM SHARKNIFE & FREINDS
REY 2005!
VISIT REYYY.COM!

REYYY.com
- DRAWINGS
- COMICS
- TREATS

Visit Today!

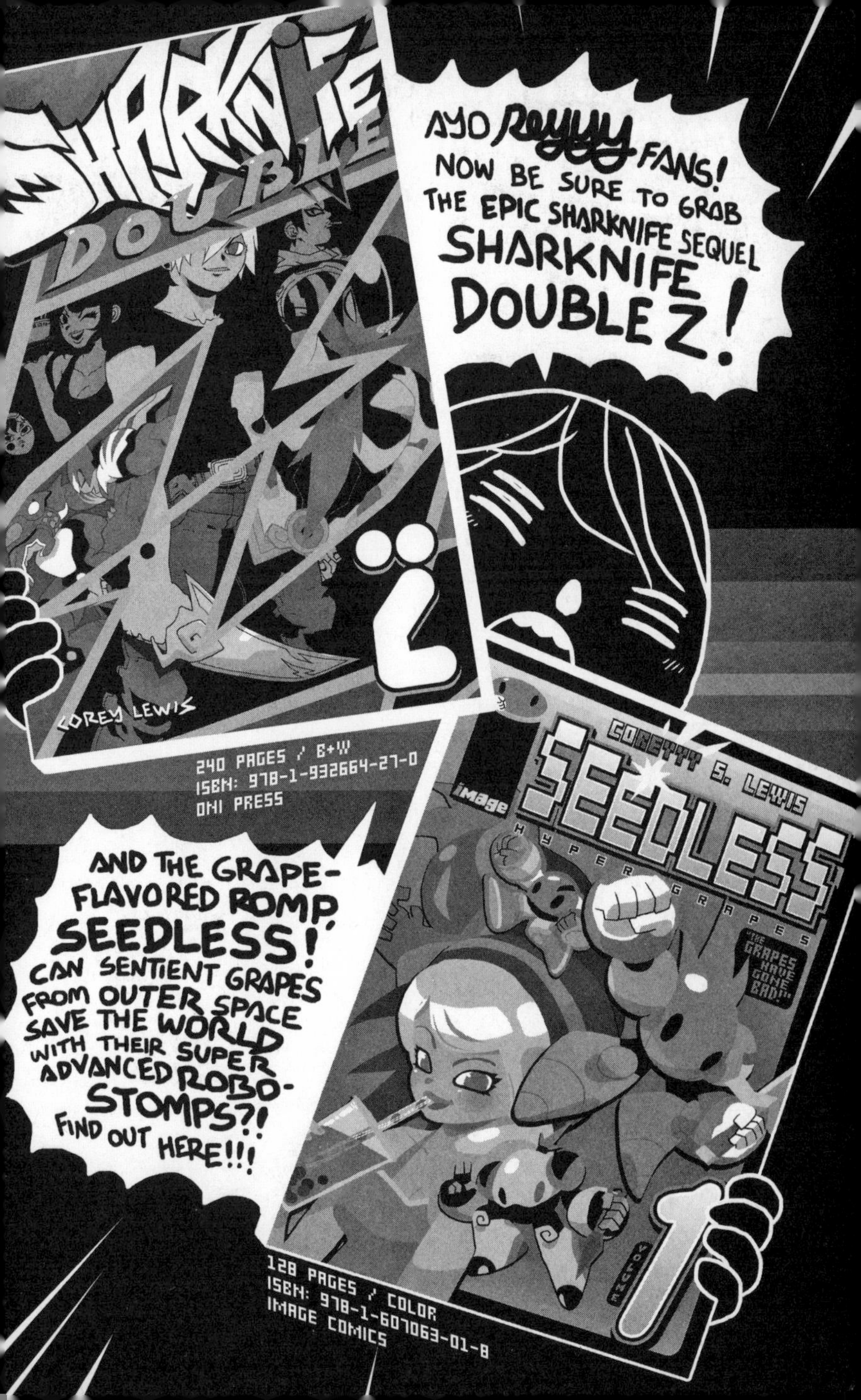
SHARKNIFE DOUBLE
AYO Reyyy FANS!
NOW BE SURE TO GRAB
THE EPIC SHARKNIFE SEQUEL
SHARKNIFE DOUBLE Z!
COREY LEWIS
240 PAGES / B+W
ISBN: 978-1-932664-27-0
ONI PRESS
AND THE GRAPE-FLAVORED ROMP, SEEDLESS! CAN SENTIENT GRAPES FROM OUTER SPACE SAVE THE WORLD WITH THEIR SUPER ADVANCED ROBO-STOMPS?! FIND OUT HERE!!!
S. LEWIS
IMAGE
SEEDLESS
HYPER GRAPES
THE GRAPES HAVE GONE BAD!!
1
128 PAGES / COLOR
ISBN: 978-1-607063-01-8
IMAGE COMICS

CHECK OUT THESE OTHER MIND-BENDING GRAPHIC NOVELS FROM ONI PRESS!

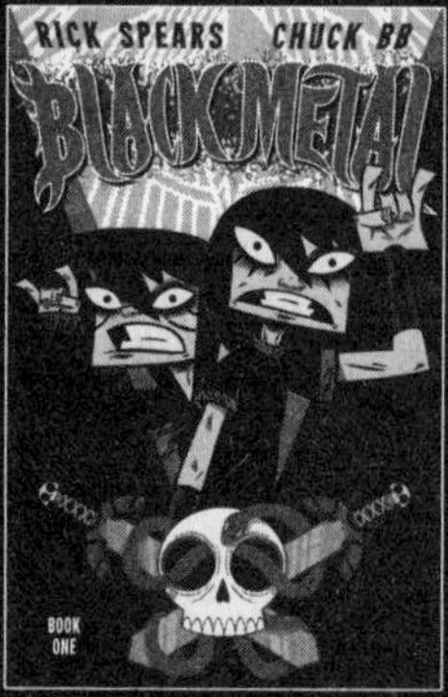
RICK SPEARS
CHUCK BB
BLACK METAL
BOOK ONE

BLACK METAL, VOL. 1
Rick Spears & Chuck BB
160 pages · Digest
B&W · $11.99 US
ISBN 978-1-932664-69-0

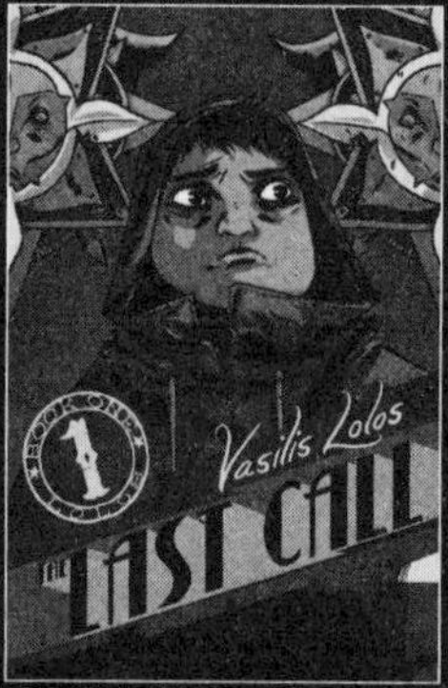
BOOK ONE
1
Vasilis Lolos
THE LAST CALL

LAST CALL, VOL. 1
Vasilis Lolos
136 pages · Digest
B&W · $11.95 US
ISBN 978-1-932664-69-0

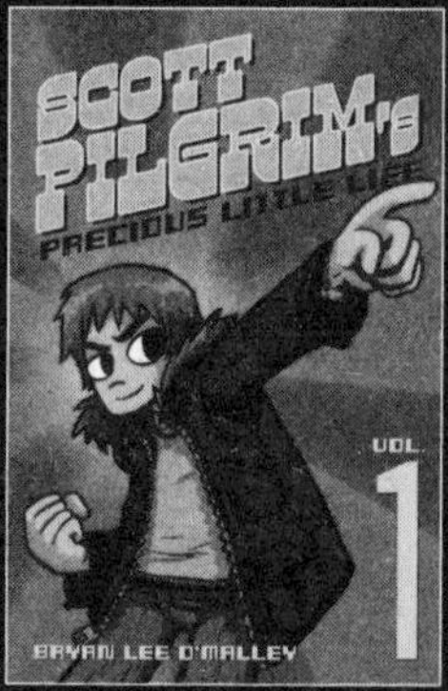
SCOTT PILGRIM'S
PRECIOUS LITTLE LIFE
VOL. 1
BRYAN LEE O'MALLEY

SCOTT PILGRIM, VOL. 1:
Bryan Lee O'Malley
168 pages · Digest
B&W · $11.99 US
ISBN 978-1-932664-08-9

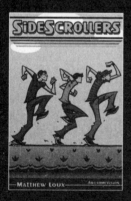

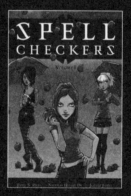

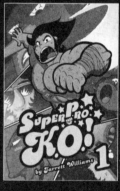

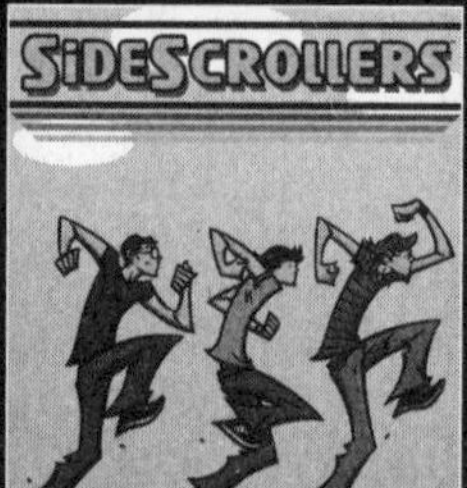
SIDESCROLLERS
MATTHEW LOUX
AWESOMEVISION

SIDESCROLLERS
Matthew Loux
216 pages · Digest
B&W · $11.99 US
ISBN 978-1-932664-50-8

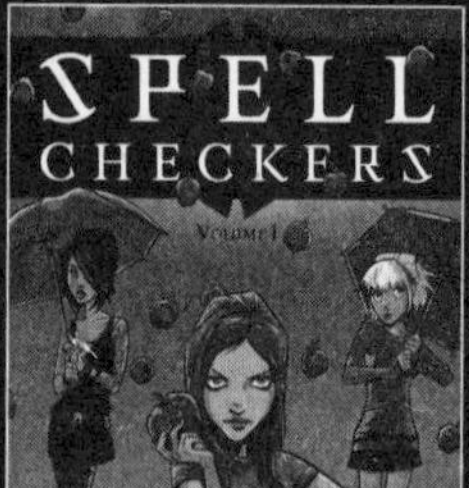
SPELL CHECKERS
VOLUME I

SPELL CHECKERS, VOL. 1
Jamie S. Rich, Nicolas Hitori De,
Joëlle Jones
152 pages · Digest
B&W · $11.99 US
ISBN 978-1-934964-32-3

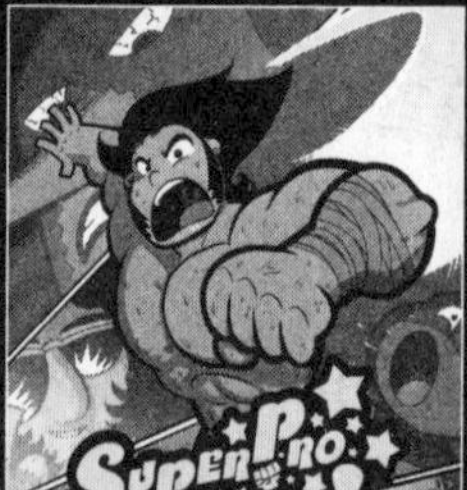
SuperPro K.O.!
1
by Jarrett Williams

SUPERPRO K.O., VOL. 1
Jarrett Williams
256 pages · Digest
B&W · $11.99 US
ISBN 978-1-934964-41-5

ONI PRESS
REVOLUTIONIZE COMICS
www.onipress.com

For more information on these and other fine Oni Press comic books and graphic novels, visit www.onipress.com.
To find a comic specialty store in your area, call 1-888-COMICBOOK or visit www.comicshops.us.